A Law Unto Himself

A LAW UNTO HIMSELF

Wyatt Earp, an American Odyssey

Book Three

MARK WARREN

TWODOT®

GUILFORD, CONNECTICUT
HELENA, MONTANA

A · TWODOT® · BOOK

An imprint and registered trademark of The Rowman & Littlefield Publishing Group, Inc.
4501 Forbes Blvd., Ste. 200
Lanham, MD 20706
www.rowman.com

Distributed by NATIONAL BOOK NETWORK

British Library Cataloguing in Publication Information available

Library of Congress Cataloging-in-Publication Data

Names: Warren, Mark, 1947- author.
Title: A law unto himself / Mark Warren.
Description: Helena, Montana : TwoDot, [2021] | Series: Wyatt Earp, an
   American odyssey ; book three | Includes bibliographical references. |
   Summary: "In Tombstone, Arizona Territory, despite a silver strike
   promising entrepreneurial opportunities, Wyatt Earp returns to law
   enforcement, posing a new threat to the rustlers running rampant on both
   sides of the U.S.-Mexican border"— Provided by publisher.
Identifiers: LCCN 2020054609 | ISBN 9781493053438 (trade paperback ; alk.
   paper) | ISBN 9781493053445 (epub)
Subjects: LCSH: Earp, Wyatt, 1848-1929--Fiction. | Peace officers—West
   (U.S.)—Fiction. | Outlaws—West (U.S.) v Fiction. | Frontier and
   pioneer life—West (U.S.)—Fiction. | Tombstone (Ariz.)—Fiction. |
   GSAFD: Western stories. | Biographical fiction.
Classification: LCC PS3623.A86465 L39 2021 | DDC 813/.6—dc23
LC record available at https://lccn.loc.gov/2020054609

♾️™ The paper used in this publication meets the minimum requirements of American National
Standard for Information Sciences—Permanence of Paper for Printed Library Materials, ANSI/
NISO Z39.48-1992.

To Susan,
for letting me read to you forever.

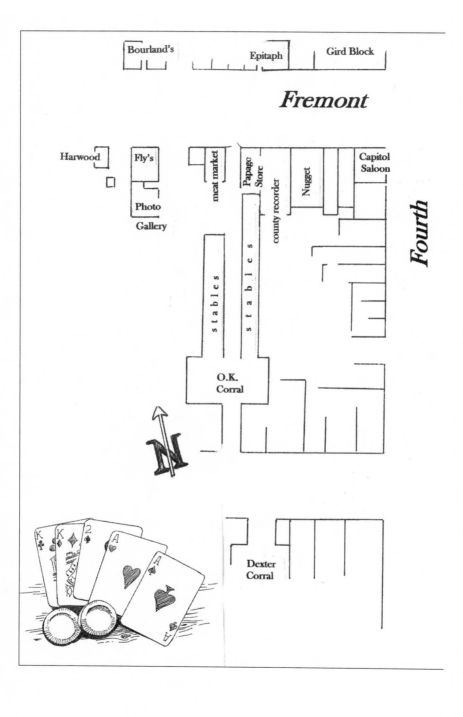

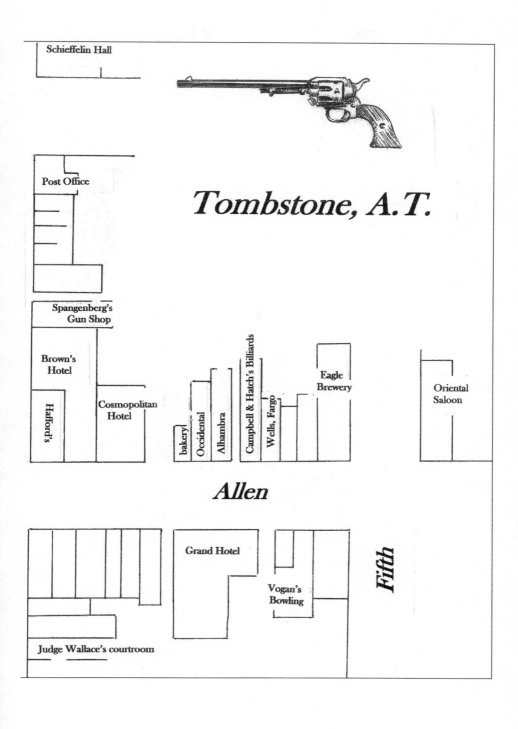

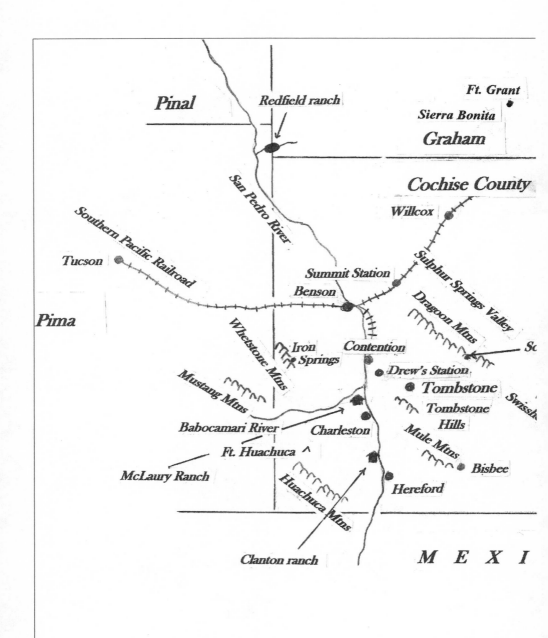

Now, I am just an actor—a mere player—seeking to reproduce the lives of those great gunmen who molded a new country for us to live in and enjoy peace and prosperity. And we have today in America . . . these men with us in the flesh . . . one is Wyatt Earp.

—WILLIAM S. HART, AS QUOTED IN THE *NEW YORK MORNING TELEGRAPH*, OCTOBER 9, 1921

CAST OF CHARACTERS

A Reader's Reference List

Bauer, Appolinar—Tombstone butcher who purchases beef from cow-boy rustlers.

Behan, Albert—Partially deaf son of Sheriff John Behan.

Behan, John—First sheriff of Cochise County, A.T., sympathetic to cow-boys.

Biddle, Colonel James—US Army officer at Fort Grant in Graham County, A.T.

Bode, Frederick—German-born teamster implicated in Morgan Earp's assassination.

Bourland, Addie—Tombstone milliner, who witnesses the "O.K. Corral gunfight."

Breakenridge, Billy—Deputy under Sheriff Behan.

Brocius, William ("Curly Bill")—Outlaw kingpin of the cow-boys.

Claiborne, Billy ("the Kid")—Cow-boy present at the opening of the "O.K. Corral gunfight."

Clanton,

> **Billy**—Hotheaded cow-boy, youngest Clanton brother, dies at "O.K. Corral fight."
>
> **Ike**—Clanton brother who instigates and runs from "O.K. Corral gunfight."
>
> **Newman ("Old Man")**—Patriarch of the Clanton clan.
>
> **Phin**—Cow-boy brother of Billy and Ike.

Clum, John—Tombstone mayor, postmaster, and editor of the *Epitaph*, the newspaper supporting the Earps.

Cos, Valenzuela—Common-law wife of Sherman McMaster and once courtesan of Wyatt Earp.

Crane, Jim—Cow-boy involved in the Benson stage holdup and murders.

Cruz, Florentino ("Indian Charlie")—Half-breed cow-boy implicated in Morg Earp's murder.

Dake, Crawley—US Marshal for Arizona Territory working from Prescott.

Diehl, Pony—Cow-boy rustler and stage robber.

Dodge, Fred—Undercover agent for Wells, Fargo and friend to the Earps.

Earp,

> **Allie**—Common-law wife of Virgil Earp.
>
> **Bessie**—Common-law wife of James Earp.
>
> **Hattie**—Teenaged daughter of Bessie Earp.
>
> **James**—Wounded war veteran, bartender, and oldest brother of the Earps in Tombstone.
>
> **Louisa**—Common-law wife of Morgan Earp.
>
> **Mattie**—Former prostitute and common-law wife of Wyatt.
>
> **Morgan**—Younger and favorite brother of Wyatt.
>
> **Nicholas**—Father of the Earp brothers.
>
> **Virgil**—Deputy US Marshal and town marshal of Tombstone. Older brother to Wyatt.
>
> **Virginia**—Mother of the Earp brothers.
>
> **Wyatt**—Wells, Fargo shotgun messenger, Pima County deputy sheriff, Tombstone deputy marshal, deputy US marshal, gambler, and investor.

Elder, Kate—Once a prostitute, an off-and-on, volatile paramour of Doc Holliday.

Fitch, Tom—Orator and attorney who represents the Earps at the "O.K. Corral inquest."

Fly, Camillus (Buck)—Photographer, owner of the boardinghouse where Doc Holliday rooms.

Flynn, Jim—Tombstone deputy under Marshal Virgil Earp.

Frank—Virgil and Allie Earp's dog.

Fuller, West—Cow-boy acquaintance who witnesses the "O.K. Corral gunfight."

Gird, Dick—Successful co-owner/operator of Tombstone Mining and Milling Company.

Goodfellow, George—Skilled surgeon and general practitioner for Tombstone area.

Goodrich, Briggs—Attorney whose firm represents Ike Clanton.

Hatch, Bob—Saloon/billiards parlor proprietor friendly to the Earps.

Head, Harry—Cow-boy involved in the Benson stage holdup and murders.

Hill, Joe—Cow-boy complicit in undercover deal with Wyatt Earp.

Holliday, John ("Doc")—Tubercular ex-dentist, gambler, gunman devoted to Wyatt Earp.

Hooker, Henry—Cattle baron of the Sierra Bonita Ranch and friend to the Earps.

Hurst, Lieutenant Joseph—US Army officer stationed at Camp Rucker.

Indian Charlie—*See* Cruz, Florentino.

"Johnny-Behind-the-Deuce"—*See* Roarke, Michael.

Johnson, Creek—Former cow-boy who joins Wyatt Earp's avenging posse.

Joyce, Milt—Manager of bar at Oriental Saloon, unfriendly to Earps and Holliday.

Judah, Theodore—Laborer at Pete Spence's woodcutting camp.

King, Luther ("Lew")—Cow-boy involved in the Benson stage holdup and murders.

Leonard, Billy—Cow-boy involved in the Benson stage holdup and murders, friend to Doc Holliday.

Marcus, Josephine Sarah ("Sadie")—Concubine of Sheriff Behan who befriends Wyatt.

McDaniels, Levi—Stage driver held up by Spence and Stilwell on the Bisbee run.

McDowell, Milton—Deputy sheriff stationed in Charleston.

McKelvey, George—Constable serving Charleston.

McLaury,

 Frank—Older of the two brothers who fence stolen cattle for the cow-boys and die at the "O.K. Corral gunfight."

 Tom—Younger of the two brothers who die at the "O.K. Corral gunfight."

 Will—Texas attorney and oldest brother of Frank and Tom.

McMaster, Sherman—Undercover cow-boy who works for Wyatt Earp.

Neagle, Dave—Deputy under Sheriff Behan.

Patterson, Frank—Cow-boy rustler and troublemaker.

Paul, Bob—Respected Wells, Fargo messenger, sheriff of Pima County after Shibell.

Philpott, Bud—Stage driver killed during Benson stage holdup.

Redfield, Len—Rancher friendly to the cow-boys.

Rickabaugh, Lou—Gambling manager at the Oriental, friend to the Earps.

Ringo, John—Moody, unpredictable cow-boy addicted to alcohol.

Roarke, Michael ("Johnny-Behind-the-Deuce")—Young gambler who murders a mining manager at Dick Gird's mill.

Schneider, Philip—Mining manager senselessly killed my Michael Roarke.

Shibell, Charlie—Sheriff of Pima County before Cochise County is sectioned from it.

Sippy, Ben—Elected marshal of Tombstone who leaves town without giving notice.

Smith, Charlie—Friend to the Earps who joins the vendetta posse.

Spence, Pete—Cow-boy stage robber, enemy of and neighbor to the Earps in Tombstone.

Spicer, Wells—Tombstone Justice of the Peace who rules on the "O.K. Corral inquest."

Stilwell, Frank—Cow-boy stage robber complicit in the murder of Morgan Earp.

Swilling, Hank—Half-breed cow-boy implicated in Morgan Earp's murder.

Tipton, Dan—Gambler and ally of the Earps who rides in the vendetta posse.

Tyler, Johnny—Seedy gambler who is adversarial to the Earps and Holliday.

Vermillion, John—Carpenter who joins Wyatt Earp's vendetta posse.

Whelan, Billy—Foreman at Henry Hooker's Sierra Bonita Ranch.

White, Fred—First town marshal of Tombstone, killed by Curly Bill Brocius.

Williams, Marshall ("Marsh")—Wells, Fargo agent in Tombstone.

Woods, Harry—Editor of the pro-cow-boy *Nugget* and undersheriff to Behan.

CHAPTER I

December 1879

Tombstone, A.T.

The Earps' three-wagon train trundled over the desert sand on the last leg from Tucson to Tombstone. The flat land on both sides of the trail bristled with dry, prickly vegetation—squat mesquite trees, bushy cat's-claw, and dagger-like leaves of yucca and agave. Tall saguaro cacti stood their ground like lone sentinels stationed strategically out in the brush. These standing giants, the startling rock formations, and the winding arroyos broke up the monotony of the terrain, providing natural mileage markers for the journey. The distant mountains completed a larger view of the Sonora Desert.

Wyatt planned to know this route with intimate familiarity as soon as his stage and transport business was up and running. Already he was committing landmarks to memory and taking note of the washouts in the road where a coach wheel could mire to the axle.

Having lived in the Arizona Territory for two years, brother Virgil and his wife, Allie, led the caravan in their sturdy Studebaker, with canvas sheeting arched high above their belongings. Their dog, Frank, trotted alongside the four-horse team when he wasn't sniffing out jackrabbits and ground squirrels. Behind Virgil came James, the oldest brother, who managed his team with his one good arm, while in the back of his sheeted spring wagon his wife, Bessie, instructed her sixteen-year-old daughter, Hattie, in the tedious methods for sewing canvas with a waterproof stitching so that the seams did not leak.

Bessie's repetitive drills and Hattie's juvenile complaints joined with the constant jingle of the harnesses and the rumble of the wheels to fill the emptiness around Wyatt and Mattie, who brought up the rear. They had barely spoken since their stop in Benson to water the horses.

It had been an uneventful journey to the southeastern corner of the territory, but now they began to encounter other migrators drifting south from San Manuel and Willcox and west from New Mexico. Just as the Earps were, all were drawn to the possibilities of a new boomtown that sat atop a trove of silver. It seemed that each group of travelers had packed in haste, stacking their worldly belongings into every manner of conveyance. Besides covered wagons like Virgil's, there were freight wagons, modified carriages, and buckboards—some of these pulling flatbed hay trailers or two-wheeled Red River carts lashed to a rear axle. Other than the occasional passenger stage or bullion wagon making a run from Tombstone to the county seat, there was no traffic moving against this flow. Silver was the new siren's song belting out its promises to a country sinking in an economic depression.

They came from the big cities of the East, from the lake country of Minnesota, from the northern plains, and from the tall timbers of Oregon. Some hailed from Wales, Germany, or Denmark. Their stations in life ranged from banking to hardscrabble farming. The geological riches of Tombstone were like an insatiable flame drawing moths of every stripe.

In spite of their differences, these travelers seemed to share one trait: Wyatt could see the same glimmer of hunger burning in their eyes. Or maybe it was hope. It seemed to set the men on edge, and out of that nervousness they prodded their teams on at an imprudent pace. In the women's faces he sensed something else. Resignation, perhaps. Or, if not that, the knowledge that they had come to a time and place in their lives where there were no other options.

From the driver's box of his wagon Wyatt constantly studied the rolling sea of desert scrub around him, so untouched by humans and nearly devoid of wildlife except birds, snakes, and lizards. Taking in the clean winter fragrance of the desert, Wyatt decided the remoteness of this land was to his liking. Despite the constant blow of fine, dun dust that found its way into every crevice of skin and fold of garment, the desert felt like the perfect place for a new start. The landscape was untouched and seemed somehow healing. Even the endless outcrops of beige, orange, and blue rocks seemed to sharpen the air with an antiseptic scent. Everything was new here. And anything new seemed full of promise.

Judging by the number of commercial coaches that had rattled past him since Tucson, Wyatt grudgingly began to accept the US Marshal's information about the stage line business in Tombstone. Wyatt had noted four different business names on the sides of the coaches, and, by the way the drivers had handled their rigs when they passed, he was satisfied that these express companies were staffed with capable men.

It would be hard to give up on his plan to establish his own stage line. For two solid months now, Wyatt had held this idea in his mind and run through the details of operation. He had even sketched a blueprint and penciled a tally of the lumber he would need to build a livery in town. The wagon on which he sat had been purchased for this very enterprise. With the help of a carpenter, he had planned to convert it into a passenger coach with a bullion trap hidden in the floor.

The string of eleven horses following his wagon on a long lead rope had been chosen for this enterprise. Each was stout and well-suited for its draft capabilities—all but the long-legged racer, of course. That stud would bring in money on private wagers and formal competitions. No matter his profession, Wyatt knew there would always be the time and the occasion for impromptu side bets as well as organized races.

*****

When the Earps watered their horses at the wells near Contention, the women huddled together at the back of Virgil's wagon and prepared a light meal of cold biscuits, dried venison, and pole beans preserved in a jar of brine. Allie hauled out a flat-topped trunk, topped it with a faded red blanket, and sat. Without invitation Bessie, Hattie, and Mattie joined her, and there they settled in to eat, each with her back to the others. Frank, the dog, sat in front of Allie, alert for any donations that might be afforded him.

The Earp brothers stood at the tailgate, and, as they picked at the food, they discussed their plans to set up a permanent camp on the outskirts of Tombstone that very night. When finished, Wyatt walked past the stage station into the brush to relieve himself. On returning he moved toward the corral, where a hostler tossed a rope over the head of a cinnamon-maned sorrel gelding. Wyatt propped a boot on the low rail of the fence, slipped his hands into his coat pockets, and studied the animals inside the enclosure.

The remuda was impressive—close to sixty well-muscled horses, all in constant motion in the brisk December air, save the sweat-soaked flanks of six at the water trough. These animals were spent and dusted gray from the trail. Together they siphoned up water through their long muzzles like a row of supplicants come to pray before a holy altar.

When the sorrel balked at being led, the hostler dug into his pocket and then teased the horse with a cupped hand near its nostrils. The big steed lipped his hand once, took a hesitant step forward, licked up the morsels of sweet grain with a thick tongue, and then followed. The man laughed with a quiet growl and smiled at Wyatt.

"Juss like some little spoilt baby awantin' his candy," he said, shaking his head.

The man laughed again and walked the horse into the barn. When he returned, he reset the loop on his lariat and threw it over the head of a bay moving along the fence near Wyatt. The bay backed away, wall-eyed, pulling the rope taut. Digging his heels into the dirt, the hostler sent a quick curling wave up the rope to give it slack, and then he jerked it twice. The bay stood firm but then nickered and surrendered to the same ruse of the cupped hand of sweet grain.

When he returned without the rope, the hostler walked directly to Wyatt and rested an arm on the top rail of the fence. Looking back at the horses, he fingered a pinch of tobacco from a small rolled bag and pushed a wad into his mouth. The man's whiskered cheek bulged like a swell on a cactus. He offered the bag, but Wyatt shook his head.

"I figure they've earn't a little spoilin', the way we use 'em up," the man said and chuckled. Chewing on the tobacco, he seemed to settle in to study the herd in earnest, but right away he turned back to Wyatt, cocked his head to one side, and raised his eyebrows until his forehead wrinkled like a washboard. "Tell you what," he said, his voice now low and confiding, "winter or not . . . I wouldn' wanna be haulin' 'round one o' these rockin' sideshows through this damned desert sand with a damned whip snapping at my ass."

When Wyatt said nothing, the hostler leaned away and spat a brown dollop into the trampled dirt of the corral. When he turned back, his eyes narrowed as he studied Wyatt from boots to hat.

"If you're awaitin' on the Kinnear stage into Tombstone, you'd best juss settle in fer a while. Stage busted a axle and broke down just this side out o' Benson. We juss got word."

Wyatt nodded back toward the Earp wagons. "Got my own rig."

The hostler looked past Wyatt and frowned, studying the small train as though appraising the soundness of each wagon for a desert cross-ing. Wyatt shifted his gaze above the herd. Beyond the corral, the Earp women walked up a low hill into the scrub brush toward a crude privy slapped together with sun-bleached boards and a door hung with baling wire. The small outbuilding was like a desert monument, listing slightly to one side as though paying homage to the constant winds. Bessie led the way with Hattie in hand, jerking the girl forward when she lingered. Allie marched behind them, muttering and fussing with her bonnet. Mattie quietly followed them all, her forearms crossed over her stomach and her head turning from side to side as she inspected the trail.

The hostler spat again and then looked at the side of Wyatt's face. "That's a purty string o' horses tied to that tailgate. Are them yours?"

Wyatt looked at the man and said plainly, "I was thinking I might open up my own stage line."

The hostler's face wrinkled like a twisted rag. "In Tombstone?" He stared back at Wyatt, waiting to see if he were supposed to laugh at a man's joke. When Wyatt's pale blue eyes held steady on him, the hos-tler's questioning expression hardened, and he began to nod, as though he were now seriously considering such an enterprise.

"Tell you what," the man said. He spat again, and then he wiped at his whiskered chin with the back of a dirty coat sleeve. "We're 'bout covered up with stages down here. The two big comp'nies are at war, each one tryin' to bury t'other." He pushed back his hat and stared to the southeast in the general direction of Tombstone. "Cain't rightly see how a new line could survive out here." He shrugged and gave Wyatt a sheepish grin. "Only so many teats to suck off, you know. I guess you got to get there early to take your place."

"This ain't 'early'?" Wyatt asked.

The horseman laughed and hitched his head with a quick jerk. "Things happ'n purty quick in Tombstone. I reckon a town can grow up too fast fer its own good." He forked his hands on his hips and tried for a show of kindness in his face. "Tell you what . . . I was you . . . I'd be thinkin' 'bout another line o' work."

When Wyatt nodded, the man turned and again watched the horses in the corral. The hostler seemed embarrassed and said nothing for a time. Finally, he twisted around and raised his chin at the Earp train.

"Tell you what . . . you might wanna talk to the station manager. He'd prob'ly buy them horses off you, if you're of a mind to sell."

Wyatt looked up the hill and saw Bessie and Hattie making their way back down the trail. At the privy, Mattie now stood alone outside the closed door, her arms still pressed against her belly as though shielding herself from the unknown dangers of this new land. For the hundredth time, Wyatt tried to imagine Mattie as a mother to the baby she was carrying. It was a difficult image to piece together. Like trying to arrange plucked flower petals floating on water. But he couldn't fault Mattie. It was no easier to see himself as a father.

Even before he climbed back into his wagon, Wyatt had accepted the fact that he might have to abandon his plans to start his own express company. Now he began to consider other opportunities. Maybe he would invest in the land itself, hire a crew, and dig up enough ore to interest another buyer. That he knew nothing of mining operations ought not to deter him. Other men foreign to the field had made their fortunes off of bold venturing and the grit to stand by their decisions.

Besides the capital to get started, Wyatt knew that such an enterprise would take some show of confidence . . . and timing. These were tools he had employed as an officer of the law—such intangibles sometimes proving equally as important as his Colt's or his fists. There was no reason he could not be one of those entrepreneurs who came out on the top of an economic free-for-all like the one going on in Tombstone.

He would have to learn the politics first. He needed to meet the right people and get them to see that he was a man to get things done. And he couldn't let a few troublesome citizens get in the way of that—people like Billy Smith in Wichita and Bob Wright in Dodge. Now that he wore no badge, there would be no reason to incur enemies as he had in Kansas. He might be able to stow his guns away for good. Like an old pair of boots he had finally outgrown.

With the Earp party under way and Tombstone only hours down the trail, Wyatt began to feel a little prickle on the back of his neck. It was the same sensation he sometimes experienced at a faro game, when he knew the next card from the box would either make him or break him. Tombstone was a gamble, the biggest for which he had anted up; but, like Virgil and James, he was all in.

Two hours later the three wagons came to a halt. At the head of the procession, Virgil erupted with an uncharacteristic *whoop* that carried back to his brothers' wagons.

"That's it!" Virge yelled, his big booming voice bringing up all eyes to a plateau nestled inside a circle of hills just below the horizon.

From his place at the center of the caravan, James turned to show his crooked grin to Wyatt. "You smell that?" he sang out in his teasing melody. "That there, son, is the sweet aroma of silver." In the wagon bed, Bessie and Hattie set aside their needlework and peered around the wagon sheets toward the town.

When Wyatt took in the flat on which Tombstone had risen, the same enigma struck him as had greeted him at every other boom town he had entered. How could a place so isolated—in the middle of so much empty space—accommodate a horde of fortune seekers and their families? How could enough food get freighted out here to sustain life? Tombstone was a level anthill of a settlement centered in a wasteland of low hills, hostile scrub, and sharp, angular stone. Only the knowledge of unseen silver below endowed the little rise of land with any sense of luminescence.

Holding up his map to square with the surroundings, Virgil called out to the wagons behind him and pointed north. There in the distance, a long mountain range stretched like a jagged set of teeth risen from a vast, flat plain.

"That there's the Dragoons. And way off behind 'em . . . the Chiricahuas. That'll be where most of the timber comes from. Apaches, too." Virge paused to wink at his wife beside him. When feisty little Allie showed no hint of being amused, Virge swept his arm from west to south. "The Whetstones. The Huachucas. That little bunch there . . . that's the Mule Mountains. And way off in the haze there . . . that's old Mexico." He laughed. "Reckon a man can see 'bout as far as he wants here."

That sounded about right to Wyatt. He took it all in and let his gaze settle back on the camp lying beyond the deep gulch, where the road appeared to have washed out. The town was already growing past the tent phase, more buildings having sprung up than he would have guessed. The distant bang of hammers and the grind of a ripsaw carried to his ears like an anthem of industry . . . and the hope of a man's resurrection, his included. All Wyatt wanted was something to carry away from this prickly desert to sustain him the rest of his life in some other place with more favorable surroundings. A big chunk of silver would do fine.

When they were rolling again, Mattie pulled her shawl more tightly around her narrow shoulders and leaned to be heard over the rumble of the wheels. "Wyatt?" she said, her small and timid voice even frailer here in the desert. "What *about* these Apaches? I overheard two men talking about them back at the station. Are they a danger to the people who live out here?"

Wyatt kept his eyes on the road ahead. Life was going to be hard enough here for Mattie without her worrying about renegade Indians. He pushed his lower lip forward and shook his head.

"If they do make any trouble, it won't be in the town. It would happen out at the fringes where the numbers of settlers are small."

She continued to stare at him, her thin eyebrows lowered over fearful eyes. "Isn't that where we'll be? At first, I mean?"

Wyatt looked at Mattie's plain face, the skin on her pale forehead creased like a washboard. Then he nodded toward her belly.

"We'll be in close enough. You and that baby are gonna be safe in Tombstone. You don't need to be worryin' 'bout Indians."

Mattie turned back to examine the rough-hewn town that was supposed to protect her. She did not appear comforted by what she saw. Wyatt thought about patting her knee to smooth out the concern on her face, but when she began fitting her bonnet to her head and fastening the ties beneath her chin, he simply stared off toward the silver-laden hills that held all their futures within its domain.

Virgil's wagon started up again and jostled its way toward the dip in the road. James snapped his reins to follow. Wyatt spoke in a low, raspy whisper to his team, and the train resumed its rattling progress over the rock and sand toward this town with a graveyard name.

CHAPTER 2

Winter 1879–1880

Tombstone, A.T.

They lived out of their wagons in the scrub at the west edge of town, close enough for the women to feel connected to the safety of numbers, but outside the grid of land lots that had been surveyed for identification and ownership. Among the three rigs Wyatt and Virgil tied up oiled canvas tarpaulins to cover a common place for meals. As a respite from the cold winds blowing in from the San Pedro Valley, they set up Virgil's wood stove in this shared ground. Crates, trunks, and barrels were dragged into a cramped circle around the stove for seating. Two latrines were dug: one due west for the brothers, the other closer to town for the women.

As it was with all boom towns that seemed to mushroom overnight, dead wood was absent from the fringe of desert bordering Tombstone. James bought a quarter cord of seasoned juniper from a dark-skinned Mexican boy who peddled his goods from a crude handcart he tugged along the streets.

The Earp women banded together quickly out of necessity, preparing meals on the stove and laundering clothes in a washtub. Their personalities made for an odd alliance: Bessie's dictatorial nature, Allie's quick chatterbox tongue, and Mattie's quiet drift at the gossamer edge of sanity.

At sixteen, Hattie should have been the one most dispossessed from her intended life, but she seemed to thrive off the friction between herself and her mother. It was Mattie who found their new venture most disconcerting. For her this move was a test of nearly insurmountable odds. The desert's inhospitable landscape—its invasive dust and hostile silhouettes of spiny plants—represented to her a disheartening step down from Kansas. Most troubling was her inclusion in this extended version of the family. The Earp women frightened her. Even Hattie lorded over her when no one else was near to hear her do it. Wyatt could see Mattie's despair, but there was nothing he could do about it. He could no more bolster Mattie's resolve than he could take the bossy sass out of Allie and Bessie.

When the brothers set out to size up the town, twice they were mistaken for bankers appraising the various establishments going up. They wore black suits and vests, and their trouser cuffs hung loose outside their boots. They carried no guns. Their sandy-blond hair and moustaches were an eye-catching contrast beneath dark, straight-brimmed hats. Between the lapels of their long, black coats, their starched shirts shone like white flames burning in the Arizona sun.

James was naturally drawn to the saloons and disappeared into each one he encountered. Wyatt concentrated his efforts on the mine superintendents to get a feel for the manpower needed to work a claim. Virgil checked into water rights and introduced himself to the owners of the buildings on Allen Street, the most important business thoroughfare in the camp. When he deemed it time to pay a visit to the mayor, Virgil asked Wyatt to accompany him.

In front of the city offices on Fremont Street, a man about Wyatt's age held the door open for them. Virgil stopped suddenly when he spotted a shield of inscribed metal on the man's overcoat collar.

"I reckon we oughta meet," Virgil said in his affable way. "Would you be city or county law?"

"Fred White, chief of police . . . or, as we used to say, 'town marshal.' " White, with the soft, rufous-tinted cheeks of a woman, shook each brother's hand in two stiff pumps. His words knotted his stiff jaw and were delivered with restraint and precision.

"I'm Virgil Earp, down from Prescott. Dake appointed me a federal deputy for the Tombstone district."

"Good," White said. "It's just me right now." He cut his inspecting eye to Wyatt.

"This is my brother," Virgil said, "Wyatt."

White narrowed his eyes at Wyatt, as though trying to remember him from some occasion of his past. "You boys putting down roots here?"

"We aim to," Wyatt said.

White looked from one to the other, noting their likeness, and then raised his chin to Wyatt. "You in the law work, too?"

"Businessman," Wyatt replied.

White nodded, waiting for more, but Wyatt turned to observe the traffic along the thoroughfare. The wide road was like a river in constant motion, eddies of construction crews swirling at the edges. Craftsmen were everywhere, erecting, nailing, and sawing. Every townsman's face appeared rapt with some blueprint for an improved life.

"Did Dake tell you the situation down here?" White said, turning his attention back to Virgil.

"Told me nothin'."

White frowned. "Well, we'd better go have us a drink and let me show you the lay of the land." He touched Virgil's elbow, and with his other hand made a guiding gesture up Fourth Street toward the heart of the business district.

"Come on, Wyatt," Virgil said and winked conspiratorially at White. "He'll need to hear this, too."

In the back of a large tent saloon, they sat around a wide plank spanning two crates set on end. Wyatt ordered coffee, the others warm beer.

"So, what kind of business are you in, Wyatt?" Fred White asked.

"Lookin' at the minin' end."

"As an investor?"

"Some. More an initiator. I'll file some claims, organize some crews, and try my luck."

White offered a wry smile. "Well, make sure your claims are tight. There's a lot of disagreement on that around here. With the town incorporating, there are men who are already making plans to renegotiate who owns the rights to what."

"How many folks in this burg?" Virgil said.

White pursed his lips and stared out the open doorway. "Going on a thousand, I'd say. Probably over a dozen coming in on the stage lines every day. And half that riding in on their own steam."

Virgil laughed. "Sounds like this town might bust at the seams b'fore long."

White sipped his beer and shook his head. "It is fast growing, but there's plenty who won't stay. Right now Tombstone looks like the answer to everybody's prayers, the economy being what it is everywhere else in the country. They'll come here and go bust or get so rich they don't have to stay." He raised his mug and swirled the contents. "Most men would rather live in a place where they can buy a beer that's *cold*."

A stagecoach rumbled down the street, and someone yelled out to clear the road. A gunshot popped in the thoroughfare, a pistol aimed high by the sound of it, the sharp percussive *crack* quickly swallowed up by the wide desert sky. Wyatt watched White's expressionless eyes flick toward the tent entrance and immediately dismiss the misdemeanor.

"Got to choose my battles with care," White said through a self-deprecatory grin. "A stage messenger firing his weapon to clear the street is not on my list of worries."

"What about the mines?" Wyatt inquired. "Are they payin' out?"

White hitched his head to one side. "Some. We're sitting on a rich lode, but it's the few big operations pulling out most of the ore. A lot of the smaller mines have played out. Some never strike a vein."

Wyatt nodded, considering his options. "I reckon the gambling has followed the money. Seems to be enough gaming houses here to keep a full police force busy."

White nodded in agreement. "I've got my hands full, there's no denying. But the real problem out here will fall to the county." He nodded to Virgil. "And to you." When he drank from his mug again, he used the time to look around the tent. Then he carefully set down the mug and leaned in closer. "There are men who have cattle ranched here since long before the strike. But now with so many people here, and the demand for beef up, a lot of them have adopted new methods for increasing their stock. Hooker's the big one out here. He's legitimate. And Ayles, too.

They lose cattle by the week to a crowd that's getting pretty damned well-organized. People call 'em 'the Cow-boys.' Mostly Texans run out of their state by the Rangers. And now they're raiding here and down into Mexico on a regular basis."

"Why ain't it stopped?" Virgil asked.

"The sheriff's situated in Tucson. It's a damned big county. Even bigger when you consider that these Cow-boys move in and out of New Mexico and Sonora at will."

"Why do the citizens stand for it?" Wyatt said. "Why don't they organize, too?"

"Like I said, it's a damned big county. And the honest ranchers don't have the manpower to fight it. And these people in town here?" White swept a hand vaguely toward the street. "It's cheap beef . . . and it's Mexican. What do they care?" He turned to Wyatt. "Best business you could go into would be town butcher."

Virgil smiled into his beer. "He done that in Wichita and Dodge."

White looked back at Wyatt, his eyes narrowed as if trying to recall a face.

Virgil set down his mug, and his voice took on a serious tone. "Do you know who these Cow-boys are?"

"Everybody knows. The Clantons, the Patterson outfit, the Redfield and McLaury brothers. They're the ones who are settled enough to *look* like established ranchers. Then there must be forty or fifty others—just saddlers, really—questionable characters who practically live on their horses. Half of them have outstanding warrants from other states. Tough crowd. Only thing they're good for is keeping the Apaches out."

"What about the army," Wyatt said, "if these boys are raiding into Mexico?"

"Both armies—ours and the Mexicans'—are going through the motions. It's just too damned big a territory." White's forehead wrinkled. He pointed at Wyatt and poked a forefinger toward him three times. "Dodge City," he whispered. "I think I *have* heard your name."

Virgil made the deep laugh that rumbled up from his chest. "Good or bad?"

White frowned. "I think I heard it from some of the Cow-boys. You know a man named Brocius? Goes by 'Curly Bill'?"

Watching Fred White gather his memory of a half-forgotten conversation, Wyatt drank his coffee and set down his cup. "Dark hair and freckles on his face." It wasn't a question.

"That's him," White said. "So, you know him?"

Wyatt recalled the embarrassment in Dodge City when he had tried to pull Mattie from Frankie Bell's line of whores in a crowded saloon. Brocius had just paid for Mattie, and Frankie had put up a fuss that quieted the room.

Pushing the incident from his mind, Wyatt laid down coins on the rough counter to cover the drinks. Then he nodded casually to the marshal.

"We've met," Wyatt said.

*****

It was dusk, the evening meal over and the dishes and cookware cleaned up. All the Earps were gathered in the adobe hut James had found to rent. The men had settled on rough benches hacked out of pine by a Mexican woodworker. There around the wood stove they smoked cigars and waited for Bessie to finish her diatribe on their living conditions.

The dust, the cold, the hauling of water—all of it was several notches down from the brothel life to which she had become accustomed. Although Allie had roughed it with Virgil for some time, she was nodding and throwing in her "amens." Mattie never spoke when more than two people were gathered. She was lost in a pent-up way, like a fawn taken from the wild to wander wide-eyed through the small rooms of the abode.

"We're gonna build some houses, Bessie," Virgil assured her, "on those properties we bought at the corner of First and Fremont."

As usual, the timbre of appeasement in Virgil's voice made all the women feel better about their situation. Even Bessie knew that when Virgil said they would do something, somehow they got it done.

"*Separate* houses?" Bessie asked, a little excitement slipping through her abrasive front.

"You and me and Hattie will find our own place closer to the business district," James said, taking over as diplomat between his wife and his brothers. "But we'll be sharing for a while, Bessie."

She sat heavily on the bench next to James. "Well, we've sure got in the damned practice for that, haven't we?"

James made a dismissive grunt. "We'll make do, pretty lady." He spoke as he always did to his wife—in a singsong fashion that would have little effect on her mood. But when she started to say more, James sat forward and interrupted her. "It's gonna take time, Bessie, so let it go." This time he put something cold in his voice to let her know that she was wearing thin on everyone.

For a moment the fire burned copper-green through the open door of the stove, but in the strained silence no one remarked on it. Allie made the face that Virgil called her "Irish pickle." She turned to face the stove, held her hands out to the radiant heat for several seconds, and then she slapped her palms to her bony knees.

"Well, let's get to building *somethin'*," she carped. When no one responded she turned a silent ultimatum on Virgil.

"We can't start building yet," Virgil explained, staring into the fire. "Our money's tied up."

"Well, untie some!" Allie shot back.

Virgil studied his cigar, so Allie glared at Wyatt.

"It's invested," Wyatt said. "Mines and real estate. There's no sense in pullin' out now." Wyatt's deep, raspy voice, on the surface, was not unlike Virgil's, only drier and with little melody to it, all of which lent it the ring of no-nonsense. When they listened to Wyatt, there was a look in their eyes that suggested they were learning something that only he knew, something they were counting on him to know. Whenever Wyatt spoke, even Virgil turned to look at him.

"If we play it smart," Wyatt continued, "we'll come *out* better than we come *into* this place."

"Takes money to make money, right?" James said and laughed as he poured himself a drink. "We'll bring some money in from these mines before too long."

Bessie scowled at James, but he was so absorbed with filling his glass, she had to lean forward to let him see the challenge on her face. "So what do we do while we're waiting to get rich?" She leaned her forearms on her thighs and stubbornly waited for an answer.

"There's a hellava lot of canvas going up in this town," James said. He avoided Bessie's stare by leaning forward to sort through the stack of firewood. "We thought you ladies might do some sewing to pull in a little extra income."

Bessie met Allie's eyes, and their female solidarity knitted together on the spot—something new for them.

"Hell, I got something better than canvas to sell," Bessie laughed dryly.

Wyatt looked up sharply, and James put some hardness into his voice. "There's to be none of that. We're makin' names for ourselves here with the folks that count. I'll be servin' drinks at Vogan's." He jammed a stick into the fire and turned a hard glare on Bessie, who set her face in a rare pout.

"I'd rather be making money off *my* business instead of just sittin' on it," she mumbled.

"No," Wyatt said.

He had not raised his voice, but his resolve brought a chill to the room that invited no discussion. In this stillness, Virgil's short-legged dog abandoned his place by the stove and stood hopefully before Allie, who picked it up, nestled it in her lap, and began stroking the cur's head and ears. With each pull, the dog's eyes narrowed to contented slits, then widened, reflecting the light from the fire.

Wyatt glanced toward the back room, where Hattie had gone to bed, and for the first time since he had left the slums of the Peoria waterfront, he thought about the price he had seen young girls pay while growing up in a brothel. Hattie's life had been no different with James and Bessie, except that she had been spared falling into the occupation. This by Bessie's mandate. Wyatt looked squarely at Bessie and, as well as he could, delivered his own pronouncement on how the Earps would operate in Tombstone.

"We'll make our money," he said, "but not that way."

Bessie propped her chin in her hand and stared at the fire. Quietly, she grunted a final complaint, but she said no more.

Virgil checked the burn of his cigar. "Well," he began, trying to bring some warmth to the family discussion, "the federal marshal—Dake—I reckon he'll have something for me before too long."

Bessie sat up straight again, but the harsh edge in her voice was gone. "That ain't like you, and you know it, Virgil . . . waiting around for something to come to you."

Now Allie bristled. "Some things have got to be waited on, Bessie!"

Bessie rolled her eyes, and then she looked from one face to the other, finally settling on Wyatt. "There's a hellava lot of people here planning to live off a one-armed bartender." She had spoken with a guarded sharpness and continued to hold her glare on Wyatt. "What are all those fancy-dancy people gonna think of that?"

Wyatt wanted to walk outside just to breathe the desert air for a while without someone to argue everything he had to say. He laid a dry stick of ocotillo in the fire, and it caught immediately, the flames licking through the woven latticework of wood along its entire length. It burned through the holes like a row of candles, until it blackened like tar and collapsed in the flames.

"Bessie," James said, capping the whiskey bottle, "if you knew my brother better, you'd know it's his own opinion of himself he knows to give a damn about." James held a hard look on her, and finally she relaxed, tilting her face into her hands, wearily rubbing the heels of her palms into her eyes.

"I'll be bringing in some money," Wyatt said. "I've got hold of a half-interest in a faro table at the Oriental. And I've got somethin' else in the works."

Bessie took the bottle from James. "Well, do we get to know what that is?" She unscrewed the cap and then hesitated as she waited for an answer.

Wyatt looked at his family, sorting the brothers from the wives, trying to understand why the women could not see the future that waited for them if they played their hands right.

"We all got to pitch in," Virgil said. "I figure the sewin' is a good idea."

The room went quiet again, Virgil's words hanging in the air like an invitation for absolution. Bessie turned a frowning face toward Virgil, but, before she could speak, Allie shooed the dog off her lap and stood.

"Well, hang it all," Allie huffed, "we didn't haul that sewin' machine out here for nothin', now did we?" She moved behind Virgil and laid her small hands on his shoulders. The dog followed and sat, its ears perked up, its dark eyes dedicated to Virgil.

Virge quietly laughed, reached to his shoulder, and patted the back of Allie's hand. "Startin' to sound like a family around here," he said and winked at Wyatt.

Mattie lay very still as Wyatt slipped into his side of their pallet. Their shared warmth had become a strained but practical commodity for the winter nights of the high desert. They listened to the distant laughter from saloons drift to them from the edge of town, the wind pushing the sounds their way like a flock of crazed birds cackling somewhere far out in the night.

"Wyatt?" Mattie whispered. "What work is it you're considering . . . besides the gambling?"

Wyatt stared up at the spaced timbers in the ceiling. He knew where this conversation would go. Weary of argument, he considered turning on his side and saying "good night," but then he thought it best to get this over with.

"Wells, Fargo," he said simply. When Mattie said nothing, he added, "They've offered me a job guarding their shipments."

Mattie's head turned on the pillow. "That's like your law jobs, Wyatt. You said you were done with that."

"It's something I know how to do, Mattie. It'll bring in some money."

She propped up on an elbow. "It's like Bessie said to Virgil . . . you're settling for something, Wyatt." She leaned closer and lowered her voice to a whisper. "You can do better than that, Wyatt. Don't settle." When she backed away and was quiet again, he heard her swallow as if to bolster her courage. "Let me get a job, Wyatt. I can probably—"

His head turned to her so quickly that the words locked in her throat. "I don't want you going into town."

When she made no reply, he lay back and closed his eyes. The room was so quiet now that he could have been alone there in the darkness. Then he heard her head slowly settle back on the pillow. She lay very still for several heartbeats, and he knew that she was trying not to cry.

"Why?" she asked quietly, the misery in her voice like a pin pricking his skin.

Wyatt took a deep breath and eased it out. "Mattie, there's people here who know you too well . . . from Kansas."

He expected her to ask more, but finally she turned her back to him, retreating into the place where she could feed her own suffering. Opening his eyes he stared at the low ceiling and tried to clear his mind of what she had said.

Don't settle.

The words crept through his head like a worm burrowing into his memory. This night brought back to him a Mexican girl's prophecy. Words spoken to him in a peach orchard in California. He could hear Valenzuela Cos's beguiling voice as clearly as if she were here in the room with him.

We all have wishes. But in the end we must settle for what we have.

She had been talking about living in a house made of mud. And a moon that mimicked the color of that mud. The adobe moon, she had called it.

Wyatt's hand touched the floor and felt the rough texture of the woven straw mat. Each of the wives had purchased one from a Mexican peddler for the three bedrooms. Wyatt clasped his hands over his belly and frowned in the dark. This mat was the only thing separating him from the dirt. Truth be told, he was surrounded on all sides by mud. Staring into the dark, he tried to see past all this for a glimpse of salvation. Not just for him. For all his brothers. And their wives.

This is temporary, Wyatt told himself.

He closed his eyes again to concentrate on what was coming. One day he would look back on this beginning as a necessary inconvenience to get a foothold in this silver-rich country. In the quiet of the room, as he smelled the mix of dirt and straw of the crude abode, something scuttled across the floor near the stool where he had undressed. He reminded himself to check his boots for scorpions in the morning.

You will settle for what you have, Valenzuela Cos had said. *The adobe moon is a better one than no moon at all.*

Wyatt wondered if that damned moon was hanging up there now in the Arizona sky. "To hell with it," he whispered to himself and turned on his side to make the mirror image with Mattie that had become their nightly habit.

CHAPTER 3

Spring, Summer 1880

Tombstone, A.T.; McLaury Ranch, Babacomari River, Pima County

When brother Morgan arrived from Montana with his quick humor and exaggerated tales of his law enforcement work in that country, the conjoined families could not help but climb a little out of the dark mood their clashing personalities had been brewing. The younger brother looked so much like Wyatt now that people no longer confused Virgil for Wyatt . . . only Morgan.

In spring, when the brothers realized their first returns on the mining claims, James moved his family into a house on Fremont and bought out the small sampling room inside Vogan's, which he now advertised as a cut above the average saloon. By doing so, he planned to serve a higher class of clientele in order to fulfill the Earps' aspirations as men of respected standing in the village.

Wyatt hired a carpenter named John Vermillion, an accomplished woodworker with a mane of dark hair flowing down his back to his shoulder blades. Under Vermillion's supervision, the first of the Earp cottages was framed up. The improved spirits of Allie showed not so much in what she said as what she didn't say. Only Mattie was unfazed by the new optimism. To her, this desert town was little more than a taunting sideshow outside the window of her prison.

Soon after they had moved into the new house, Wyatt came home from the Oriental in the pre-dawn hours and found Mattie sitting on the porch, wrapped in a light shawl, waiting. Her chin was tucked angrily into her chest as her fragile eyes looked off toward the distant lights on Fremont Street.

Wyatt checked his pocketwatch by the light of the stars and stepped up on the porch to stand before her. "It's after four. What are you doin' up?"

Her dour face came up enough to nod toward the town. "I'm two blocks from the commercial district, but I might as well be in a mineshaft." Her eyes rolled up in their pinched sockets to stare at him. "Wyatt, the most I see of you is the back of your head in the mornings. And if you're on the Tucson route for Wells, Fargo, you're gone for three days at a time. When you *are* here, you're asleep. I tiptoe around, and I feel something winding up inside me." A fierce glow hardened her eyes, and a bitter smile tightened her lips. "Is this what it's like to go mad, Wyatt?" She asked this with a boldness that seemed unnatural to her fearful ways.

"Mattie, this isn't the time. There're people asleep inside."

"Not the time?" She coughed up a rough laugh. "When *is* there time, Wyatt?"

He took off his hat and tapped it against his leg, as he watched her stare scornfully into the night. "This is part of my work, Mattie. Gambling is what I do when I'm not a shotgun messenger. It's what brings the money in."

The door opened, and Virgil stood there dressed in his black suit. "Wyatt?"

When Wyatt did not respond, Mattie stood and pushed through the door past Virgil. Both brothers watched through the open doorway as she strode down the hall and disappeared into the bedroom. When the door of Wyatt's bedroom closed with a sound of finality, Virgil stepped outside and eased the front door shut.

Wyatt slapped his leg with the hat a little harder and looked up Fremont Street at the glow of light spreading above the saloon district. "I might start stayin' in town with Morg . . . at least when I'm late coming in like this."

"With Morg?" Virgil laughed. "He's already got Fred Dodge with him living in that little shack." Virge stepped to the edge of the porch and allowed another chuckle. "Morg's having the time of his life. Drinking, gambling, shooting pool."

Wyatt nodded. "He's at the Oriental with me most every night . . . learnin' to deal faro."

Virgil laughed again and sat in the chair where Mattie had been. "Hell, all Morg wants is to be like you."

Wyatt gave Virgil a look, and the older brother shrugged. They were quiet for a time, both looking up at the brilliant array of stars arched over the skies of southern Arizona. A warm breeze whipped up dust and rattled the dry, spiny leaves of the yucca in the yard.

"I'm puttin' together a federal posse," Virgil said. "Some mules got stole from Camp Rucker. I could use you."

Wyatt's eyes sharpened, and Virgil went on.

"I'll go down and see can I find the Wells, Fargo man, Williams. He usually gambles down at the Alhambra. He might come along. And Morg, too. We'll pull out at dawn."

"Is that gonna be enough men?"

Virgil tilted his head to one side. "We'll have a lieutenant and a few soldiers, but it's you boys I'll be countin' on." They were quiet again—one of those moments when the bond of being brothers tightened around them. Wyatt walked to the door, opened it, and looked into the house. It was all dark save the faint strip of flickering light showing through the crack under his bedroom door.

"I'll try'n get a coupl'a hours of sleep," he said, his voice flat, lifeless. "I'll be ready at dawn."

Virgil stood and held the door for his brother. Chuckling deep in his chest, he growled to Wyatt's back.

"Good luck."

Mattie had lighted a candle. In the semi-dark of the room she sat on the edge of the bed and faced the wall, her spine slumped and her face pressed into the palms of her hands. She didn't turn when Wyatt closed the door, nor when he crossed the room to the clothes cabinet. After he hung up his coat, he moved to the bed and sat to pull off his boots. He paired them on the wood floor and then remained sitting in the quiet. For a time they sat like this, back to back, unmoving, their silence like a screaming match.

Finally, Mattie straightened. When she spoke, her small voice came off the wall like a sound from another room.

"I'm not married to *you*, Wyatt. I'm married to this little cigar box of a house . . . or whatever other place we happen to be living in."

Wyatt stood, laid out his money on the new bureau, and weighted it down with his revolver. He paused for a moment, leaned on stiffened arms against the bureau, and turned his head to look at Mattie's despair. Taking in a deep breath, Wyatt eased the air out and pushed himself away from the furniture. Then he walked to the open window and put his back to the glass panes to stand in front of her.

"Mattie," he said as gently as he could, "we ain't married at all."

She looked up from her cupped hands, her eyes raw and red and now hurt. Surprising him, she laughed.

"Well, whose shirts have I been cleaning and starching and ironing for God knows how long?"

He had started unbuttoning his shirt, but now he stopped and allowed a frown to show on his face. On the floor next to her were two empty bottles.

"You've been drinking."

"Yes," she hissed. "I've been drinking. Is that all right with you?"

He sat down on the bed next to her. She had tied back the curtain to let in some air. Catty-cornered across the road he could see the silhouette of the other Earp house being framed up.

"There's no baby, is there, Mattie?"

He thought she was practicing her cynical laugh again until he heard the sniffs that broke between the jolts in her body. She fell sideways onto the pillow and began to cry without restraint.

"Can't you even take me out to dinner?" she said, her voice mewling like a cat's.

The dark shapes in the scrub outside were indistinguishable. When Wyatt closed his eyes, his thoughts fared no better, his mind as barren as the land. No words came to him.

"Do you love me, Wyatt? I mean . . . in *any* way at all?"

The silence that followed seemed to stretch all the way to the Dragoons. In the quiet he chose his words carefully.

"I care enough about you to provide for you. I brought you here, didn' I?"

"Wyatt," she breathed heavily, as though he had no idea what he had said. She rose up on an elbow. "What's 'here'? Look at this house." She turned to examine the room as though she would see it for him. "This is my *world*, Wyatt." She flung an arm outward toward town. "That's your world out there . . . Tombstone . . . the whole territory of Arizona."

"I'm just trying to get ahead, Mattie. I figure if I benefit by it, so do you."

She stared blindly out the window and pushed a hand through her tangled hair. Her lack of response seemed more lethargy than acquiescence.

"When the time is right," he said, "I'm thinking on running for office."

Still propped on an elbow, she pivoted her head to him. "And so you have to hide me?"

"Mattie, you were a whore. That ain't gonna help me get votes."

She sat up and used a voice he had never heard from her. "It used to help you. Why aren't *you* the whore? What's the difference who's paying or who's getting paid?"

His face closed down on her questions. "Mattie, there was never any exchange of—"

"It doesn't matter, Wyatt!" she interrupted. "You've been with whores. It's the same thing." She raised her chin toward the door. "When you go run for your office, why don't you tell everybody that *you* were a whore? It's not fair."

He looked out at the blackness of the desert and thought about all the whorehouses he had frequented. He had never considered his part in whoring the same as the woman's. Maybe it was. And maybe it wasn't fair. But it was the way it was. He had a hold of something in Tombstone, and he wasn't letting go. He could feel it starting to gather like a force that would deliver him from every failed aspiration of his past.

If he could get elected to the sheriff's office, he would have everything he had struggled for: money, standing in the community, and the respect of any man, be that man a preacher, a businessman, or an outlaw. For all that, he could tolerate a life in the desert . . . for a time, anyway.

"Mattie, do you want to leave?" he said quietly. "I can give you money."

Her mouth tightened into a quivering seam. "Can't you just love me?"

Wyatt saw the glow first appear on the new leaves of the tall cottonwood in the vacant lot. The light gathered upon itself, pushing the dark out of the sky, leaving a hazy nimbus on the horizon. Finally, the sharp edge of the sickle moon pierced through the stark black foliage of the tree. It was like a curved blade of heated metal. Rising, the moon assembled into its double-pointed crescent, blood-tinted, like the tail feathers of a red hawk when it sailed across the sun.

He turned to Mattie, to explain to her that he and his brothers had sunk everything into the silver buried in this land. No matter how the money might come—whether by uncovering a rich ore or by dealing over a faro layout or taking a sheriff's share of collected taxes—Wyatt knew it was *his* time. He'd been prying at this door for too long. Here in Tombstone a thin possibility could turn into a fortune overnight.

But he said nothing. Mattie had buried her face into her pillow and begun to sob. Her ghostly fists gripped the sheets with a fierceness that told him there would be no more words this night.

He stood, walked to the bureau, and checked his watch again. With only a few hours left before he would ride out, he stripped off the rest of his clothes. Mattie's crying had stopped by the time he climbed into the bed. Her whiskey-scented breath had already taken on the long steady rhythm of deep sleep. Shutting himself out from every complaint she had registered, he closed his eyes. He would be no good to Virgil if he didn't get some rest.

*****

They tracked the mules from Camp Rucker southwest to the Babacomari River basin where the McLaury brothers' ranch spread from green cottonwoods and grassy flats by the river out into the rocky, dry scrub on the desert slopes. There had been no rain for weeks, so the trail had been crisply defined in the baking sand. Without talking, the trackers rode under a blue slab of sky, as waves of heat rose beneath them. Their sweat burned off in the dry air as soon as it poured from their bodies.

Coming into view of the ranch house, the posse of five soldiers and four federal deputies rode straight to a paddock where six ranch hands looked up from a conversation and stilled in collective wariness. Four mules were tied together at the rear fence. A paint mare was tethered to the snubbing post. One man, who stood apart with a boot propped on the low fence rail, straightened and squared to face the oncoming party. He was short with bowlegs and a dark, ruddy complexion. Pocketing a cigarette he had been rolling, he leaned and picked up a carbine.

Wyatt slipped his Colt's from its scabbard and held it behind his leg against the saddle skirt. As they pulled up to the fence, he nosed his horse next to Virgil's, and they sat their mounts without speaking, studying each face in the group, just as they themselves were being studied. Wyatt finally settled his gaze on the short man with the rifle. Morgan wheeled his horse around one corner of the fencing to flank the Cow-boys.

"Who's in charge here?" Virgil said, his voice shored with the authority of his federal badge.

No one spoke or moved. Virgil kicked his horse closer to a whiskered man who stood outside the paddock. This one was tall with reddish hair and red-speckled skin and a challenging sneer stretched across his face.

"Are you in charge?" Virgil said gruffly.

"I might be if there was somethin' to be in charge of," the man said through his tight grin. No one else smiled.

"What's your name?" Virgil demanded.

The man smirked at the ground, as if considering the investment of energy required to answer. When he looked up, his smile disappeared, and his nostrils flared. His slate-blue eyes burned with hostility.

"Patterson," he growled in a surly tone.

Kicking his horse forward a few steps, the lieutenant in charge of the soldiers spoke up curtly. "My name is Hurst. I have information that men named Diehl and Masters stole mules from Camp Rucker. The tracks lead right here to this ranch."

Virgil's jaw knotted at this interruption of his own chosen tempo of interrogation. Patterson gave Hurst a gap-toothed smile, his teeth the ivory yellow of worn poker chips.

"Well, hell," Patterson crowed, "it's a damned shame the army can't hold on to their livestock."

Hurst sat up straighter in his saddle. "Do you know Diehl and Masters?"

"I might," Patterson said. Then he leaned off to one side and spat.

"Do they work here?"

The Cow-boy's mouth curled again into a self-righteous sneer. "They work for theirselves . . . just like all of us do."

"But are they friends of yours?"

"Hell," Patterson mumbled, trading his show of antagonism for a shrug of disinterest. "I got lots of friends. People gener'ly try to avoid bein' otherwise."

"When did you see them last?"

"I don't keep no diary," Patterson snapped and showed his ugly teeth again.

Virgil glared at the impudent man. "Where're the McLaurys?" he barked with obvious impatience.

Patterson's smile broke at the no-nonsense timbre in Virgil's question. "Around here some'eres. How should I know?" He cocked his head sideways toward the main house and barn. "Try the corral out back."

"Hey, Virge," Morgan called out, walking his horse around the outside of the fence. He stood in his stirrups to look down into a shallow pit at the rear of the paddock. "Been a fire here recent." He pointed to the mules. "And fresh singe marks on those rumps. Looks like a burn-over to me."

Virgil kept his eyes on Patterson. "You boys been doin' some branding?"

When no one answered, Morg leaned and squinted at the mules. "Looks like *D8*." He smiled. "Kind o' fits good over *US*, don't it?"

Standing directly in front of Wyatt, the short man with the carbine took a wider stance. The rifle remained angled over one shoulder and pointed at the sky, but the Cow-boy appeared as still and taut as a trap about to spring. Wyatt hooked his thumb over the hammer of his Colt's and watched this man's beady eyes shift from one posse member to another. Inside the few seconds of silence that ticked by, no one moved. The heat beating down on the desert seemed to intensify. In all this open space of the valley, the scene around the paddock was now like a cramped room with too many bodies inside.

"Yeah, we gotta fire," Patterson snorted. "We're tryin' to warm up. We ain't used to these cool summers. Ain't like in Texas."

Wyatt checked the brand on the paint standing patiently at the post. It was an old singe and scar: an even triangle, point down. Tired of Patterson's vulgar voice, Wyatt addressed his question to the little, red-faced man before him.

"Where do you keep your branding irons?"

The group of Cow-boys continued to stand like statues, but their eyes flicked from Patterson to the feisty one with the carbine.

"Wouldn' know," the man said in a clipped manner. "Don't work here."

Virgil propped his right hand on his gun butt and swung his other hand up to point in an all-encompassing arc that included everyone inside the paddock. "You men raise your hands and stand over by the feed bucket where I can keep an eye on you. We're gonna have a look at some branding irons."

The rifleman lowered his weapon diagonally across his torso—like a sentry challenging entry. At the same time, Patterson's hand tightened on the gun butt at his hip. Wyatt brought up his Colt's, letting it float into view in a smooth, unhurried motion. He didn't cock the hammer or aim at anyone in particular, but the gleam of the blue metal was enough. Morgan brought his gun to bear on the man closest to him. Hurst and the soldiers had not moved.

"Do it now!" Virgil commanded, his big voice booming with authority. His hand remained clasped on the butt of his revolver, but he made no move to pull it.

Under the weight of Virgil's glare, Patterson released his grip on his pistol and backed to the fence, where he climbed over the rails. Trying for a swagger with his arms slightly raised, he walked toward the back of the enclosure. Following his example, the other men in the paddock lifted their hands in token obedience, their fingertips only slightly higher than their elbows. Slowly they began to shuffle toward the bucket. The red-faced man was last to comply, taking only a few steps backward in the direction of his companions. He remained defiant, with his carbine held before him.

"I'm a deputy US marshal," Virgil announced. "I'm coming in to have a look around."

Hurst dismounted, handed his reins to his sergeant, and followed Virgil into the paddock. The other soldiers sat their horses with nothing in their hands but their reins.

Without taking his eyes off the Cow-boy with the carbine, Wyatt pivoted his head a quarter turn so as to be heard by Williams, the Wells, Fargo man behind him.

"Marsh," Wyatt said quietly. He waited until Williams eased up on horseback, boot to boot with him. "Tell the sergeant to order his men to dismount with their weapons out."

Inside the paddock Virgil knelt at the fire pit and held his palm over the mound of warm, gray ash. Right away he stood and walked to the mules. There he stroked one animal's rump over its brand, where freshly scorched, blackened hairs fell away and angled on the breeze. Virge looked back to Wyatt and nodded. Then he turned to Hurst, who stood just inside the gate with his feet spread and his hands clasped at his lower back. But the lieutenant only stared blankly at the mules.

Virgil walked the perimeter of the fencing. Finding no branding irons, he walked to the knot of surly Cow-boys, stopped before them, and spread his boots.

"Frank ain't gonna like you nosin' 'round," Patterson said, his nasal voice insolent and taunting.

Virgil studied the man's sneering face and, without any show, pulled his revolver. Holding the gun muzzle down beside his leg, he pointed with his free hand to the ground at their boots.

"Unbuckle, boys. Let 'em drop."

Three heartbeats of dead quiet passed. Then the Cow-boys grudg-ingly complied, and belts and scabbards fell, thumping in the dust like so many snakes tossed into the fine powder of the paddock. The feisty one with bowlegs was the last to surrender his weapon. He bent at the knees and propped his carbine on the low rail of the fence, his glare fixed on Virgil. Then he slipped off his cartridge belt with holster and pistol and hung it over the same rail. When he straightened, his look of defiance appeared hard as a wood carving.

Virgil glanced toward the house and barn, then at Wyatt. "Let's check the house and those outbuildings back yonder." Then he strode angrily to Hurst. "You hold these men here. I ain't gonna get a straight answer from this jackleg." He jerked a thumb toward Patterson. "I'm going to find a McLaury."

Virgil waited, glaring at the officer, until the lieutenant seemed to awaken from his own inner thoughts. Only then did Hurst unsnap his holster flap and pull out his revolver.

Still on their mounts, Wyatt and Morg followed Virgil's stiff march to the house. When no one answered Virgil's heavy knock, the two horsemen parted around the house—Morgan angling toward the barn, while Wyatt took his horse at a walk downhill, where dust rose from a makeshift corral of laced mesquite branches and slender trunks of ocoti-llo. There a black stallion snorted and paced as a well-built man turned a rope around a snubbing post. Wyatt recognized him. Black, curly hair. Freckles. A smaller man squatted in the dust and rose at Wyatt's approach. Both were unarmed.

"You McLaury?" Wyatt said to the shorter man.

This one was full of spit and pepper. He hissed something to himself and walked toward Wyatt with a tight bounce in his step. The nar-row goatee and moustaches—paired with his stiff walk—gave him the appearance of a fighting cock.

"Who the hell're you? You're on McLaury land!"

"Federal posse," Wyatt said. "Name's Earp. Who am I talking to?"

The testy man tried to pull himself taller. "You can't just ride up onto my land like this." He threw out a hand and swept it in an arc at the hills around him. "This is all private, so you can turn around and get the hell out o' here."

Morgan walked his horse next to Wyatt's and reined to a stop. Smiling, he leaned a forearm on his pommel to get his face closer to the strutter.

"You hard of hearing, mister? Tell us your goddamn name."

"McLaury!" he spat. "And this is McLaury land! Now get the fuck off of it!"

Morgan laughed and carried his smile to Wyatt. Wyatt kept his face neutral and held his gaze on the hostile rancher.

"We tracked six stolen army mules here," Wyatt said. "We're gonna look around."

McLaury's face colored. "The hell you are!" He pushed through the gate. "Tom!" he yelled, walking in double-time toward a shed behind the barn. Virgil emerged from the barn and watched the man approach, so Wyatt let McLaury go.

Inside the corral Curly Bill Brocius coiled the loose end of the rope into loops and squinted at Wyatt. "I know you, don't I?" Then recognition came into his eyes, and he smiled with what seemed genuine delight. "Hell, yeah. The big-shit law at Dodge. Well, goddamn!" He looked off happily to the horizon, and his expression grew pensive. "Old Sally." Feigning a nostalgic moment, he shook his head, and then he faced Wyatt. "Now here you are down here where you got no goddamn business."

Wyatt kept his face expressionless as he recalled his last run-in with Brocius in Kansas. When Mattie had fallen back into her old profession, calling herself "Sally" again, working the line under one of Dodge's successful madams. When he had tried to pull her out of that life, Brocius had just put money down for her services.

Wyatt pushed the memory from his mind and stared at the Cow-boy. "Might be your business is mine," he said. "You work for McLaury?"

Curly Bill cocked his head as though he had heard an amusing joke. Then, taking a lot of air into his broad chest, he propped his gloved fists on his hips.

"Son, I'm free as a Mexican wolf and don't work for nobody." He smiled again, flashing his teeth. "I ain't too good at takin' orders."

"But you *are* tied to these stolen mules," Wyatt said.

"Me?" Brocius said, frowning, but keeping his smile. "Hell, no, Mister Lawman. I just stopped by for a friendly visit." A false play of concern narrowed his eyes. "But good luck finding those fuckin' mules. Prob'ly somewhere down in Mexico by now."

Joining into Brocius's theatrics, Morgan wagged a finger at the Cow-boy. "Might be you boys needin' the luck." He turned to Wyatt and held up a branding iron, his smile relaxing to a sly grin. "Look at what I found hangin' in the barn." Morg wet the tip of a forefinger in his mouth and with it touched the business end of the metal. Then his eyes crinkled with mischief as he looked back at Brocius. "Whatta you know? Still warm."

Wyatt sidled his horse next to his brother's and took the iron to inspect the brand. The lettering had been crudely hammered out, but it was distinct: an *8* followed by a reverse *D*. He looked at the stallion in the corral. On its rump was the same mark branded on the skittish paint in the front paddock: an inverted triangle.

"What's the McLaury brand?" Wyatt asked Brocius.

Curly Bill snorted a laugh through his nose and smiled at the sky. "Son, a rancher's got lots o' brands. I don't keep up with his irons."

"Looks like a triangle, far as I've seen," Morgan said. "Why the hell would a McLaury need a D-eight brand? Unless it was meant to burn over the army's."

Curly Bill made an elaborate shrug and laughed. "Hell, far as I know, a man can come up with any brand he wants."

"That's true," Morgan replied in the same tone he might use with a young child. "But what do you bet he ain't registered that brand?" He pointed to the iron.

Brocius pretended to think about that. He scratched at his whiskered chin and stared off at the barn. "Well, now . . . I reckon you'd have to ask Frank about that, now wouldn' you?" He turned to the frothing stallion and watched it pull at the rope dallied to the snubbing post. "All I care 'bout is takin' the starch out o' this black devil." When he looked back at the Earp brothers again, his face was a picture of innocence. "Tell you what, city boys . . ." Now his voice suddenly took on a vicious edge.

"Why don't you get out o' my face. Go back to your damned fancy town and give a speech or whatever it is you do there." He took off his hat, mopped his brow with the sleeve of his shirt, and plopped the hat back on his head. "I got work to do here."

Without waiting for an answer, Curly Bill spun on a heel and strolled back to the tethered stud as if he hadn't a care in the world. Morgan straightened in his saddle and called out to Brocius's back.

"If we find out you—"

Brocius turned so quickly, he cut Morgan off. "I'm done talkin' to you, young'n! Go chase your tail somewhere else!" Then, as suddenly as his anger had flared, it left him like a flame snuffed out by the wind. Trading one mask for another, he again assumed an actor's pose, extended an arm, and pointed at Wyatt. "But you, big-shit lawman, why don't you do me a favor." The Cow-boy cocked his head and squinted. "How the hell can I get in touch with Sally? I ain't really sure I thanked her proper for all she done for me back in Kansas. You ain't gotta address do you?" Now his taunting smile was like a stench invading Wyatt's space.

Wyatt's face darkened and turned hard, the angle of his jaw like sculpted stone. His eyes went cold as ice and held on Brocius for several heartbeats. The Cow-boy's smile turned garish, like a gargoyle designed to insult whoever might look its way. Wyatt urged his horse forward at a slow walk until it stopped at the edge of the mesquite fencing. Sitting his horse in his easy manner, he stared down at Brocius and spoke in a tone so low that the Cow-boy narrowed his eyes and cocked an ear forward.

"You're pretty good at yappin' your mouth. Is that all you boys can do?"

Brocius's thick, dark eyebrows lowered over his eyes, and his tongue ran across the front of his teeth, making his lips swell and then recede. "Well, I'll tell you, Preacher, I—"

"I don't care to hear you no more," Wyatt interrupted, the iron in his voice like a rail spike hammered into seasoned wood, "so I suggest you shut your mouth."

Brocius's smile broke like a taut string snapping under pressure. The two men glared at one another, the only sound the wind and the stud shuffling its hooves in the dry, rocky sand as it strained against the rope. When Wyatt reined his horse around, Morgan followed and caught up to stare at the side of his brother's face.

"What was that all about?" he whispered. "And who the hell is Sally?"

Wyatt said nothing and kicked his horse into a trot.

They caught up to Frank McLaury and flanked him with their horses, the easy syncopation of hooves making the angry rhythm of the Cow-boy's bantam walk seem overwrought and comical. Up the hill a man came from a shed behind the barn. Wiping his hands on a dirty rag, he stopped and stared at the visitors.

"Frank?" he called out, his voice rising with a question. "What's goin' on?"

"That'd be the other McLaury—Tom," Morg said to Wyatt.

Frank did not answer his brother. Virgil walked to Tom and engaged him in conversation. Like Frank, Tom was unarmed. His facial hair duplicated his brother's, but his general manner and open way of talking appeared less hostile.

When all were gathered together, Wyatt showed the still-warm brand to Virgil. Tom licked his lips and looked to his brother for a response.

"That don't mean nothin'," Frank barked. "We use a lot o' brands."

Virgil turned all his attention on Frank. "You're the other McLaury?"

"You're goddamn right I'm a McLaury! And I want all of you off my land!" Without waiting for a reply, Frank turned his head sharply toward the paddock where Hurst's men and the ranch hands were grouped around the mules. "Goddamn it!" Frank hissed. "What are those damned soldiers doin' here?" Ignoring the Earps, he marched away in his bouncy gait toward the paddock in front of the house.

"Wyatt, see what you can get out of this one," Virgil said, nodding toward Tom. Then he turned to follow Frank McLaury.

"We didn't steal those mules," Tom said, looking up at Wyatt.

"Where'd you get 'em?" Wyatt said.

Again Tom wet his lips with a flick of his tongue. He turned his head to watch his brother move down the hill toward the paddock.

"I ain't all that sure," he finally answered and looked back at Wyatt with a deep frown of bewilderment. "I figure they just strayed up the river and wandered onto our land. I reckon Frank would know."

Wyatt knew the brother was lying. Tom's eyes were open wide with a moist sheen reflecting the desert light. When he swallowed, his throat made a wet clicking sound that he tried to cover by coughing up phlegm, but when he turned to one side and spat, he came up as dry as the Sonora wind.

"The mules were stolen," Wyatt said simply. "And now you've run a brand over the government's. That's a federal offense."

Tom tried to conjure up a look of resentment, but he couldn't seem to purge the fear in his eyes. "Look, we didn't steal any goddamn mules, all right?"

Wyatt looked over the McLaury spread and then settled his gaze on the twice-branded mules. "Maybe . . . but they're in your possession. If *you* didn't steal 'em, you got to know who did."

Now voices rose in anger from the paddock, and Tom's head swung quickly that way. "I got to go see about my brother," he said and started off at a nervous, shuffling trot for the larger group in front of the house. Wyatt reined his horse around and followed.

Virgil stood outside the paddock arguing with Lieutenant Hurst, while Williams and the soldiers stood back. Frank McLaury rose up on the toes of his boots to yell at both men. The other Cow-boys lazed against the fence, watching the debate with mixed interest. By the time Wyatt and Morgan reached the volatile parley, Virgil was walking stiffly toward his horse, his face a storm cloud. Mounting, he motioned with his head to his brothers, and they joined him.

"Ain't we takin' these jaybirds in?" Morg asked.

Virgil's back was as straight as a wooden post, his jaw clamped so tightly, there was hardly room for words. He stared at Morgan, then Wyatt, and finally leveled his gaze on the army officer still conferring with the McLaury brothers.

"No," Virge said in a hard, flat tone. "We ain't."

Wyatt sat his horse and looked back at the sneering smile on Patterson's face. Williams mounted and sidled his horse alongside Wyatt's.

"Hurst isn't pressing charges, Wyatt. The jackass made some kind o' deal with Frank. All the mules are to be returned day after tomorrow." He saw the look in Wyatt's eyes, spewed air from his lips, and shook his head. "Hell, don't ask me. This lieutenant ain't got the sense God gave a watermelon."

Wyatt touched his heels to his horse and took it at a walk to intercept Hurst as the officer walked from the McLaurys toward his soldiers. When they met, Hurst stopped with a defensive glare on his face.

"You're makin' a damned fool mistake," Wyatt said evenly.

Hurst pursed his lips and seemed to be searching for an appropriate reply. Failing that, he looked off toward the river, and his face took on an impatient scowl.

"I'll have all my mules back within two or three days," Hurst insisted. "That's my major priority." He swept a hand back toward the paddock. "This need not concern you any longer. We have reached a reasonable agreement here."

Wyatt held out the branding iron, showing the soldier the *D8* stamp matched to the size of the *US* brand. "And this don't bother you?"

Hurst barely glanced at the iron. He set his jaw and stared up at Wyatt.

"No . . . not as long as I get the mules back."

Wyatt held the man's gaze. "And what if you don't?"

The officer jerked down on the front of his uniform, making the coat fit smoothly over his slight frame. "Like I said, we have an agreement. McLaury will hold up his end of the bargain. He has to. He's dealing with the United States Army."

Wyatt watched the men in the paddock pick up their pistols and cartridge belts and buckle them at their waists. The short, compact man with the carbine leaned on the fence again, exactly as he had when the posse had arrived.

"You're playing right into their hands," Wyatt replied to Hurst. He dropped the iron into the dirt at the officer's feet, where it thudded heavily and sent up a small cloud of dust. The lieutenant looked down reflexively, but he made no move to pick up the evidence. Wyatt reined his horse around to join his brothers.

"Hey, Arp!" Frank McLaury yelled. He swung his arms like scythes as he marched toward Wyatt, stopping so close that the horse started to shy. Wyatt settled his mount and watched McLaury take a wide stance in the dry dirt as his gloved fists clenched at his sides. "Don't any o' you be comin' out here no more! We shoot trespassers!"

Wyatt looked down at McLaury. He could see this hothead spitting venom for as long as he had an audience. Nodding once toward the mules, Wyatt fixed cold eyes on the livid rancher.

"You're either involved in stealing these mules or you're holdin' 'em for the men who did. But you're damned sure searing your brand over the government's. If I or my brothers have cause to ride out here again, you can be damned sure we won't have a wet-behind-the-ears stripling soldier with us."

McLaury puffed up his chest and scuffed forward a step, his entire body like one tensed muscle. Wyatt eased his boot from the stirrup on that side. McLaury was breathing so hard through his teeth, Wyatt could feel the warmth of it on his leg. Tom McLaury eased forward and pulled on his brother's arm.

"Come on, Frank. Don't you got it all worked out with the lieutenant?" Tom glanced up at Wyatt as though asking permission to remove his brother. "The lieutenant said—"

Frank jerked free of his brother's grip. "It's settled. You don't have to explain a goddamn thing to these town-shits who think they know something about this country."

When the younger McLaury led his brother away, Wyatt toed back into his stirrup. Hurst stood in conversation with Patterson, who was raising and lowering his hands in a placating gesture. When he turned, Patterson inadvertently spooked the paint, and it kicked at him, the hoof just catching his hip. Patterson snatched a quirt off the fence and lashed out at the horse, whipping it across the face, neck, and withers.

The short, bowlegged man with the carbine walked to the paint and calmed it. Then he strode coolly to Patterson, grabbed the quirt, coiled it, and slapped the bigger man over the head three times. Patterson crouched and tried to cover himself with his arms. The smaller, compact wrangler stood glaring at the cowering man. Then he flung the quirt into the dust and walked away.

Wyatt wheeled his horse around and moved down the road. Waiting by the gate, Virgil and Morgan turned to join him, and the three brothers rode side by side down the double-rutted track that led to the Charleston Road.

"That Frank McLaury," Morgan said, "now there's a half-pint rooster could stand to have his jewels clipped." He looked back at the ranch and chuckled. "I'd sure like to be the one to do it for 'im."

They spoke no more as they climbed out of the valley. Their horses lunged through a series of sand-drifts, their hooves sinking to the fetlocks and quiet as a man's stockinged feet on a hardwood floor. Cresting the hill, they gained a view of the desert that would dwarf any man's thoughts. Only the blue arch of the sky could claim dominance over such an expansive land.

When they reached the road they formed a tacit, fraternal flank and rode side by side at an easy gallop. As the cadence of their horses' hooves synchronized into a common rhythm, Virgil came out of his dark mood and shook his head.

"Camp Rucker will never see those mules. Those boys might've give their word, but they'll never make good on it."

Wyatt kept his eyes on the road ahead. "There ain't *nothin'* good'll come out o' this goddamn day," he said under his breath.

Virgil and Morgan looked at him, but no more was said as they made their way back to Tombstone.

CHAPTER 4

Summer 1880

Tombstone, A.T.

The mules were not returned. Like a child trying to make amends for his failed chore, Lieutenant Hurst printed a card in Tombstone's Republican supported newspaper, the *Epitaph*. In it he disclosed the names of the alleged thieves and named the McLaurys as accomplices. A reward was offered for information leading to a conviction.

Two nights later, as Wyatt ran his faro game at the Oriental, the two McLaurys, Curly Bill, and a big strapping boy in his late teens elbowed their way up to his table. All wore hats, as if they had just entered the establishment. The few observers who had been standing there gave ground or were bumped aside, where they stared at the intruders from a deferential distance. The heavyset boy dropped a folded newspaper on top of Wyatt's layout. It was the *Epitaph*. At a glance Wyatt recognized Hurst's juvenile plea centered on the fold of the page.

"Poor old Frank's been at home cryin' the last coupl'a nights," the boy said. "I think maybe his feelin's got hurt."

"Shut up, Billy," Frank McLaury snapped, giving the boy a sharp look.

The customers sitting in on Wyatt's game became quiet and uneasy. One player tried to rise from his chair, but the Cow-boys crowded him, giving the man no room to exit.

"If all you boys want to sit in on a game, you'll have to wait a spell," Wyatt said, his voice as calm as if he were calling for all bets. "I've only got room for one more at the moment." Like a man plucking lint from his coat, he casually picked up the paper and dropped it on the carpeted floor of the gaming room.

The broad-shouldered boy leaned forward with his fists on the table. "Game's prob'ly rigged, anyway," he huffed. When Wyatt said nothing, the boy laughed. His breath smelled of cigarette smoke, alcohol, and onions.

Wyatt looked up at Frank McLaury. "Want to sit in?"

"To hell with your game," Frank said, swatting the card box with the back of his hand. The box toppled, collapsing a stack of chips that spread across the layout. Wyatt ignored the upset and kept his eyes on McLaury, telegraphing the message that there were limits to his patience.

Curly Bill cackled. "Try him in poker, Frank. See what he's really made of."

Wyatt's gaze held on McLaury. "He knows well enough," Wyatt said quietly.

Frank pushed the oafish boy aside and took his place. Leaning on his knuckles in the same pose, he lowered his face closer to Wyatt's.

"You come out to the Babacomari again and accuse me of anything, you'd better come out in a wagon so we can haul your corpses back to this shit-hole of a town. We been here in this territory a long time before you pimps moved in. No one in Arizona has ever called my name into question."

Wyatt tipped his head toward the newspaper on the floor. "Till now," he said.

McLaury straightened to stand his full height, but the crown of his hat only leveled off at the jaw of the brutish boy standing next to him. Brocius seemed content to be a smiling audience.

"The same thing goes for the Clanton place," the boy said in a husky threat. "*I'm* a Clanton, by God. You come out there, and you'll get your-self shot all to hell for damn sure. Me, and Ike, and—"

"Ike Clanton?" Wyatt said, interrupting the blustery boy. "You're the same Clantons ran a horse ranch outside San Bernardino?"

"Why do *you* wanna know?" the young Clanton challenged, bumping the table as he rounded its corner. "What do *you* know about Ike?"

Wyatt almost smiled. "We did a little horse trading a while back. Reckon we were about your age."

Unsure if an insult had just been palmed off on him, the young Clanton frowned and looked quickly from Wyatt to Brocius and back. Wyatt turned his attention back to Frank McLaury and let his eyes go cold.

"If you boys don't know how to play proper," he said, nodding toward the spilled chips, "I'll give the seat to someone else." He righted the card box and stacked the chips.

The Clanton boy gave a sneering laugh and turned away, keeping his eyes on Wyatt as a parting message of warning. McLaury glowered a few seconds longer and then strutted to the bar. Brocius chuckled, saluted from the brim of his hat with one finger, and joined his friends. The faro customers took this opportunity to pick up their chips and relocate.

Finding himself without a customer, Wyatt noticed a well-dressed man with a finely trimmed beard and moustaches watching him from the bar. The man picked up his beer and strolled over to Wyatt's table. Slight of build, he possessed a youthful face and personable eyes.

Wyatt nodded to a chair. "Care to play? It appears my customers have vacated."

The man set down his beer and offered his hand. "I'm Charlie Shibell, sheriff of Pima County." Wyatt shook the man's soft hand. "You put a good handle on things that might go out of control, Mr. Earp."

Wyatt's eyes narrowed at the use of his name.

Shibell sat and canted his head toward the bar. "Got your name from the owner," he explained. He leaned, picked up the folded *Epitaph* from the floor, and then cocked his head as he read it. "I like the way you defused that situation. Those boys like to run roughshod over the town folk. They're not accustomed to walking away."

"Won't help my business any if I start crackin' the heads of people at my table."

Shibell smiled at the faro layout. "So, you consider this your business?"

"One of 'em," Wyatt said. "Whatever it takes . . ."

Shibell acknowledged Wyatt's persistence with a nod. Leaning in closer, he lowered his voice to a murmur.

"Marsh Williams told me about your trip to the McLaury ranch. Told me you didn't mind naming Frank McLaury for what he is to his face. I know you've got a background. Dodge City and . . . what? Wells, Fargo?"

"I'm working for Wells, Fargo now."

The sheriff sipped from his beer, careful to keep the foam from his moustaches. "I need a deputy here in Tombstone," he said in earnest. Then he made a quick appraisal of Wyatt's chest and shoulders. "My only other deputy down here is near to sixty."

"How much does it pay?" Wyatt said.

Shibell smiled at Wyatt's directness. "With mileage, court appearances, and arrest bonuses you should average well over a hundred twenty-five a month."

Wyatt nodded to show his interest.

"On top of that," Shibell continued, "you'll get a cut of the taxes you collect for me."

The sheriff waited for a reply, but Wyatt remained quiet, his face unreadable.

Shibell frowned and gestured with a hand, sweeping it around the room. Then he shook his head with a sense of helplessness.

"Pima County is too damned big. I need a good man down here."

Wyatt thought about Tombstone's unbridled growth. It was like a brush fire just before going out of control. Everyone knew that Tombstone would warrant its own county sliced out of Pima, and the new county would need its own sheriff. With that title came the big money—a sizeable percentage of all taxes collected. With the wealth accumulating from the mines and the expansion of the outlying cattle ranches—legal or not—a sheriff's income would catapult into several thousands of dollars a year. A fortune.

"Would I have the power to appoint deputies?" Wyatt asked, thinking of his brothers.

"Of course, when the situation warrants. Naturally, all invoices for expenses must be cleared through the county. As long as the privilege is not abused, I'll back you all the way."

"One thing," Wyatt said, "I understand you're a Democrat. I'm Republican."

Shibell smiled at his beer mug, then lost the smile when he looked Wyatt in the eye. "I need somebody who can handle men and is not afraid to knock on a stranger's door to serve a warrant. It doesn't matter to me if that man is a Jesuit priest."

Wyatt had already made up his mind. It could be helpful to have a badge again. And the permit to carry a gun. More importantly, the offer positioned him for the sheriff's office for the new county with Tombstone as its hub.

"Will you still be in town tomorrow?" Wyatt asked. "I'd like a chance to talk this over with my brothers."

Shibell nodded, finished his beer, and stood. "Good," he said. "I'll look for you here tomorrow evening."

Inside a half hour Virgil pulled out the same chair where Shibell had sat and dropped into it without spilling the contents of his beer mug. He carried a folded newspaper under his arm.

"Business slow tonight?"

"It's looking up," Wyatt said. "Charlie Shibell offered me a position as deputy sheriff. Wants me to police this part o' the county."

Virgil managed to frown and smile at the same time. "Like I told you . . . you were born to the badge, Wyatt."

"It'll be some extra income," Wyatt explained. "And it might lead to somethin'."

Virgil laughed. "You see the card Frank McLaury ran in the paper?" He turned the folded newspaper and tapped a column with his finger. It was a new article, this one printed in the *Nugget*, the town's Democratic voice. "Appears he don't like bein' called a thief."

Wyatt only glanced at the announcement. "He was in here a while ago . . . strutting like a peacock. Him, Brocius, and one of the Clantons—a big brawny kid with a loose mouth."

Virgil snorted. "I took some of their guff out on the street. Billy Clanton is bustin' a gut to become an honest-to-God desperado."

"He'll make it pretty quick with that crowd," Wyatt said and began loading a deck of cards into the faro box.

Virgil raised his chin at Wyatt. "This is the same Clantons from San Timoteo Canyon back in California." Virge smiled. "You remember how you snookered Ike when you pulled that one-sided horse trade?"

"I remember," Wyatt said. "It came down to us recovering a horse he'd already stolen from the freight company."

They did not speak for a time as Wyatt counted the chips in the dealer's tray. Virgil set down his beer, lighted a cigar, and looked over the crowd in the room. Finally he dug a coin out of his vest pocket and laid it on the picture of the queen on the layout. With a swirl of smoke from the cigar, he motioned for Wyatt to draw the cards.

"So . . . what about Shibell?" Virgil said.

Wyatt threw the first card into the deadwood, and then he drew a nine. He left the coin where it lay.

"I figure being deputy will help all of us. I'll have power to appoint."

Virgil nodded and raised an eyebrow. "How will that run with Mattie?"

Wyatt drew another two cards, as if Virgil had placed another bet with the same coin. The winner was a queen.

"She'll live with it . . . or she won't. It don't matter."

Virgil picked up his coin from the layout and polished off the dregs of his beer. "Reckon I got to tell you something, Wyatt." Virge looked around the room and then winked at Wyatt. "Let's go outside for a walk."

The summer night held fast to the heat of the day. It was too warm for an outer garment, but both Virgil and Wyatt were dressed in black suits without complaint. Only a few stars were visible. Clouds stacked from the western horizon and extended almost overhead, checkering the dome of night with a pattern like the scales on a snake. The monsoons would be starting soon. And with the rain came the replenishment that would increase the value of the properties they had bought for water rights.

They walked west on Allen Street past the Wells, Fargo office to Hafford's, turned down Fourth and again west on Fremont—all this with no words. When Virgil saw their houses in the distance he leaned against the high-slatted wooden gate at the back entrance of the O.K. Corral. There he pulled out another cigar and offered it to Wyatt.

"I ain't been letting Allie go into town," Virgil began. "I don't like her being there without me. And I don't need her walking next to me down Allen Street as long as I'm wearing a badge."

Wyatt looked up the street at the Gird block where the city fathers made decisions about the town's future. There, it seemed, men were getting rich just sitting in a room and talking. A few doors down was the printing shop of the *Epitaph*, which had just converted from a weekly paper to a daily. Prosperity was seeping up from the mines into every branch of business.

"Anyway . . . that's what I've been telling myself," Virgil continued. "The thing is, it don't seem right for me to let Allie go in if Mattie don't." He laughed and moved his cigar through a tiny circle in the air. It was not often that Virgil allowed himself to be embarrassed. He laughed again and shrugged. "'Course Allie don't talk to me for a day or two after I tell 'er she's got to stay at home."

A dog barked at the edge of town, the rhythm steady and insistent until a harsh voice shut it up. The pleasant scent of woodsmoke wafted from the Mexican quarter beyond the buildings across the street.

"No reason to let Mattie's life ruin yours and Allie's," Wyatt said. "Do what you want, Virge."

Virgil frowned and fixed his gaze on the assay office across the street. "How come Mattie can't go in?"

Wyatt studied his cigar and flicked a brick of ash into the street. "Mattie made some decisions a while back. Now she's gotta live with 'em."

The silence stretched out, and Wyatt knew he owed his brother more.

"In Dodge . . . she whored with Brocius."

Virgil lowered his forgotten cigar beside his leg and looked off to the jagged peaks of the Dragoons. "Shit," he whispered. Then he turned to gaze west, where two-and-a-half blocks away the Earp houses stood catty-cornered across the intersection. "Wyatt," he said and cleared his throat. "Allie was in that vacant lot next to your house . . . collectin' kindlin'. Says Mattie throws her whiskey bottles over there." He waited a moment, then turned to face Wyatt squarely. "She says there's laudanum bottles piling up out there, too. Allie says most of the time Mattie's just kind o' floatin' out on the wind."

Neither brother spoke for a time. The sound of a lively piano reached them from the Capital Saloon around the corner. The sound seemed wholly foreign to the desert spreading out from the fringes of the town.

Wyatt tossed his cigar into the street. "I can't change what she is no more than I can change what she was."

Virgil pushed out his lower lip and began to nod. "Well, I reckon that's true enough."

They stood side by side looking out toward the mountains. There seemed to be nothing more to say about Mattie.

"I'm taking Shibell's offer, Virge," Wyatt said.

Virgil blew a long plume of smoke into the night and smiled. "Hell, I already knew that." He bumped Wyatt's shoulder with the hand holding his cigar. "I keep tellin' you . . . you're born to it."

Chapter 5

Late Summer, Fall 1880

Tombstone, A.T.

The job of head sheriff's deputy for the Tombstone district quickly became one of high visibility. Investigations into crimes were more varied than Wyatt had faced in the towns of his previous law experience. There were long, two-day trips to Tucson to deliver prisoners. Then two days back. This job was often relegated to Virgil or, even more conveniently, to Morgan, who had taken over Wyatt's Wells, Fargo duties. Such an assignment brought in double pay for Morgan, who relished the rambling life, even when his common-law wife Louisa arrived in Tombstone from California.

Wyatt received the custody of prisoners from Tombstone's satellite villages, served countless summonses and subpoenas, and made arrests of wife-beaters, forgers, lot-jumpers, bribers, mule and horse thieves, murderers, an attorney who had insulted a judge, and the same judge for assaulting the same attorney in his courtroom.

With such an agenda, and with little incentive to spend time at home, Wyatt retreated nightly to the inner sanctum of the Oriental's plush gambling room. The sounds of the saloon life became his nightly anthem—the click of ivory chips, the whir of shuffled cards, the low undercurrent of men's voices weaving into the language of the card games.

On a night in late summer, Doc Holliday—sporting an impish grin—slid into the seat across from Wyatt as though he were a minute late for a scheduled appointment. Breaking his standard dealer's protocol, Wyatt laid aside the cards and smiled at his friend.

Doc closed his eyes and delivered a deep bow of the head in the manner of a royal salute. "From what I hear, Wyatt, your aspirations have gone worldly." Smiling again, Doc leaned his skinny frame to one side and adjusted his coat, allowing the material to drape loosely over the bulge of his pistol next to his ribs. "Mining capitalist, real estate broker, leaser of water rights, Wells, Fargo agent, deputy sheriff, faro dealer . . . did I leave anything out?"

"Good to see you, Doc." Their hands met across the table, and, for a moment, the flickering light of humor drained from Doc's eyes. He looked as though he might say something in earnest, but the moment passed as quickly as it had come.

"So where's the almighty badge and the requisite armory that goes with it?"

Wyatt shook his head. "Don't generally wear them at the tables." Wyatt looked at the game next to his and then turned back to Doc. "In Dodge City my problems were the drovers in town for the cattle season. They needed to see my hardware. Here it'd drive off business." He noted Doc's pallor and lowered his voice. "How's your health, Doc?"

Holliday pulled a flask from his coat pocket, raised a toast to anything or nothing, and threw back a series of swallows. "What health?" he said, exhaling heavily. Holliday wiped at his smile with the back of his hand and looked around the room, appraising the décor. "Well, are you rich yet?"

"I'm working at it," Wyatt said and idly cut the cards. "Kate with you?"

"Unfortunately, yes." Doc's head bounced once with a private laugh. Shrugging off his own romantic foibles, he eyed a nearby table. Johnny Tyler was there—a showboat gambler from Dodge City who liked to throw his weight around smaller men. "God," Doc growled. "Everywhere I go I keep running into shit like that. No wonder I'm not civil."

"You're civil enough with me, Doc," Wyatt said and produced two cigars. He laid one before Holliday. "You ever think on going back to Georgia, Doc? Be among your family?"

Holliday slowly screwed down the cap of his flask with his spidery fingers. "Family?" He chuckled. "You're about it, Wyatt. Besides, family ain't all it's cracked up to be. But friendship counts for something, by God . . . especially out here at the edge of hell."

He laughed to himself again. "This desert had better cough up a lot of silver, Wyatt, because I can't find any other damned asset to commend it." He cocked his head toward Tyler and scowled. "Same for some of the people who inhabit it." He grinned with one corner of his mouth. "But . . . I suppose shit still draws flies."

Johnny Tyler approached and stood behind Doc. "You boys playin' or talkin' about playin'?" He tapped Holliday's shoulder with the back of his hand, and Doc's eyes turned frosty.

"Care to try your hand?" Wyatt said.

Tyler bumped Doc again. "I like to sit where I can see what's going on."

Wyatt looked at Doc and waited. "You mind, Doc?"

"I don't mind being *asked*." Holliday turned his head to fix his pale blue eyes on Tyler. "But I don't like another man's hands on me. Makes me think he might be a little too sweet."

Tyler looked amused. "Well, you skinny little bastard, you'd be the one to know about that."

Holliday smiled, but his pale skin went hard as porcelain.

"Doc," Wyatt said, "why don't we get something to eat when I'm done here with business."

Holliday's eyes softened at the word that Wyatt had carefully chosen. The faro table was Wyatt's "business." It was no different from the dental offices Doc had managed in his other life. Doc stood, manufactured a cough in Tyler's face, smiled his apology, and left.

Tyler wiped his face with his sleeve and sat heavily in the chair. "Sick bastard," he said. Then his mood turned hopeful when he pulled out his money. "All right, let's buck this tiger."

Wyatt watched Doc exit the room. Walking away had been a favor, he knew. Doc was the flip of a coin. A hot fever flash on one side and a cold shiver on the other. You never knew.

*****

In the second week of October, a little after noon, Virgil sat in the kitchen drinking his coffee and talking with Allie, when Wyatt came in shirtless, heading for the washbasin. He had come in at midnight from Tucson and still wore a half-ring of trail dust on the back of his neck. Allie stood and moved a pot of water off the stove for Wyatt's clean-up. Then she stopped at the window to gaze at the roofing going up on the new Earp house across the street.

"That long-haired carpenter knows the meaning of the word 'work,' " she said into the windowglass. "He's a odd bird, but, Lordy, he'll get somethin' done in a day."

When Virgil only grunted a reply, Wyatt glanced at his brother and saw right away that Virgil had something on his mind. Virge's head came up, and he watched Wyatt wash until the sound of a handsaw began a rhythmic grind across the street.

"Holliday is in jail this morning," Virgil announced.

Wyatt's hands stopped lathering in the basin, and he turned to face his brother. Virge sipped his coffee and nodded toward the business district.

"Him and John Tyler got into it at the Oriental," Virgil continued. "When a bunch tried to break it up, Holliday shot Milt Joyce in the hand and a bartender in the foot. Joyce cracked Doc's head with a pistol."

Wyatt had been twisting a towel around his fingers, but now he stopped. "He all right?"

Holding her gaze out the window, Allie said dryly, "Which one?" Then she turned to show her arched eyebrow.

When Virgil shot her a look, Allie moved to the sideboard and busied herself with the breakfast dishes, every sound a sharp criticism spoken in ceramic. Wyatt yoked the towel around his neck and waited.

"Just bloodied up a bit," Virgil said. "Already had the hearing. Nobody showed up to press charges or testify. The judge let him plea down to assault and battery. Twenty-dollar fine and court costs."

"Why didn't they show up?"

Virgil propped an ankle on his knee and rubbed absently at the heel of his boot. "Favor'd be my guess."

Wyatt frowned. "Favor to who?"

Virgil uncrossed his legs and stood with his coffee. Lifting both eyebrows, he gave Wyatt a tentative nod. When Allie banged a pot on the edge of the washbasin, Virgil didn't move, but something changed in his eyes. Wyatt walked into his bedroom, and Virgil followed as far as the door, where he leaned against the jamb and sipped his coffee. Wyatt pulled the bedsheet over Mattie's shoulders, picked up the empty bottle from her table and set it on the floor. Gathering shirt and boots, he stepped into the hall and closed the door behind him.

Virgil kept his voice low. "Fred White and I could use you. This jackleg mayor we got is trying to void the land claims in the business district. You read about it in Clum's paper?"

Wyatt nodded. "The Townsite Company. It's fraud, pure and simple."

"Well, there's a hellava uproar 'bout it. This so-called Company is trying to charge people for what they already got. And here's the kicker: The more work you done on your building, the more it's gonna cost you to buy it back. The only ones tryin' to stop it are the marshal and Clum and some pissed-off merchants. Clum's got the *Epitaph*, and people read it, but readin' 'bout it only goes so far. Clum's organizing a vigilance committee as a show of force whenever these jaspers try to evict someone."

Wyatt led the way into the parlor, where he sat and pulled on his boots. "Who's providing the muscle for the Company?"

"Saddlers mostly. Curly Bill's crowd. They're hiring out to this damned crooked mayor like they're a special police." Virgil clamped his jaw and shook his head. "Clum's vigilance group might not be a bad idea. All the legal work has to be done in the courts at Tucson, and people can't just pick up and haul over there every time the Company tries to outmaneuver 'em. If a property owner leaves town, he's liable to come back and find new owners in his building. It's come down to a show of force."

"You working with the marshal on this?" Wyatt asked. "Official?"

Virgil nodded. "As his deputy. Me and the long-haired carpenter workin' on our other house."

Wyatt had begun to button his shirtsleeves, but his fingers froze on a button. "Vermillion?"

Virgil nodded. "He's more'n capable, and he don't back off."

Wyatt tucked in the tails of his blouse. "Why's he getting involved?"

Virgil finished the last of his coffee, his eyes smiling over the tilted cup. "I told 'im you'd be workin' with me and that you said we could use some good help." He nodded at Wyatt. "He seems to think highly of you."

"This could affect our holdings, too," Wyatt said. "Tell Fred White to call on me."

A web of lines spread from the corners of Virge's smiling eyes, just like Morgan's when he put one over on someone. "Already did." Virgil looked down at his boots. "There's one more thing. I know you got your eye on the sheriff's post when they carve out the new county."

Wyatt waited as his brother sorted out his thoughts. When Virgil's head came up, his expression showed a mix of anger and bad news.

"I know, Virge," Wyatt said. "Doc ain't helping with that. I'll have a talk with him."

Virgil shook his head. "No, it ain't just that. There's a feller I knew in Prescott—Johnny Behan—slippery as a greased snake in a fry pan. He can tell you just what you want to hear so's he'll be your best friend inside o' two minutes after meetin' you. A politician down to his dick. Democrat. Got connections in Tucson and Prescott. He was sheriff over in Yavapai and a member of the territorial legislature. Word is . . . he's a shoo-in for the sheriff's appointment."

The angles in Wyatt's face sharpened. "The Governor is Republican. He's the one'll be appointin' the new sheriff."

Virgil shook his head. "It don't seem to matter what party. Behan's got to 'im some way or other."

Wyatt had threaded a string tie under his collar. Now as he began arranging the ends into a knot, his fingers stopped moving, and the tails fell free down his shirt front.

"But this Behan ain't out making saddle sores rounding up the troublemakers in the county."

Virgil frowned. "That ain't how it works for these plum positions, Wyatt. More to who you know than what you do."

Wyatt's face soured. "I'd hate to think you're right on that."

"Well . . . ," Virgil sighed and tightened his mouth into a false smile. "Whether we like it or not, that's the way it works. I seen it too many times before."

Wyatt finished the knot and stared out the front window. He could see Vermillion hanging rafters for the roof across the street.

"This Behan . . . he got a favorable record?"

"Only with the women. He's a hound dog sniffin' at anything in a dress. And goddamn if the women don't eat it up . . . 'cept his wife, o' course. She divorced him for adultery." Virgil huffed a laugh through his nose and shook his head. "I can't figure what they see in 'im. A half-bald Irishman who could talk his way out of a case of dysentery." Virgil scowled. "He makes me feel like I need to wash my hand after he shakes it."

"Johnny Behan," Wyatt mumbled in the quiet of the parlor. "I'll be lookin' for him."

Virge stood for a moment, staring at his brother's back. "Mattie all right?"

Wyatt turned, surprised at the question. "A little sick, I think."

Virgil stared down into the cup he'd been holding. "How 'bout you?"

"What *about* me?" Wyatt said.

Virgil shrugged. "Just checkin' on my family," he said and flashed an awkward smile.

Wyatt continued to stare out the window. "We'll be movin' into the other house next week. Give you and Allie some room here. Morg and Louisa can stay with us. Mattie seems to like Lou, so . . ."

Virge pursed his lips and looked around the room. "Might go better if they stay with me and Allie. Lou's a might easier on me than she is you. Thinks you run the show just because you got ideas."

Wyatt turned, but his face showed no reaction. "I'm just tryin' to help us all get ahead, Virge."

"Hell, I know that. You just keep right on tryin'."

Wyatt turned his attention back to the window. "There's money in that sheriff's post, Virge. A *lot* of money."

"Hell, yeah," Virgil said and crossed the room. He cupped Wyatt's upper arm with his hand and nodded in earnest. "*Hell*, yeah."

*****

By that night Fred White, the Earps, and John Vermillion became known as "the merchants' saviors," lassoing the tents of lot-jumpers and exposing the bullies who had been hired by the Townsite Company. Most of these dispossessed toughs dissolved into the night only to pop up on another lot the night following. Even after four nights of this, not a shot had been fired.

On the fifth night, Wyatt ate a late meal in Billy Owens's saloon as he waited for a meeting with a Mexican who operated a sawmill at the foot of the Chiricahuas. When the man arrived earlier than expected, Wyatt stood and invited him to sit.

The dark, sun-browned sawyer removed his tattered straw hat, set it in an empty side chair, and sat across from Wyatt. His dress and posture represented a man who was more at home in the elements than inside a town, let alone a saloon full of *Americanos*. The tang of pine pitch wafted from him like a natural scent.

"Buy you some dinner?" Wyatt offered.

"No, *señor*. I eat already. Besides, I need to return to the mountains before dawn." He raised his chin at Wyatt. "You need more of the smooth planks for the inside of your house?"

Wyatt pushed his plate aside and finished his coffee. "I need the kind o' wood my carpenter can make some shakes for my roof. What do you recommend for that?"

"For that I can haul to you the gambel oak or juniper," he answered without hesitation. "The oak is more money."

Wyatt nodded. "One better than—"

A sound like the popping of firecrackers turned Wyatt's head toward the door. The current of conversation in the room did not subside, but Wyatt was better than half sure he had heard the reports of gunfire.

He looked back at the woodcutter. "I'll need to go see about that."

"*Sí*," the Mexican said, pointing east. "When I come into town, I see men with pistols down the street."

Wyatt stood and weaved his way through the tables to the front door. He had stood there for only a moment when three dull explosions of gunfire signaled something amiss at the end of the block east of him. He spotted Fred White's back as the marshal hurried down the boardwalk. Drawn to whatever misadventure was under way, men poured out of the saloons on Allen Street, among them Morgan and Fred Dodge hurrying out of the Oriental into the street. More shots erupted, and the crowd funneled toward an alley on the south side.

Wyatt walked out onto the street toward his brother. "Morg, are you heeled?"

As an answer Morg spread the lapels of his coat, but Fred Dodge offered his Colt's from under his coat. Wyatt secured it in his waistband and hurried down the block, turning into an alley, where a gray stratum of smoke hovered above White, Curly Bill Brocius, and a knot of Cow-boys. Beyond them shots were still being fired from an arroyo, some of the bullets whanging off the rock chimney of the little shack where Morgan had lived before Louisa had joined him in Tombstone.

"Wasn't me doing the shootin'," complained Brocius, slurring his words and unsteady on his feet. He smiled and shrugged, raising his hands palms-up on either side of him. "I'm just in town for a drink or two."

"Then let me smell that gun on your hip," Marshal White challenged.

As Brocius slipped the gun free, Wyatt stepped through the crowd, walked up behind the Cow-boy, and attempted to sweep the gun to one side, but Brocius, clearly not so drunk as he pretended, twisted free. Wyatt bear-hugged the Cow-boy, and White reached for the pistol, grabbing it by the barrel.

"Let go of that damned gun, you son of a bitch," the marshal ordered.

When Curly Bill did not comply, White jerked the weapon, and it exploded with a bloom of light that flashed brightly between them. Still holding the gun, the marshal groaned and fell, as Wyatt slammed his borrowed revolver into Brocius's head. Without uttering a sound, the Cow-boy slumped to the ground, unconscious, hitting the dirt like a sack of grain.

The shooting from the arroyo ceased, but a group of Cow-boys formed a loose circle around the fallen men. Fred White lay unmoving with a smoldering ring of red flame spewing smoke from his trouser material just below the cartridge belt. Wyatt swung his gun toward the onlookers and ordered them back. Morgan and Fred Dodge shouldered through the crowd and knelt next to White.

"Morg," Wyatt said, "put out that fire in his clothes." Then he spoke to Dodge, his voice as steady as if they were talking over a hand of poker. "Go fetch a doctor, Fred. Looks like he's gut-shot."

When Wyatt faced the crowd, his voice filled the alleyway. "Who else was doin' the shootin'?"

No one answered; but, though many citizens had gathered to gawk at the shooting of the marshal, Wyatt could recognize the revelers by their sullen faces: Pony Diehl, a suspect tied to several horse thefts and stage robberies; next to him, the short rifleman from McLaury's ranch; the foreman named Patterson; and a tall one with a long, brooding face—Wyatt had seen him drunk at the Oriental—John Ringo. A fifth Cow-boy—a thick-chested man in a loose buckskin jacket—carried an ivory-handled Colt's stuffed into the waistband of his trousers. Pinned in his hatband at a jaunty angle stood the long speckled wing feather of a turkey. Wyatt braced each suspect by checking for a gun. Anyone with freshly spent cartridges or a warm barrel was herded to the mouth of the alley, where Virgil had arrived to take violators into custody.

Within minutes Dr. Goodfellow pushed his way through the spectators and examined White. The doctor began snapping orders, and a trio of men lifted the marshal and carried him toward Allen Street. Wyatt pulled Brocius to his feet and jerked him, stumbling, out of the alley toward the city jail, while Virgil and Morgan followed with a loose assortment of grumbling prisoners.

With several Cow-boys locked up, the three Earp brothers gathered in the front office. Closing the cellblock door, Virgil shook his head and frowned at Wyatt.

"If Fred dies," Virge said, "there'll be a mob down here to get Brocius, sure as hell."

Wyatt nodded absently, but his attention was fixed on the short wrangler staring back at him through the open door to the street. "You!" Wyatt said moving to the doorway. "Get in here with your friends."

"I didn' do any o' the shootin'," the man shot back, his voice clear yet surly. He wore no gun.

Wyatt filled the door frame. "You can walk in or get carried in. Your choice."

The bowlegged Cow-boy stared coldly at Wyatt for a time, then finally he stepped up onto the boardwalk. When Wyatt moved aside from the open doorway, the Cow-boy scuffed into the room in stiff, angry strides. He stopped, hooked his hands over his hips, and stared down at the floor, ignoring Virgil. Wyatt closed the door and walked around the contrary man to stand before him.

"What's your name?"

At first it looked as though he would not answer. His ruddy face seemed set in a mask of obstinacy. But then his head jerked up unexpectedly, his eyes burning like hot coals fanned by a breeze.

"I already tol' you I wasn't doin' any shootin'," he repeated, this time louder. "I ain't even carryin'."

"That ain't what I asked you," Wyatt said, his voice even but brooking no insolence.

The Cow-boy sucked in his cheeks and glared at each of the Earp brothers. "Name's McMaster," he said at last.

"From Texas," Wyatt added, nodding. "I did a little checking. No warrants on you. But you don't seem to be on such good terms with this crowd." Wyatt cocked his head toward the cellblock. "Last I saw, you put it over on Patterson for beatin' on a horse."

"I beat on him same's he beat on the horse," McMaster argued. Then, with his dander up, he added, "I come here to collect money owed me by Brocius." He nodded toward the street. "I got nothin' to do with what happened out there."

Wyatt looked into the man's hostile eyes. "Maybe your problem is you hang out with the wrong crowd. Lock him up, Virge."

McMaster's anger gathered into a deadly stillness, and Wyatt knew that if the man had been heeled, he probably would have jerked his gun, regardless of the odds. "I can't be gettin' arrested tonight, goddammit. I got to be somewhere tomorrow." He fanned open his coat. "Look, goddammit, how many times I gotta tell you? I ain't even carried a gun tonight." He glared at Wyatt and let go the coat to stiffen splayed hands in the air. "I *got* . . . to be . . . somewhere . . . tomorrow!" he said, chopping his hands at the air with the rhythm of his words.

Wyatt's face showed nothing. "Your plans just changed."

McMaster was quiet as Virgil led him to the cellblock. Wyatt took down a shotgun from the wall case, broke the breach, and opened a box of shells. Morgan walked into the office as Wyatt loaded the double barrels.

"Morg, I need you to round up some boys to help discourage a mob till we can haul Brocius to Tucson."

Morgan's face took on a rare scowl. "Why'n't we just let 'em have the sonovabitch?"

Wyatt snapped shut the breach of the shotgun and gave Morgan a look. "We're either the law or we ain't." He opened the front door and eyed the crowd of citizens gathering down the street. Morgan eased past him and walked toward the Oriental.

"This might'a been a put-up job," Virgil said coming back into the room. "Get Fred White out of the way, and a lot of men stand to make some money on the new Townsite claims."

Wyatt kept watch at the door. "You think the mayor'd have his own chief of police shot?"

"New elections coming up," Virgil said and shrugged. "Ever'body likes Fred." He tried to hand Wyatt a folded paper. "Here. McMaster scribbled this. Said it needs to get to Tucson."

Wyatt ignored the paper. "I ain't too worried about notes tonight, Virge. He can post a letter. Let's see if we can keep Brocius alive tonight, then maybe we can get him hung legal."

Virgil dropped the note on the desk and joined Wyatt at the doorway. "That could've been one of us catching that bullet tonight," Virgil said, his voice sounding detached from its usual no-nonsense tone. "That's the way it happens, you know. Right when you ain't expectin' it."

Wyatt breathed in the night air of the desert, its coolness like a potion that, in the simplest of terms, defined life from death. Above the town, the stars took on that vast display of indifference that always followed a senseless act of violence.

"Then we'll always expect it," Wyatt said.

Together they moved out onto the boardwalk where they could better keep watch down both directions of the street. Neither brother spoke for a time. Inappropriate to the occasion, a string of lively piano music spilled onto the street from the Grand Hotel saloon. The mob down the street showed no signs of organizing.

"If White pulls through, maybe this will settle down," Virgil said.

"He was gut shot, Virge," Wyatt reminded.

Virgil inhaled deeply. "Yeah," he said, the word sounding like a sigh as he let his breath ease out. "Reckon I'll go and check on him."

When Virgil walked off, Wyatt spotted the Mexican woodcutter standing patiently in the shadow of the awning across the street. When Wyatt started walking toward him, the sawyer stepped down into the street to meet him at the middle of the thoroughfare.

"The marshal . . . he dead?" the sawyer asked.

"Probably," Wyatt said. "Sorry to keep you waiting." By way of explanation, he pulled back his coat lapel to show the sheriff's deputy badge pinned to his vest.

"*Sí*," the man said, nodding at the shield of authority. "I know you the sheriff."

Wyatt stared down at his boots for a moment, then into the Mexican's eyes. "Which one of those wood shingles will take longer to rot out?"

"I bring juniper, *señor*. It last you a lifetime."

A bitter smile pulled at a corner of Wyatt's mouth. "Well, let's hope it don't come to that."

The woodcutter nodded and moved off toward the alleyway beside Hatch's Billiard Parlor. For half a minute Wyatt watched the movement of the crowd down the street. Seeing no immediate threat brewing, he returned to Fred White's office.

Passing the desk, he glanced down at McMaster's note, neatly folded twice with a cursive script centered along the front. Wyatt felt the skin on the back of his neck tingle, as though a feather had lightly brushed his skin just below the hairline.

Valenzuela Cos, it read. *Pantaño Store, Benson Road, Tucson.*

CHAPTER 6

Fall 1880

Tombstone and Tucson, A.T.

Fred White lived two more days. His funeral was the biggest event in the young camp's history. By delivering Curly Bill to Tucson, Wyatt missed the ceremony, and now he was on his way back to help Virgil, who—as acting city marshal—was doing his best to hold the lot-jumpers at bay.

Just outside the old pueblo of Tucson, Wyatt reined up at the Pantaño Store and dismounted. Inside the quiet of the adobe building a hazy stratum of blue smoke hovered just below the ceiling. He looked around at the few shelves of sparse merchandise. Above a crude wooden counter and mounted on the wall was the stretched, dried skin of a six-foot-long rattlesnake nailed to a sun-bleached board.

A white-haired man lay on a cot in the back of the smoky room, where a small fire burned in a brazier. Wyatt took off his hat and walked the rough pine floor. At the sound of his boots, the old Mexican sat up and focused on the badge pinned to Wyatt's vest.

"I'm looking for somebody who gets mail here." Again the man glanced at Wyatt's badge and waited for more. "Valenzuela Cos. You know where I can find her?"

The old man raised a frail arm and pointed north. "Go past *el saguaro grande*, near *el arroyo. Con la estatuilla* in front." He leveled his hand two feet off the ground. "*De la Virgen Maria pequeña*," he explained. "*Es azul* . . . blue."

Wyatt looked around the shelves of the store. "Can I buy a can of peaches here?"

"*Si*," the man said and pushed up from the cot.

Wyatt found the adobe hut with a blue statuette out front, a Virgin Mary tilting atop a cairn of white stones. Out back of the adobe, a paint mare was hobbled, nosing at dry grass that tufted between the rocks shelving one side of a wash. Wyatt recognized it as the paint from McLaury's paddock. The triangle brand confirmed it. Outside the front door a collection of clay pots were lined up against the wall of the abode—each containing a withered vine spiraling up a stick with a few red peppers or small orange tomatoes clinging to the stem.

At Wyatt's knock a man's voice called out in Spanish. Wyatt waited for the door to open, but the voice called out again—this time much closer.

"*¿Quien es?*"

Wyatt frowned at the can of peaches in his hand and set it down between two of the tomato pots. The voice behind the door grew rough.

"*¡Dime quien eres o márchate!*"

"I'm lookin' for someone," Wyatt announced through the closed door. "Anybody in there speak American?"

"State your name or move on," said the same voice.

Wyatt propped his hands on his hips and looked down at a coarsely woven mat that served as a boot wipe. "I'm a deputy sheriff," he said in an even voice.

"That ain't a name!"

Wyatt hesitated for only a moment. "Earp."

After a time of dead silence, the lock slid with a metallic scrape, and the door dragged open on its sagging hinges. McMaster peered out, his mouth forming an unspoken word. The smell of mesquite woodsmoke was sharp inside. From a back room of the house a woman's voice asked a question, but McMaster ignored it.

"What the hell're *you* doin' here?" McMaster demanded.

Wyatt put two fingers in his breast pocket and scissored the note McMaster had given to Virgil. "Thought you'd still be in jail," he said, holding the paper before him. "Came to deliver this."

A head appeared over McMaster's shoulder. Her hair was not as black as he remembered, and a few rebellious strands on her forehead had drawn into a curl. Her mouth showed lines near the corners, and her cheekbones protruded. Her skin was the same—darkly luminescent and seemingly as smooth as the underbelly of a fawn.

"¿*Quien es*, Mac?"

She narrowed her eyes at Wyatt's badge, and when she looked back at his face, something changed in her eyes. Her lips tightened, and the lines at her mouth deepened. Wyatt heard the air escape her nose like so much regret.

"Ask the sheriff to come in, Sherman."

Only when Valenzuela Cos opened the door wider did McMaster step aside to allow Wyatt to enter. Wyatt took off his hat and stooped to clear the entrance. The dark room held its smoky scent like a permanent fixture. The dirt floor was almost completely covered by mats of woven grass or reed. Gray ash lay in the fireplace, but the room was comfortably warm. On the opposite wall hung a colorful blanket fixed into the adobe by wooden pegs. Next to it a Winchester carbine was propped in one corner.

As McMaster worked the door back into place, Wyatt stared at Valenzuela. Her dark eyes flashed with a message he immediately understood. They were to be strangers.

"The judge let me go," McMaster said. "Like I told you, I never done any of the shootin'. Wasn't even armed. But you already know all that, don't you?" He remained by the door as though discouraging a protracted visit.

Valenzuela looked flatly into Wyatt's face as she spoke. "This is the Tombstone sheriff who arrested you, Sherman? The one who suggested you were with the wrong people?"

McMaster said nothing, and that seemed to be answer enough. She pointed toward a rough wooden chair covered with a swatch of laced cowhide. Wyatt sat and laid his hat on a low table. She took a seat on a pillow perched on a saw-cut juniper stump. McMaster remained standing. Crossing his arms over his chest, he leaned his back against the wall.

"What's your business here, Earp?"

Valenzuela spoke as if she had not heard her man's challenge. "Perhaps you would like some water?"

Wyatt shook his head. "I'm all right." He turned to McMaster and looked the Cow-boy squarely in the eye, until McMaster shifted his gaze to the hearth. "Sheriff Shibell says you rode for the Texas Rangers."

McMaster tightened the lock of his arms but offered no reply.

"Yes, he did," Valenzuela said.

Wyatt nodded to her and watched McMaster walk to the mantel, where he fingered a wax-streaked bottle plugged by a candle. Finally, he turned an angry face toward Wyatt.

"Yeah, I rode with 'em. So what?"

Wyatt felt the woman's stare fixed on him, but he kept his eyes on McMaster. "And now you're riding with this bunch," he said.

McMaster lifted down the bottle and adjusted the fit of the candle in the neck. "You end up riding with *somebody*."

Wyatt met the woman's gaze as he continued. "You know where it is they're headed?" He looked back at McMaster's tight-lipped profile. "'Cause you need to know. They'll end up either in prison or dead. Brocius is behind bars right now. Fred White didn't make it." Wyatt watched McMaster's hand go still on the candle. "Did you know it was a put-up job?"

McMaster half turned and opened his mouth, but he did not speak.

"Mac?" Valenzuela said.

"No, I didn't know about that." His eyes darted to Wyatt. "Still don't, for sure."

McMaster could not hold Wyatt's stare for long. He walked to a tiny window stretched with translucent rawhide. Valenzuela searched Wyatt's face with an intensity that made him feel he should direct all his words to her, but he spoke to McMaster's back.

"Look," Wyatt began, "I don't know what your loyalties are based on with these men. I respect loyalty. But it's got to run both ways. So I'll ask you this: Would those men back you all the way?"

The quiet stretched out as McMaster glared at the dull light dappling the crude window. Valenzuela rose, crossed the room, and put a hand on McMaster's arm. The illuminated rawhide set her face in sharp profile. Light seemed to lift off her skin the same way that heat rose off the desert.

"I have a proposition for you," Wyatt said. "Will you hear me out?"

Valenzuela turned McMaster gently and guided him to the bench, where she pressed on him until he sat. She remained standing by his side. Wyatt waited until the cautious little man met his eyes, and then he made a small gesture with his hand toward the woman.

"You got a good thing here. Better'n most, I'd say." When McMaster started to protest, Wyatt added, "I ain't talking about money." Wyatt looked around the confining room. Everything laid out had its own story, he knew. A small, half-finished carving of a wooden horse. A wrinkled photograph in a frame. An oddly shaped stone that lay on a closed Bible.

"You're telling me you live in worse'n this?" McMaster challenged.

Wyatt looked down into one palm and ran his thumb along the life line. He took in a deep breath, let it out, and then remained very still until he had the words just right.

"I live in a house of mill-sawn lumber, glass windows, and even a rug or two," he began and then looked up at Mc Master. "But it ain't what you got here. It ain't got the promise."

When McMaster's face compressed into a question, Valenzuela squeezed his shoulder and raised grateful eyes to Wyatt. The Cow-boy licked his lips and waited.

"I'm going to talk to you straight," Wyatt said quietly. "Then I'll leave. What you do with what I tell you . . . that's your decision." He nodded toward the woman. "Yours and hers, I reckon."

McMaster's breathing went shallow, as though he wanted to hear every nuance of Wyatt's voice. Valenzuela knelt and pressed one cheek against her man's arm.

"I need a man who can tell me things I need to know," Wyatt continued. "I'll pay that man for this information. He would be an acquaintance of the Cow-boys . . . but *not* an accomplice."

"What you want is a backstabber," McMaster said.

"I want a man on the side of the law. A man like that ain't backstabbing a man who breaks the law. You were part of the law at one time.

I figure you've seen both sides now. So I reckon you can make up your own mind about which side to stand on."

"I rode with them boys from Texas."

Wyatt nodded. "Keep on, and you'll ride right into hell. I can promise you that."

McMaster knotted his mouth into a pout. "I don't even know you, Earp."

"Goes both ways, don't it?" Wyatt countered. "Still, I figure I see something in you." Wyatt nodded toward the arroyo, where he had seen McMaster's horse tethered. "Prob'ly got to do with that skittish paint Patterson was beatin' on." He gestured with a hand toward the room. "And maybe a little of what I see here." Wyatt kept his eyes from the woman, but he knew that she understood his meaning, even if McMaster did not.

Valenzuela tightened her grip on her man but kept her eyes on Wyatt. "I think you can trust this man, Sherman." McMaster looked at her, and that turned her face to his. She smiled at him, but he turned away. "Mac?" she said.

He began to nod. "I'll think on it," he offered grudgingly.

The woman looked at Wyatt, but her face gave away nothing.

Wyatt picked up his hat, stood, and studied the blanket on the wall. "That's all I got to say." Turning from the wall, he nodded to them and fitted his hat to his head. Then he walked out the door, leaving them in a silence that was, though fragile, not without hope.

When Wyatt mounted his horse, he looked back at the house to see Valenzuela standing in the doorway. She smiled at him for the first time since he had arrived; not enough to acknowledge a past, but enough to show gratitude. Her eyes lowered as she closed the door, and Wyatt sat his horse staring at the sun-grayed sticks and dry ocotillo lashed into an awning over the door, wondering if he had done a good thing or a foolish one.

Starting to leave, he spotted the can of peaches hiding like a child's surprise among her potted plants. He hesitated for a moment but then thought better of returning to the door. Touching his heels to the mare's flanks, he spoke to the horse and started the long ride back to Tombstone. There would be plenty of time to think about a new wooden house filled with a different kind of silence altogether.

*****

In three weeks Wyatt was back in Tucson delivering another prisoner to the county jail. Sheriff Shibell had taken a stage southwest to Palo Alto to campaign for the coming election, so Wyatt waited two days, using the layover to make some money in the gambling houses. On the day of Shibell's return, Wyatt walked into the county offices unannounced and stood before the sheriff's desk. Shibell sat frowning at a paper on which he scratched a long line through a sentence. Then he leaned forward and carefully wrote in the margins.

"Charlie," Wyatt said.

Shibell looked up, his eyes wide with surprise. "Wyatt!" he said and broke into a smile. He glanced back at the paper and snorted an embarrassed laugh. "I was just working on my speech. This campaigning is getting to be a full-time job." He propped his pen in the ink well and sat back in his chair. "How're things in Tombstone?"

Wyatt began to nod. "Stable. I reckon you know my brother Virgil got appointed temporary marshal after Fred White died. We're keepin' a lid on the town."

"That's good . . . that's real good," the sheriff said, sitting erect now, his mood bolstered by this news. "Will Virgil run for the permanent post in the elections?"

"Says he will."

"Well," Shibell said, smiling and spreading his hands with the obvious, "the more Earps wearin' badges in Tombstone, the better."

Wyatt looked down at his vest and unpinned his badge. "Came by to tell you I'm supportin' Bob Paul in the election." He laid the deputy's badge on the desk. "Don't reckon I can do that and serve you at the same time."

Shibell's face reddened as if he had been slapped. "Well, Wyatt . . . goddamn . . . doesn't mean you have to quit on me. Hell, you're the best

I've got." He frowned at the badge and slumped back in his chair. "Can I ask why you're going with Paul instead of me? Is it that both of you have a Wells, Fargo connection?"

Wyatt shook his head and looked at Shibell the same way he faced a man across a poker table. He was putting all his money on Bob Paul. It would not serve him to explain his ambitions to be a deputy under Paul, which would better position Wyatt for the job of sheriff of the new county that would be sectioned out of Pima. Furthermore, he saw no reason to insult Shibell just because the man was better suited for working in a bank or the territorial legislature rather than a sheriff's office.

"Best if I stay with Republican, Charlie. Wells, Fargo's got nothing to do with this."

Shibell took in a deep breath, flattened his hands on the desk, and exhaled as he stood. "Well, you've made my job a lot easier down in Tombstone. You've been a good officer, Wyatt." He flung one hand at the air. "Hell, you've been better'n good." He offered his hand across the desk, and Wyatt took it. The man's grip had not improved since their first meeting. "Good luck to you, Wyatt," Shibell said and produced a wry smile, "except for helping Paul, that is."

When Wyatt turned to leave, Shibell blurted out, "Say, can you recommend someone in Tombstone to take your place? Maybe a Democrat?"

Wyatt rotated his hat through his fingers and thought about the Democratic Cow-boy element spread all over the hinterlands of the county. He would be damned if he would help that crowd with a sympathetic deputy.

"Can't help you there, Charlie."

*****

On the night of the election, with the temperature bottomed out well below freezing, Wyatt sat with Fred Dodge over a poker game in Vogan's saloon. With the bar almost empty, James took off his apron and joined them for a hand, taking the pot with three queens. He was ribbing the boys about his luck with women, royal or otherwise, when Virgil came through the door wearing the stoic face that always presaged unwanted news.

"Shibell was reelected," Virgil announced. No one spoke, as they could see there was more. "And I lost by fifty damned votes."

Dodge, now indifferent to the game, lowered his cards to the table. "Lost to who?"

Virgil pulled out a chair, sat heavily, and held Wyatt's gaze as though his little brother might have something to say on the matter. "Ben Sippy, that's who."

"Well, shit!" James declared with no small amount of indignation. "How the hell did that happen? Sippy's just a miner. He don't know shit about police work."

With his face hard and angular, Wyatt closed his hand of cards and tossed them on the table.

"That's some bad luck, Virge," Dodge said. "I reckon he just shook more hands, that's all."

"Or maybe greased some," James added.

"Speaking of that," Virgil went on, all his attention directed now to Wyatt, "remember Johnny Behan? That glad-hand, slick-tongued Irishman from Prescott I told you about? Well, Shibell gave him your old post. He's the deputy sheriff here now."

Staring at the reflections in the windowglass, Wyatt picked up the deck and tapped the edges by rote. Soon he began shaking his head, then he turned back to Virgil.

"Something about all this doesn't square. I reckon Sippy could'a charmed votes out o' the citizens, even without any background in the law, but Shibell can't stand up against Bob Paul's reputation as a lawman and a Wells, Fargo agent."

James got up, poured a drink at the bar, and carried it to the table for Virgil.

"Looks like the Earps are out o' the lawin' business," Virge said and threw back the whiskey. He slapped the empty glass on the table with a sharp rap, and the cartilage in his jaw knotted.

Dodge gestured with his beer mug toward Virgil. "But you still got your federal badge." Then he turned confident eyes on Wyatt. "And Wells, Fargo will always back you, Wyatt."

Wyatt stood and slipped on his coat.

"Where're *you* going?" James asked.

"To wake up the clerk at the telegraph office. I want to send a message to Paul. We got to look into these election precincts one by one. Something ain't right."

"I'll go with you, Wyatt," Dodge said. "I'm expecting a telegram myself."

On Allen Street, Wyatt had started down the alleyway that led to the telegrapher's cottage when Dodge quietly called his name. When Wyatt stopped and turned he saw Dodge standing in the mouth of the alley with his elbows cocked out to his sides, his hands resting on his hips.

"Cross the street with me, will you, Wyatt?" Fred said, and hitched a thumb over his shoulder at the north side of Allen. "I need to show you something." Without waiting for an answer, Fred Dodge spun around and started across the thoroughfare.

By the time they reached the other boardwalk, Dodge had jangled through a collection of keys. Slipping one into Marsh Williams's lock, he opened the door of the Wells, Fargo office.

"Get on in here, and let's close the door," he advised.

Inside, amid the thick aroma of tobacco from the stock of cigars Williams sold, Wyatt stood by the residual heat of the wood stove and watched Dodge secure the door. After tripping the lock, Fred parted the shade and peered out the crack.

"How is it you've got a key to the Wells, Fargo office, Fred?"

Dodge started for the back of the room where the agent's desk stood against the wall in near darkness. He motioned Wyatt to follow. After lighting a lamp, he sat and turned down the flame as low as it would go without extinguishing it.

"I ain't told a livin' soul in Arizona what I'm about to tell you, Wyatt. If I'm wrong in tellin' it to you, then I was wrong in what I told the Wells, Fargo boys in San Francisco, about hiring you, and my word would be shot all to hell anyway."

Fred Dodge cocked his head toward the sound of boots outside on the boards. Both men waited and listened until the pedestrian had passed out of earshot. Then Dodge leaned on the desk, his forearms flat on the varnished wood, his head hanging down between his shoulders. When his face came up, it was as solemn as Wyatt had ever seen it.

"I know you're still consulting with Wells, Fargo. As a kind of off-the-books operative."

Wyatt's face remained expressionless. "What makes you say that?"

Dodge looked down at the desktop again and arched his eyebrows once, as though he were making a pact with the polished wood. When his head came up, his eyes blazed with the fire of a man confessing his soul.

"I been workin' undercover for Wells, Fargo ever since I come here to Tombstone. One o' the reasons they know to trust you is . . . well . . . on account o' me."

Wyatt stared at Dodge's stony face for a long five seconds. "Well, that explains one thing."

"What's that?"

"You told me your profession was gamblin', but I don't reckon I've seen you win a hand more'n once or twice."

Fred chuckled. "One thing I learned, Wyatt: a man will confide a hellava lot more to a gambler who *loses* his money to 'im."

Wyatt dropped his hat on the desktop, took a seat in the client chair, and looked at Dodge from a new angle. "Morg or Marsh Williams know about this?"

Fred shook his head. "Just you. And I want to keep it that way . . . *'specially* with Williams. The company wants me to keep a close eye on that jaybird. Some funds have come up missing."

Wyatt frowned at that news. "What made you tell me?"

Dodge grunted and allowed a smile. "Seemed to make sense. Now maybe I can win a few hands o' poker off you." He grew instantly serious again and threaded together his thick fingers on the desk. "Besides that, the company has got an interest in this election, too. Wells, Fargo is behind Bob Paul all the way."

"Do they know one of the Clantons oversaw the polls in the San Simon precinct?"

"That was Ike," Dodge said. "Hell, yes, they know. I'm the one told 'em." He huffed with a deep growl. "Ike Clanton! Hell, I wouldn' trust that windbag with a boot full of hot sand in the summer desert.

Only ones to ever take Ike seriously are the ranchers he's stolen from."
He shook his head. "For someone dumb as a stick, Ike's a shifty sonovabitch. All those Clantons are."

Fred began to straighten the papers on the desk. His fingers stopped
their motion when he uncovered a folder bearing Wyatt's name.
Opening it he found a Western Union telegram.

"Looks like Williams picked up a message for you, Wyatt. You seen
this yet?"

Wyatt shook his head, took the telegram, and read the two lines
typed on the paper. He took in a lot of air, and, as he exhaled slowly,
he returned the paper and reached into his breast pocket for a cigar and
matches.

"Bad news?"

Wyatt fired up the cigar. "My youngest brother, Warren, is coming
in from California."

"'Nother apple off the tree, huh?" Dodge said.

Wyatt nursed the smoke and nodded, but he was thinking less about
an apple than a prickly pear cactus. Already he was putting together the
verbal contract he would need to deliver to Warren for the sake of the
Earps' standing among the citizens of Tombstone.

"I reckon with Bob Paul as sheriff of Pima County," Wyatt said,
"Wells, Fargo stands to benefit more'n most." He made a small turning
motion with the hand holding the cigar, gesturing the obvious. "They got
the most to lose from the road agents."

Dodge laughed, but there was no humor in it. "I'd like to see Ike
Clanton's face when the election results are reversed."

"You're that sure we can turn it around?"

Dodge lightly slapped his palm to the desk. "With Wells, Fargo
behind us? I'm damned sure of it."

Wyatt turned his attention to the front window for a moment, staring through the shade as if he could see all the way across the county.
"Good," he said finally, thinking of a newly divided silver-rich county
of which he planned to be sheriff. Then he looked back at Dodge and
narrowed his eyes. "Why'd you bring me here? You could have told me
all this in the alley."

Fred held up the collection of keys by the loop of string that connected them. They clinked once and swung in a small circle, catching light from the oil lamp in quick blinks and flashes.

"Seein' is believin'," Dodge said and turned to nod at the floor safe. "And to ask you to help me—whenever you're here with Williams—to keep an eye on how he operates in this office." Fred looked back at Wyatt. "Can you do that?"

Wyatt's thoughts drifted back to Missouri to a time when he, as constable, had rationalized skimming money from a fine he had collected from a violator . . . and from the county's school funds. And then again he had done it as a deputy in Wichita.

Fred Dodge tilted his head to one side and stared pointedly into Wyatt's eyes. "Wyatt?"

"I'll keep an eye out," he replied and stood.

Fred stood and offered his hand. The two men shook with a firm grip.

"I'm sorry if this cuts against your family ties, but you can't tell *anyone*. Not even your brothers."

Wyatt made no response, neither vocal nor by expression. He snugged his hat to his head and walked to the door. There he turned the latch and looked back at Dodge.

"You gonna snuff that lamp?"

Fred made no move for the lamp. He stared down at the desk again, and, when his head came up, his brow was furrowed and his skin flushed.

"Hell, I know you'll keep it tight. It's why I told you 'bout me in the first place. I just needed to ask."

This time Wyatt nodded and peered out through the crack in the shade. When he heard Fred blow out the flame behind him, the room went dark. Opening the door, he stepped out on the boardwalk, quietly closed the door behind him, and walked west toward the Oriental to open his faro table.

CHAPTER 7

Fall 1880

Tombstone, A.T.

Within the week, the youngest Earp brother arrived by stage and moved into Wyatt's house, as Warren would have it no other way. Taller and more filled out toward being a man, he carried a certain nervous energy that kept him in constant motion. For this reason, Wyatt gave him most of the menial jobs that had to be done for both households: sawing and splitting firewood, grooming the horses, hauling water from the Huachuca Company's storage tank just outside of town, and packing in groceries for the Earp women.

On the night of the recount, as Wyatt ran his faro game at the Oriental, Warren appeared wearing a new black coat just like Wyatt's. He stood across the table with his fists clenched and his boots spread, as if trying to root to the floor.

"I'm sick o' all this women's work, Wyatt," Warren challenged, his face glowing with the heat that seemed as much a part of his identity as the dark hair that set him apart from his brothers. "I'm ready for somethin' with more grit to it. Thinkin' I might like to wear a badge."

With just a glance Wyatt passed a mute apology to his lone customer and raked the chips toward himself from the layout. "Can we talk about this later?" he suggested.

Warren's chin lifted. "I want to talk about it now."

The customer—a portly miner who, judging by the half smile playing on his lips, must have claimed a younger brother, too—gathered up his chips and dropped them into his hat. "Think I'll have a drink," he said and lumbered off toward the bar. Warren took the vacated chair.

Wyatt, watching the miner veer off to another table, stacked the loose cards onto the deck, shuffled, and loaded them into the box. When he closed the box, he looked pointedly at Warren.

"Badges are not so easy to come by these days."

Warren frowned at the layout and fingered the painted king on the layout cloth. "Then what about Wells, Fargo? I could ride for them, couldn't I?"

Wyatt surveyed the room and took in a lot of air. As he eased out the breath, he watched a slender, well-groomed man with a receding hairline enter the saloon and belly up to the bar, where he bought drinks for several men standing there. Even without having met him, Wyatt knew the newcomer was Johnny Behan, confirming it when the man draped back one side of his coat to slide a hand into his trouser pocket. On his vest he wore the same badge that had been pinned to Wyatt's chest just a few weeks before.

"Warren," Wyatt began, his manner relaxed, "b'fore you start workin' with other people—outside the family, I mean—you're gonna need to understand how to deal with 'em."

Warren's face flushed and closed down with anger. "What the hell is that s'posed to mean?"

Wyatt nodded toward his faro table. "Take right here, for example. You just cost me some money."

The youngest Earp glared at the card icons imprinted on the cloth. He opened his mouth to argue but then only frowned at the layout. When he looked at Wyatt again, his heated face was wrestling with the first traces of contrition.

"I did?"

Wyatt nodded. "I figure you can pay me back tomorrow. My mare and my gelding need a washin' b'fore it gets too cold."

Warren's shoulders sagged, and he cursed under his breath. Dropping an elbow on the table, he buried his fingers into his dark hair and then propped his chin in his hand as he stared into his brother's eyes. Wyatt nodded to a chair two seats away.

"Sit over there and watch the game for a spell. See what you can pick up."

Warren's hand dropped to the table as he perked up. "You mean about faro?"

Wyatt shook his head. "About the people who play it."

Warren pushed back the chair and stripped off his coat as he rose. "I'll stand," he said. "So you can give the seats to your customers."

Right on cue, the stout miner was back, taking the chair Warren had vacated. Wyatt watched Johnny Behan conclude his social obligations at the bar, then talk pleasantly to each man he encountered on his way to the gaming tables. Finally, he stopped across from Wyatt's layout and smiled.

"Mr. Earp?" Behan removed his hat and swept it toward an empty chair. "May I?" His Irish accent carried a lilt that was almost musical, delivered like an actor on a stage.

"Have a seat," Wyatt invited. "We were just about to place bets."

Behan widened his smile, stepped around the corner of the table, and offered his hand. "I'm Johnny Behan, the new deputy sheriff in Tombstone. I've heard good things about you."

Wyatt took the man's willowy hand and shook. "Wyatt Earp."

A cloying, rose-scented pomade lifted off the deputy's body, and Wyatt regretted that he now carried that scent on his own hand. When Behan took a seat beside the miner, he fanned open his coat to free the tails, and the badge flashed briefly like a teasing wink. Digging into his inside breast pocket, Behan produced a long wallet and removed a sheaf of bills.

"Let me have twenty dollars worth of chips, Wyatt. Better make them dollar chips." He smiled at the men sitting around him. "That way I can enjoy losing my money over a long stretch." He laughed as if he had said something amusing. "You know, rather than all at once. It's so depressing when you go broke on the first play, eh, boys?"

Behan's silky voice elicited modest laughter from the miner. Warren studied the deputy but made no response. Two small-time bettors joined them at the table and stacked their chips before them. When Wyatt called for the bets to be laid down, Behan was the last to decide. He placed one chip on the king, then one on the queen.

"It's an old tradition I've learned to be loyal to," he said, his eyes already glowing at his newest performance. "If you're going to lay down on a lady—" he paused to point to the queen on the layout. Then he tapped the chip he had laid over the king's face. "Always cover up her husband's eyes first." He laughed and clamped a dry cigar between his smiling teeth. Everyone laughed this time. All but Wyatt.

For the better part of an hour, Johnny Behan lost all but two of his bets, taking his failures as good-naturedly as a man awaiting his dinner at a fine restaurant. He handed out smokes until his silver pocket case was empty, then he bought more chips as though his pockets were bottomless.

"Well, let's have another go," Behan laughed. "My luck can't get any worse."

"Hell, Johnny," Warren said, "there appears to be no limit as to how bad you play this game."

Behan turned and smiled, as though it were impossible to raise his dander. "Don't believe I've had the pleasure," he said, offering his hand.

"Warren *Earp*," Warren said and hitched his head toward Wyatt. "Brother to the man that's taking all your money." Warren's face glowed with pride.

Behan affected a dismissive laugh and winked for the other men around him. "Well, now, I don't see how you can be an Earp, friend. Not with that dark hair."

Wyatt looked up from loading a new deck into the faro box. Warren's face had flushed red again, and his jaws knotted as he stared at the side of Behan's face.

"He's the youngest," Wyatt said. "Just come in from California."

Behan pretended to inspect Warren more closely, his gaze traveling the length of him. "I don't know. Just doesn't have that Earp look about him, you know? Those unforgiving eyes that can make a man think twice about what he says."

Wyatt held his gaze on Warren as a warning, but it was too late. "I ain't met a man yet I couldn't look eye to eye," Warren huffed. "There ain't none of us Earps met that man."

Wyatt's hands lay idle on the table, nothing about his expression changing, yet the onlookers standing around his table were focused on him. "Warren, go find Morgan, will you, and tell him the three of us need to ride out to the Huachucas tomorrow to map some water rights."

Warren frowned and glanced at the other men, but no one would look at him. "All right," he said and stood. "I'll be back in a few minutes."

"No need," Wyatt suggested. "I'm about done here. I'll see you at home."

The youngest Earp sniffed sharply and began thrusting his arms into the sleeves of his new black coat. All the while he held a smirk on his face and glared at Behan.

"You just keep on throwing that money away, Deputy."

Behan smiled at no one in particular. Warren shrugged his shoulders to adjust the hang of his coat. He looked around the room once and strode out as if he had broken the bank.

The men at the table were quiet as Wyatt swept cigar ash off his layout and called for bets. Behan laid down chips on the nine, jack, and queen.

"When I was a young pup," Behan began in his melodic story-telling voice, "my papa said I used to sing louder than anyone else at mass. He told me years later, it used to embarrass the hell out of him. So I said, 'Well, that's why I did it, Papa, to get the hell out of you.'"

While everyone else laughed, Wyatt tended to business. "All bets in," he announced. He drew a card from the box and set it aside. The second card went face up. Behan had lost again.

"I believe you are imperturbable, Wyatt," Behan said, propping his elbows on the table as though settling in to study the man before him. Wyatt drew the next card, another disappointment for Behan, who didn't seem to care if he won or lost. "Well, gentlemen," he said, laughing, "I think that's enough punishment for me."

"Reckon it's time for me to call it a night," Wyatt announced.

The players and spectators shuffled away to another table, leaving Wyatt and Behan alone. Losing his smile, the new deputy struck a match to relight his cigar. Baring his teeth, he talked around his hands cupping the flame.

"Too bad about Virgil not taking the chief of police post. He did a fine job as a temporary." Behan tilted his head thoughtfully. "I'm sure you boys were counting on the money."

Wyatt racked his chips and rolled up his layout. "We're doing all right," he said. He opened a tally book and penciled in the night's profit. "You hear about the recount for sheriff?" Wyatt said idly. "There were over a hundred fraudulent votes cast in the San Simon district. Bob Paul is in as sheriff. Looks like you and Charlie Shibell will be out of a job."

Behan offered an amused smile, showing that this was not news to him. "Shibell will still hold the position a few more weeks until the courts make it official. Besides, I'm not worried. I've got other irons in the fire." He blew on the coal of his cigar and then tried to suck life back into it.

"Wyatt," Behan said, letting his voice soften with a personable melody, "I know you're interested in the sheriff's job when the new county is formed." Behan lowered his chin and raised both eyebrows to look up at Wyatt. "I think we might consider working together on that."

"How do you mean?" Wyatt said, his voice clear and in sharp contrast to Behan's conspiratorial whisper.

"Well, you see," the deputy said and pushed out a nervous laugh, "I'm interested in the job, too." He pointed at Wyatt with the cigar. "I appreciate a man like you. Your expertise could be useful alongside mine."

"What would yours be, Mr. Behan?"

"Oh, call me 'Johnny.' All my friends do." He drew on the cigar again, but it was dead.

"What kind of record have you built up since you became deputy?" Wyatt asked.

Behan had a way of broadening his smile, even when it seemed to have reached its limit. "A sheriff's station is political, Wyatt. A man has to know his way through the channels in the territorial office. I've got a background there. To be honest, I think that gives me an edge over you."

Wyatt watched the man's performance and then let quietness gather around them. Behan used the time to speak to two men leaving the room. He seemed incapable of discomfort.

"Here's the way I see it," Wyatt began. "We got a Republican president. Territorial governor is Republican. On this first go-round, the sheriff's post will be an appointment. Not an election. You're a Democrat; I'm a Republican. I see that edge the other way."

Finally acknowledging that his cigar had expired, Behan laid it aside. "It's not so clear as you think, Wyatt. I'm telling you this as a friend." He looked from side to side and leaned in closer. "Back out of the running, Wyatt. My appointment is a done deal, all right? But I want you for my undersheriff."

When Wyatt started to rise, Behan half stood and raised his hands, palms forward, and gently pushed them toward Wyatt. "Now wait; hear me out. I'm good at administrating. You're good at enforcing. Hell, I'm betting you'd hate administrating . . . just like *I'd* hate the enforcing." He shrugged and sat back in his chair. "It's a perfect combination."

"If it's such a done deal," Wyatt said, settling back in his chair, "why're you so set on me pulling out?"

"Wyatt, if you look like you're going after the office and you lose"—he dipped his head to one side and smiled an apology—"well, you'll look like a loser. And, frankly, I don't want that for you. Or, more to the point, I don't want that for the man who would be my undersheriff." Behan's eyes took on the warmth and steadiness of an earnest man. "That's the God's truth." He leaned closer and lowered his voice to a whisper. "I don't want you embarrassed, Wyatt. I want you with me. Withdraw your application and agree to sign on with me as undersheriff. That way we both win."

"How is that?" Wyatt said, his voice deep and relaxed in contrast to the deputy's secretive mumbling. "The sheriff stands to make a lot more money than the men under him."

Behan shook his head. "The big money comes from the tax collecting. And *that*, you and I can split right down the middle. Plus, we've got our regular salaries, and you, as undersheriff, would have bonuses on travel time, arrests, and court appearances. That would even us up pretty square. You'd be doing what you do best." He opened his hands and smiled again. "And so would I."

Wyatt stood and cradled the faro box and layout under one arm. "I'll think on it."

Behan stood and offered his hand, but Wyatt filled his free hand with the tray of chips and balanced it between them. "Any businessman would," Behan said agreeably. "I like a man who thinks things through." He patted Wyatt's upper arm. "You think on it, Wyatt."

Johnny Behan strolled out, speaking to the owner and to the man sweeping up. Wyatt looked down at Behan's cold cigar in the glass tray. The man just couldn't keep the thing burning.

At the bar Wyatt counted out the house share of his winnings and stacked the bills beside the manager's till. Virgil appeared beside him and leaned on the countertop.

"Just passed Johnny Behan when I came in," Virge said and nodded at the money. "Some o' that his contribution?"

"Most of it," Wyatt said.

Virgil's quiet laugh narrowed his eyes. "He make you his best friend yet?"

"Wants me to be his undersheriff."

Losing all signs of mirth, Virgil frowned. "How's that gonna work?"

"Wants me to pull out of the sheriff's race." Wyatt looked at Virgil, and for several seconds neither man spoke. Wyatt reached over the countertop and secured the faro box on a shelf under the bar. Then he did the same with the tray of chips. "Says he's already got the deal sewn up."

Virgil scowled. "The hell he says."

Wyatt slipped the tally book into the inside pocket of his coat, and, when he caught the owner's eyes, he pointed to the till. Then the two brothers walked out the door and stood together at the corner looking west on Allen Street. The night air was invigorating, and the noisy, lighted saloons gave the town a sense of economic momentum.

After a time Wyatt said, "You know what 'imperturbable' means?"

Virgil frowned at the cross-hatched pattern of wheel ruts in the dusty street. Then he turned to Wyatt.

"I got no idea."

Chapter 8

Winter 1880–1881

Tombstone and Charleston, A.T.

At noon the next day Wyatt carried his breakfast plate to the sideboard, thanked Louisa, and poured himself more coffee. Morgan sat at the table reading the newspaper. Warren stood before the framed portrait of the elder Earps hanging in the hallway, using the reflection in the glass to knot his string tie.

"So Curly Bill goes free," Morg said, backhanding the paper with a slap. "Explain that one to me."

Wyatt walked to the window and sipped his coffee. "Even Fred White said it was an accident. Said he shouldn't have jerked on Brocius's gun like he did. Told his family that before he died."

"You hear how Bill celebrated his release?" Morgan laughed.

Wyatt nodded.

"Well, *I* ain't," Warren spoke up. "What happened?"

Morgan slouched back in his chair to tell the story. "Lou, you might wanna close your ears for this."

Louisa frowned, and at the same time her eyes narrowed to a shy smile.

"Well, it appears that Curly Bill and his boys drank the saloons dry in Charleston the other night. Once they figured they were drunk enough, they busted into the dancehall where there was some kind o' social event goin' on. They locked the door and commenced to force everybody to strip down and dance naked as a flock o' plucked chickens."

Warren whooped a single high-pitched note. "I would'a liked to a' seen that!"

Morgan studied Wyatt's face and dropped his boyish smile. "Ain't much law in Charleston," Morg said, using his big-brother voice for Warren's sake. "I reckon that'll change when you get to be sheriff, Wyatt."

"Undersheriff," Wyatt corrected.

Morg's face closed down. Even Warren went still.

"You made the deal with Behan?" Morg probed.

Wyatt continued to stare out the window, his eyes fixed on Virgil's house across the road. "I had someone from Wells, Fargo look into it for me. Behan wasn't lyin'. It's a sure thing for him." Wyatt turned his head to drive home his point. "Least now, bein' undersheriff's a sure thing for *me*."

Morgan's eyes searched Wyatt's face. "But it's *under*sheriff, Wyatt . . . under *Behan*!"

"For a while. Next time it'll be an election, and I can beat 'im. Being undersheriff will give me a chance to show people how I operate at a higher level." He waited for his brothers to grasp his logic, but Morgan only carried his frown to Warren.

Wyatt turned back to the windowglass, leaned to look across the yard, and set his cup on the sideboard. "Somebody untie the gelding?"

Warren moved to the window. "He ain't out under the cottonwood?"

Wyatt put on his heavy coat and stepped out the door to walk a circle around the house. By the time he walked out onto Fremont Street, Morgan and Warren came from the porch, buttoning their coats and checking the ground for tracks.

"Must've wandered off," Warren said.

Morgan made a grunt deep in his chest. "Or somebody wandered 'im off for us."

"Somebody needs to go out to the Huachucas today about those water rights," Wyatt said. "I'm the one who knows where the claim is. Would you boys ask around about my horse?"

Morgan frowned. "Maybe you ought not go out there alone, Wyatt. Long's we're sharin' this territory with the Apaches."

Warren squared himself to Wyatt. "I'll go with you, Wyatt." He lifted his chin as though trying to stand taller. "Maybe we can kill us some Indians."

Seeing the fever building in his youngest brother's face, Wyatt spoke quietly. "Doc'll go with me. You boys know my horse. I'd be obliged if you could handle that end for me."

At dusk, having located the spring and marked it on a map, Wyatt and Doc were four miles out from Tombstone when a lone rider came up behind them at a fast trot. Sherman McMaster pulled up next to Wyatt and matched his speed until Wyatt reined up. Doc coughed through a long racking fit, and the three sat their horses until Doc could get down several swigs from his flask.

McMaster took off his hat and propped it on his pommel. Then he pursed his lips and looked directly at Wyatt. "Can I talk to you?" he said. "In private?"

Doc took another drink, slowly screwed down the cap, and urged his horse forward at a walk. McMaster returned his hat to his head and lowered his voice.

"You missing a bay gelding?"

"Was when I left home this mornin'."

McMaster jerked a thumb back down the road toward the crossing on the San Pedro. "Might find that horse in Charleston 'bout now. Might find Billy Clanton sittin' on it." He pursed his lips again, this time conveying his doubts. "Says he found it loose out in the scrub." Wyatt looked at him sharply. "Oh," McMaster chuckled, "he knows whose horse it is, all right."

The two men sat their horses for a time. Doc waited fifty feet ahead and stared at the stars just beginning to twinkle in the fading light.

"That all?" Wyatt asked McMaster.

McMaster nodded. "That's all I know."

When Wyatt said no more, McMaster leaned and reined his horse off the road, weaving his way through a prickly maze of cat's-claw and cactus. Wyatt walked his horse to Doc.

"Ride with me to Charleston. One of the Clantons has my horse, and I aim to get it back."

Doc looked off in the direction where McMaster had gone. "Isn't that one of the reprobates who rides with Curly Bill?"

"I'd appreciate you keepin' this to yourself," Wyatt said and tilted his head in the direction McMaster had ridden. "He done me a favor. Right now I just want to go get that horse."

Darkness had settled over Charleston as they rode unnoticed down the main thoroughfare. The town had a rawer feel than Tombstone. More remote, untouched by social amenities, and less confined by the strictures of the law. They moved slowly through the side streets, checking the stables, until across from Ayer's saloon they found the bay in a stall at an unlighted livery. Perched on its back was a high-cantled saddle with a rifle stuffed into a tooled scabbard.

"Doc, keep an eye out here. I'm going to find a sheriff's deputy."

"Hell, let's just take the damned thing. It *is* yours, isn't it?"

"It's in his possession. We're not on friendly ground here. And I ain't the law yet."

*****

In a half hour Wyatt found Doc in the alleyway next to the livery corral. Doc was fending off the night chill with the burn of alcohol from his flask.

"Where the hell'd you go?" Doc quipped. "To the Bureau of Horses in Washington?"

"I talked to a deputy. Then I sent a wire to Tombstone. One of my brothers is comin' with papers on the horse."

Doc lowered the flask and looked past Wyatt toward the saloon. "Well, he'd do well to hurry. That looks like some Clantons right there."

Wyatt turned to see three men silhouetted by the window of the bar as they walked diagonally across the street for the stable. Wyatt bent at the waist and scissored through the corral fence to follow them through the livery entrance. Doc brought up the rear.

The gelding nickered when the loutish Cow-boy began rummaging through his saddlebags. Even when the three men noticed Wyatt's dark figure standing behind the horse, their manner remained familiar and relaxed.

Billy Clanton yawned. "When I get back to the ranch, I'm gonna sleep for two days."

"You'll prob'ly need to," Wyatt said. "You got a long walk ahead o' you."

Billy squinted and moved closer, his drunken haze trying to burn out of him. "What the fuck do you want?" The other two Cow-boys turned from their horses and stood very still.

A revolver double-clicked to full cock as the acid tone in Doc's voice broke the silence. "If any of you degenerates are anxious to meet the devil, then please do jerk your pistol."

"I *found* this horse," Billy snapped. "Figure the shit-brain who let it go didn't care to hold on to it." He wavered, trying to put a foot into the stirrup while the horse was still in the stall. Wyatt grabbed the heavyset boy by his collar and jerked so hard, Clanton fell back against the stall divider.

"Goddamn you," a squat curly headed man snarled. "That's my kid brother."

Wyatt turned to face him, and the man stopped suddenly. "Then why ain't you taught him about stealin' another man's horse?"

Doc laughed. "That's probably exactly what he did teach 'im. Right, Ike?"

Ike Clanton turned on Holliday. "You talk big holding a gun, you puny bastard."

Doc pressed the cocked revolver into Ike's belly. "I *do*, don't I. See, one of the advantages of holdin' a gun is talkin' big. You, on the other hand, talk big all the time and everybody knows it's about as meaningful as the air you squeeze out your ass."

Billy Clanton stood up to his full height. "I'm gonna stomp you into the dirt, Earp."

Wyatt's gun appeared in a slow, steady movement. Ike and Billy went still as mannequins in a store window. The third man edged toward the street one step but then decided to freeze.

"We're gonna sit tight for my papers on this horse. After that, you can try some of that stompin', if you're still of a mind."

Ike Clanton spat. "You can't prove a damn thing on how that horse come into our possession."

"Maybe not," Wyatt said, "but I can prove he's mine."

*****

In an hour Warren arrived with the local deputy sheriff, McDowell, who hung a lighted lantern on the gatepost and ordered all the men into its pale nimbus of light. McDowell sorted through the papers and walked around the horse, touching the identifying marks as listed.

"Looks like the right horse." He turned to Billy. "*You* got papers?"

"Hell, no! I found this horse wanderin' out in the mesquite!"

McDowell handed the papers back to Wyatt. "You pressing charges?"

"Hell," Billy growled, and then he smirked. "He ought'a be thankin' us for findin' the damn flea bag."

Wyatt unhitched Billy Clanton's saddle and let it and the saddle blanket fall into the street. Billy bulled his way in, bumping Wyatt as he bent for the saddle. Wyatt casually turned the horse in a half circle until the young Clanton was caught inside all four legs. Ike and the third Cow-boy backed away quickly as the gelding nickered nervously, tensed, and stutter-stepped. Clanton fell and cried out like a child when a hoof stamped down on his fingers.

Crowding Wyatt, Ike fumed, his breath so offensive that Wyatt put a hand on the older Clanton's chest and moved him back. Ike tried to resist but lost his footing.

"You don't push us Clantons!" he screeched. "You hear me?"

Doc laughed. "I believe he just did, Ike."

The deputy stepped between them and faced Ike. "You boys simmer down now. Let's ever'body get off the street."

Billy Clanton got to his feet, picked up his saddle and blanket, and angrily swung the rig over the top rail of the corral fence. Then he turned and extended an arm to point at Wyatt.

"I ain't afraid of you, Earp."

Doc laughed again and shook his head in thespian regret. "You'll learn the foolishness of that soon enough."

"I ain't afraid of you neither, you little skinny bag o' pus."

Doc's eyes lost all their philosophical wit. "If that was my horse," he said, "you'd be dead right now. Now get the fuck out of my sight."

Herded by the deputy, the Cow-boys shuffled toward the middle of the street. Billy Clanton swiped at the deputy's hand and turned so that he was walking backward to glare at Doc and Wyatt.

"If you got any more horses need findin'," Billy called out, "let me know!"

McDowell prodded the boy on. Grumbling and scuffing their boots in the street, the trio of Cow-boys strode toward the saloon, with Billy turning every few steps to glower.

"Why'd you let 'im off, Wyatt?" Warren whispered. "You should'a locked 'im up! Or shot 'im! Hell, I would have!"

Wyatt removed Clanton's bridle and slung it into the fence. Then, using a length of rope from his saddlebags on the mare, he fashioned a hackamore.

"Wyatt?" Warren pressed.

Wyatt fitted the rope snuggly over the gelding's long muzzle and did not look at his brother. "I aim to be sheriff of Cochise County," he said so quietly he might have been talking to the horse. "Won't help me to be shootin' anybody or wastin' time in court over somethin' that will never get sorted out." He turned his head to Warren, driving home his point with the ice in his eyes. "This here was just a moment in time with a few Cow-boys who will eventually dig their own graves. Being sheriff can set me up for a long time to come. You understand that?"

Warren spat to one side and stared at his brother. "Morg says you used to crack a man's head if he looked at you wrong."

Wyatt walked the gelding by a lead rope to his mare and tied the free end behind the cantle of his saddle. "Things are different here in this country, Warren," he said. "We got to live with these people. They don't go back to Texas at the end of summer like they did in Kansas."

Warren frowned and checked Doc's face, but Doc only offered a quizzical smile. "Shit," Warren said, "I'd'a just killed 'im."

Wyatt studied his brother for a moment and then turned to Doc. "Who was the third man with the Clantons?"

"Frank Stilwell," Doc said, pronouncing the name as if he were recalling a gum disease. "If anybody in that crowd needs killing, it's *him*."

Wyatt booted into his stirrup and mounted. "Do me a favor, Doc, and don't point out everybody who you think needs killing. My brother seems to put some stock into your considerations."

"Well, hell," Doc huffed, "somebody ought to."

CHAPTER 9

Winter, Early 1881

Tombstone, A.T.

Two weeks into the New Year, at midday, Wyatt knocked on the locked door of the Wells, Fargo office and waited. After the shade was opened a crack, the lock clicked, and Marsh Williams swung open the door, a pistol in his hand. Wyatt went inside and watched Williams peek out past the shade and then lock the door.

The warmth of the room was welcoming, the aroma of the agent's humidor rich and exotic. Without a word of greeting, Williams sat back down on the bench near the wood heater, laid his pistol next to him, and continued to stack money from the safe into a strongbox.

"Let me finish this, Wyatt," Williams mumbled without looking up. "Eighty, ninety, a hun'erd. That's thirteen." He tongued the point of a pencil and wrote down a figure in his ledger.

Wyatt eyed the stacked and banded bills inside the strongbox. If Williams was a man with sticky fingers, he certainly had the opportunity to short the company. He waited until the agent closed his book.

"Now, what can I do for you, Wyatt?"

"My brother, James . . . his stepdaughter is gettin' married to a machinist who opened a foundry on one of our mine properties. I wanna put in a word for him with Wells, Fargo. He can make most anything you need out o' metal." Wyatt pointed to the strongbox. "Buckles, locks, and such."

Before Williams could reply, his head came up at the clatter of hooves in the street, and his hands dropped protectively to the money. He rose, hurriedly crossed to the door, parted the shades, and peered out.

"Ain't that your racehorse?" Williams said, his voice rising with the question.

Wyatt unlocked the door and stepped outside to see his double-mounted Thoroughbred sliding to a halt in front of Hatch's billiard parlor. Virgil lowered a slight young man from the horse's rump, and then he himself dismounted. The horse was lathered and breathing hard, its long legs rippled with swollen veins and its flanks dark and wet with perspiration. Morgan walked out of Hatch's, followed by Fred Dodge, and then Doc Holliday.

"Where's Wyatt?" Virgil bellowed to the trio on the boardwalk.

"Right here," Wyatt called out. Only then did he recognize Virgil's passenger—a feckless gambler who regularly lost money playing faro at the Oriental.

Virgil handed the reins to Morgan, clamped a hand on the boy's upper arm, and walked him to where Wyatt stood. "There's a mob on the way from Charleston to get at this'n," Virgil explained. "The constable, McKelvey, was haulin' 'im here to Tombstone in a wagon. That's when I run into 'em." Virgil pulled the prisoner closer, and the boy bobbled like a puppet. "Apparently he's kilt the manager at Gird's smelter."

Squirming in Virgil's grip, the accused boy licked his lips and looked beseechingly at Wyatt. "It was self-defense, Mr. Earp. He come at me with a knife."

Wyatt looked west down the street toward the Charleston Road. "How far back are they?"

Virgil wiped at his cold nose with his coat sleeve and shook his head. "Last I saw of 'em was about two miles back. We outran 'em easy on the racer, even ridin' double." He nodded toward the Wells, Fargo office. "We'll need a place to hole up till we can handle the crowd."

Wyatt walked back to the Wells, Fargo doorway and saw Williams strapping up the strongbox at a frenzied pace. Wyatt immediately ruled out using the office as a safe haven.

"I'll need your shotgun, Marsh."

Without interrupting the rhythm of his hands, Williams bobbed his head toward the back of the room. "Beside the desk. There's shells in the bottom drawer. But before you run off with it, how 'bout making sure nobody robs me!"

Wyatt pocketed extra shells and carried the double-barreled ten-gauge out onto the street, where Virgil and the fidgeting prisoner waited. A small crowd had begun to gather to watch from the boardwalks.

"What's your name, kid?" Wyatt asked.

"Rourke," he replied eagerly.

"Which manager did you kill?"

"Schneider," he said, turning testy. "That sonovabitch come askin' for it. He—"

A swell of voices turned their heads to a cluster of men on horseback pouring into Allen Street several blocks to the west. They milled about, fronting pedestrians, and yelling into the liveries and shops that they passed.

"Don't let 'em hang me, Marshal!" the boy whined, looking quickly from Wyatt to Virgil with a heightened anxiety flickering in his eyes.

"We ain't the marshal, son," Wyatt said, "but we won't be allowing any hanging today." He turned to Fred Dodge. "You'd better find Sippy."

"To hell with Sippy," Virgil interrupted. "Consider yourself a federal deputy."

Wyatt pointed with the shotgun across the street. "Take him over to Vogan's, Virge. The bowling alley is long and narrow and has got only two ways in. Tell James to put two men on the backdoor with scatter-guns. Morg, go fetch us a wagon and team and bring it around front." With a decisive jab of his index finger, Wyatt pointed to the curb in front of Vogan's. "Park it right there, pointed west," he instructed. "And do it quick! Sooner we get this boy started for Tucson, the better."

Wyatt took up the reins of his racer and walked the horse across the street to Vogan's, where he tied it to an iron hitching ring bolted to the tread boards. Cradling the coach gun in the crook of his left arm, he stood on the boardwalk, leaning his shoulder into an awning post, waiting and watching the crowd of twenty or so mill workers dismount in front of the Grand Hotel and advance toward him. From the sidewalks, others joined their ranks—curious onlookers mostly—swelling their number to fifty. Most were unarmed, but the ones in front carried pistols and rifles in their hands, openly defying city ordinance.

"Where *is* the little murderin' sonovabitch!" a man yelled from the mob.

Wyatt remained as still as the post on which he leaned. He recognized Dick Gird, the owner of the mill works, shouldering his way to the front of the crowd and speaking to the men he passed in a low, angry tone.

When the mob crowded in close, stopping only a few yards from the boardwalk, Wyatt studied the men in front, appraising each one's capacity to incite the others into action. Finally, when they saw he was not going to shy from the numbers, the men at the head of the mob went silent, and gradually the stillness worked its way to the back of the crowd.

"Bring him out!" ordered a broad-faced man standing in back. Wyatt set his gaze on the one who had spoken, and a graveyard quiet returned to the street.

"I'll bring him out when I'm ready."

The man appeared to be puzzled at this reply. When he started to speak again, Wyatt cut him off.

"But you boys are going to be in the way here." Wyatt nodded across the street. "I want you to move over there to make room."

"What the hell for?" challenged another of the mill workers. Wearing stained canvas coveralls, this man marched forward through the crowd, his hand gripping a heavy revolver stuffed in his pocket. "If that little bastard Rourke is in there, you're the goddamn one needs to move."

Wyatt straightened from the post, seated the stock of the shotgun to his shoulder, and raised the barrels until they bore down on the advancing man. The man's angry face went slack, and his momentum stopped as if by some involuntary rebellion of his legs.

"Step back," Wyatt ordered, his voice low and raspy.

The man hesitated only long enough to release his grip on the pistol, and then he edged his way backward into the crowd. Wyatt nodded to the narrow opening in the street before him.

"A wagon's comin' in here directly to take Rourke to Tucson, where he'll stand trial."

"Stand aside, Earp!" someone yelled. "You ain't a sheriff's deputy no more!"

Wyatt cocked the hammers on the shotgun, and the clarity of the metallic clicks fixed the crowd into photographic stillness. In this sudden quiet, the wind pushed the sign in front of Hatch's into a small pendulum arc, setting up a steady cadence—the sound like someone diligently working the handle of a stubborn pitcher pump.

"That's right," Wyatt said evenly, "but it doesn't really matter what I am, does it? 'Cept I'm the one standin' up here between you and the mistake you're considerin'."

For a time, no one spoke. Then a voice from the back broke the silence.

"He's bluffing! Let's go in and get Rourke. Earp can't stop all of us."

Shifting his aim, Wyatt trained the shotgun on Dick Gird, who had said nothing. "You're right. I can't stop all you boys . . . but I'll kill these men up front. Then you'll have to step over them to get to Rourke." Wyatt kept his face empty. "Then there's two more Earps inside."

The door to Vogan's opened, and Doc Holliday stepped out, his nickel-plated revolver in his hand, catching quicksilver light from the winter sky. Stopping beside Wyatt, he spoke loud enough for all to hear.

"I think I'll start with that brave sonovabitch in the back with the big mouth."

Just then, Marshal Sippy fast-walked up the middle of Allen from Fourth Street. He was hatless, and his overcoat hung askew where he had mismatched the buttons with their holes.

"All you men there!" he called out hoarsely. "I want you to disperse!"

"Stay out of this, Sippy!" someone replied. "We didn't vote you into office just to protect a killer."

Sippy slowed his walk and then stopped to turn at the sound of a wagon coming on hard and fast. Morgan slapped the reins on a team of wall-eyed bays harnessed to a utility wagon, and he charged recklessly past Sippy toward the crowd. Boots began to scuffle, stirring up clouds of dust from the cold street. The wagon skidded sideways as it carved a tight turn in front of Vogan's, forcing the men closest to Wyatt to back away in undignified haste. When the wagon stopped with its team facing west, Holliday climbed up into the bed and swept his shining revolver in a wide arc, like a man at pistol practice choosing his target.

The crowd began a slow retreat, until Virgil stepped out of the bowling alley with Rourke in hand. James followed and walked quickly to the edge of the boardwalk, a Colt's revolver in his good hand. The crowd now gravitated toward the wagon's tailgate, and Virgil paused. Wyatt gathered the young gambler's coat lapel in his left hand and forged ahead. With the shotgun extended before him in one hand, he walked slowly, parting a path to the rear of the wagon, letting his eyes convince each man of his single-minded intent.

The millworker in coveralls blocked his way, but Wyatt's momentum was set. "Step aside," he said in a low, even tone. "I'm bringing my prisoner through." The challenger held a hostile glare but backed away, his pistol still filling his pocket. Marshal Sippy climbed up into the bed of the wagon and extended a hand to Rourke. Then Virgil climbed up, his pistol still holstered but his face set with purpose. Fred Dodge stood by the wagon with his hand inside his coat.

"I want all you men to get back to your work," Sippy announced, but no one paid him any mind. Doc Holliday sat the prisoner down with his back to the driver's box and stood in front of him as a shield. Wyatt worked his way through the milling bodies, mounted his racehorse, and rested the butt of the scattergun on his thigh, the muzzle pointing to the cold, gray sky.

"Morgan, get that team movin' up the street," Wyatt ordered quietly. "Now."

James remained on the boardwalk, nodding at Wyatt when their eyes met. The jingle of the harness and the roll of the wheels had the effect of energizing the men nearest the back of the wagon, and they followed as if they did not know what else to do. Wyatt insinuated his horse between the wagon and the crowd, reined the stud around to face the mob, then coaxed the racer into a shuffling reverse gait. When voices began to swell and a knot of men started to rush forward, Wyatt lowered the barrels of the shotgun to those inspired few and kept his mount back-stepping with the wagon.

"This ain't worth you boys dyin' over," Wyatt said. "You'd best lay off."

Most of the millworkers had lost the fire that had brought them to Tombstone. While scanning the crowd, Wyatt spotted Johnny Behan across the street in the shade of the Alhambra saloon's awning. Behan still wore the sheriff's deputy badge, as the official transfer of the shrievalty had not yet passed to Bob Paul. When Behan realized that Wyatt had seen him, he jumped into the street and began making broad gestures with his arms.

"It's all over, boys!" Behan announced. "Let's clear off the street now and let the law take care of this." He nodded and smiled at a few faces he seemed to recognize. "Come on now, gentlemen, let it go!"

Behan strutted backward down the street, like a bandleader called up to lead the parade in reverse, but by the time the wagon was passing the Grand Hotel, he hurried past Wyatt and climbed aboard the wagon bed, taking his place with the other lawmen.

When the wagon had gained enough distance from the angry crowd, Wyatt reined the spirited stallion around and held it to a walk behind the prisoner and his entourage of protectors. Fred Dodge walked beside the right rear wheel like a man participating in a funeral cortege.

Now, away from the crowd, Johnny Behan launched into a flowery speech about the prudence of settling affairs like this one in the courts. When the wagon turned down Fourth Street, Wyatt eased down the hammers of the shotgun and watched Rourke hold his fearful gaze on the corner at Hafford's. Finally, the young gambler's eyes settled on Wyatt, and he offered a sheepish nod of gratitude. When Wyatt looked at Holliday, Doc made a wry grin.

"We missed a fine opportunity back there, Wyatt. We could have gone out in a blaze of glory."

Wyatt said nothing, but Morgan twisted in the driver's box and crinkled his eyes. "Maybe next time, Doc. Fred Dodge owes us too much money for us to cash in now."

Dodge only shook his head at the banter.

On Fremont Street John Clum came running from the *Epitaph* office in an ink-stained apron, his shirtsleeves rolled to his elbows, his hands blackened with the dark pigments of his trade. He looked from Virgil to Wyatt.

"What's happened?" he said excitedly. He studied the face of young Rourke, who sat in the wagon bed hugging his shins, his chin wedged between his knees. When the prisoner did not offer an explanation, the editor singled out Sippy. "What the hell happened, Ben?"

The marshal appeared flustered. He took in a lot of air, inflated his cheeks, and exhaled in a rush, like a man who had just surfaced from deep water.

Morgan kept the wagon moving, and Behan yelled over the rumble of the wheels. "It's all under control, John. Just a little scare with a lynch mob."

"Lynch mob!" Clum chirped up. His eyes snapped to the young prisoner balled up behind the driver's seat.

Sippy cleared his throat and found his voice. "They say this boy killed Schneider at Gird's mill in Charleston."

Clum looked back at Virgil and Wyatt for confirmation, but neither spoke.

"What's your name, son?" Clum asked the boy.

"Rourke," he replied quickly. "Michael Rourke."

Matching his walk to the wagon, Clum pulled a small notepad from his apron pocket and found a stub of pencil behind one ear. "Why did you kill him?"

Rourke pointed to the notepaper and frowned. "I go by 'Johnny-Behind-the-Deuce.' That's how people know me." Then his blue eyes narrowed. "Schneider, the uppity bastard, he needed killin'."

At the rear gate of the O.K. Corral, Holliday stood to climb down from the wagon, so Morgan halted the team. "I believe my services are no longer needed, gentlemen," Doc said, cocked his head at Clum, and smiled. "Just leave me out of your story, if you don't mind."

Sippy cleared his throat. "Mr. Holliday," he said, his voice now deeper, "how is it you are carrying a weapon inside the town limits? Were you deputized for this?"

Holliday turned a cold stare on the marshal. Then he smiled and nodded toward Wyatt.

"My friend needed help, Marshal," he said, as though the logic of it was obvious. Sippy looked at Wyatt, then at Virgil, but he said nothing more.

When Doc walked toward Fly's boardinghouse, Clum directed his focus on Behan. "Did they try to take him by force? Were they armed?"

"Most were," Behan answered.

Clum began scribbling. "Was anyone hurt? Who was in the crowd?"

Behan climbed down from the wagon and dusted off his trousers. "It was a modest attempt, I'd say. The millworkers are just upset, John, that's all. We've got it under control."

"Prob'ly fifty . . . sixty men," Sippy volunteered. "I'd say about a third were carrying guns." He hopped down to the street to talk to Clum. "But no shots were fired. There was plenty just come to watch. All in all, by my estimation, the town kept its order. But damned if it weren't a powder keg for a minute there."

Clum looked up at Wyatt, who sat unmoving on the racer. "Wyatt? Anything to add to that?"

Wyatt's face showed nothing when he met Clum's eyes. "They wanted at him," he said, nodding toward the prisoner. "But they didn't get 'im. That's all there was to it."

"That damned Schneider pulled a knife on me," Rourke blurted out. "The sneaky sonovabitch! Always thinkin' he's better'n the rest've us. You can ask anybody works over on the San Pedro. He wouldn' hardly talk to you. 'Less maybe you're Dick Gird! Or God!"

Morgan snapped the reins once, and Clum walked alongside the wagon, taking notes from the boy, who seemed now ready to relate his story at length. Wyatt handed the shotgun to Dodge.

"Fred, will you get that to Marsh Williams for me?"

Dodge took the Wells, Fargo ten-gauge. "You bet," he said but hesitated and lowered his voice. "If nobody else is gonna say it, Wyatt, that was a hellava thing you done back there. Why *did* you do it?"

"Somebody had to," Wyatt said and nudged the stud forward to follow the wagon.

CHAPTER 10

Spring 1881

Tombstone, Drew's Station, and Redfield Ranch, Cochise County, A.T.

In the gambler's hours of a frosty March night, Virgil stepped from the cold into the Oriental. Wyatt looked up and watched his older brother march straight to his faro table, his face set hard with a no-nonsense look. When he stopped at the end of Wyatt's table, every player looked up at him.

"Bob Paul just telegraphed from Contention. He was riding shotgun on the stage to Benson. Some road agents stopped them, and Bud Philpott and one of the passengers were shot dead."

Without apology to his customers, Wyatt closed his game and began gathering his cards. "Where did it happen?"

"Inside the new county. Just this side of Drew's Station. Behan wants you, Morg, and Marsh Williams in his posse. Meet at the Gird block in a half hour." Virgil watched Wyatt gather up his faro layout. "Looks like it's time for the new sheriff of Cochise to show his cards."

Wyatt looked up at Virgil. "Are you pulling together a federal posse?"

Virgil shook his head. "I'll ride with you boys. Wasn't nothin' taken off the stage: no mail, no strongbox . . . nothin'. Paul opened up on the sonzabitches with his scattergun. Thinks he hit the one who killed Bud." As Wyatt stood with his hands full, Virgil peeled open Wyatt's coat by the lapels and searched his vest. "Johnny ain't given you a badge yet," he said, more an observation than a question.

"Pending," Wyatt replied.

Virge pursed his lips and nodded. "And you're still countin' on it?"

Wyatt met his brother's eyes. "We shook hands on it."

Virgil nodded again and stuffed his hands into his overcoat pockets. "You know Warren'll be wantin' to go with us," he said in a flat tone.

Wyatt only shook his head as a reply. Then he walked past his brother to the bar.

"Well . . . he *will*," Virgil argued as he watched Wyatt reach over the bar to store the accoutrements of his gambling trade. "*You* wanna tell 'im?"

"I'll tell 'im," Wyatt said.

The posse members met outside the new county offices—eight men sitting their horses in the dark street, each sufficiently armed, lightly provisioned, and dressed for the cold of the high desert night in early spring. The new sheriff of Cochise County came through the door and stood before the somber group of horsemen, spreading his boots on the boardwalk, and repeatedly referring to a two-line telegram in his hand. Behan wore a long, gray dress coat with a burgundy strip of velvet sewn onto each lapel. His hat was new—pearl gray like the overcoat—and perched on his head like a colorless rooster's comb.

"Boys, you know my new deputy, Billy Breakenridge." Behan lifted the telegram toward his deputy hurrying around the corner as he led two horses. Dressed in new trail clothes, Breakenridge cradled two repeater rifles against his chest with one arm. He stopped before Behan, who relieved him of one of the rifles, then looked out upon the group, his eyes darting from one face in the posse to the next, as if seeking someone's approval.

Wyatt waited for Behan to acknowledge him as new undersheriff, but the sheriff's attention was again riveted to the telegram. When Behan's head came up, his eyes panned the posse in an all-encompassing arc as if he were about to deliver a speech.

"My first priority," he said, "is our safety." He cleared his throat, seeming unfamiliar with the practice of using his voice at such a volume.

"I don't want any man taking unnecessary risks. We ride together, and we back each other. Now . . . who here is experienced as a tracker?"

With no answer forthcoming, the new sheriff, looking mildly confused, frowned at the faces before him.

"We're all experienced, Johnny," Virgil said finally. "Let's get going."

One-handedly Behan folded the telegram against his chest. "All right," he announced, trying his damnedest to sound official. "Let's get going."

*****

From Drew's Station they tracked the highwaymen to the ranch of Len Redfield, a known consort of the Clantons and Curly Bill. Behan spoke to Redfield in a tone closer to apology than authority. The others in the posse sat mutely listening to the conversation, growing equally irritable at Redfield's reticence and Behan's lax manner of questioning.

With dawn breaking over the hills in the east, Wyatt walked his horse to the barn and inspected the stalls. He didn't need to dismount to see that four of the horses inside were still damp from a hard ride. When he returned to his party to share this information, Morgan tapped him on the arm.

"You see that?" Morg whispered, pointing toward a copse of mesquite behind the barn. He spurred his horse that way, and Wyatt followed. After a few passes through the brush, Morgan drew his revolver, and yelled into the thicket. "You can get on out o' there on your own or get *shot* out!"

A man rose with his hands raised high and made his way through the brush. With Morgan and Wyatt riding behind him, the frightened man moved toward the barn. When Redfield saw their approach, he visibly paled.

Stopping at the barn, Wyatt and Morgan dismounted and took the man inside amid the sharp tang of horse sweat and manure. The man turned to face them, but his eyes kept darting to the played-out horses in the stalls.

"Talk and talk fast," Wyatt said, "startin' with who you are."

"King," he answered and swallowed. "Lew King. Talk about what?"

Wyatt slapped him across the face, and King fell backward into a stall gate. The horse inside snorted and backed away. Wyatt stepped closer and leaned his face into King's.

"Two men died on the Benson stage tonight." Wyatt grabbed the man's lapels. "Let's start there."

"Wyatt?" Behan called from the yard. Wyatt looked at Morg and nodded toward the barn entrance. Morgan walked off to intercept the sheriff.

Wyatt jerked King's lapels, and the man dangled limply in his grip. "Give me names, or you're gonna die in this horse shit."

"I didn't do nothin'," the sniveling man insisted, his voice dry and hoarse.

Wyatt swatted King's hat off his head, took a fistful of hair, and shoved the back of his head into the gate. The horse kicked wildly at the boards and nickered. When King volunteered nothing, Wyatt flung open the gate and pushed him into the stall with the panicked horse. In the grainy light of the barn, the frightened man's eyes shone like bright coins.

"I didn't shoot nobody—I swear it!"

King's desperate eyes fixed on the barn door. He could hear Behan's voice getting louder as he argued with Morgan. Wyatt walked into the stall, and King raised his arms over his face.

"If I tell you, you got to protect me."

Wyatt slapped him again, and the frightened man fell into the hay where he tried to squeeze himself into the corner of the stall. Wyatt drew his revolver and held it down by his leg. When he hooked his thumb over the hammer, it looked as though King's terror would burst from his eyes. The horse stamped and snorted but kept its distance.

"It's me you better worry about right now," Wyatt said, his voice humming with malice.

King checked the door again, but all that could be seen was the silhouette of Morgan's back. Behan had dropped the authority from his voice and was now arguing with reason. Wyatt grabbed a handful of King's hair and jerked his prisoner toward the horse. Panicking, the animal half turned and kicked, its hooves ringing on the stall boards.

"Damn it to hell," King said finally. "It was Jim Crane, Harry Head, and Billy Leonard. I'm tellin' you I didn't shoot *nobody!*"

Wyatt pushed King ahead of him out of the stall just as Behan managed to slip around Morgan.

"Who's this?" Behan demanded, but his eyes sharpened in recognition. Before the sheriff could say anymore, Wyatt pushed his prisoner out the barn door, where Marsh Williams took hold of his arm.

"Jim Crane, Harry Head, and Bill Leonard are the men we're after," Wyatt reported. He jerked his head toward the stalls. "They used up these horses and picked up fresh mounts from Redfield." He nodded outside, where King was being shackled. "He was part of it."

"Billy Leonard is in business with Ike Clanton," Williams said from the door. "All three of those men he named run with Curly Bill." He jostled the man in his grip. "Don't know this one though."

Behan stood up straighter and turned from Wyatt. "I'll question him myself. Alone."

"I already did that," Wyatt said, moving in front of Behan. The sheriff stumbled backward a step before catching himself. "We're losing time here, Johnny. Morg and I'll pick up the trail." He nodded toward King. "You keep him away from Redfield. Don't give 'em a chance to spin up the same story." Wyatt mounted the chestnut and reined the mare out into the mesquite with Morgan following.

In the growing light, the two Earp brothers found fresh tracks heading north in the gulch behind Redfield's house. Returning at a gallop, Wyatt spurred his horse toward Behan, who was in conference with King and Redfield. Behan faced Wyatt's glare and screwed his neck up through his shirt collar.

"I'm taking King back to Tombstone," the sheriff announced and lifted his hands out from his sides. "Well, we can't haul him around the territory with us now, can we?" He cleared his throat as he faced his posse. "I want you boys to keep going after the others . . . and get word to me where I can meet you. I'll join you when I can."

Virgil stepped into the conversation. "You've had two prisoners escape out of your jail since you took office, Johnny." He thrust a finger at King. "Keep this man under guard."

Behan took a freshly filled canteen from Breakenridge and busied himself securing it to his saddle. "Once we get him to Tombstone," the sheriff said, avoiding Virgil's eyes, "he's not going anywhere."

"What about Redfield?" Virgil asked.

Behan shook his head. "He's likely a victim in all this. Says his horses were stolen." Behan's hands fumbled with the tie-downs on his canteen.

Virgil scowled. "Guess he forgot to tell us that, Johnny."

"Says he didn't know," Behan snapped as he mounted. "Get King mounted!" he called out to Breakenridge. "We're heading back to Tombstone." It was his first convincing command.

Wyatt sidled his horse next to Behan's and waited for the sheriff to look him in the eye. "Which part do you figure all this to be, Johnny? The administratin' or the enforcin'?"

Behan frowned and began stuffing his hands into his gloves. "I don't know what you mean. And, frankly, I don't—"

"I advised you to keep King and Redfield separate," Wyatt reminded. "You told me as undersheriff I—"

"Look, Wyatt," Behan interrupted, giving him a look of saintly patience. "I've already got an undersheriff." And with that, he reined his horse around to head back down the same trail by which they had arrived. Breakenridge climbed into his saddle, took the reins of King's horse, and followed.

Wyatt raised his chin to Williams. "Go with 'em, Marsh," he said in a low monotone. "See he gets to the Tombstone jail and that the goddamn door gets locked." Wyatt turned a stony face to the rest of the posse. "Let's go find the rest of these sons of bitches."

*****

In the course of the weeklong hunt through the mountains, Wyatt's chestnut began to favor a foreleg. The other horses were playing out fast, too. Finding no sympathy from the outlying ranchers, who benefited from the rampant cattle rustling along the border, the lawmen were not offered replacement mounts—neither for rent nor for sale. The tracks showed the fugitives had secured fresh mounts all along the trail.

With his horse lame, Wyatt had no choice but to walk the mare some twenty miles back to Tombstone on foot, while the others pushed on.

Six days later Virgil and Morgan returned to town with the posse. Wyatt stepped out of the post office, raising a hand against the afternoon sun, and waited for his brothers to dismount. Virgil's big jaw was clamped tight as a steel trap, and Morgan's face was drawn, his eyes empty, as though he hadn't slept in days.

"We got nothin'," the younger Earp said, "no news at all . . .'cept I'm bone tired."

Virgil climbed stiffly up to the boardwalk and began pulling off his trail gloves. He cut his eyes to Wyatt, but he was too angry to talk.

"You seen Behan yet?" Wyatt said.

Virgil clamped the fingertip of a glove in his teeth and shook his head.

"King's gone," Wyatt informed him. "Slipped out the back door of the jail, free as you please."

Virgil stood stock-still and stared into Wyatt's eyes. His face reddened beneath the weathered tan he had acquired on the manhunt.

"We ride around this whole Godforsaken country, and our new sheriff can't lock a goddamn door on a man." Turning his fierce gaze on the county offices across the street, he bunched his gloves into one hand and whipped them against his pant leg.

"Here's the rest of it," Wyatt went on, and Virgil turned around to hear it. "Behan ain't payin' us. Says Wells, Fargo needs to pick up Morg's tab . . . and the federal marshal, yours."

The ill humor in Morgan's face sharpened his eyes. "Got a answer for just about everything, don't he? But what about you, Wyatt? Since when's an undersheriff not get compensation?"

Wyatt turned his head to glare at the county offices. "I ain't the undersheriff."

Virgil and Morgan stared at Wyatt for the time it took an ore wagon to rumble down Fremont Street. "Sonovabitch must'a forgot his promise," Virgil grumbled. "Hell-fire . . . Dake and Wells, Fargo didn't ask us to do nothin'. Why should they pay?"

Morgan laughed. "Christ! Talkin' to Behan's like tryin' to hold on to the wind."

Virgil spat into the street. "How's the chestnut, Wyatt?"

"Still swole-up," Wyatt said. "Was a hell of a walk back, and she's paying for it."

"Least somebody's payin'," Morgan said, something of the usual twinkle back in his eye.

*****

After a ride south of town to check on one of their mines, Wyatt and Virgil stabled their horses at the O.K. Corral and walked out the back entrance to Fremont Street. Because neither brother was in a hurry to return to his home, they strolled under the awning at Bauer's Meat Market. There they stood in the soft violet haze of twilight and lit cigars. Virgil chuckled and tilted his head to the store behind them.

"Prob'ly more stolen beef runnin' through here than there are lies passin' through Johnny Behan's smilin' teeth."

Wyatt said nothing. He faced northwest, where the Rincons and the Santa Catalinas stretched in a blue haze out on the horizon. He had covered much of those ranges during the search for the men who had attacked the Benson stage, and now these mountains—like all the vast desert around them—had come to symbolize for him the futility of being a lawman in a sprawling territory where the general populace of ranchers supported the law breakers.

Virgil coughed up another laugh from his chest. "Morg says you eat enough of Bauer's beef, you might start speaking Mexican."

Wyatt drew on his cigar and listened to the evening sounds gather around them. Now there was a purple tint to the desert—not something you could point at . . . more like an infusion spreading from the heat rising off the land. The aroma of beans, peppers, and onions wafted from the Mexican quarter, reminding Wyatt of the bare kitchen he would be going home to. He considered, once he had talked to Virgil, going straight to the Oriental to his faro table. He could get something to eat at the bar.

"I got something I want to talk over with you," Wyatt said, keeping his eyes on the mountains.

Virgil leaned a shoulder into an awning post and waited as Wyatt sorted out his words. A Mexican girl led a burro and cart from the business district toward the arroyo that opened up beyond the Aztec House. Wyatt had seen her in the neighborhood going door to door, quietly offering her produce of tomatoes, peppers, and herbs. When the girl waved, both Wyatt and Virgil nodded.

"McMaster tells me Ike Clanton is the weak link in the Cow-boy crowd," Wyatt began.

Virgil grunted. "Ike'd be the weak link in a line of ducks walking across Arizona."

"Seems he's got his eye on a ranch belongin' to one o' the stage robbers—Bill Leonard." Wyatt checked the burn on his cigar. "I'm considerin' makin' Ike a proposition."

Wyatt waited for a reaction from Virgil, but he got none.

"Wells, Fargo is offerin' a reward for Leonard, Head, and Crane. It's a lot of money. I figure it's enough that Clanton would guide us to 'em."

Virgil narrowed his eyes at Wyatt. "You think he'd do that?"

Wyatt cocked his head in a barely perceptible shrug. "Ike keeps the reward. Leonard's ranch is up for grabs. I make the arrests. Come time I run for sheriff in a regular election, I figure that'll give me a leg up."

Virgil was quiet for so long, Wyatt already knew his opinion of the transaction.

"He can't afford to let it go bad," Wyatt explained. "If word got out, he wouldn't last a week among his San Simon crowd."

Virge nodded at that part of the idea. Then he narrowed his eyes and slowly rotated the cigar in his lips.

"Might be *you* can't afford to let it go bad, too. If people think you're making deals with the likes of Ike Clanton, how's that gonna help you win the sheriff's post?"

Wyatt waved the question away with his hand, leaving a trail of smoke that hung in the air. "Using informants is part of the work, Virge. You know that. I got a man ridin' with Brocius working for me right now." He turned to meet Virgil's eyes. "The short, feisty one with the bowlegs—McMaster."

Virgil's breathing checked as he stared at his brother. "How the hell do you pay for that?"

Wyatt shook his head. "Not me. Wells, Fargo."

Virge frowned out into the night for a time. Wyatt waited for his brother to come around.

"What if Ike don't accept it?"

"Then he don't," Wyatt said simply.

Virgil remained still for a time. In the fading light the mountains had darkened to a solid flat backdrop. They were like a background prop used in a theatrical production, something snipped from roofing tin and painted black.

"You're pretty set on doin' this?" Virgil pushed.

"I'm set on doin' *somethin'*. This seems good as anything."

"Well," Virgil said and studied the label of his cigar. "You'd better keep this tight." He looked at Wyatt. "If Clanton's old man finds out, he'll kill Ike himself." Then Virgil laughed at his own words. "Maybe this idea does have some possibilities." He stepped down into the street and looked up at the night sky. "Lotta stars down here in Arizona. One of the Mex in our neighborhood told me it's 'cause of all the silver in the ground."

"Lot o' stars in Kansas, too, Virge," Wyatt reminded him.

Virgil laughed deep in his chest. "Well, hell, Wyatt, you think we ought'a go back and dig for silver there?"

Wyatt flicked ashes into the street. "I think we're in it up to our ankles right here."

Virgil turned his attention back to the broad desert plain that opened up beyond the arroyo. "Or our necks," he said quietly.

CHAPTER 11

Late Spring, Summer 1881

Tombstone, A.T.

When the Kinnear stage rolled to a stop in front of the Wells, Fargo office, Marsh Williams clamped a cigar in his teeth, picked up his ledger, and stepped outside. Seated at William's desk, Wyatt finished writing the letter to his parents in California—explaining why Warren was coming back to live with them. The message grew wordier than he had intended, but he felt the need to convince his father to steer Warren into a line of business that would not involve a badge. Or a gun.

Williams came back inside, grinning broadly around his cigar. "Hey, Wyatt, take a look at this, would you?"

The spring day had warmed up like mid-summer. Outside, Johnny Behan was helping a young woman step down from the coach. He was dressed in a new suit and hat—both the color of sand—and, when he turned, Wyatt saw that his badge, which he usually wore on his vest, was pinned to the front of his coat.

"You ever see a woman like that?" Williams muttered into the windowglass. "She looks good enough to spread on a biscuit and eat."

Wyatt admired the hourglass shape of her body and watched her laugh at something Behan said. The melodic sound of her voice drifted into the office, taking Wyatt to a place he did not know still existed inside him.

"Nobody in Tombstone can touch *that*," Williams said, and then he snorted. " 'Cept maybe Johnny."

When Behan playfully reached for the woman's hat, she turned her head away with a minimal effort, and the movement reminded Wyatt of a mother tolerating mischief from her child. Behan laughed, but the woman busied herself dusting her travel skirt with modest strokes of her hand.

"Word is," Williams said, "she's come from San Francisco to marry our august sheriff." Wyatt gave the Wells, Fargo agent a look. Williams shrugged. "If anyone could tame ol' hound-dog Johnny," Marsh said, nodding at the woman in the street, "be somebody like that."

They watched through the window as Behan paid two boys to gather the luggage lined up on the boardwalk. The young woman lifted her arms and tied back her hair with a ribbon beneath the brim of her hat. Her hair was black as the wing of a raven.

"Who is she?" Wyatt asked.

"Actress, is what I heard," Williams said. "And a Jew." His voice turned sly. "Johnny probably stands to make some money off this deal."

When she turned away to take in the town, Wyatt studied the woman's back. She was like water, shifting from one inspiring posture to another. Her waist was small, her breasts full, and her hips mirrored this fullness in a perfect symmetry. She looked strong somehow—strong-willed, Wyatt guessed. As Behan instructed the boys with the luggage, she became still for a moment and looked in earnest at the business establishments lined up along Allen Street.

In the profile of her face Wyatt saw a restrained hunger, as though she were looking through a door she was determined to enter at all cost and claim whatever waited behind it. Her eyes were dark like her hair, and the smooth outline of her jaw was etched clean and flawless.

From the near sidewalk John Clum approached Behan and then turned and became animated as he introduced himself to the woman. Wyatt heard Clum refer to himself as "the new mayor" twice in the same sentence. Forfeiting a measure of her grace, the young woman made a deferential bow with her head. Suddenly she seemed flustered beneath that dark beauty, a little girl trying hard to be a grown-up. Clum laughed with her, making her feel at ease. When he spotted Wyatt in the window, he waved, and in that same moment the girl turned her dark eyes on Wyatt and smiled. It was a passing thing of no importance, he knew, but the image burned into his mind, and he held it there, even as Clum approached and spoke through the doorway.

"Wyatt, can you and Virgil come by my office at the newspaper? First let me get my sorters started at the post office. Then I can meet with the two of you at the *Epitaph* in an hour."

Wyatt nodded to the mayor, and Clum stepped back out into the street, calling up to the stage driver for the mailbag. Behan and his woman angled across Allen Street toward the Grand Hotel, Behan talking continuously to the side of her face. Her walk was not confident but unflagging, a little scared and a little brave at once.

Wyatt wondered what could bring such a person from San Francisco to a man like Behan. Had it been any other woman, he might have dismissed her as a fool. But the way she carried herself, the way she moved . . . there was nothing about this woman he could deem foolish.

John Clum wiped at the ink on his hands with a hopelessly stained rag and led the Earp brothers into the back room of the *Epitaph* offices. After closing the door to the clanking rhythm of the press, he walked behind his desk. Leaning on his fists, he leveled fiery eyes on Virgil, then Wyatt. His flair for a dramatic moment never surprised Wyatt. It matched the tenor of the man's editorials.

"First, gentlemen, what is said here, stays here." Clum waited, prepared to hold the pose all day. His bald head reflected the light from the back window as if he had oiled his skin.

"That goes without saying, John," Virgil said.

Clum sat and threaded his fingers together on the desktop. "I'm not at all happy with our law enforcement officers—town or county. Our citizens are fed up with this ring of politicians getting rich off the land-lot situation. This ring has its hooks into Behan, and he'll back them." Clum paused to check for the Earp brothers' reaction, but there was none to see. "And the marshal . . ." he went on. "Well, Sippy just doesn't see eye to eye with the town council. He doesn't understand the town politics." Clum's eyes slanted with regret. "Frankly, he just doesn't make a good officer."

Virgil and Wyatt betrayed no expression. When neither brother made a reply, Clum swept a hand to the south.

"Cattle rustling and smuggling across the border is on the rise. It goes both ways, but the Cow-boys are getting the better of it, so they're getting bolder even here around Tombstone, waylaying traffic, taking whatever they want. If there's no money, they'll take their share of whatever is being transported. Some commerce on the county roads is shutting down. This is going to hurt us. The governor wants a militia formed down here, but the legislature is tight with money, saying there're already enough soldiers down here to handle the problem." Clum scowled. "But we've got this *posse commitatus* act. Washington won't let the army meddle in territorial affairs. And . . . they won't let them cross the border. Their official job is one thing only . . . Apaches."

Virgil cleared his throat. "We know all this, John."

"Well, here's what you don't know. We've formed a vigilance committee. We're keeping it tight." Clum looked from one Earp to the other and frowned. "What!" he said, intoning the word as if he'd been challenged.

"It ain't as tight as you think, John," Wyatt said.

Clum's brow furrowed as he looked to Virgil for verification.

"Sippy told me," Virgil said.

Clum fidgeted with the inkwell on the desk and squared it with the blotter. "Sippy is no more happy with us than we are with him. He's told me he's considering leaving Arizona. If he does, Virgil, I want you as police chief. Is that agreeable to you?"

Virgil slipped his hands into his trouser pockets and rocked once on his boots. "It is."

Clum looked at Wyatt. "When the next county election comes around, I want to see you sheriff of Cochise County. The newspaper will back you boys. How does that sit with you?"

"Sits good," Wyatt said.

Clum nodded, and, just as quickly, he frowned. "One thing, though." He glanced obliquely at Wyatt and then adjusted one of the apron straps on one shoulder. Sitting back with a worried look, he worked up a show of determination. Finally, he looked Wyatt in the eye. "There is a rumor that Doc Holliday was in on the Benson stage holdup. They're even saying he was the one who killed Bud Philpott."

Wyatt shook his head once. "That's Behan talking, John. That's the way he works. He knows I want his job, and he tries to get at me through Holliday. He's thinking about that next election, too."

"Well, what do we do about it?"

Nothing outwardly changed in Wyatt, but when he spoke there was a certainty in his voice that would brook no debate. "Doc Holliday is my friend. Like you said . . . it's a rumor."

"Well, yes," Clum sputtered, "but it can hurt us." He rubbed distractedly at an ink stain on his palm. Wyatt was quiet for so long, the mayor finally spread his hands and gave a reluctant shrug. "Well, I guess we can't do much about rumors," Clum admitted. "So we'll concentrate on what we *can* do." He lowered his gaze and shook his head. "But it would be good if no more rumors circulate. It doesn't do us any good if your friends are suspected of robbing the stage."

The mayor sat back and grasped the arms of his chair as though it might try to buck him off. When Wyatt still said nothing, Clum nodded as if everything was now clear. He stood and shook hands with each brother. The Earps quietly walked out of the office, through the pressroom, and crossed Fremont to start up Fourth Street.

They were past Spangenberg's Gun Shop before Virgil broke the silence. "Might be a good time to have a talk with Doc, Wyatt."

Wyatt made no reply. Turning onto Allen Street they walked with the same stride, dressed so much alike, they would have appeared near identical but for Wyatt's slightly leaner physique. When they reached the alley beside Vogan's, they stopped, and Virgil jerked a thumb toward the telegraph office.

"I got to get off a wire to Prescott . . . let Dake know I plan to wear two badges now. You got any ideas how we can reverse that rumor about Doc?"

"Might be a good time to offer that deal to Ike Clanton," Wyatt said.

Virgil pursed his lips and looked down the street at the steady traffic moving through the intersection at Hafford's. Gradually, he began to nod.

"Just might be."

*****

It was never hard to know when Ike Clanton was in the Oriental. His whining voice rose in complaint each time the cards worked against him in a poker game at the front of the room. McMaster had named that voice well: "a mule braying among a church choir." Wyatt kept a casual eye on Ike, watching his slovenly eating habits at the poker table. The tall, melancholic Ringo was with him. Wyatt bided his time. Ringo would not be right for the deal. It would have to be just Ike.

When Clanton finally strutted alone to the faro tables, he surveyed the games and chose one far from Wyatt's, where Lou Rickabaugh dealt. During one of the breaks in his game, Wyatt sent the bar-sweep to Rickabaugh's table to arrange a switch of dealers. At his next break, Wyatt sat down across from Ike, meeting Clanton's hostile glare with a straight face.

"Hope you gentleman don't mind a change-up." Wyatt looked at each man. Clanton was quiet for once, and no one else voiced an objection. "Place your bets for the winning card, gentlemen."

Wyatt groomed the professional courtesy that his work required, showing Clanton that business was business . . . that at the gaming tables, at least, he held no grudge about the stolen horse. Ike won enough times to keep him in the game, and at each of these occasions Wyatt nodded his congratulations. Before an hour was up, Wyatt called for a break, leaned to the floor, and came up with a ten-dollar chip.

"Must be yours, Ike," Wyatt said and slid the chip across the layout.

Clanton's eyes darted to Wyatt's unreadable face. "Yeah, probably is." He picked up the chip and looked around his chair as though there might be more scattered there. The other players left the table for refreshments.

"You do pretty well at this game, Ike."

Clanton smirked. "I'm game for most any kind o' gambling. I like keno better."

"Wherever the money is," Wyatt agreed.

"Hell, yeah. I'll take the swag however it comes." Clanton smiled, and both men knew he was talking about Mexican cattle and army livestock. Wyatt sorted the chips before him.

"I remember you now," Ike said, raising his goateed chin at Wyatt. "You pulled a switch on me with a gimpy horse. You were running freight for Taylor out o' San Berdoo." Ike smirked, as though by merely remembering the incident, he had somehow evened the score.

"I'd say you came out pretty good on that deal," Wyatt said.

"Yeah, how's that?"

Wyatt let his hands go idle, and he looked directly into Ike's dark, beady eyes. "That horse you traded me didn't cost you anything. It was stolen."

"Yeah?" Ike shot back. "But the nag you traded me went lame."

Wyatt allowed one corner of his mouth to lift. "It was already lame. But I'm bettin' you made some money off it."

Ike could not mask his gloating smile. "Hell, yeah, I did. I'm a businessman. I'll tackle most anything if there's some money in it."

Wyatt nodded, as if approving such a philosophy. "You might be interested in a deal I'm working on, Ike," he said casually.

Clanton's eyes tightened, even as his vanity opened wide to possibility. "What deal is that?"

Wyatt loaded the cards into the box. "Thirty-six hundred dollars worth."

Clanton laughed and spewed air from his lips, but when Wyatt's face remained stoic and focused, Ike leaned forward and stacked his forearms on the table, allowing his curiosity to prod him. "Thirty-six hundred? For what?"

"Wells, Fargo is offering a reward for the men who tried to rob the Benson stage. Same ones who killed Bud Philpott and a passenger. Leonard, Head, and Crane. Twelve hundred each. I'm offering it all to you."

Clanton looked to either side and leaned closer, baring his teeth in a forced smile. "The hell you say." But his eyes had already glazed over with a private calculation.

"I'm offering a business deal," Wyatt said. "I need information. In return, you keep all the money."

"What information?"

"I want to find those men. You tell me where and when. That's all."

Clanton tried for disdain. "Why the hell would I do that . . . even if I could?"

Wyatt was as dead-faced as a poker player about to triple the pot. "Like I said, thirty-six hundred dollars."

"Shi-it!" Clanton huffed and rotated his beer glass with his thumb and forefinger. He looked around the room again and finally settled a challenging glare on Wyatt. "Why would you do that?"

Wyatt gritted his teeth to get out the words he had already chosen for the moment he was asked this question. "For the glory."

Clanton squinted as though he had been spoken to in an arcane language.

"I've got business ambitions with the county, Ike," Wyatt explained. "Bringing in those men might help me."

Letting his head tilt back, Clanton looked down his nose at Wyatt, then smiled until his wax-tipped moustaches rose. "Ohhh," he purred, drawing the sound out with a coarse laugh. "You mean 'cause those boys made you look like the horse's ass when you chased 'em all over the territory." Ike snorted. "What makes you think I'd give 'em up like that?"

Not in the habit of repeating himself, Wyatt breathed out a silent sigh and made on-the-spot adjustments for dealing with Ike Clanton. "Again," he said as plainly as he could, "the money." His voice was full of reason. He stacked his chips in the order of their value. Then he looked up into Clanton's eyes to toss in the prime bait for the transaction. "And that ranch of Billy Leonard's."

Ike's smile dried up. He licked his lips and began fidgeting with the ten-dollar chip Wyatt had supplied him from the floor.

"I'm gonna get these boys one way or the other," Wyatt said simply and pushed back from the table. "Just thought you might like to make some money in the deal." He stood, picked up his tray, and started to walk away. Ike touched Wyatt's sleeve, stopping him.

"Well, what if I want to talk to you some more 'bout this?" Ike said in a rough whisper.

"Can always talk. But I got other irons in the fire."

Wyatt carried his tray from the back room into the saloon, feeling a gritty vibration running through his fingers, as though he had just had hold of a rattlesnake. Setting down the tray he saw Ike in the mirror's reflection, his head down, turning his glass in circles again.

*****

They met the next night in the alley behind the Oriental—Wyatt, Ike Clanton, a nervous Frank McLaury, and a sullen man squinting through the lazy drift of smoke from his cigarette. With three Cow-boys present, Wyatt considered how this proposition might have already jumped track. He stopped six feet away and peered into each man's face, his focus settling last on Ike.

"For a man who might need to keep his business dealings private, I'd say you're off to a poor start."

"I ain't gonna do business with you without some witnesses," Clanton snapped. "Besides, Joe here is the one who will be able to locate them boys if anybody can."

"Joe?" Wyatt said.

"Joe Hill," Clanton replied and jerked his head toward the Cow-boy slouching against the rear wall of the building.

Hill slowly removed the cigarette from his lips, his stare an open challenge. McLaury shifted his weight from one leg to the other and glared at Wyatt.

"They're gonna need to hear all this from you," Ike insisted. "So start from the beginning."

In the dark of the alley with the muted sounds of gamblers' voices and the clink of glassware reaching them from the gaming room, Wyatt explained the deal in the same terms that he had offered to Clanton. Ike's eyes focused on one Cow-boy to the other and back, waiting for their expressions to manifest some sign of credulity, some appetite for the reward . . . like his own. McLaury held on to his God-given scowl, but Wyatt could see the idea of easy money begin to lure Frank in. When the proposition had been laid out in full, Joe Hill spewed smoke and shook his head.

"Them boys won't go easy. Not without killin' 'em, maybe."

"Or them killing you," McLaury added with a malicious grin.

Clanton stepped forward. "Yeah, what about that? Is the reward for dead *or* alive?"

"Wells, Fargo wants those men off the books. I don't reckon it matters how it goes."

McLaury hissed through his teeth. "What you 'reckon' don't mean shit to us. You're asking a hellava lot of us, sticking our necks out like this."

"Who else is in on this?" Hill asked. "On your end, I mean."

"Just my brother Virgil. No one else."

Hill frowned. "He's the marshal now, ain't he?"

Wyatt nodded. For a time no one spoke. The three men stared at Wyatt as though waiting to see if the combined force of their innate distrust might crack his composed demeanor. A congratulatory roar of voices swelled inside the building, announcing a winning hand for someone.

"All right," Frank said. "Find out about the reward for dead men, and we'll meet again. Bring your brother so we can see this thing is on the square. Meet us at noon tomorrow behind the Eagle Brewery."

"Noon," Wyatt said and walked back inside the Oriental.

*****

The day following, just before noon, Wyatt met Virgil in front of Spangenberg's on Fourth Street. For a moment the two brothers simply looked at one another, and then, without speaking, they turned down the alley and worked their way through the back lots to the last building in the block.

When the Earps appeared from the alley, McLaury and Hill looked up from their conversation. Ike sat on a wooden crate with his head in one hand. The two standing Cow-boys stepped apart a few feet, and the sound of their boots in the dust brought up Ike's head. The three men stared at Virgil, their eyes gravitating to the new chief of police badge pinned to his vest. Ike slowly stood, looked uncertainly at Wyatt, then at Virgil.

"How'd you get to be the new marshal?" Ike said. "What happened to Sippy?"

"Left town on extended leave," Virgil said. "We don't expect him back."

Frank huffed a laugh and shook his head. "You Earps like bein' in charge, don't you?"

Virgil opened the front of his coat and splayed his hands on the sides of his cartridge belt, his elbows cocked outward as a sign that there was only so much guff he would take off McLaury. He turned his impatient glare on Wyatt.

"I heard from Wells, Fargo," Wyatt said, opening the negotiations. "The reward is for dead or alive. That's official."

Ike could not keep the excitement from his face, but Frank's mouth crimped into a knot. "We're gonna need something better'n your word on that," McLaury said.

"I just got the telegram." Wyatt's voice had a calming effect on Ike and Hill, but it was clear from the look on Frank's face that he needed more.

"Then we'll see that telegram," McLaury said testily. Holding the contempt on his face, he turned to Virgil. "You backing this with your word, too?"

"I am," Virgil said, his voice filling the alley.

Wyatt hitched his head toward Allen Street. "I'll need to walk to the Wells, Fargo office."

McLaury turned on his heel. "We'll be at the Alhambra. Bring it there."

Virgil and Wyatt walked out to Fifth Street, Virgil crossing to the Oriental and Wyatt walking toward the corner, making for Marsh Williams's office.

Virgil stopped halfway across the street and turned to Wyatt. "You still think this is a good idea?"

Wyatt halted at the question and looked at his brother. He said nothing.

"Like parleying with a trio of vultures over a carcass," Virgil said and continued across the street. "I just hope we don't regret this," he murmured, as much to himself as to his brother.

Wyatt turned the corner, carrying the image of Frank McLaury's surly face in his mind. Sometimes, he knew, it took a certain boldness to get to a place that was not easy to get to. In the end, if everything went well on this deal, the reward would be worth the trouble. It was up to Wyatt to see that it ran smoothly.

Marsh Williams was curious about Wyatt's tight-lipped request for the telegram, but he detached it from his files without a question. "I'll need that copy back," Williams said. "We got to keep all the official communications. Company rule."

Five minutes later, after showing the telegram to Frank McLaury under the awning outside the Alhambra, Wyatt folded the paper and watched through the saloon window as McLaury returned to his friends and engaged in private conversation. Looking east down the boardwalk he saw Williams standing in front of his office staring at him, his arms folded across his chest. Turning, the agent walked back inside and closed the door.

Wyatt slipped the paper into his coat pocket and walked west. He was in no mood to answer any questions Williams might have.

*****

Within the week Ike Clanton appeared in the back room of the Oriental. Well past midnight, the tables were filled with gamblers. Clanton paced around the room, keeping his distance, and then he settled at the bar and ordered a drink. Finally, he signaled Wyatt, nodding toward the rear of the building with a nervous tic around his eyes. Ike threw back what was left of his drink, slapped the glass on the bar, and marched out through the front door.

At his break, Wyatt found Ike pacing in the alleyway where they had first talked. As soon as Ike saw him, he hurried forward, his face creased with worry.

"Leonard and Head are dead," Ike said in a rush. "The Heslet brothers kilt 'em over in New Mexico."

Wyatt hid his disappointment and nodded. "There'll still be a reward on Crane."

Ike shook his head. "Listen, Earp. This whole thing is feeling like a bad idea. Some of our boys shot the Heslets all to pieces." Ike's face hardened, and his eyes burned bright with fear. "That's what could happen to me! Let's just forget about this! To hell with Crane! And to hell with the reward money! I'd rather save my own skin!" Ike poked a finger at Wyatt. "You tell your brother, too. I don't want no part o' this deal!"

Wyatt removed his cigar from his mouth. His face went cold as stone. Though Wyatt made no other movement, Ike took a step backward in the narrow alley.

"I'll be waiting to hear from you about Crane," Wyatt said, his quiet voice as hard as his expression. Clanton started to protest, but Wyatt quickly held up his palm, the cigar sketching a red arc in the air. "I don't want to hear anything about you backing out, Ike. Either you deliver Crane up, or be ready to have this thing blow up in your face."

Ike paled. "What do you mean? This can blow up for you just as bad."

Wyatt almost smiled. "What makes you think I give a damn if your crowd knows I want Crane? Me going after him is one thing. You giving him up is another. You're gonna hold up your end of this bargain, Ike."

As Wyatt held unforgiving eyes on Clanton, the Cow-boy found no words to argue. He managed to swallow, and the sound of it crackled in his throat. Wyatt spun on his heel and walked out of the alley back toward the front of the building.

CHAPTER 12

Summer 1881

Tombstone, A.T.

On a hot day in June, in front of the Arcade saloon, the bartender rolled out a barrel of whiskey as he argued with the delivery man who had just freighted in the shipment by wagon. After dipping a measuring stick into the bunghole, the saloonkeeper gritted his teeth around his cigar and squinted in the bright sun to read the calibration.

"We ain't buyin' no more air from them damn chiselers. Either these barrels arrive full or—"

As he railed against his wholesalers, a red brick of ash broke from the tip of his cigar and disappeared into the bunghole like a bright orange bee homing in on its hive. The men scrambled away as the explosion flared like the surprise of a photographer's flash.

A bright flame leaped to the boardwalk awning, and burning pieces of barrel staves tumbled through the air, crashing into the windows of nearby shops. Within minutes a section of the dry tinderbox of Tombstone was burning out of control, the angry flames moving with alarming speed from the Oriental east to Seventh Street, from Fremont south to Toughnut.

Despite the efforts of firefighters and volunteer citizens, the conflagration raged with what seemed an insatiable hunger to consume the sun-bleached buildings. The blistering waves made the heat of the surrounding desert seem a refuge. In only an hour four city blocks had been reduced to a charred hole of blackened building frames and the scorched relics of furniture and goods that had filled the stores.

After the initial, frantic scramble to save lives, douse flames, and tear down walls that could spread the flames to other blocks, the spectacle of ruin became an altar to which citizens came to grieve over their own losses or those of their friends. Already there was talk of rebuilding. Even before the flames subsided, a vision of a bigger and better Tombstone was taking root.

But the disaster opened the scene for other opportunities, both nefarious and calculated. That night hired muscle from the corrupt county ring surfaced to stake claims on contested properties. They were like nocturnal snakes come out of their holes to slither through the darkness. Each mercenary employed speed and intimidation to back off his quarry.

To counter this, Virgil deputized Wyatt, Morgan, Fred Dodge, and John Vermillion, their former carpenter. Throughout that night the lawmen patrolled the streets, tearing down the tents of lot-jumpers wherever they appeared. Against these four, every contest was a brief one.

The larger timbers of the storied buildings glowed well into the night, as unnamed items from various businesses plumed steam or spewed black, acrid smoke that fanned into the night as if it were the source of the darkness itself. There was an unaccountable beauty to this aftermath of calamity, and the citizens gathered in the dark to witness it like an impromptu though somber social event.

On one of his vigils riding the perimeter of the embers, Wyatt recognized Behan's woman standing outside the Russ House. She leaned to a young boy and pointed at something, and their heads stayed together in conversation. As Wyatt approached on his horse at a walk, she looked up, saw him, and slowly straightened.

"Marshal?" she said.

Wyatt reined up and turned in his saddle. "No, ma'am. You're thinking of my brother."

"You're Wyatt, aren't you?"

He dismounted and took off his hat, which was more than half ruined by the day's work. "That's right," he replied. His shirt was torn and soot-smudged and his body covered with sweat and grime from the endless hacking at timbers with an axe or sledgehammer. Though he felt ill at ease standing before her beauty in such disarray, there was an accompanying sensation of baring his soul. His was a smoke-stained portrait capturing him in the act of living. Nothing to show but himself. Somehow he knew she saw through the charred exterior right into the center of him.

He turned to stand beside her, and together, like a man and woman come to hear a selection of musical pieces at a concert, they witnessed the glow of orange coals that breathed in the night air. The smoke lifted at an angle, riding the slight breeze like an incantation on the folly of men's plans. The crowd kept up a continuous overlay of muted conversations, all deferential to the sobering memory of the fire's earlier domination, when it had raged uncontrolled. The assembly of the townspeople was like a final ritual meant to mark this day in Tombstone's history.

Wyatt turned, wanting to see her face this close, and when he did, he knew he preferred the whites of her eyes to the glowing embers across the street. Her eyes shone like pale moons against the dark of her skin. She bent to the boy, and Wyatt was surprised at the strength in her voice so close to his ear.

"Albert, this is the man who carried the woman out of the burning building." The boy looked up, squinting with his front teeth pinched down on his lower lip. She straightened, smiled at Wyatt, and tapped her own ear, conveying a message. "He's hard of hearing," she whispered. The communication was like a secret, settling them onto a common ground that strengthened their connection, and at the same time it set them farther apart from the others gathered there.

Wyatt looked at the ruins of the brothel—the place where he had broken through a wall and carried out the unconscious whore. When he saw the boy still studying him, Wyatt bent from the waist and spoke close to his ear.

"She'll be all right. Just breathed in a little too much smoke." Straightening, he returned his eyes to Behan's woman. "This your son?"

"Albert is Sheriff Behan's son."

Wyatt studied the boy again, looking for a resemblance. All the while he felt the woman's attention on him.

"My name is Sadie Marcus," she said.

Wyatt looked at his hat in his hands, and then at her. "I've seen you around town."

"Yes, I know. And I've seen you."

He didn't know what to say to that, but he was comfortable in the silence that followed. It isolated them even more from everything else. He liked standing with this woman, Sadie Marcus. He thought of Mattie in their bedroom sucking her life from a brown bottle and quickly fed this image to the lingering flames across the street.

"Were there many people hurt today?" she asked him.

Wyatt shook his head. "I reckon we were lucky on that count. There was some, but—"

He could not interpret her smile as one wholly reacting to this news. The smile gathered him into its domain in some way that he could not define. Across the block Wyatt heard Virgil's booming voice, ordering someone off a piece of charred property.

Sadie's smile all but dissolved. "Looks like it will be a long night."

He nodded and was surprised at the words he composed on the spot. "Some parts of the night might not be so bad."

Her wan smile did not alter, but her lambent eyes absorbed a part of the smile, until her face filled with a gracious warmth. Hers was an uncommon beauty, but she wore it with an effortless grace. Something else lay beneath her looks—something daring and determined—like the soul of a traveler who was willing to go wherever the next journey beckoned.

"How'd you know who I was?" Wyatt said.

"Johnny pointed you out." It was a clean, honest statement, like a drink of cool water.

He almost laughed. "I reckon there was a little more to it than that. Johnny and I don't exactly—"

"I asked him who you were," she interrupted.

John Vermillion rode up on his big dapple gray, his long, dark locks of hair fanned out behind him and bouncing with the horse's stride. Standing in his stirrups he searched the faces in the crowd.

"Wyatt!" he called out. "Better git over to the backside of the block. We got more lot-jumpers to drag out." Vermillion spun his horse around and galloped off around the corner, his fast exit spurring the crowd to more lively conversation.

Wyatt pushed his battered hat onto his head and tipped the brim to Sadie and the boy. As he walked away, he felt something tugging at him—a part of himself trying to stay with this woman. It was an unexpected connection, one he would have to think about. But one thing he knew: He would see this woman again, if only to hear her speak in the timbre of honesty that made him feel so comfortable around her, Behan's fiancée or not.

*****

He let two days go by. There were half a dozen reasons not to go to the Grand Hotel—where Sadie Marcus lived—Mattie being at the head of that list. He only needed one reason to enter. Coffee would do. The Oriental had burned to the ground. He had to get his coffee somewhere.

After entering the lobby he nodded to the clerk behind the desk and crossed to a sofa in the front corner and sat. Several newspapers were strewn across a low table before him. Picking up a copy of the *Nugget*, he opened the paper but did not read. Casually, he peered over the paper and scanned the upstairs landing where a few numbered doors could be seen. After several minutes of seeing no one, he turned his attention to the window that looked out on Allen Street.

Workers were laying out a new foundation amid the rubble where the Oriental had stood. Vermillion was there stringing a chalk line. Wyatt watched the workers begin the resurrection of the building and considered the effects of the fire tripling business at the saloons that had survived the fire. Folding the paper he stood, dropped the paper on the table, and approached the desk.

"Miss Marcus in?" he asked in a low murmur.

The clerk looked up open-mouthed, squinted at Wyatt, and then turned to the wall to check the panel of keys hanging on rows of hooks. "I'm not certain, Mr. Earp. Her key is gone, but sometimes she doesn't turn it in when she comes in. Have you checked the bar?"

"Not yet," Wyatt said.

The hotel bar was a semi-dark palace of gleaming bottles and glasses located in the basement below the lobby. Crowded with miners just off the late shift, the room was noisy, making it difficult to hear the musicians who played at the far end. Most tables were filled, and, at one of these, Joe Hill drank with four other men. One was the gloomy-eyed Ringo, slouching in a chair like a corpse that had been propped up for appearances. Frank Stilwell, recently acquitted on a murder charge and now Behan's deputy, hunched forward with his elbows on the table, a shot glass held by fingertips hanging below his limp wrists. A surly smile stretched across his face as he held court to attentive ears. Next to Stilwell was Pete Spence, thin with a sly ferret face, who lived with a Mexican woman across from Wyatt's house. The fifth man was McMaster.

Wyatt approached the closer end of the bar where it made an L-shape with the longer counter. When the bartender saw him, he strode the length of the bar with a pleasant smile.

"What can I get you, Mr. Earp?"

"Coffee." Wyatt pushed a coin across the bar. "Miss Marcus been down?"

The bartender reached below the counter and set down a mug. "Usually comes down about noon." He waited with his fingertips on the edge of the bar and a question on his face, but when Wyatt said no more, he walked to the far end of the bar and exited through a door. In seconds he was back carrying a kettle by its loop handle padded by a cloth. As he poured, a deep guttural laughter erupted in the room.

Using the mirror Wyatt checked the men at McMaster's table, where most of the men were howling their delight. Only Ringo was not smiling. Wyatt carried his coffee to an empty table at the front corner of the room. He sat, set his new hat in the neighboring chair, and sipped his coffee. As he set the mug down, a woman with painted lips and rings of jangling bracelets appeared next to him and leaned on his table.

"Which Earp are you, honey? You're Wyatt, aren't you?"

Wyatt nodded and studied her face, but he came up with nothing. He started to stand, but she pushed him back into his seat.

"Don't get up, sugar." Something changed in her eyes, and an impudent smile pushed her mouth to one side. "You don't remember. You carried me out of the fire."

Wyatt let his eyes rove freely over her, inventorying her by portions. "I reckon so."

She leaned and kissed him on the cheek. "I'm Nina," she whispered into his ear. She stepped back, her face showing more mischief than gratitude. "I believe I am in your debt, Mr. Earp."

Wyatt looked her in the eye. "Do you know Sadie Marcus?"

Her playful eyes seemed to look through him. "Sure. We worked together over in Tip Top."

Wyatt frowned. "She came in from San Francisco."

Nina's eyes slid away, and the smile on her painted mouth turned sly. "Well, yeah . . . she came from there, all right." She turned to Wyatt and bobbed her eyebrows. "Then she was at Tip Top. Now she's here."

"She livin' here permanent at the Grand?"

Nina tilted her head as if looking at Wyatt from a different angle might explain something more about him. "She's with Johnny Behan mostly, I guess."

Wyatt nodded. "She really his fiancée?"

The girl sat and crossed her forearms on the table. "So she says." Her head sagged between her shoulders and bounced once with a quiet laugh. When she looked up, smiling, her eyebrows rose again and remained in a double arch.

"You know something she don't?" Wyatt asked.

She shrugged. "I know Johnny," she said dryly.

A disheveled woman stumbled through the stairway entrance, stopped, and eyed the crowd. It took Wyatt a moment to recognize Kate Elder, Doc Holliday's consort. When she began to reel, Wyatt excused himself and walked to her, taking her arm to offer support. Her head came around quickly, and her eyes flashed with a fury that suggested he ought to grab both her arms.

"Let me go, godt-damnt you!" Whiskey slurred her words and thickened her Hungarian accent. She scanned the room with angry jerks of her head. "Where is dat damnt whore?"

Wyatt pulled her as gently as he could back toward the stairs. "Let's go outside, Kate. You don't want—"

"Don't you tell me vhat I vant!"

Her face had turned vicious, and she tried to slap him. In one motion he caught her wrist and swept her into the stairwell. After dragging her up the steps and out the lobby door, he swung around the side of the building. In the alleyway he pressed her back against the side of the building.

"Maybe we should go and find Doc," Wyatt suggested.

She exhaled a whiskey-soaked screech. "*You* findt him! He loff to see *you!*" Her voice was shrill, like a rough stone scratched against glass. She tried to jerk free, but when she couldn't, her eyes clamped shut and tears squeezed out, running in silver streaks down her cheeks. "You vant to beat me, too?"

"I don't want to beat on anybody, Kate. But I can't have you beatin' on me. Where is Doc?"

She turned her face away. "How do I know! Maybe vit dat whore."

"Kate, you've been with other men. You know how it works."

Her eyes lost some of their fire. "Not since I say I von't! I am goodt to him." She shook her head violently, as if to cast off her self-pity. "Who else stay vit a man like dat?" Then her scorn gathered in her eyes, and she coughed out an airy laugh. "He treat *you* better dan *me!*" She tried to shake him off again. "Let me go, godt-damnt you!"

"Kate, you can't be making trouble. I don't wanna have to take you down to the jail."

She let her head fall back against the building. "I make no more promise to any man." When he relaxed his grip, she went limp and almost collapsed. "I make him sorry," she said, her voice now just a whisper. Pulling herself upright, she walked past Wyatt and into the street, where she quickened her pace and was soon gone from view.

*****

At noon the next day, Wyatt rolled out of bed to answer the pounding on his front door. Pulling on his trousers, he studied Mattie, who lay still as a corpse, purring rhythmically with a soft, medicated snore. An empty, brown glass bottle lay on its side on the bed table. He hooked the suspenders over his bare shoulders, picked up his revolver from the dresser, and headed for the front room in his stockinged feet. He opened the door to find Virgil waiting.

Wearing a grim face, Virgil stepped into the parlor without a word, anchoring himself to the center of the room with his boots spread. He looked down at the gun in Wyatt's hand and then out the front window. Finally, he met Wyatt's face eye to eye.

"Behan locked up Doc," Virgil announced in his no-nonsense voice. "For the Benson stage holdup. And for killin' Bud Philpott. Says Doc is the one who planned the whole damned thing."

Wyatt pushed the loose strands of hair from his forehead, moved to the front window, and stared out at the edge of town. "This is Kate Elder's doin', ain't it?"

Virgil was quiet until Wyatt turned to him. "Got no idea," Virge said. "Just got the news myself."

"Let me get dressed," Wyatt said and crossed the room, the quietness of his step seeming inadequate to match the anger he felt building inside his chest.

Together Wyatt and Virgil marched to Behan's office, reaching the front entrance just as Billy Breakenridge tried to leave. The deputy's face went slack, and he backed up into the room, causing Behan to look up from his desk and slowly straighten in his chair.

"What the hell is this about Doc and the Benson stage, Johnny?" Wyatt said.

The sheriff feigned a look of regret as he opened a drawer. "Pretty simple really, Wyatt. Attempted armed robbery and murder." He dropped a paper on his desk, his eyes simmering with pleasure. "That's a signed affidavit. Says Holliday admitted to the attack on Bob Paul that night."

Virgil picked up the document and read. "Signed by Kate Elder? Are you serious?"

"Of course, I'm serious," Behan said. "Read it. It couldn't be clearer."

Wyatt leaned on the desk, keeping his voice low. "You get her drunk, Johnny?"

"She knew well enough what she was signing. I have witnesses."

Virgil skipped to the bottom of the page and read aloud, "'J. P. Ringo' . . . 'W. Breakenridge.'" He tossed the paper to the desk and huffed out a sarcastic laugh. "That the best you could do, Johnny?"

"What of it?" Behan shot back. "Anybody can be a witness!" He looked away from Virgil, but found himself equally unable to hold Wyatt's stare. The sheriff straightened the paper on his desk, aligning it with the blotter. "You use whoever is convenient at the moment," he explained, his tenor voice sounding as if his shirt collar were too tight.

Wyatt turned to Breakenridge. "How 'bout it, Billy? Any money or whiskey involved in this confab?"

The deputy glanced at the sheriff and then back at Wyatt. Stuffing both hands into his trouser pockets, he frowned, shifted from leg to leg, and managed a shrug.

Behan made a show of shuffling papers. "It's a legal affidavit, Wyatt."

Wyatt's jaw knotted as he straightened from the desk. "I want to talk to Holliday."

Without looking up, Behan shook his head. "You can see him at the arraignment."

Wyatt glared at Behan, but the sheriff continued to sort items on his desk. "Then I think I'll go have me a talk with Kate Elder."

"Fine," Behan said pleasantly. "I've had *my* talk with her."

*****

They found Kate drunk in the Grand Hotel barroom. Virgil took her to the city office and force-fed her coffee while she kept up a steady spate of slurred profanity. Finally he put her in a cell with a piss bucket in one corner and tin of fresh water beside the bunk.

When Wyatt checked on her in two hours, she was still splayed out on the bunk but coherent. He entered the cell and stood beside the small bed, looking down at the side of her pouting face as she stared at the wall.

"Kate?" Wyatt said quietly. "Do you want Doc dead?"

"He deserff to be deadt," she said and tightened her forehead into a web of wrinkles.

He waited the better part of a minute, knowing she could probably stare at that wall for hours. "I ain't talking about punishing him for what he's done to you, Kate. We all make mistakes on that count. I'm asking: Are you prepared to see him hanged?"

She sniffed and swiped a palm across her cheek. "He treat me badt. He *shouldt* hang!" she said, but the fire had gone out of her complaint.

Gently taking her shoulder, Wyatt rolled her to face him. "Kate, Doc prob'ly ain't got much time left anyway. As I see it, every day he can get is worth somethin'. Especially when you know he had nothin' to do with that stage holdup."

Fresh tears sprang from her eyes, and she covered her face with her hands. "Why can't he be goodt to me? Vhy duss he alvays hit me?"

"I don't know, Kate. I reckon he got a raw deal from life, but not much place to show it."

Virgil appeared in the cellblock and stood with his forearms resting through the crossbars of the cell. When Wyatt looked at him, Virgil laced his fingers together and looked down at his boots.

"Kate," Wyatt continued, "Behan is using Doc to get to me. He wants to keep me from making sheriff when the next elections come around."

Kate blew a short laugh through her nose. "You men. You and your damnt offices. You make all da rules."

"Behan's the one making the rules," Virgil said, his harsh voice unmindful of her misery. "He'll hang Doc if you let him."

She uncovered her eyes and stared at the wall again.

"You played right into it," Virge said. "If Doc swings, it'll be your doin'. You'll have to live with that."

Her face screwed up like she might cry. "Ringo and Behan," she mumbled. "Dey treat me goodt."

"Did they talk you into signing something?" Wyatt pressed. "And maybe you didn't know what it was?"

"They keep pouring, and I drink too much," she admitted, her voice wavering like that of a child making a confession. She turned to look at Wyatt. "I don't remember signing anyt'ingk."

Wyatt nodded. "All you got to do is say that to a judge. Can you do that?"

Gradually she began to nod; then she settled into silent weeping. Wyatt looked at his brother. Virgil nodded once and walked back into his office. Wyatt reached to Kate's shoulder to give her a reassuring squeeze but thought better of it. He watched her sob into the dirty mattress for a time, and then he left.

CHAPTER 13

End of Summer 1881

Tombstone and Bisbee, A.T.

The nights were cooler. After a five-hour stint of poker at Hafford's, Wyatt and Doc Holliday walked toward their respective homes. When Doc went his way at Fly's boardinghouse, Wyatt continued out Fremont Street, slowing just after passing Second Avenue. A solitary horseman appeared from the shadows of the big cottonwood in the vacant lot next to Virgil's house. The rider came out at a walk, his relaxed body bending easily with the rhythm of the horse's gait. Wyatt had come to know the silhouette well. When the man circled his horse back into the shadows, Wyatt followed.

After an exchange of terse greetings, McMaster sat his horse and stared off into the dark. Wyatt gave him time. Finally, the horseman looked over both shoulders, leaned, and spat.

"Mexican regulars kilt Old Man Clanton and a dozen others in Guadalupe Canyon."

Taking in this information, Wyatt began to calculate how this news might affect his aspirations for the sheriff's office. "What about Brocius?" he asked.

McMaster shook his head. "That man leads a goddamn charmed life." He removed his hat and scratched vigorously at the crown of his scalp. After pushing his hat back on his head, he leaned on his pommel and arched his back.

"You make the ride from Tucson to tell me that?" Wyatt asked.

McMaster shook his head and spat again. "Coupl'a stage robberies bein' planned." He faced Wyatt. "I don' know how I can keep avoidin' bein' part of it. You wanna give me any advice on this?"

Wyatt reached inside his coat for an envelope. "I been carrying this for days." McMaster took the envelope. "You're gonna have to let me know which stage, Mac. I can't be paying somebody to rob Wells, Fargo."

McMaster chewed on that for a while. "What if I can't get word to you in time?"

Wyatt looked off toward the mountains, knowing full well that one of the deterrents to enforcing the law in southeastern Arizona was the vastness of the territory. "Then I reckon you can't."

McMaster let some anger show in his face. "Look, it ain't easy walkin' both sides of the line. Maybe you ought'a get somebody else to do this for you."

Wyatt kept his expression neutral. "Already got one," he said. "But I need both of you."

McMaster's brow tightened. "You got another informant with the Cow-boys? Who?"

Wyatt shook his head, and McMaster glared at him.

"He know about me?" McMaster demanded.

Wyatt shook his head again.

"Well, shit-fire, Wyatt!" the horseman said and spat off to the side again. Still angry, he looked behind Wyatt's house over the broad expanse of desert that stretched all the way to the Dragoons. Raking his upper teeth across his lower lip, he gradually cooled, seeming to accept his situation. The horse snorted and jangled its bit.

"One more thing," McMaster said, shaking his head and avoiding Wyatt's eyes. "You won't like it." He shifted in his saddle, stretching the leather in a crackling groan. "Jim Crane was at Guadalupe." Mac's cautious gaze turned to Wyatt. "He's one o' the ones got kilt."

The horse stamped a front hoof, tossed its head, and nickered. McMaster stroked his mount's neck and spoke to it in a low murmur.

"Wyatt, these killin's at Guadalupe . . . that'll likely shut down raids across the border for a while. If these boys can't git what they want out o' Mexico, they'll git it right here." Mac lowered his voice as though talking to himself. "That's all there is to it."

Wyatt nodded. "Just let me know what you can, Mac."

McMaster picked up his reins but hesitated. "You gonna tell me who else you got workin' undercover?"

Wyatt looked up into his informant's face. "Best if neither of you know."

McMaster stared off into the dark for a time, his mouth tightened into a humorless grin, as though he were the brunt of some joke. Finally, he adjusted his hat, shook his head, and nudged his horse from the shadows onto the road to Tucson. The horse eased into a lope and melded with the darkness, its hooves clopping softly in the dust until the sound dropped into the wide arroyo past Boot Hill and disappeared.

Wyatt listened for the horse to rise on the other side of the swale, but only the desert wind could be heard. He thought about the prize at the end of McMaster's two-day journey, wondering how much Mac told his woman about their conversations. Probably everything. Valenzuela Cos was not the kind of woman you held back on.

He looked toward town. Sadie Marcus would be that kind of woman, he wagered. He imagined himself talking to her in a room at night, a lamp turned low and the quiet wrapped around them like a buffalo robe. She would listen. She would probably have something to say about each thing that mattered to him. He walked toward his house, feeling the numbness begin to sink into him as it did every night when he lay next to Mattie's inert body curled in the bed. He might as well keep walking out to Boot Hill and sleep with all the strangers buried there. It made about as much sense.

*****

A week into September, late in the evening, the Western Union clerk found Wyatt at Hafford's saloon. Wyatt unfolded the telegram and read McMaster's pseudonym at the bottom of the page. He began standing as he read the message: *Bisbee stage tonight.*

Within a half hour, Wyatt and Morgan were riding hard by moonlight for the Mule Mountains, but they arrived too late at the holdup site. An open Wells, Fargo strongbox lay in the road, and empty purses and satchels were strewn among the brush beside the road. Even as the Earp brothers examined the tracks, Fred Dodge, Marsh Williams, and Behan's deputies, Neagle and Breakenridge, rode up on the scene.

"Looks like two men came out o' the south from Hereford," Wyatt said. "We found the same tracks leaving the road about a hundred yards that way." He pointed down the road toward Bisbee. "If it's the men we want, they're cutting across country to get there ahead of the stage."

The combined posse followed the trail to a broken-down windmill, where the tracks were lost in the wide trampled swath of a cattle crossing. The lawmen divided into two natural factions: Behan's deputies in one, the Earps, Williams, and Dodge in the other.

Half a mile out, Dodge cut the trail of two horses and right away spotted a dark, smooth, crescent shape contrasting sharply against the rough texture of rock and sand. Wyatt dismounted and picked it up—a worn boot heel, the points of its tacks shining brightly in the dawn light. He pressed it into the sand, studied its impression, and looked up at his companions.

"Like that print we saw all around the holdup area," Wyatt said.

"Look here," Dodge said, dismounting and pointing to a scrape on a flat platter of shale. "His horse slipped. Sonovabitch probably stiffened and pushed the heel off his boot with the stirrup."

They followed the tracks to Bisbee, which appeared of a sudden, nestled as it was in the narrow canyon beneath the ridge trail. The work day had begun, with mining machinery hammering out a jarring, redundant dirge that echoed through the town. In all directions the land was scarred and rough with scree and tailings from the gutted terrain—even intruding so close to private homes as to be a liability. All through the canyon, the slopes were studded with flat-topped stumps, like grave markers for the trees that had been sawn to feed the boiler furnaces for the stamp mills. Just as in Tombstone, mining took precedence over everything. Here, instead of silver, it was copper.

As they rode into town, Wyatt doled out instructions. "Morg, check the stage office. See if you can get a description of the holdup men from the driver and passengers. Fred, check the saloons. Marsh, watch the main road. If any of you see a man missing a boot heel, throw down on him and hold tight. It'll be a federal arrest, so don't let Breakenridge and Neagle take him. I'm going to the boot maker."

"We got federal authority on this?" Morgan asked. "Without Virge?"

"There was mail on the stage, so we'll make it federal. Us bein' here is the same as Virge bein' here. I don't want another Cow-boy walkin' out of Behan's jail."

Wyatt had just stepped out of the boot repair shop when Fred Dodge found him. "Frank Stilwell and Pete Spence own the saloon across the street," he reported. "They're in there right now." He gave a sly laugh. "Stilwell's got a brand new heel on his boot, Wyatt."

Morgan rode up at a brisk pace, reined his horse to a stop, and leaned on his pommel. "Wyatt, I was just over at the stage livery. Levi McDaniels was driver on that stage. He says one o' the men who waylaid 'em climbed up in the box, put a pistol to his gut, and asked did he have 'any sugar' to add to the sack." Morgan smiled at Dodge, whose eyes burned with certainty.

"That's Stilwell talkin', by God," Fred said. "He uses that word all the time."

Wyatt stared across the street at the saloon and nodded back toward the boot maker's shop. "Stilwell was here this morning," he said. "Purchased a new heel and asked the shop keeper how much 'sugar' did he owe."

"God, they almost make this easy." Morgan laughed.

"Stilwell and Spence will have friends here," Wyatt reminded them. "Morg, you and Fred go round up Williams and Behan's deputies. I'll watch the saloon."

"You wait on us, now, Wyatt," Dodge warned. "Stilwell is still a deputy sheriff." When Wyatt did not respond, Dodge added, "B'sides, I want to see his face when you show 'im that boot heel."

For fifteen minutes Wyatt stood across the street from the saloon in the shade of a grocery store awning. With the sun up over the canyon rim now, Stilwell and Spence came out, mumbling to one another with their heads down, laughing. They appeared to be unarmed. Wyatt stepped into the street and called their names, and both men raised a hand to shield their eyes from the glare of the sun. As Wyatt approached, Spence slowed and then stopped, grabbing Stilwell's sleeve to halt him. Stilwell's head jerked one way, then the other, checking the street.

"You boys have been out in the hills this morning," Wyatt said and kept walking.

Stilwell jerked a thumb at the saloon. "Been right here, if it's any o' your business."

Wyatt slid his Colt's from its holster and stopped three paces short of the men. "Take off your coats so I can see what you've got."

"You go to hell!" Spence said.

Stilwell broke into a chattering laugh. "Hell, Earp! I'm a goddamn deputy sheriff in this county. As I remember, you ain't nothin' at all."

"I'm serving as a deputy US marshal. You're both under arrest. Take off your coats."

Morgan, Williams, and Dodge rode up and sat their horses stiffly, each man with an elbow cocked high, his hand gripping a pistol butt. A crowd had started to gather on the boardwalk in front of the saloon. The two cornered men grudgingly removed their coats.

"Morg, climb down and go through Stilwell's pockets," instructed Wyatt, and then he stepped close to Spence. "Turn around."

When Spence did not comply, Wyatt holstered his gun and spun him. Spence lashed out with an elbow, but Morgan changed course from Stilwell and slammed Spence facedown into the street. Dodge dismounted and placed a boot on Spence's back while Morgan rifled his pockets.

"You damn Earps are gonna pay for this!" Spence screeched.

Wyatt walked to Stilwell. "Your turn." Stilwell started to back away until he saw Breakenridge and Neagle coming in at a gallop. Bolstered by their presence, he faced Wyatt and smiled.

"You got nothin' on me, Earp," he snarled, but he lost his smirk when Wyatt pulled the boot heel from his pocket. Stilwell licked his lips. "That s'posed to mean somethin' to me?"

Morgan wedged between them, his face inches from Stilwell's. "Is everybody in your crowd as ignorant as the two of you?" Morgan threw him face down into the street.

Breakenridge dismounted but stood back, pulling up his belt and frowning. "What're you doing there with Frank, Wyatt? He's a sheriff's deputy, you know."

"Ain't you heard, Breck?" Morgan laughed. "He's a deputy *and* a damned stage robber."

"Go find their horses," Wyatt said to Breakenridge. "We're taking them to Tombstone."

"We ain't gonna rest up a spell first?" Breakenridge asked. "We just got here."

Wyatt turned to face the deputy. "No, we ain't."

*****

On the front porch of Wyatt's house, Virgil and Wyatt sat in the rocking chairs John Vermillion had pieced together from the lumber scraps of house construction. The late afternoon light brought out a honey-gold hue from the desert around them. A light breeze from the west brought the scent of woodsmoke. Savoring their cigars, the two brothers watched two dark-skinned girls carry armloads of stove wood along the sandy road toward the Mexican district. The brothers didn't speak as Mattie set a tray on the ground between them and then returned to the house. Virgil tried the lemonade she had brought out.

"She don't look too good," Virgil said, glancing at Wyatt. Then he held up his glass, studying the flecks of fruit and sugar suspended in the water. "Lemonade's good though."

Wyatt's eyes were fixed on Pete Spence's house across the street and next door to Virgil's. "How is it we come to live in the same neighborhood with a stage robber?"

Virgil followed Wyatt's gaze. "He didn't like being arrested, did he?"

"Son of a bitch threatened all of us when he left the courthouse. Same as Frank McLaury did."

"You mean 'Frank Stilwell,' don't you?"

Wyatt picked up his glass and shook his head. "Stilwell doesn't have the sand. It was McLaury. He told Stilwell he'd never speak to 'im again for lettin' us arrest 'im."

Virgil made a sound deep in his chest—something meant to sum up the likes of Spence and McLaury. "Frank McLaury seems like he was born all in a lather about somethin', and he don't know what. But Spence is sly. He's a damned snake. I doubt we'll see him coming if he decides to make good on that threat."

Wyatt sipped from his glass and then set it in the dirt. "How're we gonna make any headway with these Cow-boys when all they gotta do is get their friends to lie on the witness stand?"

Virgil made the sound in his chest again and watched Allie back out of their front door and sling a basin of gray water into the yard. Their dog jumped down from the porch and sniffed at the water, as Allie looked across the intersection at the two brothers. Allie's posture was stiff, poised as if she might yell out something to her husband, but she only clamped the bowl under one arm and went back inside. The dog climbed back onto the porch and curled up next to the wood box.

"Hell," Virgil said, his voice sounding tired now. "I don't know. Long as men will lie in a courtroom, we ain't got much of a system, do we?" He continued to stare across the street where Allie had stood. After a moment he set down his half-drunk glass, made the deep grumbling sound in his chest, and pushed up from the chair. "Hell, I'd better go." He started across the intersection, squaring his shoulders and setting a deliberate pace.

Wyatt picked up both glasses and carried them to the house. Sidestepping inside, he eased the door shut with his boot. With both Louisa and Warren back in California and Morgan rooming with Fred Dodge again, the new abode was a house of cards. Whatever room Mattie occupied seemed filled with a misery that made Wyatt want to walk quietly past that door. In the kitchen he set the glasses on the sideboard and looked at the open doorway of the bedroom. He would have liked to have heard some movement to suggest Mattie might be doing something—anything—but the room was still and quiet, just like the rest of the house. Wyatt moved quietly to the threshold and looked in, but he stopped short of entering the room.

"Lemonade was good," he said, his words seeming to come back at him like a senseless exercise in breaking a silence.

Mattie sat on the side of the bed, her fingers fumbling idly with the tie sash of her robe. Her bloodshot eyes remained fixed on her hands, the corners of her mouth pulled down in a dedicated scowl. On the floor beside her was a corked brown bottle.

"Want to put something on and walk down to the ice cream parlor, Mattie?"

Mattie gripped the edge of the bed frame and turned angry eyes on him. "No."

The word hung between them, sufficient to undermine anything else he might say. Wyatt walked into the room, draped his coat over his arm, grabbed his hat, and left the fragile atmosphere that had become a permanent fixture inside the house.

The heat of the day was lifting, and the coming evening brought with it a cool crispness that hinted of autumn. Before he had passed the back entrance of the O.K. Corral, he heard a piano and a chorus of men's voices pouring out of the Capitol Saloon at the corner. Across Fourth Street, the ice cream parlor showed no activity. When he reached the window, he leaned close to the glass and verified that the shop was empty. Then he read the paper notice fixed to the door: *All melted. No ice till next week.*

The revelry of song swelled across the street—the Irish miners pouring their hearts and accents into an anthem of their homeland. The sound was like a magnet pulling in more laborers from Allen Street. Among the latecomers were Johnny Behan and Sadie Marcus.

Behan's head was lifted to the music, mouth open as though he were breathing in the notes of the song. When Sadie jerked from his grip, Behan spat a string of angry words at her and waved her away. Continuing alone, he picked up his pace as he neared the celebration spilling out of the saloon. Unmoving, Sadie stood alone in the street and searched her purse for something. Wyatt walked into the street and headed toward her. When he stopped ten feet away, she still had not seen him.

"Miss Marcus."

Turning at the sound, she blinked, her moist eyes reflecting the yellow light glowing in the saloon windows. When Wyatt approached and pulled a handkerchief from his coat pocket, she took the linen with an embarrassed smile.

"Can we get off this street?" she whispered.

He offered his arm, and they turned the corner onto Fremont and started east with no destination in mind. They walked past the red-light district and then on to a winding trail that wove through a maze of yucca, sage, and agave scattered among the loose rock. The path dissolved into an incline of scrubby soapberry and left them perched above the broad plain of the Sulphur Springs Valley with no remarkable feature but the emptiness of the land that terminated in the distant mountains, mute and gray.

Standing with their backs to Tombstone, they listened to the wind keen over the flat land below them. From a nearby shrub a night bird twittered, its wings fluttering as though it were caught in the brush. Then it shot free into the air and flew careening from side to side low over the land until it was lost to sight in the growing dark.

Wyatt had never experienced the comfort of silence like this—not with a woman he barely knew. He imagined that she, like himself, was trying to take from this place some measure of relief from past disappointments.

"You're married, aren't you, Wyatt?"

"Close enough, I reckon."

She glanced at him, and then she refolded his handkerchief and touched it to her eyes. "Is it what you had hoped it would be?"

He had never been asked such a question. Of course, the answer was easy enough, but it was this moment of putting it into words that made him realize what separated him from the people he deemed important in any town he had lived. It was family. Not the one a man had no choice about . . . but the one he tried to build.

She bowed her head and folded her arms across her stomach. "I'm prying, aren't I?"

"I reckon it's hard to answer when you don't like what you'll hear yourself say."

She looked at him with a question narrowing her eyes. "You're a man. You can just pick up and start over anywhere you want. Why don't you? Other men do it all the time." She turned back to the broad valley, and her voice grew smaller. "Women just stay behind and learn how to surrender their last shred of dignity . . . just to stay alive."

He looked at her curiously. "I heard you were an actress. From San Francisco."

She laughed, but there was more misery in that laugh than when she had cried. "I ran away from my parents in San Francisco. I was only thirteen, pretending I'd be an actress."

Wyatt nodded. "That took something . . . to leave like that."

"Not really. I was gravely deluded . . . about Johnny."

"You ran off with him?"

She blinked back more tears. "I thought I had met the most charming man in the world." She laughed ruefully. "And I guess I had. I just didn't yet know what 'charming' really means."

Wyatt frowned and tried to read her face in the dark. "And you're still his fiancée?"

"That's his word for me," she admitted. "I think you know what I am."

Wyatt's face stung for a moment, as if hit by an icy wind. Sadie smiled wanly.

"You didn't know our sheriff had other business ventures?"

Her confession was like a private room into which she had just invited him to hear the truths rarely shared. With anyone else he would have been silent, aloof. But she had included him in that space, and he would not treat the invitation lightly.

Wyatt forced an even timbre into his voice. "All this time . . . you been doing that for Johnny?"

She nodded. "Prescott. Tiptop. And now Tombstone." She pressed the cloth over her eyes and began to sob. He wanted to touch her, but his hands hung useless at his sides.

"What about being an actress?"

She sniffed and wiped at her cheeks. "I was just a stand-in . . . for a season. We traveled and put on our shows, and Johnny would show up and—" She turned her sad smile to the vast openness of the desert.

Wyatt took off his hat and ran a finger around the sweatband. "You seem to me the kind of woman who could do most anything she sets her mind to. It's easy enough to see you're blessed with looks. But there's more to it under that. You're more alive than most."

Staring out at the valley, her eyes seemed to glow from an internal light. "This is only the second time we've talked," she said in a whisper, "and yet you can say that?"

Inside his mind, he listened again to the words he had said to her. He had not spoken from such a place since Missouri . . . and Aurilla. The image he had carried of his dying wife was like an old battle scar he could not hide. Now, when he allowed his gaze to rove freely over Sadie's face, he was surprised how quickly the memory of Rilla was swallowed up by the rest of his past. He saw an unexplainable familiarity in this woman's dark silhouette, as though everything he had gone through . . . and everything she had endured . . . they had somehow done it together, in separate lives, in different parts of the country.

"Nobody really knows who you are," he said, "but sometimes, maybe when you least expect it, you get a chance to show somebody the part of yourself that counts . . . and maybe that person can see the value of it."

"I'm not sure I understand that, Wyatt."

"I ain't sure we're meant to."

She smiled at that. "You don't usually talk this much, do you?"

He looked down at the hat in his hands. "I reckon not."

He believed she was smiling now, but he couldn't be certain in the dark. Before he said something he might want to think through, he turned to face Tombstone. The lights of the town shone brightly against the dark land—like stars floating low over the desert. It was, he realized, the first time he had attached any concept of beauty to the mining village.

"You have a way with words, Wyatt. Johnny has that, too; only you can't believe him."

Wyatt nodded. The cool air was perfect now, making his skin feel clean. The Arizona sky had blackened to ink, and the stars swam like jewels suspended in a bottomless lake.

"You can believe me," he said.

She turned to stand with him, and they watched the lights blink and shimmer through the heat still rising off the land. She slipped her arm through his, and the only sound was the wind.

CHAPTER 14

Fall 1881

Tombstone, A.T.

Another stage was waylaid near Charleston, and, though McMaster had not been able to get word to Wyatt before the holdup, the Cow-boy informant did volunteer the names of the men who had perpetrated the crime: Curly Bill, Spence, and Stilwell. Virgil deputized Wyatt, and they arrested the latter two, only to see a parade of Cow-boy witnesses take the stand and, yet again, lie for the accused.

Outside the courthouse, Stilwell flashed a snide smile at the Earp brothers until Frank McLaury grabbed his arm. "Stilwell," McLaury declared loudly, "I told you I'd never talk to you again if you let these town-shits arrest you." He spat and faced Morgan. "You boys ever try that on a McLaury, somebody's gonna find your bones out in the desert."

"Give us a reason to come find you," Morgan said, smiling, "and we'll show you how to make a capon out o' a cocky little rooster."

John Ringo walked from the building and stopped two feet in front of Wyatt, his body turned in profile, his lips pursed and his eyes narrowed as if he were working out the details of a riddle rolling around inside his head. He looked down at the hat in his hands, which he began to turn slowly as if appraising the shape of the brim.

"Getting to be too damned many lawmen in this part of the country," he said loud enough to be heard by all around him. He took his time fitting his hat to his head and then turned his morose smile on

Wyatt. "Way too damned many." Ringo lipped a crudely rolled cigarette, snapped a lucifer into flame with his thumbnail, and lighted the twisted end of the paper. Exhaling a plume of smoke over the flame, he flipped the match into the street. When he stared at Wyatt again, there was a cold and predatory hardness in his eyes. Wyatt ignored the performance, turned, and walked south toward Allen Street.

The bar at the Grand Hotel never provided music this early in the day. Only a handful of patrons occupied the room. Wyatt ordered a cup of coffee and took it to a table to read the town's rival newspapers.

"Like some company, Mr. Earp?" It was the whore he had carried from the fire. She smiled down at him, somehow displaying equal measures of gratitude and sauciness.

Wyatt lowered his newspaper. "Thought I'd read the paper a bit."

She pushed her lips into a playful pout. "Am I not ever gonna be able to repay you?" When she saw he would not answer, she pulled out a chair and sat down. "If you're still looking for Sadie, she's moved out." Her smile widened at the change in his eyes. "She moved out on Johnny, too."

"I reckon that's her business," he said.

"Oh, really? Then why do I have the feeling I won't see you drinking your coffee in here after today?" She leaned closer and lowered her voice. "She's at a boardinghouse on Safford Street." Turning sultry, she slid her hand across his sleeve, but Wyatt's attention had shifted.

Frank and Tom McLaury, Joe Hill, Billy "the Kid" Claiborne, and Ike Clanton filed into the room and grouped at the bar. Ike slapped the bar with the flat of his hand and ordered drinks.

The whore shielded her face with her hand. "Oh, God," she drawled. "Spare me a go-round with Ike Clanton."

The conversation at the bar ceased when Frank spotted Wyatt in the mirror. The two McLaurys and Claiborne twisted at the waist. Tom turned back to nurse his drink, but Frank's eyes burned a hole into Wyatt's corner of the room. He picked up his glass and walked his cocksure walk to Wyatt's table. Ike and Claiborne followed in his wake.

"I want to talk to you, Earp," Frank said.

"Yeah, me, too," Ike blustered.

Wyatt drank from his coffee mug and set it down with barely a sound. "Then talk."

McLaury glared at the girl. "Well," she announced, rising, "I have to go see the doctor about a little problem." Giving the Cow-boys an icy smile, she sashayed away.

Tom called from the bar, "Frank, I'm going to Bauer's to price the beef."

Frank turned but made no response, except to tap Claiborne's arm. "Go with him."

Claiborne scowled but mustered no complaint. Scuffing his boots, he followed Tom out the door. Joe Hill slapped Claiborne's shoulder as he passed, and then he carried his drink to Wyatt's table. The three Cow-boys pulled out chairs.

"No need for that," Wyatt said. "You won't be here that long."

Ike Clanton hesitated, but McLaury perched a boot in his chair. "How many people have you told about that damn deal you tried on us?" Frank said.

Wyatt let his eyes go cold. "Same as I told you before. Just Virgil."

Ike Clanton leaned forward and jabbed a finger at Wyatt. "You're lying. That Wells, Fargo man, Williams, he knows about it. Told me any deal I made with you was good with him. That's what he said." Clanton's breath touched Wyatt's face like a damp spider web soaked in vinegar.

"Ike," Wyatt said, his voice so low that Clanton cocked one ear closer. "Get your stinking breath out of my face." With a startled pinch in his eyes, Ike slowly straightened.

"I bet you told that skinny-ass Holliday, too," Frank said.

Wyatt held McLaury's gaze and spaced his words for emphasis. "Just . . . Virgil."

McLaury's lips pulled back, exposing the tips of his teeth. "Then how's Williams know?"

"He *don't* know," Wyatt said. "He's guessing."

"Bull-*shit!*" Ike spat and pointed at Wyatt. "If you or your brothers—"

Quickly, Wyatt pointed at Ike, his eyes hardening to ice. "Threaten me or my brothers, and I'll kick your teeth down your throat right here."

With his face coloring, Ike glanced quickly at McLaury and then at Hill. Fisting his hands at his sides, Ike frowned like a sullen child.

"Well, goddammit," he whined, "Holliday knows—I can tell—and now he's out to get me 'cause he was friends with Billy Leonard." Ike's frantic eyes demanded reassurance. "What's to keep *him* from talkin'? You tell me *that*!"

Hill spoke out of the side of his mouth. "Stop your bellyaching, Ike. If you're so afraid of Holliday, why don't you just kill 'im?" He held his stare on Wyatt and smiled.

McLaury dropped his boot heavily to the floor. "Our threats stand."

"Suit yourself," Wyatt said. "I've stuck by my word."

"What about Holliday?" Ike pushed. "Ask him if he don't know."

"Doc's in Tucson, gambling," Wyatt said. "Ask him yourself when he gets back."

The Cow-boys walked out, their spurs ringing on the floor like a jangle of loose parts in a coffee grinder. The sound filled the stairwell as they climbed to the lobby.

Wyatt tried his coffee but it had cooled. He surveyed the room and watched each patron look away from him. The bartender held up the coffee pot with a question lifting his eyebrows. Wyatt shook his head, stood, and left.

*****

Two nights later, Wyatt ate a late meal in the Alhambra and listened to Ike Clanton's drunk and abrasive mouth carrying across the long ornate counter that divided the lunchroom from the saloon. Morgan leaned on the bar, at once amused and irritated. He looked at Wyatt as though asking a question, but Wyatt shook his head.

When Doc Holliday walked into the saloon, Wyatt laid down his fork and stopped chewing. Over the countertop, he watched Holliday move past Clanton to the far end of the bar. Clanton stared at Doc for a time and then groped his way along the backs of the customers until there was no man between him and Holliday. Ignoring Ike, Doc threw back the contents of a shot glass and ordered another.

"You looking for me, Holliday?"

Doc deigned to turn his head but did not answer.

"I know what the Earps told you 'bout me," Ike slurred, "and I don't give a shit *what* you think!" He spewed air from his crooked scowl. "It's all lies anyway!"

Holliday drank his second whiskey and set down the glass with a sharp rap. "What the hell are you talking about, Ike?"

"I ain't afraid of you *or* the Earps." Ike spun his back to the bar and raised his voice to the crowd. "I don't give a goddamn what this man Holliday says about me! He's a liar! The Earps, too! They're all liars!"

Holliday's pallid face flushed with color. "Clanton, you're being damned loose with my name and the names of my friends."

But Ike had his audience. As he continued to rant, Morgan sat up on the counter, raised his boot heels, and spun around to drop into the saloon. He insinuated himself between Clanton and Holliday, leaned an elbow on the bar, and smiled at Ike.

"Oh, great!" Clanton snapped. "A fuckin' Earp."

"Gettin' a little loud, Ike," Morgan said. "Why'n't you go outside and cool off."

"Tell it to that sick bastard behind you. He ain't nobody special just 'cause *you* know 'im. He's throwin' 'round lies about me, and I aim to do somethin' about it."

Doc slipped his hand under his coat. "Then for God's sake, get to it! I'm game."

Morgan threw a hand out in front of Doc. "Hold on, Doc. Help me out here."

"I intend to. Step aside. I'm going to clean some scum off the heel of Tombstone."

"I'll fight you!" Ike screamed, stiffening an arm to point at Doc. "You skinny lung-er!" Clanton came at him, and Morgan had his hands full from both parties. Wyatt tossed down his napkin and stood. Doc's hand was still inside his coat, and he was trembling with rage.

"Pull your shooter!" Holliday cried hoarsely and stepped back two paces.

"I ain't heeled, damn you!" Ike returned. He pushed at Morgan and backed away.

"Well, then go fix yourself," Doc yelled, "and let's see if there's more to you than mouth."

Clanton lunged again, and Morgan grabbed a handful of Ike's curly hair, dragging the Cow-boy outside. "Owww!" Ike squealed, turning his rage on Morgan. "You goddamn town-shits!"

Wyatt walked outside in his shirtsleeves just as Morgan heaved Ike across the boardwalk into the street. "If you're hot to make a fight, Ike," Morgan taunted, "you can start right here with me."

Virgil came at a fast walk from across the street. "Morgan!" he called. Virgil stopped, spread his coat lapels, and rested his fists on his hips. His pistol was tucked into his waistband. He glanced at Wyatt and then turned back to Morgan. "What the hell is this ruckus?"

"The ruckus has not yet started, Virgil," Doc said. "I'll be waiting right here, Ike."

Ike got to his feet. "You better be looking for me, you skinny bag of pus. You'll see me sooner'n you want!" He pointed at Morgan. "All o' you!"

"God willing," Doc mumbled.

"Get off the street, Ike," Virgil ordered. "Go get some sleep and sober up."

As he turned to leave, Ike snarled at Virgil, "You're the marshal. See that they don't shoot me in the back."

"Go home, Ike," Virgil barked and turned to Holliday. "You, too, Doc. I want both of you off the street now, or you'll spend the night in jail."

Holliday started to say more, but, when he met Wyatt's eyes, he closed his mouth. Snapping down the front of his vest, Doc turned and walked east toward the rebuilt Oriental.

Virgil gave Morgan a big-brother look. "You go home, too."

"Hell, Virge, I'm on duty."

"Then go be on duty at home." Virgil glared at him until Morgan pulled a sulky face and walked off, mumbling something that could not be heard over the scrape of his boots on the boards. Virgil turned to Wyatt. "I still consider you an active deputy." He waited, but Wyatt made no response. "This is about that goddamn reward money, ain't it?" Virgil asked.

"There ain't no reward money," Wyatt said. "All the sons of bitches are dead."

Virgil frowned and turned his head to watch Ike stumble down the street. "Not all of 'em," he said and walked away in the same angry stride with which he had arrived.

The temperature had dropped. Wyatt went back inside, paid his bill, put on his coat, and walked to the Eagle Brewery to check on the faro dealer who was running a game for him there. As he left the Eagle, someone called his name from the alley. When Wyatt stopped and turned, Ike Clanton moved from the shadows, his eyes darting up and down Allen Street.

"He knows, don't he? Holliday knows! I know he does!"

Wyatt did not bother to answer. "You're a damned fool, Ike."

Ike pointed repetitively at Wyatt and struggled to sort out his words. "You told 'im so he would want to get rid of me. I know your game. By God, if I'd been heeled in there—" Ike wiped his mouth with the back of his hand and then thrust his chin forward. "Nobody insults me like that! I ain't afraid to fight him or *any* o' you. You hear that? Hey! Where're you going?"

"I ain't interested in fighting," Wyatt said over his shoulder. "There's no money in it."

"Well, you might have to fight!" Ike called to his back. "All o' you!"

Wyatt stopped and turned. "Go home, Ike. You talk too much for a fightin' man."

At the Oriental, Wyatt found Doc counting his money at the bar. Doc looked up to acknowledge him and then resumed his tally. When he finished, he folded the money and slipped it inside his wallet.

"Is that loudmouth bastard back on the street?"

"Let's turn in, Doc," Wyatt suggested. "Come on, I'll walk with you to your room."

Holliday's nickel-plated revolver blinked brightly in the dim lighting as he stuffed his wallet into the inside pocket of his coat. "I'd rather stay up and kill that son of a bitch," he said. "But I suppose I can use some sleep." He grabbed his overcoat from the wall peg and followed Wyatt outside.

They turned at Hafford's Corner and walked down Fourth. Doc coughed, and his breath plumed gray in the cold. He turned up his coat collar and pressed his lapels against his chest.

"God," he growled, "this feels like Philadelphia." When they turned west on Fremont, the wind was in their faces, whipping the tails of their coats behind them. "I know you asked me, Wyatt, but I couldn't very well avoid Clanton tonight. There's only so much you can take off that filthy bastard. I can't even understand the idiot most of the time."

Wyatt nodded but wanted no more conversation about Ike Clanton. They walked the boardwalk past the Papago Cash Store, stepped down at the back gate of the O.K. Corral, and up onto the boards again at Bauer's Meat Market. When they reached Fly's boardinghouse, Doc turned to face Wyatt.

"What the hell was Ike talking about back there?"

Wyatt removed his hat and turned it like a wheel on the axle of his hand. "It's complicated, Doc. Clanton thinks you know something about a deal he might have made. He's afraid you'll tell it to the wrong people. Or maybe act on it yourself."

Doc's eyes narrowed and studied Wyatt's face. "*You* made a deal with *Ike?*"

When Wyatt did not answer, Doc laughed and coughed at the same time. "God, Wyatt, is the faro table just not doing it for you anymore? What was the deal?"

Wyatt stopped the motion with his hat and looked inside the crown as if he might find an answer there. "Just trying to catch some stage robbers, Doc."

Holliday offered a wry smile. "This is about Billy Leonard's ranch, isn't it?"

"For Ike, maybe," Wyatt said. "For me, it was about votes." He raised the hat toward Doc and lowered it. "I'm asking you to stay away from Ike, Doc."

Holliday laughed. "Hell, why don't we just kill 'im? That ought to get you some votes."

"We don't need that kind of trouble, Doc. I'm still aiming to be sheriff, and running up against Clanton ain't gonna help me do that. Ike's a piece of shit, but he's connected to all the other shit in the yard. We'd be stepping in it everywhere we turned."

Still smiling, Doc nodded. "All right, I'll try to restrain myself." The wind whipped up dust and rattled the gate back at the corral entrance. Doc opened the door to the boardinghouse. "For as long as you need me to, anyway."

" 'Preciate it, Doc," Wyatt said. He fitted the hat to his head and continued down Fremont to his home.

After Wyatt closed the bedroom door on Mattie's drug-induced snoring, he spread a copy of the *Nugget* over the kitchen table. For an hour, he cleaned and oiled his gun, giving each working part of the Colt's its due. He listened to the wind gust outside, sometimes moaning like a deep-throated animal as it carved around the eave of the roof on the west side. All the while he worked, he thought about Sadie Marcus.

CHAPTER 15

October 26, 1881

Tombstone, A.T.

Wyatt was seated at his kitchen table reading the *Epitaph* when Virgil came through the side door. The noon wind was blustery, whipping up at unexpected moments and pushing the rocking chairs outside into a hollow, rumbling rhythm. Crystals of snow dusted Virgil's hat and the shoulders of his heavy coat. When Virge opened his coat to the cast-iron wood stove, Wyatt saw his brother's pistol stuffed into his waistband.

"You heard?" Virgil said.

Wyatt set down his coffee and wiped his moustaches with a napkin. "Ike?"

"Hell, yes, 'Ike,' " Virgil grunted. "He's on the street threatening all of us."

"That's Ike's fight . . . his mouth. Why don't you just arrest him? Let him sleep it off in jail." Wyatt sipped his coffee and watched his brother angrily re-button his coat. "You going into town now?"

"Don't reckon I can put it off any longer," Virgil answered, his face set hard with purpose. He turned his head to look squarely at Wyatt. "I'll be wantin' you on duty again today."

Wyatt downed the last of his coffee and stood. "I'll walk with you." Buttoning his collar, he crossed the kitchen to the bedroom. Mattie lay in bed with her back to him. He slipped into his wool vest and stared at her as he pushed the buttons through their holes. Her limp hair splayed on the pillow in a nest of tangles. It had been so long since she had tended to herself in the way that females did that he had come to think of her as a presence without a soul. An empty brown bottle lay on its side on the small table next to her. He couldn't remember an exact time she had abandoned the idea of hiding the laudanum. Its presence had simply become a part of her daily fare.

He donned his frock coat and then the heavy mackinaw that cut out the wind. In the mirror he squared his hat on his head. From atop the dresser, he lifted the Colt's revolver and checked the loads. The smooth *clicks* of the cylinder filled the room like a surrogate message to Mattie: *There was business he needed to tend to*. But he doubted she heard it. He tucked the gun in his coat pocket and dropped a handful of cartridges into the other. When he left the room, he felt Mattie's misery peel away from him like a rotted cloak.

On the street Morgan walked to his brothers in a direct, purposeful line, his boyish face drawn and focused. "Ike's carryin' a Winchester and a pistol. He was down at Fly's askin' for Doc." Morg shook his head to the unasked question. "Nothin' happened."

The brothers split up to scour the business section. Wyatt was on Allen Street crossing to Hafford's when he heard the deep boom of Virgil's voice. He spun in time to see Virgil just past the gun shop, one-handedly trying to twist a rifle from Ike Clanton's grip. With his other hand, Virge drew his pistol and slammed its barrel against the side of Ike's head. Ike dropped heavily, face-down in the street. When Morgan appeared from the alley and stooped to pick up Ike's dropped revolver, Wyatt relaxed his grip on the gun in his pocket and walked to his brothers.

"He was coming up behind you, Wyatt," Virge said.

"I'm growin' damned tired o' this loudmouth sonovabitch," Wyatt growled.

When Ike moaned, Virgil handed the rifle to Morgan and jerked Clanton to his feet by his coat lapels. "He's drunk. Let's haul him to Judge Wallace and see if that takes some of the fight out of him."

"You mean 'some of his mouth,' " Morg corrected.

In Judge Wallace's courtroom Morgan pushed Ike onto a bench, where the battered Cow-boy sat hunched forward, cupping the cut on his head with one hand. Then he looked up to glare at Wyatt and Virgil.

"A second later, and they'd 'a been carryin' some o' you Earps to the coroner," Ike snarled.

Wyatt felt the prelude to violence crackle across his skin like sparks from a fire. Townspeople had begun to crowd the doorway, their faces full of curiosity and expectation.

"I'll go find Judge Wallace," Virgil huffed. "Try not to kill the sonovabitch."

As Wyatt and Morgan waited for the judge, Ike let go with a litany of complaints to anyone in the room who would listen. When he stood to further remonstrate, Morgan shoved him back onto the bench and used the muzzle of the Winchester as a prod to keep him there. One of Behan's deputies looked on uneasily from the other side of the room. When Ike resorted to screaming his insults, everyone turned to watch his antics.

"You goddamned Earps are gonna pay!" Ike screeched. "All o' you!" He tried to shunt aside the rifle pressed into his gut, but Morgan leaned in with his weight. Ike winced at the pain and screamed again. "You goddamn pimps . . . you come here to leech off the rest of us. You cheat at your cards . . . strut your badges . . . and you rob the goddamn stages. Then you make a big show of ridin' out to catch the bandits when you're really chasin' your own tails. There ain't none o' you fit to live here among us ranchers who been makin' a livin' off this land. Hell, the people of Arizona would thank us for killin' you."

Ike knotted his mouth to gather saliva, and then he spat at the two brothers. He seemed surprised when he hit his mark. Wyatt looked down at his trousers, at the beads of white foam clinging to his pant leg. Morgan tightened his hold on the rifle and checked Wyatt's face. In the silence that followed, Ike seemed to shrink on the bench.

Then the stillness broke as Wyatt moved as quick as a cat and lifted Ike by his throat to pin him against the wall. Morgan backed away, lowered the rifle, and watched.

"You goddamned dirty cow thief," Wyatt began in a whispery growl, his face so close to Ike's that the Cow-boy had to turn a cheek to the wall. "I'd be justified in shooting you down like a dog. You've threatened us for the last time. I'll fight you any place you name, even if I have to come over among your crowd in the San Simon."

Clanton's one visible eye was ringed in white. When he swallowed, the bulge in his throat bobbed with a dry *click*. Then, just as quickly as the fear had seized him, he mustered bravado.

"All right, I'll fight you!" he snapped, his voice cracking like cold glass. "All I need with you is four feet o' ground."

Wyatt pushed Ike back onto the bench, and Morgan slammed down Ike's revolver next to him. "Here's your chance right here," Morgan purred. "You damned yellow windbag."

Behan's deputy rose from his chair. "Now wait a minute!" He approached the Earps but stopped as Judge Wallace came through the door with Virgil right behind him, both carrying a fresh dusting of snow on their shoulders. Reading the tension in his courtroom, the judge quickly started proceedings, fining Ike twenty-five dollars for carrying weapons inside the town limits.

At this announcement Wyatt let his boot drop heavily from the bench, and he walked out the door, his hard face shining like polished stone. Slamming the door, he bumped headlong into a man hurrying to enter. When he recognized Tom McLaury, the fire in his chest fanned into a flame again. The younger McLaury's face—usually open and friendly—was set with hostility, making the physical similarities to his brother suddenly apparent.

"What the hell've you boys been beating on Ike for?" Tom demanded. With his arms swelling from his sides, he widened his stance and glared at Wyatt.

"I'll knock down any man who threatens me or my family," Wyatt said, his voice like iron. In his peripheral vision, Wyatt saw the crowd backing away. They were voters all, he knew, but the heat of his anger trumped reason. "Are you a part of that threat?"

The fingers of McLaury's right hand spread and stilled next to his hip. Only then did Wyatt spot the gun butt jutting from the Cow-boy's deep trouser pocket.

Tom's forehead furrowed. "I'm with Frank and Ike," he blurted out. "Whatever they say goes with me, too. We're damned sick of you Earps always pushin'." Tom scowled and licked his lips. "You're all just trespassers, suckin' this land dry, while us ranchers have been scraping out a livin' long before you ever got here." He looked so much like Frank now that Wyatt let the differences between the two brothers dissolve in his mind.

"I ain't waitin' around to get back-shot by the likes of you," Wyatt snapped. "Jerk your gun!"

For a moment nothing happened. Tom's moist eyes darted from Wyatt's face to the bulge in his coat pocket and then back to Wyatt's icy eyes.

"Jerk it!" Wyatt ordered.

With his left hand Wyatt slapped McLaury across the face, and with his right he pulled the Colt's. The violent energy that had gathered inside him in the courtroom now funneled into a long slashing arc of gunmetal. Tom dropped backward into the street, a red gash opened on his head. Wyatt looked up when "Kid" Claiborne shouldered through the crowd, but the young Cow-boy's hostile gaze could not hold on Wyatt's.

Virgil stepped out onto the boardwalk, and Wyatt nodded at McLaury. "Here's another for the court to collect a goddamned twenty-five-dollar fine. Never mind he threatened our lives. That don't seem to mean a damned thing around here." Wyatt jammed his gun into his pocket and strode away, mumbling under his breath, "We ought to 'a killed 'em both."

At Hafford's, Wyatt bought a cigar and then stationed himself outside in front of the saloon to keep watch over the main intersection. The heat of anger had passed. He watched "Kid" Claiborne, Ike, and Tom move up Fourth Street and disappear into Dr. Gillingham's office. Virgil and Morgan came up the street from Wallace's courtroom and stood beside Wyatt. In their dark coats and hats and starched white shirts, the three Earps stood like businessmen who might be considering some new entrepreneurial proposition. At the same time—looking so much alike with their wheat-straw hair and moustaches—there was a menacing and powerful sense of solidarity.

"You reckon we knocked the fight out of 'em?" Virgil wondered.

"Hell," Morgan said, "they could stand a lot more knockin' than that."

Billy Clanton, Frank McLaury, and a third man appeared a block down, astride their horses, all moving at a walk down the middle of Allen Street. Each wore a revolver on a hip. Ignoring the Earps, they passed the intersection and dismounted at the Grand Hotel. They didn't see Doc Holliday approaching from behind, and they stopped at the front door when he spoke to them. Doc carried a walking cane and with his free hand made a cavalier salute. When he offered his hand to Billy Clanton, the surprised boy reacted by rote and shook Doc's hand.

"Could be a hell of a day," Doc said in his sly and jaunty way. Wearing his long, gray overcoat and matching hat, Doc never broke stride as he veered toward Hafford's. An impish grin twisted his ashen face. Frowning and a little confused, Frank and Billy disappeared into the Grand Hotel's lobby.

"You reckon somebody wired to them in Charleston?" Morgan said.

Virgil opened his pocketwatch. "Maybe," he said. "Might be more comin' in."

"Hell, bring 'em all in," Morgan said. "Let's shoot the lot of 'em."

When Doc stepped up onto the boardwalk at Hafford's, he pulled down briefly on the brim of his hat as he checked the faces of the Earp brothers. "Morning, gentlemen," he said and turned to stand beside Wyatt. "You boys look rather serious today."

Wyatt made no reply. Across the street Frank and Billy emerged from the Grand, untied their horses, and walked them west on Allen. This time as they passed by, they glared at the Earp party with eyes that seemed molten with hostility. Moving down the next block, they passed Doling's saloon and turned into the Dexter Corral.

"My, my," Doc said with a lilting melody. "Are we grooming bad relations with the local cattle thieves?"

"They didn't check their guns at the Grand," Morgan said.

"Let's not push it," Virgil advised. "They can check 'em at Dexter's."

Snow fell in sparse swirls of dull white flakes. "I'm having a drink," Doc said and coughed once into his fist. He turned at the door. "Don't start the party without me."

Virgil blew into his hands, rubbed them briskly, and then followed Doc inside.

Morgan started to join them but hesitated. "Ain't you cold?" he said to Wyatt's back.

Wyatt shook his head. "Go on in and get warm. I wanna keep an eye on things."

Alone, Wyatt stood in front of Hafford's. Within minutes both set of brothers—Clantons and McLaurys—came back up Allen Street toward him. Ike walked in front, his hat in his hand, a bright white bandage crowning his head. Tom's dressing was a simple narrow strip of gauze tied around his forehead. Glaring at Wyatt, Tom peeled off the bandage and eased his hat onto his head. Still armed, Frank and Billy led their horses.

Wyatt turned to face them, clamped his cigar in his teeth, and let his right hand hang at his side, where the Colt's weighted down his overcoat pocket. At the corner Tom McLaury peeled off from his friends and continued down Allen Street. The other three Cow-boys turned down Fourth, and, as they did, Frank leaned and spat into the street, never taking his eyes off Wyatt.

When they moved out of his view, Wyatt walked to the corner and watched them file into Spangenberg's Gun Shop. Frank McLaury's untied dun mare clopped up onto the boardwalk and pushed its head into the shop's open doorway. Wyatt threw his cigar into the street and started along the walkway toward Spangenberg's.

Through the windowglass he saw them gathered at the counter, Ike arguing with the owner as Billy and Frank pushed cartridges into their belt loops. Wyatt took the horse's loose reins and backed it away, its high steps awkward and percussive on the boards. At the sound, Frank turned around, and his face colored. He came on quickly, lunging out the door, grabbing for the reins.

"Get your fuckin' hands off my horse!" he shouted, his words like fat popping from a hot skillet. Now Billy Clanton's broad shoulders filled the door frame, his hand clenched firmly to the butt of his holstered gun.

"Keep your horse off the sidewalk," Wyatt ordered. "City ordinance."

The moment drew out like a fine thread stretched to its limit. The Cow-boys glared at Wyatt, their faces boiling with resentment, as he considered in which order he would shoot them if someone jerked a gun. Frank tied the reins to the awning post and, stepping back up on the boardwalk, spun around to face Wyatt.

"I've seen enough of you damn Earps to last me a lifetime," he snarled.

Virgil's boots rang on the boards, and the Cow-boys turned as one to see the marshal's double-fisted grip on a ten-gauge shotgun. The twin barrels of the scattergun angled downward, but Virgil's presence shut down all conversation. Ike, who had pushed his way outside to join in the taunting, backed into the shop. Frank and Billy followed, scuffing their boots, making a show of it, mixing indignation with insult.

Wyatt walked past Virgil back to Hafford's Corner and lighted a new cigar. Joining him, Virgil propped the shotgun, muzzle down, on the boards. Their eyes met for only a moment, but in that glance was the understanding of what it meant to be brothers who backed one another, no matter the occasion. Morgan came out of the saloon to stand with them in time to see the Cow-boys retrace their steps, marching around the corner to head west on Allen. Again they disappeared into the Dexter Corral.

"What happened?" Morg asked.

"Those sonzabitches are gettin' right on the edge of it," Virgil grumbled. "I'm just about mad enough to give 'em the fight they want."

"They're just struttin'," Wyatt said. "Let 'em. They don't know what else to do."

Virgil picked up the shotgun but grew still again when the Cow-boys and their horses crossed Allen Street from Dexter's into the O.K. Corral. "Maybe that's it," Virgil said. "Maybe they're leaving town."

Just then a man dressed in coveralls fast-walked up the street and looked from Wyatt to Virgil and then down at Virgil's badge. "Them men back yonder at Dexter's . . . they're armed and talking trouble. Your name come up, Marshal. They say they'll shoot you on sight."

From across the street at the barber shop, Behan called out, "Virgil! What's the trouble?" Behan's face was plum red in the cold. Clinging to one of his ears was a streak of shaving lather. A crowd had begun to gather and moved in closer to hear the sheriff and the marshal confer.

"Clantons and McLaurys are makin' threats and carrying guns," Virgil said, letting his anger show. Behan's eyes flicked uncertainly toward the shotgun.

"Well, what are you planning to do, Virgil?"

"Long as they're in the corral or leaving," Virgil said, "we'll let it sit. But if they push this, we'll give 'em the fight they want."

"You can't do that, Virgil. It's your job to disarm them."

Virgil gave Behan a cold stare. "What about you walking down there with us, and we'll do just that?"

Behan touched his cravat as if checking to see that it was centered on his neck. Frowning, he stretched his neck upward through his shirt collar.

"Look, I know those boys," he said. "Let me go talk to them alone."

The Earps watched Behan hurry down the street. A few of the onlookers fell in behind the sheriff, but most remained at Hafford's Corner, their curiosity fixed on the Earps. A heavyset man in a business suit and bowler sidled up to Virgil and clasped his upper arm.

"Marshal, I'm with Clum's vigilance committee. You say the word, and I can have two dozen men to back you."

Virgil shook his head and eased his arm from the man's grip. "I don't want any more guns on the street. Long as those boys stay in the corral—that or they get out of town—I'll let 'em be."

"Marshal? Dos men are not in da corral!" Virgil turned to see the stout German who ran the furniture store on Fremont Street. "Dey're standing out on Fremont right now . . . saying how dey kill you and your brodders."

Virgil's jaw clenched as he looked down the street. Wyatt slipped his Colt's from his pocket, set the hammer at half-cock, and opened the loading gate. He rotated the cylinder a click, took a cartridge from his pocket, and slipped it into the empty chamber that the hammer had rested on. Virgil tested the fit of his own pistol in his waistband and took a step forward so that he stood in profile right before Wyatt.

"I don't like dodgin' threats," he said quietly. He pivoted his head to look at Wyatt.

"It's past due," Wyatt said. "Either we're the law, or we ain't."

Tapping his cane on the tread boards, Doc shuffled out of Hafford's smiling and smelling of whiskey. "What's the plan?" he drawled.

Morgan nodded toward Fremont. "We're goin' down the street to make a fight, Doc."

Holliday cleared his throat and looked at Wyatt. "Well, hell . . . let's get to it."

"This is our problem, Doc," Wyatt said, thinking of his bid to become sheriff of the county. "No need you gettin' mixed up in it."

The mirth in Doc's face closed down—his mood as changed as the raw weather. "That's a hell of a thing for you to say to me," he snapped. But it was hurt, not anger, filling his eyes.

Another citizen stepped sheepishly into the conversation. "Marshal Earp?" he said, looking questionably back and forth between Virgil and Wyatt. "Those Cow-boys are next to Fly's in that little lot where Harwood sometimes stacks lumber. They're talking up a fight."

"That's right outside my room," Doc said.

Virgil nodded and took the shotgun by its forestock. "All right, Doc, come along with us." He held out the scattergun to Holliday. "Here, hide this under your coat and give me that." He nodded toward Doc's cane.

With the exchange made, Virgil leveled his gaze on Wyatt, but both knew that the time for words was past. The four men turned and started down Fourth Street, and the crowd opened to give them passage. Their pace was unhurried but deliberate—their strides naturally coalescing into a common rhythm as they walked four abreast. Along the way citizens paused in conversation or stilled in their daily tasks to watch them pass. Some followed behind in a belated procession of the curious, intent on seeing what drama might unfold. Wyatt was aware of this growing presence of spectators only peripherally, and he gave them no more attention than the diminishing spit of snow angling on the wind.

Wyatt's mind was clear. The boil of anger had settled to a simmer. His momentum was set with one purpose only—the one that burned at the center of what it meant to be an Earp: a sense of duty. Despite his show of rage with Ike Clanton in Judge Wallace's courtroom—and his manhandling of Tom McLaury—Wyatt believed he had shown restraint. He and Virgil had given them plenty of room, but some men did not recognize salvation when it slapped them in the face. The time had come to educate these Cow-boys in the error of their ways. The townspeople would see the way that the Earps could put men like these in their places and, in so doing, restore order to the village.

Wyatt doubted the Cow-boys would fight, due in part to the unequivocal certainty that the Earps *would* fight. And that threat only intensified with Doc along. He was the wild card. If the Clantons and McLaurys believed the Earps would show restraint as lawmen, they would not make the same mistake with Holliday.

When they turned west on Fremont, Wyatt spotted Frank McLaury in the street conversing with Behan partway down the block. The sheriff made broad gestures with his hands, but his posture appeared retiring and his manner uncertain. When Frank looked over Behan's shoulder and narrowed his eyes at the Earps, the sheriff turned and stood paralyzed. Even as Frank backed into the vacant lot beyond Fly's, Behan stared at the Earps like the odd man out on a dance floor.

As the four lawmen walked toward the sheriff, Doc whistled quietly, a thin melody weaving into the push of the cold wind—like a distant, playful tune insinuating itself into a funeral dirge. Keeping his attention on the corner of the boardinghouse, Wyatt slipped his revolver from his coat pocket and pressed it into the folds of the mackinaw. Morgan saw his movement and did the same.

Virgil carried only the cane, but his gun butt protruded from the front of his waistband, where it offered quick access. When the wind whipped up the tails of their coats, Doc reached across himself with his left hand to hold his overcoat over the shotgun.

When Virgil veered for the boardwalk, the Earp party formed a double rank—Virge and Wyatt in front, Doc and Morg in back. As they stepped down from the tread boards at the Papago Store to pass the rear entrance to the O.K. Corral, Behan finally hurried toward them, his eyes glazed and unfocused, all poise abandoned.

Virge turned his head to speak to his deputies. "There might be others on their way into town," he said quietly. "Doc, you stay on the street and keep your eyes open. If anybody shows up and tries to box us in, use the scattergun."

"I don't care to get back-shot today, Doc," Morg said. "So let 'em have it."

"All right," Doc replied and then laughed quietly at the panic on Johnny Behan's face as the sheriff stopped before them and began to walk backward in a moving parley.

"Now wait a minute!" Behan said, trying to inject some authority into his whining, tenor voice. "There's no need for you to go down there!" Behan announced this breathlessly, his voice cracking twice. "I won't have any trouble, Virgil."

When he got no reply from the Earps, Behan abandoned all attempts at presenting any kind of official persona. "Virgil!" he yelled. "For God's sake, don't go down there! I'm the sheriff, and I won't have any trouble!"

Without turning his head to acknowledge the sheriff, Virgil spoke in a quiet, firm voice. "We're just going to collect their guns, Johnny."

"I've already disarmed them!" Behan shot back, frantically backstepping to stay ahead of the Earps.

At this announcement, Virgil slid his pistol far to the left side of his waistband under his coat. He then took the cane in his right hand. Wyatt thrust his Colt's back into his coat pocket.

At Fly's boardinghouse Behan stopped abruptly, as if only now realizing the importance of distancing himself from what was coming. As the Earps brushed past him, Wyatt studied the vacant lot, noting the position of each man. Besides the Clantons and McLaurys, there was "Kid" Claiborne standing deeper in the lot. And West Fuller, a friend to Ike Clanton. Fuller was approaching the Cow-boys from the rear of the alleyway, but, seeing the Earps, he began backing away, stumbling and catching himself when his boot heel caught a piece of scrap lumber lying in the dust.

Billy Clanton and Frank McLaury wore their pistols in plain sight, each gun holstered on a cartridge belt and angled at the left hip for a cross-draw. The Cow-boys stood diagonally across the lot between Fly's and the Harwood house, their conversations suspended and their heads turned upon the arrival of the Earps. Two saddled horses took up room in the alleyway. One—Billy's big bay—partially concealed Tom McLaury, who reached over the horse's withers to take a grip on the stock of a rifle booted in a saddle sheath.

When Virgil and Wyatt approached the corner of Fly's building, they stepped over a small ditch recently dug for a water pipe. Just a few paces into the lot, they stopped with Virgil deepest in the alleyway and Wyatt closer to the front corner of the boardinghouse. Morgan took a position near the ditch, and Doc remained in the street, where Tom McLaury now began to sidle toward the boardwalk as if he might bolt. Doc moved quickly toward Tom and pressed the muzzle of the shotgun into McLaury's belly.

"You don't want to leave the party early, do you?" Doc said through a tight smile. When Tom retreated back into the lot, Doc backed into the street for a better view of the thoroughfare.

West Fuller broke and ran for the gap in the buildings between the boardinghouse and the photographic studio that connected to it by a short walkway covered by an awning. Seeing Fuller's retreat, "Kid" Claiborne began to sidestep along the same route.

Frank McLaury and Billy Clanton stiffened as though every muscle in their bodies had tensed. Tom peered over the bay again, only his head and shoulders showing above the bow of the saddle. Beneath his new gauze bandage, Ike Clanton's eyes widened, showing a lot of white. His attention darted back and forth between each of the dark-suited men before him, until finally he focused on Wyatt. With his tongue flicking around his lips, Ike wiped his palms against his trousers and took two steps forward. Wild-eyed and mouth agape, he repeatedly pushed his palms at the air, as though the motion might somehow appease the lawmen.

"Where's all your fight now, you little sonovabitch," Morgan hissed to Ike. "It's what you been askin' for, ain't it? Now you can have it."

Virgil cut off all conversation by pointing the cane forward, sweeping it from Frank McLaury to Billy Clanton. "I want your guns!" he ordered. "Throw up your hands!" Virgil's deep voice boomed off the building walls and filled the lot.

Frank reached across his body and gripped the butt of his revolver, and Billy did the same. Both men froze with their elbows cocked, their eyes flashing with nervous glints of light as they tried to keep watch over each of the lawmen spread out before them.

"Hold!" Virgil called out, raising the cane skyward, as if it might somehow take command over the moment. "I don't mean that!"

Wyatt's hand was buried in his pocket, his thumb hooked over the hammer of his Colt's. He raised it enough to clear the hammer spur from the hem of the pocket and waited. Then the hammer on Frank's holstered gun clicked back. Billy's followed immediately.

Every man stood motionless, as if the cold day might offer one last chance at sanity. They were like a living photograph. Then one of the horses shifted and nickered, and the wind gusted and kicked up a swirl of dust between the two parties. "Kid" Claiborne had almost reached the safety of Fly's buildings, leaving four men to face four in the lot, the parties standing not twelve feet apart. The moment hung as though a distant bell had been rung in a dream. All were listening to the plangent tone as it faded into the gray void of the sky—all trying to understand its meaning.

The town around them dissolved into irrelevance. For three heart-beats the small lot comprised the whole of the world. Wyatt's vision relaxed to take in the scene as a whole, to see any motion that might arise. *Frank first*, he thought. *Then Billy.*

Growling some unintelligible grunt of defiance, Billy drew his gun in the instant before Frank pulled his. Both men bore down on Wyatt, their faces contorted with hatred as they aimed their revolvers. In a single smooth motion, Wyatt swung his gun up from his pocket, cocked the hammer, and fired. Two quick explosions shattered the silence in the small lot, and, in some peripheral outpost of consciousness, Wyatt acknowledged the ruin of the tacit shell of order that citizens expected to envelop a community.

Billy's bullet whined past him, as Wyatt's echoing shot buckled Frank McLaury at the waist. Frank groaned and clapped his free hand to his midsection, his belligerent face suddenly pale and open with shock.

An eerie pause held the fight in check. Even Virgil hesitated, the cane still held high in his right hand. Wyatt cocked his gun and held it steady on Billy, who had half turned, distracted by Frank's guttural cry. Then rage flooded through the youngest Clanton, and he crouched down, aiming wildly, and fired.

Wyatt put a bullet in Billy's chest, this followed immediately by a shot from Morgan into the stout boy's gun arm. Billy fell heavily against the wall of the Harwood house, but he did not go down. Suddenly, the alley came alive with the explosions of gunpowder—Virgil on Wyatt's left, Morgan on his right and, across from them, Frank and Billy, both staggering, managing to get off more shots. The air seemed to tear apart with the rending sounds of ripped cloth as clouds of smoke began to coalesce between the two parties. Dreamlike and disjointed, every movement seemed unnaturally slow and yet almost too quick to follow.

With empty hands raised before him, Ike rushed at Wyatt and grabbed his arm and shoulders. "I ain't heeled, Wyatt," Ike pleaded. "Don't shoot me! I don't wanna fight!"

"It's commenced!" Wyatt growled. "Go to fightin' or get away!" He slung Ike against the clapboard wall of the boardinghouse and turned back to the fight. Behind him he heard Ike claw his way up to Fly's front porch.

Gunshots popped in erratic bursts. Billy and Frank would not quit. Then Virgil was down, cursing, then up again, firing his gun. Frank stumbled into the street, keeping himself upright with a white-fisted grip on the cheek strap of his panicked horse's bridle. He gawked at the ground, his mouth open, drooling a string of spit.

Tom McLaury fired from beneath the other horse's neck, but Wyatt took aim at Billy again and fired. Billy Clanton, who had kept up a left-handed fight, jerked and began a slow slide down the window of the

Harwood building. He screamed something that was lost in the gunfire, and then he let go a wild shot, the bullet whining off the cold ground near Wyatt's feet. Then Billy's arm lowered as though the weight of the gun was too much for him.

"I'm hit!" Morgan yelled.

Wyatt glanced toward his younger brother and saw Morg getting back on his feet, aiming in the direction of the horse still in the lot. Then Morgan backed into the water ditch and fell again. Wyatt shot high into the haunch of the horse. When it bolted, the deep roar of Doc's shotgun filled the street, and Tom McLaury staggered back, lost to view as he stumbled down the sidewalk toward Third Street.

As Billy struggled to cock his revolver again, Wyatt moved toward Morgan, who had pushed up on one arm to take aim at Frank McLaury in the street. Behind him he heard Virgil yelling at Billy Clanton to lay down his gun. Just then a gun report spun Wyatt to the alleyway between Fly's house and photographic studio. He leveled his gun, but no one was there—only a cloud of smoke suspended at the corner of the building. Turning back to the fight, he found Billy Clanton sitting in the dirt, legs stretched out before him, his arms limp at his sides. Frank McLaury was weaving across the street, struggling to keep his balance, teeth bared as he snarled at his enemies.

Doc turned sideways to Frank, arm outstretched like a duelist, his small nickel-plated pistol gathering unnaturally bright light from the gray of the day. Releasing his horse, Frank McLaury raised his gun, using his left forearm as a rest.

"I got you now!" Frank growled at Doc, his raspy voice scraping from his throat like a strained cough.

"You're a daisy if you do!" Doc taunted. "Blaze away!"

Doc fired, and, simultaneously, Morgan, half-sprawled on the ground, fired, too. McLaury's gun went off as he crumpled headlong to the street. Immediately, Doc recoiled and lost his balance. In a flash he was up, hurrying toward the felled Cow-boy, Doc's nickel-plated revolver outstretched before him as though the gun were pulling him forward. But it was over.

Acrid smoke hung in the air and drifted in a ghostlike curtain across the alley, the memory of the gunfire still lingering between the buildings like a sustained echo.

Carrying a Henry rifle, Buck Fly ran out of his house in his shirt-sleeves and entered the lot. Cautiously, he approached Billy Clanton and wrested away the boy's gun.

"Gimme some goddamn bullets," Billy begged, but he hadn't even the strength to raise his hand.

Virgil hobbled backward and leaned against Fly's building as he pulled up his trouser leg to examine his wound. Morgan sat in the street, blood soaking through his coat at either shoulder. Doc, with a hand clapped to his hip, hovered over Frank McLaury and screamed something that Wyatt could not hear for the blurred memory of muted gunfire still trapped inside his head.

Working on rote, Wyatt tapped the empty shells from his gun, let them drop into the lot, and then he reloaded. When Virgil nodded, Wyatt moved to Morgan to inspect his wounds.

"Wyatt?" Morg said, his face a mix of anger and regret.

Wyatt knelt. "Quiet, Morg. You rest easy. We'll get a doctor."

"Wyatt, I've got a wagon ready." It was Fred Dodge, who seemed to materialize out of nowhere. "The doctor's on his way."

Cradling the back of Morgan's head in his hand, Wyatt looked toward the crowd gathered at the corner of Third Street. Through the copse of legs he glimpsed Tom McLaury's dark vest and blue shirt, all of it now glistening with red.

"Take my brothers to Virgil's house, Fred," Wyatt said. "We need to get 'em off the street."

"Wyatt!" called a strident voice, loud enough to be heard by the crowd gathering in the street.

Wyatt turned to see Johnny Behan marching out from Fly's covered walkway, ordering people back from the alley. His face was set with unnatural determination. The sheriff slowed at the ditch and then stopped six feet away from Wyatt. Clasping his coat lapels Behan took in a deep breath. His pistol hung at his hip, more ornament than tool.

"Wyatt," Behan announced, "I'm going to have to arrest you."

The words were forced, as if rehearsed in front of a mirror. When Wyatt stood and turned squarely to face him, Behan lost the erect carriage of his shoulders and seemed to be at a loss for more words. The onlookers edging past the two lawmen looked back to see Wyatt's face.

"I'll see any decent officer, but you won't be arresting me today, Behan."

"I am sheriff of Cochise County and—"

Behan closed his mouth when Wyatt took two steps toward him. The sheriff still smelled like a flower garden from his visit with the barber. His body leaned back as if a stiff wind had caught him unawares, but his boots remained fixed to the ground. Wyatt's Colt's was still in his hand, hanging down at arm's length. Tightening his grip on the gun, he held cold eyes on Behan and watched the man's attempt at bravado yield to a pallid fear. Wyatt despised everything about the man, but it would do him no good in the polls to knock the county sheriff senseless.

"You threw us, Johnny!" Wyatt said, his voice contained and private, yet carrying the ring of a blacksmith's sledge. "You told us you'd disarmed them."

Behan licked his lips and stared at three men in the vacant lot who were picking up Billy Clanton. With a visible effort the sheriff covered the sheepish frown on his face with a veneer of indignation.

"No. I did not say that!"

At the absurdity of the reply, Wyatt felt the flame of rage roaring in his chest now unexpectedly subside. Behan was no better than the men who lay dead in the lot . . . or the scourge of saddlers spread throughout the county who lived off the spoils of cattle rustling and stagecoach robberies. They all covered their tracks with lies, every Cow-boy willing to perjure himself for the sake of any other. Allowing the ice in his eyes to melt, Wyatt pushed his revolver snug into his waistband and turned away from Behan the same as he would ignore a whimpering dog.

Morgan gritted his teeth as several men lifted him into the wagon. Virgil sat next to him, his bloodied leg stretched out on the wagon bed. When the wagon lurched forward, Virgil winced and grabbed for the side panel. Then Allie was there, her head bare in the raw weather. Breathing hard from running she walked alongside the wagon, her tiny hand clamped over Virgil's big fist.

In front of Fly's, Doc Holliday stood away from the crowd, fishing a handkerchief from his coat pocket. After carefully folding it, he worked the linen under his waistband to his hip. When he looked up, he saw Wyatt staring at him above the heads of the citizens milling about on the street. Doc made the same little salute he had given Billy Clanton earlier in the day. Wyatt gave the barest of nods.

The young boy who did odd jobs for Fly was picking up the spent cartridges where Wyatt had stood when he had reloaded. Beyond the Harwood house two teams of men carried Tom McLaury and Billy Clanton around the corner on Third Street. Tom was limp, his mouth moving but making no sound. Billy screamed to be left alone so he could die in peace. In the middle of Fremont, Frank's lifeless body could wait for the coroner's wagon.

Following the wagon carrying his brothers, Wyatt walked through the crowd, his back erect, the Colt's in his waistband pressing its weight against his belly. He passed under the shadow of the big cottonwood and turned into Virgil's yard. Virge's dog sat on the porch staring attentively at the door, listening to the voices inside, giving Wyatt only a glance before keeping watch on the door again.

Before going inside, Wyatt stopped and looked back at the distant crowd still gathered in the street. It seemed everyone in town had turned out. With the reverberation of gunshots still clouding his ears, he used the distance to examine a broader picture of what had just happened. This day would affect a lot of things, he knew, including his chances in the elections, but it was too soon to know if he had done a constructive thing or a damaging one. He only knew that he hadn't really been given a choice. It simply had to be done.

Looking across the street, he saw Mattie standing in the doorway of their house. *How long had she been there?* he wondered. They stared at one another across the cold and dusty road, one as silent and unmoving as the other, until finally she backed slowly into the house and closed the door. The more Wyatt took the simple dwelling's measure, the more it began to take on the appearance of a squat casket, its contents as lifeless as that of any pine box lowered into the ground.

The doctor's voice carried through the house behind him, asking for Allie to bring clean rags. Wyatt turned and went through the door to check on his brothers.

CHAPTER 16

After the Street Fight, 1881

Tombstone, A.T.

At dusk Wyatt walked to Fly's boardinghouse, where Kate was tending to Doc's wound. Wyatt entered the room, set his hat on a table, and sat in the cushioned chair by the wall. From there he watched Kate saturate a folded cloth with antiseptic. When she pressed it to Doc's hip, he jolted as if the bed had bucked. Doc craned his head around to sneer at her, but Kate would not look at him.

"Why don't you just shoot me?" Doc hissed.

Kate capped the bottle. "You not haff enough shootingk for one day?"

Wyatt felt the comment directed as much to him as to Doc.

Doc gave her a spiteful smile. "I might shoot *you* before we're done here."

With bloodied rags and a porcelain bowl in tow, Kate left the room. Wyatt stood and approached the bed. Doc's scrawny buttocks and thin legs were as pale as the bed linens. Pulling the sheet over himself, Doc rolled to his side, his wry smile dropping away as his eyes fixed on Wyatt's.

"Why in hell didn't you shoot Ike? This was his party, you know."

"He wasn't heeled," Wyatt said and nodded toward the wound. "How bad is it?"

Doc frowned and shook his head. "Superficial . . . just plowed across the side of my ass." His eyes traveled down and then up the length of Wyatt's torso. "You weren't hit?"

Wyatt shook his head. "Morg got the worst of it. Bullet went through both shoulders and clipped his backbone. Virge was shot clean through in the lower leg. Didn't touch the bone."

Doc tilted his head toward the door. "What's the consensus out there?"

"Town's behind us, seems like . . . but Behan's already changed his story . . . twice."

Doc coughed up a caustic laugh. "I wish he'd been out there with his friends when the ball opened. We could have freed up that sheriff's post for you right quick, Wyatt."

Wyatt looked around the room. Doc's gray coat was streaked with dust and draped over the beveled top of a trunk. Wyatt remembered seeing Doc fall in Fremont Street when Frank McLaury had fired his last shot.

"Wyatt," Doc said, "did you see West Fuller out there? He's a friend of Ike's, you know. He got to Tom McLaury pretty damned quick after it was over. I heard him tellin' folks that Tom was unarmed." Doc produced his ironic smile. "It was Tom who shot Morgan."

Wyatt nodded. "Fred Dodge said they didn't find Tom's gun. Fuller must've picked it up."

"Him or Behan," Doc said through a sneering smile.

The two friends stared at one another, weighing the consequences to come. Wyatt picked up the bottle of antiseptic, read the label, and set it back on the night table.

"You gonna be all right?" Wyatt asked.

Doc frowned. "Oh, hell yeah. Go see about your brothers."

Wyatt hesitated. "I wanted to see about *you*."

Doc grimaced as he repositioned himself in the bed. "All right, well . . . you've done that. Now go on and see to Virgil and Morgan."

Wyatt picked up his hat and stopped at the door. "Doc," he said, half turning and looking down into the crown of the hat as he fingered the sweatband. "I'm obliged . . . we all are . . . for you standing with us." He looked back at his friend.

Doc reached for his silver flask on the table. "Well, Wyatt," he said, his voice finding its melodic wit. "If you don't have something worth standing for, maybe you don't have much."

As he drank, Doc stared at Wyatt over the flask, and for a moment his pale and sickly eyes filled with what seemed a childlike devotion. Wyatt nodded and walked into the front room, where Kate stood by the window that overlooked the vacant lot.

"He risk hiss life for you," she said. Her voice reflected off the cold glass in a harsh whisper meant only for his ears. "Seems like he hass a habit uff dat." She flashed a whimsical smile as though she were alone in the room. "You t'ink he ever do somet'ing like dat for me?"

Having no answer for that, Wyatt looked around the walls of the room at the picture frames enclosing Fly's photographic work. When it seemed Kate would say no more, he fitted his hat to his head.

"Let me know if he needs anything, Kate."

Her head bounced with a soundless laugh, and she turned to show her contempt. "Needt? Only two t'ings Doc needt, and I take care of one. The ot'er is up to Godt." She faced the window again, and Wyatt looked past her to the shades of twilight beginning to soften the details in the lot where the fight had taken place. He thought of telling her what it meant for friends to stand together, but then he remembered the affidavit that Kate had signed against Doc. She would not understand that kind of loyalty. *It's probably easier to be Doc's friend*, Wyatt thought, *than his woman.*

"Evenin', Kate," he said and left her standing alone in the room.

Back at the house Virgil lay in bed with his exposed leg swathed in fresh bandages. His Colt's lay on top of the sheets next to him. James sat in a corner of the room with a Winchester balanced over his knees as he kept watch on the street through a crack in the curtain. In the front room, John Vermillion stacked firewood from a pile he had split out back.

Allie, uncharacteristically quiet, moved in and out of the room supplying wet cloths or dishes of food or hot tea—anything within the scope of Virgil's needs. She seemed to bestow upon Wyatt a new measure of respect, which he took to be a sign of gratitude for standing shoulder to shoulder with Virgil in the street fight. Bessie rattled cookware in the kitchen, from where the aroma of pan-fried bread spread through the house.

"Behan came by after you left," Virgil said and made a pained look that soon disappeared behind his stoic eyes. "Clum says our sheriff's been proddin' the vigilance committee to deal with us with a rope. 'Course Behan denies it. Says he's my friend, and we done just right out there in the fight." He forced a low grumbling laugh. "Behan's a damned fool. Hell, the vigilantes are backin' us all the way. Said they wish we'd a' killed Ike, too."

Wyatt remained standing with his hat in his hand. "It'll come to more killin' before it's over."

Allie came to the door and stood looking at Virgil, her face anxious with the need to do something. "Go on and eat something, Allie," Virgil said. "Wyatt and I are havin' a talk."

She looked at Wyatt and then at James. "Who's ready to eat something?"

James narrowed one eye. "*You* cook it, or Bessie?"

"I made cornbread and greens," Allie said, raising her chin like a challenge.

James leaned the rifle against the wall. "Then, hell yes, I'll eat," he said with a chuckle and followed her into the kitchen. Virgil pushed himself higher on his pillow. Wyatt dropped his hat on the bed and sat in James's chair.

"Did you know that Frank McLaury told Behan to come to Hafford's and disarm *us*?" Virge quipped.

Wyatt nodded absently. It mattered little to him what Frank had or hadn't said.

"They didn't find a gun on Tom," Wyatt said quietly.

"Yeah, well, to hell with that!" Virgil's eyes flashed with anger. "He shot twice from behind the damned horse. His arm was stretched out right under the horse's neck. He's the one that hit Morg."

Wyatt nodded. "Somebody picked up his gun, hoping it would go hard on us."

Cursing under his breath, Virgil repositioned his leg. Wyatt leaned forward in the chair, settled his forearms on his knees, and kneaded the knuckles of one hand.

"I went to the undertaker's. The McLaurys and Billy Clanton are in the front window, dressed up like bankers. Got a sign in the window: 'Murdered on the streets of Tombstone.'"

Virgil grunted. "That's Ike's work."

They were quiet, listening to James dole out his playful banter about Allie's good cooking. It was a simple sound of family that reminded Wyatt of better times.

"Oh, an' listen to this this," Virgil said. "Behan said we misunderstood him. Claims he never told us he had disarmed those boys. Said he'd gone down there for the *purpose* of disarming them." He huffed a quiet laugh through his nose. "Reckon the Irish sonovabitch just forgot to mention he was unsuccessful at it."

Wyatt threaded his fingers together and waited for Virgil's temper to settle. "Somebody took a shot at us from behind Fly's."

Virgil's eyes pinched as he chewed on that information. "Could'a been Ike," he said.

Wyatt shook his head. "Ike wasn't heeled. They found him hiding over on Toughnut in the back of a saloon. I doubt he would'a stopped running long enough to aim at anything."

"Yellow son of a bitch," Virgil said. "You should'a shot him when he took hold o' you."

Wyatt looked down at his boots. "Virge," he said in the flat tone he used whenever he had to repeat himself. "He wasn't heeled."

Virgil's mouth curled in disgust. "He needed killing more'n them others." When Wyatt made no response, Virgil pushed himself higher in the bed. "Go see Morg. He's got a hell of a pain runnin' down his arms."

Wyatt stood and picked up his hat. Softly slapping the brim against his leg, he stared down at his brother's wound.

"What about Doc?" Virge asked. "I hear he got shot in the ass."

"You know Doc. He's drinking his medicine right now."

"We owe him, don't we?"

Wyatt raised his hat before him and turned it once as though inspecting the straightness of the brim. "Reckon I'll always be owing Doc," he said and left the room to check on Morgan.

*****

The funeral—the largest event in the town's history—would have convinced a newcomer to Tombstone that the founding fathers had died. Most attendees were there simply to witness the aftermath of the town's most dramatic fight. Others wanted to see Ike Clanton's face, to see how grief mixed with humility and cowardice. As for the rancher friends of the Cow-boys, they represented a tribute as much to cheap Mexican beeves as to any sort of friendship with the rustlers.

At the coroner's inquest, Johnny Behan worked his smooth tenor voice to spin a story touched both by professionalism and personal regret. "The Earps would not heed my order," Behan swore. "They walked past me into the lot, and Billy Clanton called out, 'Don't shoot me!' and 'I don't want to fight!' He raised both hands above his head. Then Tom threw open his vest to show he was unarmed. I had already checked Tom—and Ike, too—and found no weapons on either of them."

Ike and "Kid" Claiborne told identical stories: that the Cow-boys had thrown up their hands at Virgil's order . . . that Holliday and Morgan Earp had opened fire on defenseless men. A gambling friend of the McLaurys swore that at Hafford's he had overheard Virgil say that he would not arrest the Cow-boys but shoot them on sight. With these testimonies flying about town, there were now questions that seemed to have contradictory answers.

In the last days of October, Ike Clanton filed murder charges against the Earps and Holliday. With Virgil and Morgan still convalescing at home, Wyatt and Doc appeared before Justice of the Peace Wells Spicer and had their bail set at ten thousand dollars each, a sum quickly amassed by the businessmen in town. Spicer agreed to a preliminary hearing to decide whether enough evidence warranted a trial by jury.

The hearing began with redundant but damning testimonies by prosecution witnesses, all swearing that Tom McLaury had not carried a gun.

And, worse, that Doc Holliday had precipitated the fight by shooting first while the Cow-boys held their hands in the air.

With the sheriff's contrived testimony printed in the newspapers, the swell of culpability fell back upon the Earps, and public support for them spiraled steadily downward. Even Mayor Clum, in his editorials, began to distance himself from his chief of police's actions.

Will McLaury, a mourning brother and Texas lawyer, joined the district attorney and milked the town for sympathy while pouring money into the expense account of the county's investigation into the shoot-out. He convinced the judge to revoke bail, and Wyatt and Doc were remanded to the county jail, where they would spend the next sixteen nights. At the insistence of pro-Earp townsmen, four men on the vigilance committee stood guard outside day and night.

In the courtroom, each time the defense took its turn, Tom Fitch—the most eloquent and most expensive attorney in the territory—mounted a skillful rebuttal to every false claim made against the Earps and Holliday. But his finest hour came during an unexpected windfall of support from one of the prosecution witnesses. It was as if a surprise witness had surfaced on behalf of the Earps. The turn in momentum was something no one on either side could have predicted. The witness was Ike Clanton.

Ike sneered as he looked at everyone but Wyatt. "Yeah, he offered me a deal, but I declined it." Ike sat back in the witness chair and cocked his head to one side. "I asked him why he wanted these boys so bad—Leonard, Head, and Crane." Ike nodded toward Wyatt but still would not meet his eyes. "Said he had some business dealings with these boys and couldn't afford for them to be taken alive on account o' they might talk."

Clanton wiped at a smile with his fingers and kept his gaze angled to the floor. "He told me him and his brother, Morgan, piped off money from the Wells, Fargo shipment to Doc Holliday and Billy Leonard." Ike looked up quickly at Fitch. "This was the money supposed to be on the Benson stage last March, you see."

Fitch arched an eyebrow. "But at the coroner's inquest, Mr. Clanton, you testified that you *did* have a deal with Wyatt Earp . . . and *that* was why he wanted to kill you."

"That ain't what I meant. I meant he *tried* to make that deal so he could capture them boys . . . I mean, kill them. That's what I meant to say. He needed to kill them."

The lawyer pushed his hands deep into his pockets and rocked back on his heels. "So, you say that Wyatt Earp admitted to you that he was stealing Wells, Fargo money." He held a straight face and stared at Ike.

Clanton frowned sideways at his interrogator as the district attorney objected. Spicer sustained the objection, but now the illogic of it all had been set free inside the courtroom.

"And, Mr. Clanton," Fitch continued, "if Wyatt Earp, as you say, 'piped off' money from the strongbox before the shipment departed—" The lawyer smiled here, taking his time. "Isn't it curious that there was no money missing from the Kinnear stage once it arrived at Benson?"

Doc leaned close to Wyatt. "I believe Ike just sat right back into his own shit."

"I'm just telling you what he told me," Ike huffed. "Doc Holliday told me . . . or rather Billy Leonard told me that it was Holliday killed Bud Philpott. And Virgil Earp told me to get word to those boys they needn't worry 'bout a posse trackin' 'em . . . that it was all for show." Ike flung his hand toward Wyatt and Doc. "See, they wanna kill me 'cause of all this that I know 'bout the Earps."

"And yet," said Fitch, "you alone were spared in the fight . . . you, who could have been killed most easily." He frowned and flung his hands out to his sides, posing like a man thoroughly confused. "By your own testimony, Wyatt Earp called for you to fight or to get away."

Clanton sat back and sulked. "Well, I didn't have my damned gun, now, *did* I?"

The defense attorney waited, still frozen in space with his arms extended. "And he spared you because of that?"

"Well, sure. They can't shoot an unarmed man, can they? Not right there in town."

"And, yet, you say they killed an unarmed Tom McLaury . . . *'right there in town.'*"

The room was quiet, all the spectators waiting for Ike to smooth out the wrinkles of his story. But the silence drew out. With the thread of Ike's fabrications so thoroughly unraveled, the lawyer grinned and waited.

"*What!*" Clanton snapped.

Ignoring Clanton, Fitch let his arms slap against his sides. "No more questions of this extremely reliable witness, your honor."

On the day following, Wyatt took the stand and read from a prepared written statement that chronicled the animosity between the Earps and the Cow-boys, starting with the theft of the army mules. He worked his way through the threats made by the Clantons, McLaurys, and Ringo concerning the arrests of Stilwell and Spence. When he outlined the terms of the Wells, Fargo deal with Ike, Frank McLaury, and Joe Hill, the Cow-boys in the room grew painfully quiet. Throughout the telling, Ike vehemently shook his head to anyone who would look at him.

After describing the street fight, Wyatt ended his testimony by offering two documents: one from the people of Wichita and the other from Dodge City. Each paper was signed by fifty leading citizens attesting to his character. The Dodge petition even referred to him as their marshal, though technically he had never actually held that post. The people of Dodge City had apparently considered him their chief enforcer. When Wyatt stepped down from the witness box, his back was straight as a fence post.

The defense witnesses who followed completed the disintegration of the case against the Earps. Chief among these was a railroad engineer, who had come into town on the morning of the fight. It was he who had warned Virgil of threats he had overheard near the Dexter Corral. Curious, the railroad man had followed the lawmen to Fremont Street, where he witnessed the fight from start to finish. He corroborated Wyatt's version of the details in every respect, reasserting that it had been Frank and Billy who pulled and fired on Wyatt first, only Wyatt, quick and cool, still managed to hit his man.

Both an army surgeon and a hotel manager swore to seeing a gun in Tom McLaury's pant pocket just before the fight. Addie Bourland, a milliner, witnessed the initial confrontation in the vacant lot from the front window of her shop across the street. She testified that no person in the lot had raised his hands to surrender, and that the shooting had started simultaneously from both parties.

It was enough. At the end of November—one month after the hearing had begun—Spicer set the Earps and Holliday free, not to be bound over to a grand jury.

*****

The political battles that manifested in the rival newspapers proved as lively as the fight in the vacant lot. The Earps' enemies predictably spoke through the *Nugget*, whose editor was Behan's undersheriff. The *Epitaph* strove for a counterbalance, printing articles that championed Wyatt and his brothers. But balance proved to be an impossibility with the coming January elections. Tombstone's citizens were either pro- or anti-Earp. There was no middle ground.

Threats to the family forced Wyatt to move his clan into the Cosmopolitan Hotel, where he could better protect them from Cow-boy attack. A cadre of friends flocked to him, offering their services as bodyguards, and, of these, Wyatt chose proven gunmen he could depend on: Doc Holliday, McMaster, ex-carpenter John Vermillion, and gambling friend Dan Tipton.

When a fifth man joined their ranks on the night of their second meeting inside Wyatt's room, McMaster visibly tensed, pushed away from the wall where he had been leaning, and stood with his hand resting on the butt of his gun. As he stared at the man, Wyatt stepped beside McMaster.

"Easy, Mac," Wyatt said. "He's with us."

McMaster narrowed his eyes at Creek Johnson, a broad-chested Cow-boy who had ridden at various times with both Ringo and Brocius. Mac's face wrinkled with questions as he turned to Wyatt.

"He's the other one been workin' undercover for you?" Mac whispered.

Wyatt motioned Johnson over, and the big man approached with an open smile, a long turkey wing feather pinned jauntily into his hat brim.

"How ya doin', Sherm?" Creek said. He offered his meaty hand to McMaster and allowed a chuckle. "Reckon we've been hidin' in the same shadows for a while."

Shaking his head, McMaster took Johnson's hand and cut his eyes from Wyatt back to the ex-Cow-boy. "How the hell'd he rope you in?"

Creek propped his hands on his hips and looked down at the toes of his boots before answering. "Gotta brother in the Yuma pen." He nodded toward Wyatt. "Wyatt's workin' with Wells, Fargo . . . says they'll help to git 'im out if . . . you know—" His eyes angled down again, and, when they came up to look at McMaster again, all trace of humor had disappeared from Johnson's face. "That is, if I could see my way to git on the right side o' things and let slip a little information to Wyatt here from time to time." Creek raised his chin and pushed it at McMaster. "What about you?"

McMaster snorted a soft, airy laugh through his nose. "I still ain't sure how he did it, but I'm in for keeps now."

Creek Johnson laughed outright, his big voice filling the room. "That's for damned sure." He arched his eyebrows and leaned forward. "We've crossed a line, *amigo*," he said quietly, "and it ain't one we can cross back." Creek straightened, spewed air through fluttering lips, and shook his head. "Not that I care. I'm sick o' takin' my orders from the likes o' Brocius . . . and that damned moper, Ringo." Johnson tapped a finger twice to his temple. "Ask me, that sour-faced sulker is better'n half loco. Don't care who lives or dies . . . includin' hisself."

When the six men settled in to talk, Wyatt laid out the rotating schedule for guarding their hallway of the hotel. Two men would always take posts on the Earp floor, while two others covered the front and rear entrances of the ground level.

"Wyatt," Creek Johnson said, "for what it's worth, there was a midnight meetin' the other night out in some canyon near Bisbee. Ringo and Brocius and about ten others. Word is, they made up a list for ever'body they plan to put under the ground. O' course, ever'body in this room is on it."

Wyatt nodded. "That's why we're here. We need to see 'em coming." He looked to each man for agreement, and he got it. "Every man here will be paid for his services. There'll be money coming in from Wells, Fargo soon. And from some of the businessmen in town who back us. I'll let you know when that comes in. Right now, get out there to your positions and keep your eyes open. Any shot you hear near or in the hotel, assume it's trouble and get back here to my brothers as quick as you can."

Wyatt and Doc walked down the stairs together into the hotel lobby, Holliday leaning on his cane with every other step. Tipton and Vermillion followed and then separated, one to the front and one to the rear. Outside the street was darkening, and the clerk moved about the lobby lighting the oil lamps bracketed to the posts and walls.

"How are Virgil and Morgan?" Doc said.

"Startin' to move around. Mostly feeling cooped up. But the wounds are healing."

Doc waved the cane around the lobby. "This has got to be expensive, Wyatt."

"Our houses are too exposed. Easier to keep an eye on 'em here in town."

Doc offered an expression of regret. "Virgil know about losing his badge?"

"I told him. He don't like it, but he knows he can't do any marshalin' from his bed. Still, it don't seem to matter to a lot of people that Spicer judged us to be in the right." Wyatt looked around the lobby and catalogued each face as friend or enemy. When he spoke again, he kept all emotion from his voice. "The Cow-boys finally got whipped in court, but it don't seem to count for much. We lost something in all this, Doc. It seems like whatever Behan swore to—no matter how much it was disproved—people remember it."

"That's the nature of the beast, my friend. All you've got to do is plant the seed of doubt, and human beings will provide all the manure to make it grow."

A woman sat at the piano in the barroom and began touching the first notes of a doleful melody Wyatt had heard somewhere in his past. He watched the woman's hands float over the keys, and it might have been the first time in his life that he took music to be some sort of conversation—this one between a man's hopes and his disappointments.

"Wyatt, what about this recent attack on the Benson stage just the other night? Are you going to look into it?"

Wyatt clenched his jaw and stared out the door at the sparse traffic on Allen Street. "I'm not a lawman now, Doc. All I want to do is look out for my family."

Doc nodded. The hotel clerk put a match to the lamp nearest them, and Wyatt leaned in closer to Doc's face.

"What the hell happened to *you*?"

Doc's mood went frosty. "Kate," he said simply. The skin grew tight around his mouth. "Can you believe that bitch was with Ringo when you and I were in jail?"

Wyatt looked back to the sway of the piano player's back. "She still in town?"

"Who knows?" Doc made a sour smile and put on his hat. "Maybe she's with Ringo right now, spreading my disease. Come on. Let's go for a walk."

The December night was bracing, but after the crowded quarters of the hotel, the ring of the boardwalk under their boots and the voices spilling from saloons were liberating. Wyatt chewed off the nub of a cigar and spat it into the street. Doc stopped and struck a match.

"Wyatt, there's a little more to that Cow-boy pact Creek Johnson mentioned. It appears our illustrious enemies engaged in some theatrics . . . built a fire and performed a little ceremony." Doc coughed up a sarcastic laugh. "Written in blood supposedly." When he looked down the walkway, his smile melted into an inanimate shadow. "We're not the only ones on that list. There's Spicer, our lawyers, Mayor Clum, Marsh Williams, and a few others."

"That's just talk," Wyatt said.

"Well," Doc purred, "Mac and Johnson suggest we listen to it." He lifted an eyebrow. "Clum was traveling on that stage to Benson. He thinks they were after him."

"Well," Wyatt replied, "we won't be getting on any stages any time soon."

Holliday offered a fraternal smile. "Wyatt, you don't have to leave Tombstone to find trouble with these boys." He raised his cane to the hotel across the street. "The clerk at the Grand passed on some interesting information to Vermillion. Some o' the Cow-boys are checked into rooms right now—Ringo, Hill, Stilwell . . . several other scum."

Wyatt's face hardened as he surveyed the windows of the Grand Hotel directly across the street from the Cosmopolitan. "Maybe I should get back," Wyatt said, "keep an eye on things."

Doc put a hand on Wyatt's arm. "I'll do that. You've got another appointment." He turned and pointed with the cane through the stagecoach office into the dining room of Brown's Hotel. "Someone's waiting for you." Doc's voice was uncommonly gentle, his head bowed to hide his eyes. "I'll be with your brothers." He gave Wyatt's shoulder a pat and limped away.

As Wyatt passed by the stage line's ticket counter in the hotel lobby, the agent laid down his newspaper. "Hotel kitchen is closed, Mr. Earp. But you're welcome to sit a spell."

Wyatt nodded and stepped into the semi-darkness of the dining room. The tables were empty save for one figure sitting motionless in the back corner. Wyatt removed his hat and moved across the carpet, weaving through the tables, his eyes fixed on the woman's silhouette. He stopped a few feet away and breathed in a scent he remembered.

"Wyatt," she said quietly.

He laid his hat on a nearby table and sat before her. The stillness in the twilit room was like a balm to his problems. This restaurant seemed far removed, a place where no one knew them . . . or *of* them. The sounds from the street arrived muted and irrelevant, while the clean white linen on the table became a pristine altar upon which he might sacrifice all his misdeeds to the past and, with this woman, lay out what was left of his future.

"I'm sorry about your brothers," Sadie said. "I'm thankful, though, that you weren't hurt."

He stroked the linen with his fingertips. "My brothers'll be all right."

She reached across the table and stilled his hand with her own, her touch at once both firm and gentle. "Wyatt, when I was with Johnny, I met some of these men who are against you." Her face drew up with worry. "They're not *like* Johnny. He's all talk, you know. But these men, Wyatt. They're vicious." Her eyes narrowed, and she shook her head. "They have nothing inside them . . . no conscience, no sense of honor . . . nothing. They seem to enjoy the evil that rises up from inside them."

Studying the dark outline of her face and hair, Wyatt considered what it had taken for her to come here . . . to set up this meeting. "I've known men like them all my life, Sadie."

"I know," she said, and she meant it. "Only there are so many of them."

Wyatt looked down at the shape of their combined hands. "All I ever wanted to do was make a good name for myself . . . and, you know, make some money . . . for me and my brothers."

She squeezed his hand, and he looked up at her. "I just need you to be careful, Wyatt. Don't underestimate Johnny."

"It ain't people like Johnny I need to worry about."

She leaned toward him. "Yes, it *is*, Wyatt!" she whispered, pushing the words at him. "It's not just the men who do the killing who are dangerous. In fact, in some ways, they're the least of the problem."

Wyatt looked toward the street beyond the closed sheer curtains, thinking of his brothers lying bandaged in their hotel rooms. For a moment, he could hardly feel her grip on his hand.

"Johnny can't do the hard things, Sadie," he said, turning to her, making a conscious effort to take the edge from his voice. "And, right now, that's mostly what I'm thinkin' about."

She sniffed wetly and wiped at her cheek. "I need you to be safe, Wyatt."

He ran her words through his mind, knowing he would hold on to them when he had to leave her. "I will," he promised. She pulled his hand a few inches closer. The soft sound of their skin on the linen was as intimate as a declaration of her feelings. Her grip tightened.

"I just had to see for myself you were all right," Sadie said and pulled her hand away.

He waited, knowing that she had more to say.

"I'm going back to San Francisco, Wyatt."

He listened to the sound of her breathing and tried to fix her image in his mind. In the dark of the restaurant, the lines of her face were elusive, but he held to what the dim light offered.

"That's where I'll be, Wyatt . . . in San Francisco." She took a folded piece of paper from her purse and pushed it into his hand. Then she stood and pressed her handbag to her stomach. "You'll know when it's time to leave, too," she said. "And now you know where I'll be." With that she turned and walked soundlessly from the room.

He listened to the front door of the hotel open then close. Then he listened to her shoes tap on the boardwalk outside the window, until there was nothing left to hear.

CHAPTER 17

Winter 1881–1882

Tombstone and Cochise County, A.T.

Three nights after Christmas, Virgil—recently returned to his role as chief of police—left Wyatt's game at the Oriental and limped across the street as he headed for his room at the Cosmopolitan. Wyatt was gathering cards from his faro layout when three thunderous explosions from outside stilled the gaming room. By the time Wyatt reached the barroom, Virgil was staggering through the doorway, the left sleeve of his black overcoat shredded at the elbow. The dark fabric was darker still with blood soaking through from his wounds.

"Wyatt," Virgil gasped, his voice bottomless and wavering. The bystanders looked on in shock and came forward only after Wyatt grabbed his brother. "Shotguns," Virge managed in a raspy whisper, "from the building goin' up 'cross the street."

Several men acquired guns from the bartender and rushed outside to investigate, but Wyatt sent for a doctor and a wagon and stayed with his brother. After Virgil was stripped of his coats and laid out on one of the tables in the front room, Wyatt turned his head to see who stood beside him. It was Dan Tipton.

"Before he left, Virge told me to stay here with you, Wyatt," Tipton said. His voice was all-business, unapologetic, but regret was working into his eyes. "He wouldn' let me walk with him. Said it was only half a block to the damned hotel." Tipton shook his head and frowned at Virgil's bullet-riddled arm and back. "Goddamnit!" he hissed. "I should'a gone with 'im."

"Tip, get some help and then get back here to watch the doors and windows. This might not be over."

Doc Goodfellow had Virgil transferred to the Cosmopolitan, where he dug shattered bone from the marshal's arm and shotgun pellets from his back. Finally, Goodfellow dropped his forceps into the porcelain bowl, shook his head, and sat down on the edge of the bed. He stared at Allie. She had been wiping Virge's face with a damp rag, but now the motion of her hand stopped, and her teary gaze fixed on the doctor.

"The arm has got to come off," Goodfellow reported in his no-nonsense voice. "It will be useless after this. There's no bone left in the elbow to connect upper and lower arm."

"Nobody's takin' my arm," Virgil growled. He reached to Allie and laid his good hand in her lap. "Don't you worry, Allie-girl. I still got one good arm for huggin' you."

Wyatt left Virgil's room and moved into the hallway, where Doc Holliday stood guard with McMaster. Both men carried holstered pistols. McMaster held his carbine in one hand. When they turned to Wyatt, their faces carried the same questioning expression.

"How is he?" Holliday asked in his gentlest Southern drawl.

Wyatt was too angry to respond. When he walked to the end of the corridor and stood before the window, Doc followed quietly and stood beside him.

"Wyatt, we found a hat in the construction site where the shots came from. Ike Clanton's name is inked into the sweatband."

Reining in his feelings, Wyatt stared across the street at the windows of the Grand Hotel. "I'll telegraph the US marshal in Prescott. Ask for an appointment and the power to deputize." He turned to let Doc see the hardness in his eyes. "Ride with me?"

Doc straightened, all the customary humor drained from his face. "Hell, yes, I'll ride with you."

Morgan's voice turned them in unison. "When do we go?" He stood two doors down with his shirt puffed out at the shoulders where the bandaging was packed on his wounds.

Wyatt considered him a moment, then worked the buttons of his coat. "We won't leave till I see how it's gonna go with Virge. I'll let you know."

Morgan made a fist and circled his elbow in a rolling motion, testing his shoulder. "James sent word to Ma and Pa. Got a wire back tonight. Warren's comin' into town." His mouth tightened to a vindictive smile. "God help the men that see *us* comin'."

Doc chuckled and glared out the window. "God won't have a damned thing to do with it," he whispered, his words matching the raw cold of the night.

*****

Over the next weeks, Virgil gained strength—except for his left arm, which continued to hang useless at his side. When Warren arrived in Tombstone, he was assigned full time to Virgil and Morgan, while the rest of the coterie of gunmen rotated through their posts around the hotel. No incidents with the Cow-boys developed in town, but out in the hinterlands of Cochise County the story was different. Two stages were held up, one near Contention and the other near Hereford. It seemed the outlaws were taking advantage of a time when the Earps were staying close to town.

As soon as Virgil's voice regained enough strength to declare the certainty of his recovery, Wyatt rode out with his posse to find the men who had back-shot his brother. Under the mantle of both a deputy US marshal and a Wells, Fargo operative, he and his hand-picked gunmen combed the territory. They were looking for any one of nine men named on a list supplied by McMaster. Ringo headed that list. Following him were Ike Clanton, Curly Bill, Frank Stilwell, and Pete Spence. It mattered little to Wyatt what part a man had played in any crime. To him they were all a part of the same spreading disease. Any Cow-boy, by Wyatt's definition, was vermin.

After four days the posse returned empty handed, and Wyatt learned that Ike Clanton had come into Tombstone and surrendered to Sheriff Behan. Based on the evidence of the hat, Clanton stood trial for the ambush on Virgil, but a parade of witnesses swore that Ike was in

Charleston on the night of the attack. After the trial, as jubilant Cow-boys shuffled out of the courtroom, the judge, lingering at his bench, summoned Wyatt with the curl of a finger. After Wyatt approached, the judge held an expectant look on his face as he waited for the last spectator to leave his courtroom.

"Wyatt," he finally said, leaning closer to compensate for his whis-pered message, "it appears the judicial system is not working too well in Cochise County."

Wyatt narrowed his eyes at the man's conspiratorial tone. "What would you have me do?"

The judge looked pointedly into Wyatt's eyes. "Why don't you just leave your prisoners out in the brush and let the coyotes deliberate over them?" He stared at Wyatt for several heartbeats, the whites of his fiery eyes bright as molten metal. Then he rose from his bench and marched in a long angry stride to his private quarters at the back of the room.

When Wyatt left the courtroom, he found Doc and Dan Tipton waiting for him just outside the door. Beyond the boardwalk, a knot of Cow-boys stood talking and laughing in the street. Ike Clanton pointed at Wyatt, and the others turned, each man holding the same sneering smile on his face.

"Wanna thank you boys for findin' my hat, Earp," Ike called out.

Holliday started for Clanton, but Wyatt clasped a hand to Doc's bony elbow. "He's all wind, Doc. Don't let him goad you."

The Cow-boys in the street huddled together again to mumble and gloat, only Stilwell and Spence continuing to glance over their shoulders at Wyatt. Joe Hill, Pony Diehl, and the others laughed at Ike's nonstop monologue. Ringo stood alone on the other side of the street, his hang-dog expression like a mask of apathy. Leaning against an awning post he seemed content to watch from the shadows. Then something changed in his eyes. With his gaze fixed on Holliday, he stepped midway into the street, stopped, and squared his boots to face the Earp party.

"What's the matter, Holliday? Daddy won't let you come out and play?"

When Doc stiffened, Wyatt reached for his arm again, but Doc jerked away before he could be restrained. "Doc," Wyatt whispered. "We don't need more trouble."

Keeping his eyes on Ringo, Doc pivoted his head slightly. "Maybe *I* do," he replied pleasantly.

Stepping into the street, Doc seemed as relaxed as a man about to greet an old friend. Stopping little more than an arm's reach from Ringo, he adjusted his stance enough to put his right shoulder ahead of the left.

"On the contrary, I'll be your daisy. I even brought my toys." Smiling, he slowly raised his right hand to pat the bulge in his coat at his left breast.

Ringo's sullen face became oddly animated, as though he were remembering a forgotten joke from his past. His eyes became jittery and took on a new light. Following Doc's example, he carefully raised a hand, but his fingers slipped into the side pocket of his coat. Doc slid his hand inside his own coat, and both men stood in that pose, their attention locked on one another with a resolve so fierce that passersby in the street began to give the two a wide berth and look back over their shoulders lest they miss the town's latest eruption of violence.

The group of Cow-boys began a slow retreat from the line of fire, their boots making a quiet scuffle in the cold street. Other pedestrians on the sidewalk went about their business, unaware of the violent potential building beneath the seemingly civil confrontation.

"Must be hard on you, Holliday," Ringo taunted and canted his head toward Wyatt on the boardwalk. "Your daddy over there making all the rules for you." Ringo's smile widened. "And your mama . . . Kate . . . signing affidavits to have you locked up."

Doc was unfazed. "If you will be so kind as to initiate this transaction, suh," he purred and glanced down briefly to indicate Ringo's pocketed hand. Then Doc smiled with one corner of his mouth. "That's for the sake of the judicial charade that is sure to follow after I put a bullet into your black heart. So please, pull that shooter whenever you feel lucky."

Wyatt walked into the street. "Doc?"

Big Jim Flynn, a current deputy marshal who had worked under Virgil, came out of the county recorder's building rolling a cigarette. Spotting the trouble brewing between Ringo and Holliday, he stuffed the cigarette into a pocket and called out from the boardwalk.

"Hold on there!" he commanded, his deep voice freezing the other Cow-boys in place but having no effect on the two antagonists.

Flynn hurried into the street in his lumbering gait, came up behind Ringo, and locked him in a bear hug with his long arms. At the same time, Wyatt pulled Holliday away.

"Why are you boys carryin' guns?" the deputy demanded. He loosened his hold on Ringo enough to extract a Colt's revolver from the man's pocket. Flynn stuffed the gun behind the buckle of his cartridge belt. Then, out of deference to Wyatt, he held out his flattened hand to Holliday. Doc handed over his weapon.

"Let's the four of us walk down to the city jail and sort this out," Flynn suggested.

After paying fines for carrying firearms against city ordinance, Ringo and Holliday were given staggered releases, with a strong encouragement to go their separate ways. At the request of Deputy Flynn, Wyatt stayed behind to parley.

Flynn sat at the desk and motioned Wyatt toward the visitor's chair. "How's Virgil comin' along?"

Wyatt remained standing and shook his head. "His lawing days are likely behind him. The arm is no good to him."

Flynn frowned at the papers on the desk and nodded. "Listen, Wyatt," he began and brought up a sober face, "Behan and his crowd o' politicians have got their fingers in a lot o' the pie. I ain't just talkin' about Cochise County. They got connections in the territorial government. These men know how to stir up a lot of talk about a fellow."

"I know that," Wyatt said.

Flynn took in a lot of air, inflated his cheeks, and exhaled so quietly it might have been a sigh. "Yeah, well, what you might not know is they're pushin' the federal marshal in Prescott to cut you loose . . . both you and Virgil."

"Dake wouldn't do that," Wyatt said.

The deputy raised an eyebrow like an apology. "He might not have a choice." Flynn nodded to the gun strapped to Wyatt's waist. "Only reason you can carry *that* is your badge. I can't extend that right to your temporary deputies." He nodded toward the street. "Like Holliday. Not unless he's on official assignment with you." He leaned his forearms on the desk and shook his head with a show of regret. "If you lose that badge, Wyatt, you're going to be an easy target for the Cow-boy crowd."

"I'll be all right," Wyatt said and waited to see if there was more.

Seeming reluctant to let the conversation end there, Flynn nodded and stood, and the two men shook hands. "Watch your back, Wyatt," he said, "and give my best to Virgil."

By the time Wyatt returned to Virgil's room to check on his brother, Flynn's warning had planted doubts in his head. He knew that the machinations of politics were too abstract for him, and, as a result, he had always relied on physical action to speak for him in the public eye. Now, as he relayed Flynn's words to his brother, he began to realize the full potential of the threat to his aspirations.

"You still plan to run for sheriff against Behan?" Virge asked.

Wyatt dropped his hat on the foot of Virgil's bed and took the chair by the window. "It's about all I got," Wyatt said, his voice atypically soft in the privacy of the room.

Virge pursed his lips and stared out the doorway, where Allie prepared a meal on a table she had converted to a sideboard. "Maybe we oughta make the first move on this, Wyatt. Turn in our resignations. That way, if Dake really does plan to fire us, we come out better by pulling out first." Virge turned to check Wyatt's expression. "Better on your record that way."

Wyatt frowned. "How's that going to look good for me . . . quittin'? I can't see people wantin' to vote for a man who does that."

"You quit on Shibell, didn't you?"

Wyatt's jaw clenched, and his eyes hardened with the memory. "That was about loyalty to Bob Paul."

Virge pursed his lips again and nodded. "All right, then we make this about loyalty, too."

"To what?" Wyatt said.

"To the citizens," Virgil replied, his voice more animated now. "If the people are saying the Earps are too powerful or ambitious or whatever it is they're thinkin', we'll show 'em we ain't." Virge adjusted himself higher in the bed. "Look, we'll get our lawyer, Fitch, to write a letter to Dake, and we'll post it in the *Epitaph*."

Wyatt looked away for a time and fixed his attention on Virgil's revolver lying on the bed covers. Shaking his head once, Wyatt cleared his throat.

"Don't feel right to me, Virge. Seems too private to print in a newspaper." He let Virgil see the distaste on his face. "It's like somethin' Frank McLaury would do."

Virgil smiled with his eyes. "This'll work for us, Wyatt. Hell, I wouldn' bet on Dake acceptin' our resignations anyway. We're the only real law he's got down here."

Wyatt scowled. "So, we're puttin' this in the paper just for show?"

Virgil's smile worked its way over the rest of his face. "Hell, yes. We'll let the damned newspaper work in our favor for a change. I'll take care of the whole thing. Fitch is coming to talk to me tomorrow."

Wyatt studied his brother for a time, seeing the contrast of optimism in Virgil's face compared to the ruination of his arm. He stood and picked up his hat. When he looked at Virgil again, Wyatt opened the lapel of his coat and tapped the badge pinned there.

"Be a shame to lose this right now. We might have as many enemies as we've got friends."

Virgil stared for several seconds at the bright metal shield that he, himself, had worn. "This could help you get that sheriff's badge, Wyatt."

Wyatt narrowed his eyes. "You really believe that?"

Virgil flattened his good hand in the air before him and tottered it back and forth, like a spun coin coming to rest on a tabletop. "Might," he said and then smiled. "Regardless, I can tell you Dake ain't gonna let us go."

*****

Two weeks later, the Earps' lawyer, Tom Fitch, drafted and published the resignation letter in the *Epitaph*, but it was the card he ran in the *Nugget* that got the most attention. This article was an open letter to Ike Clanton. In it the writer proposed a conciliatory meeting to settle all the acrimony between the Earps and the Clantons. The announcement was offered as an invitation to end hostilities. The bottom of the card bore one name: Wyatt S. Earp.

When Wyatt read the *Nugget* article in Virgil's room at the Cosmopolitan, he felt his skin flash with a prickly heat. Then right away he went cold, as though a damp fog had penetrated his clothing. He tossed the paper on his brother's bed and walked to the window, where he looked out over the alleyway between the hotel and the bakery.

"That ain't what I had in mind," Wyatt said, watching his breath condense on the glass. "Why would Tom Fitch think Ike Clanton would agree to such a meeting with me?"

"He don't, Wyatt," Virgil said. "He wants the people of Cochise to see what you're willing to do . . . and what Ike ain't."

Wyatt turned and let concern show through his deadpan expression. "I would never ask any Clanton for such a parley." Wyatt raised the hat he was holding and fanned it at Virgil's maimed arm. "I know Ike was part of the ambush that did that. He wanted you dead, same as he wants me and Morg and Doc. McMaster overheard Ike in Charleston . . . said when Ike found out you were still alive, he said he'd have to come back and finish the job."

"Well," Virgil growled and slapped his good hand down on the pistol lying on the sheets beside him, "if he does, he'll have to come up here to this damned hotel room to do it." In an effort to lighten both their moods, Virgil forced a chuckle. "Look, Wyatt, Tom Fitch knows what he's doin'." He picked up the folded newspaper and held the article facing Wyatt like a piece of evidence. "He's just wantin' people to see a side of you they might not know. It'll get you some votes."

Wyatt stared at his brother until Virgil looked away. The room grew so quiet, they could hear Allie turn the pages of her Bible in the front room.

"That ain't a side of me, Virgil."

Virgil made a dismissive gesture with his hand, waving away his brother's concerns. "Clum came up to see me earlier. Told me Dake has already publicly refused our resignations. And Ike Clanton has spread the word all over town that he won't see us . . . said he'd rather shoot an Earp than talk to one." Virgil paused to let that news sink in, but Wyatt would not be appeased.

Letting his impatience show, Virgil dropped his head back onto the pillow. Staring at the ceiling, he took in a lot of air that wheezed through his nose. When he expelled it, his breath came out in a rush.

"Don't hurt to do a little politickin' sometimes, Wyatt." Virgil rolled his head on the pillow and offered an apologetic smile.

"That what this is?" Wyatt said.

Virgil put on his no-nonsense face. "Just let it go. It's all a sharper's play, but it'll accomplish exactly what Fitch wants. Besides, he didn't charge us. Said he had a stake in all this, too . . . with his name bein' on that blood list." Virge cracked a grin and pointed at the badge on Wyatt's vest. "You're still a federal marshal, ain't you? Now you got to win that sheriff's post and send Behan packing with his tail between his legs."

Wyatt returned to the window and looked out over the rooftops of the business establishments lined up on Allen Street. Most were saloons that never closed, to accommodate all the shifts of the workers in the silver mines.

"Virge, you remember our plans when we first come down here?"

When Virgil did not answer, Wyatt turned at the waist to see his brother pursing his lips and staring at Morgan, who stood in the doorway. Virgil's dog stood behind Morg, looking into the bedroom. When no one spoke for a time, the dog turned and paced back to Allie.

"Seems like a long time ago, don't it?" Morg said quietly. "I guess things didn't go quite like we expected down here in Tombstone."

Wyatt returned to staring out the window and relaxed his eyes to see the whole of the town. Tombstone no longer resembled a low constellation of stars as it had the night he had walked with Sadie Marcus. Now the scattered lights were like the dying embers of a fire, still trying desperately to burst into a flame from any combustible material it could conjure.

"A man can't always count on his plans runnin' like he wants 'em to," Virgil said.

For the time it took a Chinaman to pull his hand cart the length of the block on Allen Street, Wyatt gazed out the cool glass pane and tried to see the town as the repository of some good fortune he might still squeeze out of it. Neither of his brothers spoke. In the other room they heard Morgan's wife, Louisa, speaking in low tones to Allie.

"Well, Lou-Honey," Allie blurted out, "there ain't none of us can fault you for that."

Wyatt turned at the waist again and waited for his younger brother to answer the unasked question. Morg tried to smile, but his eyes dulled and turned away.

"Lou's wantin' to pull out," Morg said.

Wyatt thought about the prospect for several seconds, and then slowly he began to nod. Glancing at the pink-stained seepage on the gauze wrapped around Virgil's arm and side, Wyatt turned back to Morgan and considered the bullet that had torn through his younger brother's shoulders from one side to the other. As much as Morg tried to hide it, there was a new and fragile tilt in his posture, as though he were constantly seeking a position that lessened his pain. With a steady look of support in his face, Wyatt nodded again . . . this time with resolve.

"Might not be a bad idea," Wyatt said plainly. "Where will you go?"

Morgan's face twisted with a scowl. "I'll send *her* out to Ma and Pa in California. *I* ain't goin' nowhere." He pulled his shoulders back and tried to stand a little straighter, but his expression turned apologetic. "She just ain't cut out for all this. She'll do better in a more civilized place."

Virgil grunted and lifted his head enough to look Morgan in the eye. "Maybe you ought to think about goin' with her, Morg. Hell, out there in California she might find somebody prettier'n you."

Not taking the bait, Morg kept his face as sober as a mortician's. Then a steely blue glint hardened his eyes, reminding Wyatt of the moment he had seen his little brother finish off Frank McLaury on Fremont Street.

"I figure there's more we got to do here," Morg replied. After leaning back to check on the proximity of the women in the other room, Morg eased a few steps closer to Virgil's bed and lowered his voice. "We got a goddamn score to settle, boys." He looked from one brother to the other and then let his gaze settle on Wyatt. "There's too much vermin down here in this territory, and I figure nobody else is gonna do a goddamn thing about it long as this pissant sheriff rules the roost. Am I right?"

Wyatt pivoted back to the window. In his mind he watched a parade of faces flash before him like half-formed portraits etched into the glass: Ike Clanton, Brocius, Frank Stilwell, Joe Hill, Pete Spence, John Ringo . . . and Behan.

"Right," Wyatt said so quietly, the echo of his voice off the window barely reached his own ears.

CHAPTER 18

March 18, 1882

Tombstone and Cochise County, A.T.

Just after mid-March, on the night before Wyatt's birthday, rain streaked the windows of Virgil's hotel room where the five Earp brothers had gathered to commemorate the event. Morgan stopped pacing long enough to stare down at the lighted saloons on Allen Street.

"Let's go celebrate," he said to the room behind him. "Hell, it's Saturday. They're puttin' on that play, *Stolen Kisses*, again. And it's a damn good one." When he turned to convince his brothers they needed a night on the town, he passed over Wyatt and instead channeled his enthusiasm on James and Warren. "Let's go to Shieffelin Hall, boys . . . b'fore we start shootin' each other."

"Not a good idea, Morg," Wyatt said. "Not tonight."

Virgil heard the tone in Wyatt's reply. "You hear something we ought'a know?"

Wyatt tilted his head at the irony. "From Ike Clanton's lawyer—Goodrich."

Warren blew a stream of air. "To hell with Clanton's lawyer. Let 'em come."

"Listen to Wyatt, Morg," James said. "B'sides, you already seen that show once."

"That's how I know it's a damned good one," Morgan laughed and tried to establish some momentum by working his arms into his coat.

The pain in his shoulders showed in his face. "Come on, boys, have some pity on a man without his woman." He gestured toward Virgil's dog, who lay sleeping at James's feet. "Lou's been gone so long, that damned dog is startin' to look a little appealin' to me."

"Frank's a boy," James reminded.

Morg opened his hands palms up at either side and froze in that position. "See? See what I'm goin' through?"

James laughed. "What you mean is, we should have some pity on a man dumb enough to let his woman take off like that. Is that what you're sayin'?"

Morg kicked at James's boot, but James dodged it and in the process awoke the dog. Frank jumped up and trotted from the room.

James widened his smile until the skin around his eyes creased into a fan of lines. "Now you got the dog worryin' about your intentions, Morg."

Morgan started to kick again, but James pointed a finger at him and raised an eyebrow.

"I may be a one-armed bartender, but I can still whip your ass." James held his smile in place, but there was a steely tone to his voice.

"Well, I'm goin' to see the show!" Morg announced. "With or without you sourpuss preachers."

Wyatt knew better than to challenge his little brother's stubbornness. "If you're goin', take some of the boys with you—Doc or McMaster."

"Hell, I'll go with 'im," Warren announced, grabbing his own coat. "I'm sick o' being cooped up."

Wyatt gave his youngest brother a sharp look. "I'd guess Virge is pretty sick of it, too. But he ain't got much choice. Your job is here with him, understand?"

Warren sulked and threw his coat in an empty chair, but he didn't argue.

"Why don't you come, Wyatt?" Morgan prodded. "Hell, it's your birthday, big brother."

Wyatt shook his head. "I'm tired. I'm turnin' in."

"Goddamn, Wyatt." Morg laughed. "Would you listen to yourself? You *are* gettin' old."

Wyatt watched Morgan try not to show the discomfort of his wounds as he buttoned his coat. "Just keep your eyes open, you hear me?"

Morgan clowned it up, leaving the room with his eyes pinched shut and his arms outstretched before him, feeling his way along the wall. In the hallway John Vermillion and McMaster frowned at Wyatt and Warren as Morgan tried to identify Vermillion's face with his hands. The ex-carpenter slapped at him, and Morgan headed down the stairwell, laughing.

"Better go with him, Mac," Wyatt said to McMaster. "Tipton, too."

Wyatt started down the hall. Inside his room, he undressed and slipped into the bed beside Mattie's lifeless shape, but he didn't sleep. For almost an hour he listened to rain tap on the window and thought about the message he had received from Goodrich. Quickly, he threw back the covers, got up, and dressed for the weather. Within minutes he closed the door on Mattie's soft snore and left the hotel.

When the play let out, Wyatt was standing under the awning of the post office, watching the crowd spill out into the rainstorm. Thunder rumbled across the sky, and men ran for carriages while the women clustered under umbrellas near the brightly lighted door. As Morgan, Doc, and McMaster crossed the intersection, Wyatt stepped out into the rain and met them in the street.

"You should'a come," Morgan yelled over the rain spattering the ground. "Even better the second time around."

Taking his brother's elbow, Wyatt said, "Let's get back to the hotel."

Morg pulled his arm free and laughed. "Are you mother-hennin' me?"

Doc coughed into his fist. "Can we have this conversation under a roof somewhere—preferably one with a liquor license?"

"Got a billiards match over at Hatch's," Morgan announced. "Tip is already over there warming up the table. Come on down with me, Wyatt, and watch me take Bob Hatch's money. Just one game."

Holliday touched the brim of his hat, and a string of water dribbled before his face. "I'll leave you gentlemen to your game then, as I have one of my own lined up at the Alhambra."

At Hatch's parlor, several men had gathered to watch the match. Dan Tipton took up a post just inside the front door. McMaster stood beside the entrance to the card room.

"Come on into the lion's den, Morg," Bob Hatch said, raising a steaming mug of coffee. "I hope you're soakin' wet, 'cause I'm all warmed up and ready to crack your balls."

Morgan winced and clutched his privates. Wyatt hung his wet slicker on a rack by the door and took a chair against the wall near the billiards table. He lighted a cigar and tilted the chair back on its rear legs. The room quieted as Hatch lined up to make the break.

The precision click of the balls was rhythmic and musical. The players' concentration seemed magnified by the muted patter of rain on the roof. Wyatt liked watching his brother's face transcend under the rigors of the game. It was the same expression he used when sighting over a gun or pointing out a track in the dirt. For Wyatt, it was a brief glimpse into a mirror. Then, as suddenly as Morgan had been gripped by his inner discipline, he broke the spell by smiling and moving to a new position around the table. It was a dance. Morg loved this game.

As Hatch leaned in for a shot, the rear door exploded in a shower of glass and wood splinters. Another shot followed immediately, and a board cracked above Wyatt's head. Morgan pitched forward onto the floor, and Wyatt rolled out of the chair to crouch over his brother, his gun trained on the back of the parlor. Tipton and McMaster broke open the shattered door and charged outside into the storm, hatless and with pistols cocked. A gust of wind invaded the room, and the sound of the rain droned and rattled in the back alley. At the front of the table a bystander cried out and hobbled backward to a chair, where he clutched his bleeding leg.

Wyatt could only look at Morgan, just healed from the goring wound of October . . . and now ruined again. "Help me get him in the other room," Wyatt called to Hatch.

When they tried to get him on his feet, Morg cried out with a voice that twisted Wyatt's gut into a knot. It was a wretched and desperate sound Wyatt hardly recognized as his brother's, and it was this ungodly shriek, even more than the blood painting Morg's blouse, that announced the severity of the wound. Immediately he and Hatch lowered him back to the floor.

"Don't stand me up!" Morgan gasped. "I can't take it." His face was drained of all color.

Four men carried him horizontally into the card room and lowered him to the sofa, each man hardening himself against the grimace on Morgan's face. Wyatt dropped to one knee and gripped his brother's hand as Morg struggled to swallow between labored breaths. McMaster came into the room, his hair plastered to his skull, clothes soaked and heavy. When Wyatt looked at him, the former Cow-boy shook his head and holstered his gun. Taking in Morgan's bloodied body, Mac's eyes went dead with the unspoken severity of the wound.

"Hurts like hell," Morgan whispered, his words squeezed from his chest. "Someone set my legs out straight."

Everyone was quiet as Wyatt's voice emerged, hollow and helpless. "They are straight, Morg."

Thirty minutes later, when Doc Goodfellow gave up on his horrific probing with a forceps, he eased Morgan's drugged body back to the sofa. Turning to Wyatt, he said nothing. His grim expression was sufficient to deliver the news. Two other doctors arrived, stamping the rain from their shoes, but after seeing the copious blood and the expression on Goodfellow's face, they gathered around the man who had taken a bullet in the leg.

Looking up into the ceiling, Morgan wet his lips. "Wyatt," he breathed, "looks like Lou was right. I should'a gone with her."

When Wyatt said nothing, Morg raised his chin slightly and tried to form another word, the movement costing him a bolt of pain that seemed to run the length of him. With a fierce grip on Wyatt's hand he shut his eyes as his face contorted in a garish show of teeth.

Wyatt leaned close to listen, and Morgan's warm breath—when he spoke again—moved across Wyatt's face like death itself. "Find the ones did this," Morg whispered. "And kill 'em." And then, unaccountably, Morgan seemed to relax. His voice became steady. "They can't touch you, Wyatt. They're empty inside . . . hollow . . . without a soul. They ain't got what you got." Morg's grip tightened as he tried to pull himself closer. "Kill 'em and then get out, Wyatt. Get away from this goddamn place."

Wyatt waited to hear more, but Morgan lowered himself back to the sofa. When he seemed settled, his breathing scraped in and then out, the sound wet and clotted. Morg swallowed with an effort, and then his breath eased out as gently as a child in sleep. His hand went limp.

Dr. Goodfellow leaned in close to Morg and then looked at Wyatt. "He's gone," he whispered. He held his gaze on the side of Wyatt's face, but Wyatt said nothing. Wyatt could only stare at the peaceful expression on his dead brother's face. The doctor stood and began wiping his hands on a clean white towel he unfolded from his bag. By the time he had finished, the towel appeared more red than white.

Picking up his bag, Goodfellow hesitated. "I'm sorry, Wyatt." When Wyatt still did not respond, Goodfellow hitched his medical bag under his arm and pointed into the billiards room. "I'll just go see about this other man, Wyatt . . . see if the other doctors need my help."

After a few seconds Wyatt nodded once, but he could not take his attention from Morgan. Goodfellow moved away to the next room, stepping quietly like a man leaving early from a church service.

The rain drummed the roof. The other men in the room were motionless and seemingly uncertain, as though waiting for something they knew could never arrive. The quiet in the entire saloon was absolute but for the rain and the low voice of the doctors as they administered to the leg wound of their patient. When Wyatt walked out of the card room and into the billiards parlor, every eye fixed on him, but he crossed the room without speaking to anyone.

At the front window he watched a gutter spout water into the slick mire of Allen Street. Watching the rain, he felt the ethic of his career as a lawman begin to wash away—vague images of right and wrong . . . useless definitions of the law. There was no law in this territory. Not with night-stalkers who shot men in the back. And smirking confederates who lied against God on the witness stand in a courtroom.

Quietly, under his breath, he spoke the names of every man for whom he held a warrant, and some he did not, certain that the men who had killed Morgan were on that list. When he had locked those names in memory, he heard the judge's voice clearly in his head, putting the final terms on the contract that he was now brokering: *Leave your prisoners out in the brush, Wyatt. Let the coyotes deliberate over them.*

CHAPTER 19

March 19–20, 1882

Contention and Tucson Train
Depots; Back to Tombstone

Under the guard of six gunmen on horseback, Wyatt and James transported Morgan's casket by wagon to the nearest train depot at Contention. From there James would accompany the corpse to Tucson to connect with the train to California, where Morgan's wife would join the elder Earps in burying their son. Returning to Tombstone, Wyatt readied Virgil and Allie for the same trip on the day following, as Bessie had agreed to stay behind to help prepare Mattie for a later journey.

In late afternoon when Wyatt returned to his room at the hotel, he found McMaster and Tipton standing in the hallway, one on each side of Virgil's door. The three men nodded to one another. Then McMaster shook his head at Wyatt's unasked question.

"No trouble," Mac said. But he glanced tentatively down the hall, where Bessie stood at the south window, a bottle of whiskey clutched in one hand as she stared out the glass at the town. " 'Cept maybe—" It was all McMaster was willing to say.

When Bessie turned and saw Wyatt, she tried to smile, but her mouth curled with a scowl. Glancing at the door to Wyatt's room, she just shook her head and then pivoted back to the window. Unscrewing the bottle cap, she took a swig and said something into the glass he could not make out.

When Wyatt entered the room he found the shades drawn and Mattie lying in bed with her curled back to the door. He walked around the bed and found her staring at the wall, her unkempt hair pinned up on her head in a failed attempt at propriety. Wyatt knew this had been Bessie's effort. Two brown glass bottles sat on the bed table, one empty, the other half full. When he spoke her name, Mattie still did not move. Wyatt opened the window shade and stood staring out over the roofs of the business district.

"You don't have to pretend, Wyatt," Mattie said in her lifeless monotone. "I know you won't come for me once you ship me off to California." Her words ran together in the fog of her drug-induced lethargy.

He turned and waited for her to look at him, but she was as settled as a corpse. "Won't do you any good to stay in Arizona, Mattie. There's nothing here for you. You need to start new somewhere and get your feet underneath you."

Her attempt to laugh was little more than a stir of air through her nostrils. "So I'm supposed to go off to the Earps." She turned her head enough to show him the bitterness in her smile. "Will they teach me to be strong like you, Wyatt?"

When he reached and picked up one of the brown bottles, he watched her eyes go desperate. "Lou will be there, Mattie."

"Is that where life is waiting for me, Wyatt? I get to start over there among all those Earps?"

Wyatt raised the bottle between them. "This is no kind of life, Mattie."

She sat up and snatched the bottle from him, the speed of her reaction surprising him. "It's the life I got!" she spat and twisted around, trying to turn her back to him. But she only surrendered to gravity as she returned to her recumbent position.

Wyatt watched her body sag into a listless heap, and he did his best to dredge up a final measure of pity. "You can find something better, Mattie, but you'll have to want it. Nobody can do it for you."

Clutching the bottle, she glared at the wall as though she could see right through it to condemn all of Arizona to the violent death it deserved.

With nothing more to say, she uncorked the laudanum, took a draw, and lay back in the sheets with the open bottle still in her hand. By the time her eyes closed, Wyatt felt as though he were the only one in the room.

*****

At the Contention station, as Warren stayed with Virgil and Allie in the passenger car, Doc Holliday, McMaster, and Creek Johnson climbed onto the loading platform and spread out along the depot. Wyatt walked to the telegraph office to wire Bob Paul and there found a telegram waiting for him. When he returned, his party gathered to hear him read directly from the paper.

"Ike Clanton and Stilwell are at the Tucson depot watching the loading and unloading of trains."

When he looked up at his three companions, he watched each man's mood transform. Every one of them had been a friend to Morgan. But now whatever grief they had carried internally was supplanted by purpose and deliberation.

"We're going on to Tucson with Virge," Wyatt instructed. "Once he gets away from there, won't be any more stops until Yuma."

The engine built steam, and the whistle sounded, followed by the conductor's call to board. "When we pull in there," Wyatt warned, "keep your eyes open." The line of cars began its slow, labored turn of wheels on the iron rails. "And when we get off there, I want all of us to stick close to Virgil."

Without a word, the four gunmen stepped up onto the moving train. Wyatt was last to board. Standing alone on the coupling platform, he watched the distance grow between the small depot and himself. If he had been a praying man, he would have asked God to keep Clanton and Stilwell in Tucson until he could get there. Instead, he hardened himself to the task before him, believing those cowards would wait for him only because he willed it so.

*****

When the train pulled into the Tucson train yard, darkness had begun to settle in over the complex of buildings and the sprawl of side tracks.

Lights spilled out from the depot windows, and new gaslights provided a scattering of halos along the sidewalks and around the establishments beyond the terminal. With shotgun in hand, Creek Johnson stepped off the moving passenger car and stationed himself at the near end of the boarding platform. McMaster took the other end. Wyatt and Doc checked the depot, leaving Warren to guard Virgil and Allie.

When they had gathered back inside Virgil's car, they decided to eat while they waited for the connection to California. It was a short walk from the station to the nearest restaurant, but they covered the distance with shotguns at the ready, speaking only when necessary.

Inside the dining room, while Allie pressed a handkerchief to her eyes and retired to the privy, Virgil took Wyatt aside to the hat and coat rack. When Warren followed, Virgil put a hand on the youngest Earp's shoulder.

"Warren, go tell Mac and the boys to sit at the other table. I want them between Allie and the front entrance." Warren turned around to survey the set-up of the dining tables. Virgil squeezed his shoulder and gently shook him once. "I want *you* facing that goddamned back door. If we have trouble, that's where it will come from."

Warren nodded eagerly and started for his post, only to stop when Wyatt spoke his name. "Before you open up on somebody, be damned sure o' what you're shootin' at."

Putting on a sulk, Warren marched off stiffly. After watching the youngest Earp oversee seating arrangements, Virgil turned to Wyatt, lifted both eyebrows, and inhaled a deep breath that whistled through his nose. Virgil let the breath ease out and began shrugging his coat from the sling that supported his crippled arm.

"Allie all right?" Wyatt asked.

Virgil pursed his lips and shrugged his head to one side. "It ain't just about Morg. We had to leave Frank."

Wyatt frowned.

"Our dog," Virgil explained. "Left 'im with that Mexican girl who sold us produce from her cart." Turning to put his back to Wyatt, Virge spoke over his shoulder. "Help me with this, will you?" After surrendering his overcoat, he readjusted his sling and studied Wyatt's face. "What are you aimin' to do once we're gone, Wyatt?"

"Head back to Tombstone. Bessie said it will take a few days before Mattie can travel with her."

"I mean after that?"

Wyatt hung up Virgil's coat and then produced a folded paper from his pocket. He opened it on the bar and ironed it flat with the palm of his hand.

"This is the coroner's preliminary report on the men who killed Morgan," he said. "Pete Spence, Frank Stilwell, a German named Bode, and a couple o' half-breeds—Swilling and Indian Charlie."

"Who supplied the names?" Virgil asked.

"Spence's wife."

Virgil pursed his lips and narrowed his eyes. "Who's this Bode?"

Wyatt shook his head. "Don't know. I hear he hauls wood for Spence's sawmill." He nodded toward Virgil's crippled arm. "I figure Ike Clanton, Stilwell, and Curly Bill for you. And Ringo is in this somewhere."

Virgil clenched his massive jaws. "I reckon most of those boys have lit out by now. But with your federal badge, you can go all the way to hell and back, if you need to."

Wyatt showed no expression, but his voice seemed to come from a hollow place inside him. "Don't need a badge to do what I'm gonna do, Virge."

Virgil watched his brother for a time and then turned to appraise the gunmen seated at their assigned tables, their chairs all turned toward the front door. Warren had taken his post facing the rear door, his hand gripping a revolver lying at the center of his place setting. All in all, there was more weaponry reflecting light from the oil lamps than from the flatware on the tables.

"These boys here," Virgil said quietly, "keep 'em close to you, you hear?"

Wyatt nodded. "They're making five dollars a day plus meals and livery rentals. Ammunition, too. Dake has promised us more money." He looked over his shoulder at his posse. "I reckon they'll stick."

Virgil's face compressed with a curious smile. "You think they're doing this for the wages?" He coughed a modest laugh, leaned in, and softened his deep voice. "Hell, Wyatt, these men will walk through fire for you." Again Virgil looked over the posse men, his eyes finally lingering on the youngest Earp. "But you'd better look out for Warren, much as you can." He raised an eyebrow. "Even if he don't wanna be looked out for."

"He needs to be in on this," Wyatt said. "He's spent more time with Morg than any of us."

The silence between them drew out, until Allie entered the room through the rear door. Her hair was freshly groomed, but her eyes remained raw and teary. The two brothers watched Warren lower his revolver back to the table linen. Virgil began fussing with the hang of his sling.

"What about Mattie?" he said. "Once she gets to us in California?"

Wyatt folded the coroner's report and stuffed it into his coat pocket. "See can they get her off that damned opium to start with."

Virgil's face broke into a map of creases. "Who the hell is '*they*'?"

Wyatt shook his head. "I don't know. Maybe Louisa? She liked Mattie. Mattie needs to be able to get along on her own." Wyatt's eyes went dead. "I'm done with her, Virge."

Virgil watched Allie squint at a menu. "Well, Mattie's been done with *us* for a long time," he said as gently as he could. "God help 'er." He looked back at Wyatt. "She'll need it."

"She will," Wyatt agreed. "When I get out there with you, maybe I can steer her toward something with some promise. Something that don't involve me."

*****

It was overcast and dark when they left the restaurant, and little was said as Virgil and Allie boarded the train bound for San Bernardino. The Earp gunmen spread out on the loading platform, turning in slow circles, eyes vigilant, their artillery throwing off glints of reflections in the depot's lamplight. Inside the car, Allie shook Wyatt's hand, and he sensed from her expression that she never expected to see him again.

"You might as well kill as many of them heathens as you can find, Wyatt," she said. "Do it for Morgan." She turned her head and nodded toward Virgil, who was struggling again with his coat. "An' what's left of your big brother."

Seated at the rear of the car, Virgil motioned for Wyatt to come closer. "We'll be waitin' for you in San Berdoo. You take care of your-self, you hear me?" Allie sat next to Virge and locked onto his good arm. "Wyatt," Virge said, taking Wyatt's wrist, "don't be thinkin' 'bout Mattie. We all make our own choices. Mattie made hers. Do what you gotta do, and then get out of Arizona Territory."

When the two brothers shook hands, Allie's moist eyes reflected the lamplight like the sheen off two new silver coins. "Wyatt," she said and cut her teary gaze away, embarrassed. "God bless you, Wyatt," she man-aged before her throat tightened.

For the departure, Wyatt had his men spread out over the rail yard, while he, himself, stood in shadows on the coupling platform just outside the door. When the whistle blew, the train jolted into motion, and he stepped down to follow Virgil's car, his shotgun in hand. Then, unex-pectedly, the train banged to a stop.

Forty yards away in the dark of a side track, two shadows darted onto a stationary flatcar coupled to a string of boxcars. Wyatt squatted to backlight the figures against the faint glow spreading from the engine's headlamp. Not seeing anyone drop off the other side, he circled around the idle cars. Virgil's train continued to hiss steam and bang its coupling joints, masking the sound of his boots as he moved down the far side of the track. Stopping ten feet from the corner of the first boxcar, Wyatt raised his shotgun to his shoulder and inched forward. Right away, the shotgun clanked one clear note, metal on metal, and he stood stock-still. In the inky dark, he hadn't seen the iron ladder bolted to the car.

Ahead of him in the flatcar two prostrate figures rose up and scrambled off the far side. Jumping through the coupling, Wyatt gave chase and closed on a man carrying a shotgun. The ambusher's coat flapped wildly, seeming a great hindrance to his escape. Over the crunch of gravel made by their boots, Wyatt could hear the man gasping for breath.

Breaking into the stark light of the engine's headlamp, the run-ner unexpectedly stopped, whirled around, threw his weapon to the ground, and raised both hands. With the light carving him out of the black desert night, Frank Stilwell stared into the train's glaring light, his chest heaving, his eyes wide and bright. Wyatt walked toward him past the loud grumbling of the engine, and the whistle shrieked again, causing Stilwell to lower one hand to press against his groin. He spread his coat and looked down at himself, where his trousers had darkened with urine.

The train lurched for another start, and the long chain of passenger cars rumbled and banged and grated as the pull of the engine passed down the line. In the bright light, Stilwell's face was as white as chalk. Squinting, he tried to shadow his eyes with one hand.

"Who is it!" he called out, his words clipped and desperate. "What do you want with me!"

Wyatt walked closer, his shadow stretching far down the tracks like a messenger moving ahead of him, a dark wraith carrying the prophecy of death. He walked slowly until he pressed the shotgun into the cavity below the Cow-boy's sternum. Stilwell's face contorted with the horrible revelation he found in Wyatt's eyes, and then his hands flattened out before him, as though he might reverse his fate by a simple deflection off his palms.

"Don't!" he begged, his voice quavering with the certain futility of his words. "*Please!*"

"For Morgan," Wyatt said in a low growl, the words piercing Stilwell with such finality that terror burst from his eyes in rivulets. Frozen in the beam of light, the tears clung to his whiskered face like beads of clear glass. Then he panicked and grabbed the barrels of Wyatt's shotgun. So violent was his shaking that he could gain no advantage over Wyatt's grip on the gun.

"Morg!" Stilwell cried in a hoarse scream. "*Morg!*" he repeated louder.

The blast from both barrels lifted him off the ground for an instant before delivering him back into the long shadow of his body, a pool of black that gathered beneath him even as he fell. There he lay motionless on the loose gravel, a gaping wet hole opened in his chest.

Doc Holliday and McMaster came at a run along one side of the train, as Warren and Creek Johnson materialized from the other side. Each man looked silently at the body, and then at Wyatt.

Doc stepped forward, and the ring of men opened a step as he leveled his pistol at Stilwell's corpse. He fired once, stepped back, and looked to McMaster, who levered a round into his carbine, aimed from under his arm, and fired.

"Is he one of the men who killed Morg?" Warren yelled over the hiss of steam from the train.

Wyatt nodded once. "Stilwell, Behan's deputy."

Warren sidestepped to straddle one of the dead man's legs. Bending, he jerked Stilwell's pocketwatch away, breaking the chain.

"You won't need this in hell," Warren said in a seething, flat tone. He flung the watch aside into the rail yard, and then he drew his revolver. "You goddamned back-shooter!"

Warren's gun roared four times. After holstering his gun he spat on the corpse and stepped away. Then Creek Johnson added his signature to the body—one bullet fired casually from the hip. The five men stood unmoving as the engine began to steam past them, building a sluggish exit from the yard.

Matching its crawl along the track, Wyatt walked to the car nearest the caboose. There were no lights showing inside. He tapped lightly on the glass with the barrel of his shotgun. The shade rose, and Allie's face appeared. Holding Virgil's gun in both hands, she turned and spoke to someone. Then the shade on the neighboring window opened, and Virgil leaned toward the glass. Wyatt held up one finger as he walked beside the moving train.

"One for Morg," he called out over the metallic grinding of the wheels.

Allie's face tightened with approval, and she nodded once with a quick jerk of her head. Virgil's somber expression remained unchanged, but the message telegraphed by his eyes was clear: *Keep it up.*

Wyatt stopped and watched the train slide out into the vast darkness stretching to California. Now the avenging had begun. The federal badge he wore on his vest was little more than a false front on a building, giving him the image of something other than what he was. But he would use it without qualms, without mercy. There were more men upon whom he would dispense such swift justice, and he knew he probably had limited time in which to do it.

*****

In Tombstone on the day following, Wyatt and Doc walked out of the Cosmopolitan Hotel into the cool of the evening. Behind them followed Warren, Vermillion, Johnson, McMaster, and Dan Tipton. Each man carried saddlebags over a shoulder, a cartridge belt and two revolvers strapped to their hips, a Winchester repeater in one hand, and a double-barreled shotgun in the other.

As they turned west for the stables at the O.K. Corral, Sheriff Johnny Behan crossed the street toward them. Just behind him were his deputy, Breakenridge, and the new town marshal, Dave Neagle. Neagle cradled a shotgun across one forearm; the other two lawmen carried holstered revolvers. Behan stopped in the middle of the street, raised a paper above his head, and shook it with a smart snap.

"Wyatt!" he called out. "I want to see you!"

Coming to a stop on the boardwalk, Wyatt's posse turned dispassionate eyes toward the emboldened bureaucrat. A dozen townspeople gathered along the boardwalk to watch from a distance. Behan tried to hold Wyatt's stare but could not keep from surveying the abundance of weaponry displayed by the small army he faced.

"You're going to see me once too often," Wyatt said, his voice deliberate and final.

Inside the bubble of silence that gathered around them, the sheriff looked down at the telegram in his hand as though searching for instructions. When it was clear that Behan could think of nothing more to say, Wyatt turned and continued down the street. His posse followed, none of them so much as glancing back at the three officers left standing in the street.

CHAPTER 20

March 22-24, 1882

Dragoon and Whetstone Mountains

By early afternoon Wyatt and his posse breached the South Pass of the Dragoons and rode up on Pete Spence's wood camp from the east. Two Mexicans looked up from repairing a wagon axle in the main yard. Beside them, smoke raced off at an angle on the wind from a pit fire. Wyatt reined up before a crude open shelter canopied with torn canvas. An old man sat up on a cot and swung his bare feet to the dirt. Wyatt sat his horse as the man pinched the sleep from his eyes.

"Who are you?" Wyatt said.

The man looked surprised at the directness of the question. "Judah . . . Theodore Judah."

"Where's Spence?" Wyatt continued.

"We ain't seen 'im for a few days." The old man's voice trailed off with the recognition of the man before him. His head pivoted to take in the full array of armed riders looking back at him. Slowly he straightened his spine and spread his hands on the canvas bedding.

"If I find 'im here," Wyatt informed the man, "I'll kill you. You stayin' with that story?"

The man swallowed. "He ain't here, Marshal. I'm tellin' the truth. He told me he was turning himself in to the sheriff."

"Turning himself in?" Wyatt repeated, a trace of anger putting a rough edge to his words.

Judah swallowed and averted his eyes. "For protection," he explained and dared to meet Wyatt's eyes again. "That's what he said anyway."

"Mac!" Wyatt called over his shoulder. "Ask the two at the wagon."

McMaster rode to them and broke into a quiet cascade of Spanish. In front of Wyatt, the man named Judah remained motionless on the cot.

"What about a man named Swilling . . . or Bode . . . or Indian Charlie?" Wyatt said. He watched the man's eyes flick to the Mexican workers and back.

"Florentino, the half-breed," the old man admitted, "he goes by 'Charlie.'" He raised his chin and thrust it to the west. "He's roundin' up some mules over that hill yonder."

Wyatt kept his eyes on the frightened man as he called behind him, "Warren!" When the youngest Earp reined up beside him, Wyatt spoke in a quiet tone that brooked no argument. "You and Tipton see that these men stay here in camp."

He took four men over the rise at a brisk canter before seeing a lean, bronze-skinned man some fifty yards off walking through a copse of palo verde, herding three mules ahead of him with a long limber switch with a swatch of white cloth tied to its end. When Florentino Cruz spotted the posse, he spun so fast his pale straw hat sailed off his head, his long, black hair flashing in the sun like a crow's wing. Dropping the stick, he bolted diagonally up the far hill toward a scattering of boulders, his boots clawing for purchase in the loose scree.

"Mac, stop 'im before he makes it to the rocks," Wyatt ordered. "Don't kill him."

McMaster levered a round into his carbine, took careful aim, and fired once from the saddle. Cruz went down, one leg flying out from under him as though it had been yanked by a rope. The riders fanned out as they climbed the hill, but the wounded man made no effort to escape. When they reached him, his face was stretched with pain, his left leg losing blood from the back of the thigh. Wyatt dismounted and stepped into the man's line of sight.

"I look familiar to you?"

Cruz's moist eyes burned with white rings of pain and terror. "*¡No se de que me hablas!*"

"You helped kill a man who looked like me two nights ago."

Cruz shook his head stiffly. "I no keel!" he insisted. "Only keep watch!" Frantic, he searched the horsemen for sympathetic eyes but found none. "Spence . . . he my boss," he whined, as though that had been reason enough to take part in an assassination.

"Who else besides Spence did the shootin'?" Wyatt demanded.

Cruz shook his head again, vehemently. "We use hees house to make plan, but Spence too scared to shoot. Steel-well, Curly Beel, Sweelling, and two more, I theenk. They shoot. I only watch from street. Spence, he say I have to watch."

"Ringo?" Wyatt pressed.

"*Si*," he said, nodding. "He shoot." Then the half-breed seemed to forget the pain in his leg for a moment, his eyes turning eager. "But Steel-well, he brag *he* the one keel your brother."

"He won't be bragging anymore," Doc quipped.

As Cruz stared at Holliday, the question on the half-breed's face gave way to understanding. He looked quickly at Wyatt, his bloodless face begging for mercy.

"I *work* for Spence," he sniveled. "He pay me. I juss do what he say."

Wyatt kept his voice calm, steady. "How much for bein' look-out?"

Realizing that the question of money had opened up a darker subject, Cruz searched for an answer in the long, sloping walls of the Dragoons. "What he always pay." His tongue flicked across his lips. "Twee-ny-five dollar," he volunteered. "Thees man they keel . . . *el muy importante.*" Cruz nodded encouragingly.

As the wretch tried to curry favor, Wyatt felt a tingling on the back of his neck. "Twenty-five dollars," he repeated in a cold monotone.

"*Si*, thees man *muy importante.*"

Wyatt's face turned to stone. "Say the name of the man you killed."

Cruz shook his head more emphatically now. "I no keel."

"Say his name!" Wyatt commanded, the change in his voice causing Cruz to recoil.

"Earp," he finally said, pushing out the word as gently as a prayer.

"Say his first name!"

Unsure of Wyatt's intent, Cruz looked at the others, but they only stared silently, their eyes vacant, distant. With nowhere else to turn, he faced Wyatt again.

"Mor-can?" he whispered.

Some of the tension fell away from the cowering man, as if in remembering the name he believed he might have attained absolution. But when Wyatt pulled his Colt's from its holster, the riders tugged gently on their reins, widening the circle.

"You're gonna die here," Wyatt said simply.

As if to steady himself, Cruz dug his fingers into the sand. His head turned frantically toward the wood camp, as though there might be help for him there. As Wyatt's gun cocked, the wretched man began to wail.

"*¡Por el amor de diós, no me mates!*"

The gunshot cracked and bloomed inside the circle of men and horses, and Cruz dropped back into the sand. As he lay limp, the gun's report tapered away to nothing in a sky too vast to contain it. Wyatt stood looking at the silenced assassin through a skein of gray smoke, until Warren and Tipton rode up at a gallop. Warren looked from face to face to see what he had missed.

"Is he one of 'em?"

Wyatt's face was answer enough. Expressionless, each man sat his horse, their collective stillness like the permanence of the mountains around them. Without another word, Warren jumped down from his horse and fired three times into the lifeless body. Still fuming, he kicked at the ground in front of the dead man's face, and flecks of stone and sand peppered the still-wet mouth. Each posse member had drawn a pistol to fire a shot into the body in a somber procession of solidarity, but after Warren's vent of rage, each gunman holstered his weapon and in his turn took his horse at a walk down the slope to follow Wyatt.

*****

After sending Tipton into Tombstone to collect the funds that had been promised by the federal marshal, Wyatt led his posse down the San Pedro Valley through the scrub of a trail-less tract of desert. In the late hours of the afternoon, after leaving Warren to guard their pack horses at the foot of the Whetstones, Wyatt and his men wended their way up the wash toward Iron Springs, where they expected to rendezvous with Tip and the expense money.

Wyatt rode well ahead of the others through the dry stream bed, his horse's legs slithering through the tall, shimmering grasses with a dry, whispery sound. The wind pushed at his back but did little to offset the heat of the day. As he rode, he unbuttoned his vest and loosened his cartridge belts. He could only hope that the spring was not dry. If it was dry, there was little likelihood that any of the Whetstone watering holes could provide their mounts with enough hydration to last the night.

Climbing to the open mesa before the spring, Wyatt dismounted lest his horse spook at the sudden appearance of someone waiting. With his feet on the ground, he listened and felt his senses sharpen to a fine edge. It was just a feeling, but it was strong enough that he eased the leather thong off his saddle horn and gripped the sawed-off shotgun in both hands. When Vermillion and Holliday came into view forty yards behind him, Wyatt led his horse toward the edge of the grassy flat that would put him in sight of the spring.

Woodsmoke rose above the grasses below and streamed away into the willows and cottonwood saplings covering the embankment beyond the spring. Wyatt started to call out to his men, when someone at the spring yelled an alarm. Immediately, the full torso of a man holding a fry pan bobbed up above the grasses. Four others scrambled up the bank into the trees. Wyatt heard the pan fall on the rocks as the lone man lunged toward a gnarled mesquite tree and snatched up a shotgun. One of the tree's branches toppled the man's wide-brimmed hat, and sunlight reflected off Curly Bill Brocius's unmistakable wavy, black hair, as dark and shining in the hard light as if it had been slathered with lard.

The shallow draw exploded with gunfire, guns popping from the grass, from behind the spring, and from the trees on the higher ground.

Amid the fusillade, Wyatt steeled himself against sure death and willed himself to survive long enough to exact his revenge on Brocius for Morgan's murder.

In this state of mind, Wyatt heard the tattered volleys of gunfire become a muted series of reports, as if from a battle too distant to harm him. A surreal calm gathered inside him. Immersed in a cocoon of semi-quiet, he felt an ineffable sense of protection surround him, like a silken web suspended in the air, shielding him from anything the Cow-boys could throw at him. Morgan's voice whispered in his ear, as clearly as if the two brothers were conferring over coffee during the midnight hours in Wyatt's kitchen.

They can't touch you, Wyatt, Morg said. *They're hollow . . . empty inside . . . without a soul.*

In a smooth, steady arc of motion, Wyatt raised the shotgun, thumbed back both hammers, and seated the stock to his shoulder. But his horse—still a part of the other world—shied from the gunfire, and the reins in Wyatt's hand pulled and jerked, interrupting his aim. Bullets from the willows tore through his hat and coattails and whined off the rocks behind him. Then Curly Bill's gun roared. Scattershot scoured the grass and tugged at Wyatt's coattails. Brocius was cocking the second hammer when Wyatt leveled his eye over the twin barrels of his gun and pulled both triggers. The outlaw leader screamed and disappeared behind a pale cloud of smoke, but not before Wyatt saw the Cow-boy's striped shirt burst into a pattern of crimson flowers.

In front of Wyatt, bullets whanged off stone, showering pieces of rock and dust into the air. His horse reared, tugging at the reins still wrapped around his hand. Tossing down the shotgun, he reached inside his coat for the Colt's at his hip, but his hand slid across the bare cloth of his trousers. Looking down he discovered the loosened gun belts had slipped to his thighs, the pistol scabbards having worked their way around behind him. He tugged up on one belt, found the gun, and, turning his body sideways to the fusillade pouring out of the trees, he fired five times at three silhouettes, two of those shots rewarding him with high-pitched cries.

Struggling with his horse, he tried to grab the Winchester from the saddle boot. A glimpse back down the slope showed that no one was backing him. Only Vermillion was on the mesa, hatless and trapped beneath his prostrate horse, pushing with a boot in the bow of his saddle to free himself.

Bullets continued to pluck at Wyatt's clothing as he hopped on one leg, trying to get his boot into the stirrup. The wall-eyed mare danced in a wide arc, and Wyatt could do nothing but swing with it. In a dream-like lethargy, he tried to mount, but the cartridge belts still shackled his thighs. Losing his grip on the saddle horn he grasped a handful of the horse's mane and hung on. Inches from his nose, a bullet hit the pommel and tore it from its metal post with a rank, sulfurous smell. Leaning into the saddle, he yanked up on the gun belts and finally managed to straddle the horse.

He saw Vermillion pull out of his trapped boot and yell to the men behind him as he limped a retreat on one bare stocking. Perched atop his horse, utterly exposed, Wyatt snapped awake from the trance that had dulled his sense of hearing. The sound of gunfire was now thundering and chaotic. He did not know how he had survived the hail of bullets for so long. He knew he was still alive by the acrid smell of spent gunpowder that burned his throat. Now it was only a matter of seconds, he knew, before one of the Cow-boy's bullets would find him.

Then Morgan's image in the pool room filled his mind—shot in the back, collapsing in a shower of glass and emptying his lifeblood onto the dirty floor. Under his breath, Wyatt growled something unintelligible and, when he finally inhaled, a preternatural strength surged through him. Again he felt invincible, but this time he experienced the power coming not from somewhere outside of him . . . but from the core of his being.

He pulled the Winchester free and leveled it at the willows, firing and cocking the gun repeatedly from the saddle in a sustained and deafening roar that filled the air with smoke. And then, a bullet struck him, numbing his leg from toes to knee. The bones of his lower leg seemed to hum, as if a swarm of bees had been stirred up inside his marrow.

His guns were empty. Before the breeze could disassemble the gray haze of smoke hanging like a protective curtain around him, he reined his horse around, kicked its flank with his good leg, and made for the boulders, picking up the hobbling Vermillion on the way.

As Wyatt dismounted behind the palisade of rocks where his posse had gathered, Doc reached out to him, his hands tentative, his face slack with shock. "Good God, Wyatt!" Doc's inspecting gaze moved up and down the bullet-riddled coat. "You must be shot all to pieces."

Sitting in the grass behind one of the boulders Wyatt pulled up a trouser leg to examine his lifeless leg. He could find no blood, no mark anywhere.

"Bullet's in the heel of your boot, Wyatt," Vermillion said, his voice filled with awe.

Wyatt stared at the gouge in the leather and thought about how many pieces of flying lead had tried to find him out in the open space on the mesa. He realized then how tightly the muscles of his body had cinched around his torso. It was as though he had physically constructed himself a suit of armor.

"What do you want to do, Wyatt?" Creek Johnson said.

Wyatt removed his hat, closed his eyes, and let his head settle back against the rock. The posse men were as still as the boulders around them as they waited for his answer.

Doc leaned in closer and lowered his voice. "Wyatt? What do you—"

"I reckon I already done it," Wyatt snapped and opened his eyes, letting a flash of anger show on his face. Doc eased back and sat on his heels as he stared at the hard veneer of his friend's face.

"Is it Brocius?" McMaster asked.

Wyatt settled the back of his head against the rock again. "Not no more, it ain't."

Creek Johnson poked a finger at the air, silently counting the holes in Wyatt's long coat. Giving up the calculation, he shook his head in wonderment.

"How in hell'd you not get shot, Wyatt?"

When Wyatt said nothing, Vermillion peered out over the rock. "Well, they sure as hell shot my goddamn horse dead enough." He spun back around. "You boys want to make a charge on the rest o' them bastards?"

Wyatt cocked his head and half raised a hand to hush them, his eyes fixed on the middle distance as he listened. When the others grew still, they heard horses scrambling up the slope beyond the spring. Each man in the posse looked to Wyatt.

"What about it, Wyatt?" Doc said. "Want to make a run in there?"

Wyatt opened the gate on one of his revolvers and snicked out the empty cartridges. "I've already been there." He pushed fresh loads into the chambers and gave Doc a stony look. "You go ahead, if you want to."

Standing, Wyatt holstered the gun and repeated the loading process with his other pistol. Then he stamped his boot in an attempt to bring life back into his numbed leg. When he could walk, he limped to his chestnut mare and began to examine the animal for wounds. Slowly he ran his hands down the legs and across the flanks, cupping the thick muscle in the chest, patting the haunches. Like himself, the horse was untouched. He scratched the wiry coat around the base of the mare's ears, and the horse nickered and nuzzled him, pouring warm breath over his cheek and ear, and it was as if Morgan were there with him again, whispering something about immortality.

Wyatt looked past the spine of the Whetstones into the valley of the San Pedro. The final colors of the day were starting to gather in the sky. Minutes before, he had not expected to witness such a thing again. He looked down at his bullet-riddled coat and felt the heel of his boot give where the bullet had gored a trench into the leather. He had bucked the odds, and he wondered if, somehow, Morgan had played a hand in that. *How else could it be explained?* he thought.

Doc picked his way carefully through the rocky scrub and stood beside Wyatt. For a time neither man spoke. Holliday's unnatural stillness was a sound unto itself.

"Is she hit, Wyatt?" he asked quietly and nodded toward the mare.

Wyatt's anger had subsided. Now a cool breeze moved across his skin like a post-battle ritual of ablution. He ran his gaze over the unscathed horse once again.

"She's all right," he said.

Doc fingered the bare metal post jutting up from the front of Wyatt's saddle. Staring hard at the place where the pommel had been, Holliday started to say something, but then he closed his mouth and breathed out a long and heavy sigh. It took half a minute before Doc could get his words out.

"We thought you'd ride back for cover with us, Wyatt."

Wyatt said nothing. He stroked the long muscles running the length of the mare's neck.

Doc coughed once lightly and pressed the fist of his left hand to his lips. When the usual spate of coughing did not develop, he lowered his hand.

"When Vermillion's horse went down, hell, we just figured it was every man for himself," Doc said, his voice full of contrition.

The wind soughed, making a soft, whistling sound around the boulders. Off to the north a hawk called a raspy *scree, scree* somewhere high in the sky, scratching its whispery notes against the quiet susurrus of the wind.

"I couldn't get mounted," Wyatt said, letting the hardness fall away from his voice.

Furrowing his brow, Doc looked at him quickly as though he had not understood.

"I'd loosened up my gun belts, and they slipped down my legs."

Doc held an incredulous look on his friend. "Shit, Wyatt," he whispered.

Wyatt looked back toward the colors stacked in layers on the horizon. The sky was turning to fire.

"I'd'a prob'ly got out o' there, too," he said, "but I had Brocius right there in front of me, not twenty-five paces away."

After a long stretch of quiet, Doc clapped a hand to Wyatt's shoulder. "God himself must have been with you out there, my friend. I don't know how else you could have walked out of that hornets' nest untouched."

Wyatt thought of Morgan . . . and that serene mantle of otherworldly protection that had wrapped around him in the open grassy space above the spring. Inside that suit of immortality, every sound had been muffled by the impervious nature of the shield itself. And then, just as unexpectedly, the sensation had reversed. He had been privy to every tap of grass blade, every crunch of sand and grit, and every click of hammer and cylinder as the fusillade rained down on him from the willows.

And it was that way now . . . every utterance of the hard, dry land finding its way to his ears in crystalline detail. He could hear the coursing of his own blood in his ears and out his extremities to his fingertips and toes.

"Morg," he said so quietly that Doc leaned closer.

"What?" Doc probed gently.

Wyatt turned to look at Doc squarely in the eye. "It was Morg."

Gradually, the lines in Doc's face relaxed, and—slowly—he began to nod. He tightened his grip on Wyatt's shoulder.

"All right, Wyatt," Doc allowed, but a question remained in his eyes.

When Wyatt reached to the mare to loosen the cinch, Doc's hand slid from Wyatt's shoulder. "We'll water the horses here," Wyatt instructed. "Then we need to find Tipton. We're out of supplies and out of money, Doc."

"Where do you want to go, Wyatt?"

"We'll look for Tip in Tombstone. After we get those funds, we'll see if we can find Ike Clanton, Ringo, and a few others."

Doc looked east toward town and pressed his lips into a thin line. His nostrils flared, and then he nodded once.

"We're with you, Wyatt."

When Wyatt said no more, Doc moved quietly back toward the others waiting in the rocks. Wyatt slid saddle and blanket from the mare, dropping the rig in the grass. He watched Doc wend his way through the yucca scattered among the rocks, returning to the other posse members to deliver his message and, as he studied the faces of the men who rode with him, a sudden fatigue washed through his body in a wave. Leaning into the boulder, he waited for the sensation to pass.

After a moment, Vermillion walked purposefully toward Wyatt and took the mare's reins. "I'll take your horse to the spring. You ought to get some rest."

Still anchored by the rock, Wyatt removed his hat and let the breeze touch his scalp like a preacher's hand at the river. "My shotgun is out there. Would you get it for me?"

Vermillion nodded, walked away a few steps, and stopped. "We're with you, Wyatt . . . as far as you wanna take it." Without waiting for a response, the ex-carpenter led the mare up the slope to the mesa and past the dead horse. The rest of the men filed one behind the other and followed him to the spring.

Wyatt untied the bedroll from behind the cantle of his saddle and rolled the blanket out on a grassy strip of sand. There he lay down with his head on his saddle and his eyes taking in the scorched dome of the sky arching over the mountains. The tiny vibration in his left foot was slowly receding just as the smoldering colors of the heavens began to fade to gray.

CHAPTER 21

March 26, 1882

Cochise and Graham Counties, Arizona Territory

At the outskirts of Tombstone, Wyatt and his men met a lone rider coming out of town at an easy lope. As they approached one another in the dark, both parties slowed. Each man in Wyatt's posse quietly slid his revolver from a holster at the ready.

"Marshal Earp?" the man called out from thirty yards.

Wyatt reined up, and his deputies fanned out into a flank on either side of him.

"Who is it?" McMaster demanded.

"O. C. Smith," the man replied. "I'm a friend of your brother James . . . and Fred Dodge, too. You remember me, don'cha, Wyatt?"

When the interloper stopped in front of them, Wyatt recognized the short, compact man from his time gambling at the Oriental. His cleft lip was partially hidden behind bushy moustaches that spread from under his nose like an unkempt nest. Smith looked from one posse man to the other and finally let his questioning gaze settle on Wyatt.

Creek Johnson leaned to Wyatt. "I know 'im, Wyatt. That's Harelip Charlie."

"I remember you," Wyatt said to Smith.

Charlie nodded encouragingly. "I was just on my way out to try an' find you."

Wyatt sat his horse quietly and watched the man's tongue dart around his lips. The posse horses shifted their weights and snorted, adjusting to this sudden respite on the dark road.

"You found me," Wyatt said.

Charlie pushed his hat to the back of his head. He appeared relieved to be recognized, crossed his hands on his pommel, and leaned his weight on his arms.

"Did them two boys find you with the money?"

"What two boys?" Wyatt said.

"Some o' the mine operators and businessmen chipped in a thousand dollars for your expenses. They sent two riders to fetch it to you . . . up to Iron Springs."

"We're expecting money from Dake in Prescott," Wyatt said.

Smith was shaking his head before Wyatt finished the statement. "It ain't come."

"How the hell did they know to go to Iron Springs?" Doc tested.

At the tone in Doc's voice, Smith pushed himself erect in the saddle. His forehead creased with three deep lines as he jabbed a thumb over his shoulder toward Tombstone.

"Well, that's where Dan Tipton said to take it."

"Why didn't Tip bring it himself?" Warren said brusquely. "I waited the whole damned morning for 'im and missed out on killing Curly Bill."

Smith narrowed his eyes at the youngest Earp and then again fixed his gaze on Wyatt. "You kilt Brocius?"

"Sonovabitch was cut into two pieces," Warren crowed.

Smith hitched his head once in regret. "Damn, I'd liked to 'a seen that." Then he checked Wyatt's face and smiled. "Did you know that Curly Bill and his men was sworn in as a posse to find you?"

McMaster laughed. "Curly Bill . . . deputized? Well, he sure as hell found us."

"Why didn't Tip bring the money himself?" Wyatt asked. "That's why he went into Tombstone."

"Well, he couldn't. He was in jail with me. Still is, in fact . . . but not with me, o' course. Behan arrested 'im soon's he come into town. Trumped up some charge about resisting an officer and conspiracy."

Doc laughed. "That's Behan trying not to look like a neutered pussy cat after you brushed him off in front of the hotel, Wyatt."

"Why'd he arrest you?" McMaster asked Smith.

"For bein' with Tip," Charlie said and shrugged.

No one spoke for a time as the news sank in. The horses' breathing had settled to a quiet, steady rhythm. The cool night air lay heavily on the land, and out in the scrub brush and mesquite, there was only the sound of a dry muted wind sleaving through the bare branches. Doc cleared his throat roughly, leaned from his saddle, and spat in the road.

"We didn't receive any money," Wyatt said. "Who'd they send with it?"

"Coupl'a boys you can depend on. If they missed you, they'll bring the money back in and get it to you some'eres else."

"What about Tip?" Wyatt said.

Smith waved away the worry on Wyatt's face. "One o' your lawyer friends . . . he'll be postin' bail and gettin' Tip out in a day or two. Tip says not to worry. He'll catch up with you. He says don't come back into town. There's six deputies holed up around the sheriff's office just hopin' you'll make an appearance." Smith nodded out into the dark. "And some'eres out there there's three posses lookin' for you. Behan has hired all the riffraff he can dredge up from around the county."

"What about Bob Paul?" Wyatt asked. "Is he huntin' me?"

Smith allowed a smile. "Sheriff Paul made a show o' lookin' for you 'bout killin' Stilwell, but he ain't pushin' it. He won't have nothin' to do with Behan. Says the men Behan deputized are unfit to be lawmen."

"Who'd Behan hire?" McMaster asked.

Charlie Smith curled his deformed lip to make a sour face. "Ringo . . . the Clantons, both Ike and Phin . . . a handful o' Curly Bill's boys."

"God!" Doc said. "And here I thought I was somebody special because I'm wearing a badge."

No one laughed at Doc's joke. Smith licked his lips again and fixed worried eyes on Wyatt.

"Behan's tryin' to stack it against you," Smith explained, "but Wells, Fargo came out with a public statement supportin' ever'thin' you done.

They say the territorial governor is comin' into Tombstone to back you, too."

Doc leaned on his pommel and smiled at Wyatt. "Governor! How'd you get friends in such high places, Wyatt?"

Wyatt kept his eyes on Charlie Smith. "That's Wells, Fargo's doin'. They know who's been holdin' up their stage shipments."

"Hell, yeah, they know," Smith cackled. "Who don't?" Then his face sobered. "Where will you go now? Them posses are combing the hills for you boys."

"I'm going after the rest of the men who shot my brothers," Wyatt said plainly.

Smith nodded. "I don't reckon you heard . . . those men named by the coroner's jury—the ones who kilt Morgan?—they ain't all available to be found. Hank Swilling—that half-breed who ran with Stilwell—and that German named Bode . . . they both turned theirselves into the law for protection. Pete Spence, too." Charlie coughed up a humorless laugh. "They're still shakin' in their boots though. They say Behan give Spence a gun to keep in his cell, if you can believe that."

"Let's give 'em what they want, Wyatt!" Warren blurted out. "Let's go into town and kill 'em all!"

Wyatt said nothing. He turned his head to look out into the dark expanse of the empty desert. A tendon in his jaw knotted, causing a shadow to pulse there as steady as a heartbeat.

"Say," Smith said, changing course. "Could you boys eat somethin'? I know where you can get your fill without goin' into town." Then he pointed at Vermillion perched double on the wide rump of Creek's spent roan. "We'll get this man a horse, too."

Wyatt turned to either side and studied the faces of his companions. No one made the slightest gesture as a response, but he could see the sag of their shoulders and the fatigue in their eyes. The horses were tired, especially Johnson's, which had carried double weight after the fight in the Whetstones.

"We could eat and rest a spell," Wyatt said. "Horses, too."

Smith nodded sharply and turned his horse a half circle in the road. The other animals perked up at the movement. As the group started off at a walk, Smith twisted around and propped a hand on the cantle of his saddle.

"After you eat and rest up," Charlie said, "I'd like to ride out with you. Can you use another hand?"

Wyatt heard the ring of sincerity in the man's voice. He stared into Smith's eyes, looking for something that would inform him about the man's grit.

"What's your stake in this?"

Smith's whiskered face took on a surprising hardness, while his eyes remained soft as a woman's. "Your brother, Morgan . . . he was a friend of mine. And besides that . . . I'm damned sick o' these low-life Cowboys runnin' it over on ever'body in the county."

Wyatt nodded once. He remembered Morgan telling a story about O. C. Smith leveling a man twice his size for poking fun at his deformed mouth. Morg had said that no man made that mistake twice.

"Can you shoot?" Wyatt asked.

Smith smiled and cut his eyes to Creek Johnson.

"He can shoot," Johnson spoke up.

Wyatt studied the confident gleam on Smith's face. "When I find these men who killed my brother, I won't bring them into court to walk free on the perjury of their friends."

Charlie lost the smile and raised his chin. "You just point out the ones did the killin', and I'll help you *not* bring 'em in."

Smith sat forward in his saddle and coaxed his horse into a trot. The other horses followed without a cue from their riders. The soft sound of hoofbeats on the sandy road melded into a common deep rumble, like the far-off throb of drums marking the advance of a phantom army moving somewhere across the desert.

*****

The next morning Wyatt and his posse rode north up the Sulphur Springs Valley into Henry Hooker's Sierra Bonita Ranch in Graham County. It was a sprawling grassland still in its winter grays and yellows, bordered on east and west by mountains and shadowed through its beveled interior by occasional hills and bluffs. The valley was generously veined with a network of clear streams that would promise lush growth come spring and summer. Both the acreage and the size of Hooker's herds spoke of an empire—one he protected with a small army of loyal hands against the constant threat of rustlers and Apaches.

A lone horseman showed himself on a low ridge at a distance, and then he was gone. By the time Wyatt's party had traveled another three miles inside Hooker's holdings, nine riders appeared on their flank, coming forward at an easy gallop from higher ground.

"Wyatt," Creek Johnson announced.

"I see 'em," Wyatt replied and reined up.

Stopping, the posse turned their mounts to face the oncoming men. One rider wearing a sky-blue shirt beneath a buckskin vest rode a little in front with a Winchester carbine propped vertically on one thigh. The others balanced their rifles crosswise over the bows of their saddles. Wyatt crossed his wrists over what was left of his pommel and waited.

The Hooker party pulled up, and their mounts stamped and snorted and sidled as though the apparent trespass were as much resented by the horses as the cattlemen who rode them. The leader was a wiry man with ink-black hair and a steady gaze. His roan mustang was well-muscled and attentive to the reins. Though young, with a clean-shaven face, this man was clearly the group's leader. He carried himself like a seasoned frontiersman. Looking over Wyatt's posse, he gave a nod to Charlie Smith and then settled his piercing blue eyes on Wyatt.

"My name is Earp," Wyatt said and prodded his horse forward a few steps. He reined up boot to boot with Hooker's spokesman and then cocked his head to indicate the men behind him. "These men are my deputized US marshals."

"Billy Whelan," the young man said, showing no surprise at the identity of the visitors. He sheathed his carbine and nodded to his companions, who put away their weapons and appeared to take on a more relaxed manner. "I'm foreman here," Whelan said and offered his hand. Wyatt took it. When the handshake ended, Whelan squinted one eye in what might have been a stalled wink. "Mr. Hooker's 'xpec-tin' you."

Wyatt patted the neck of his travel-weary mare. "Our horses are played out, and we're pretty much the same. We'd like to rest up for a spell. Feed and water for our mounts, if you can spare it. I can pay you soon as my man comes in from Tombstone."

Whelan looked south down the long valley of sepia-tinted grasses that lay like a ragged winter coat over the land. "Anybody else comin' up that draw we ought'a know 'bout?"

"Could be," Wyatt said. "Coupl'a sheriff's posses are looking for us."

Whelan cracked a grin but held a steely glint in his eyes. "And that'd be Sheriff Johnny *Be-hind*, I'm guessing?"

Doc laughed and then coughed twice to clear his throat. "Sounds like you are acquainted with our sheriff's inflated virtues."

The foreman smiled coolly at Doc and then directed his attention back to Wyatt. "Ain't sure what that means, but it don't matter what anybody thinks of the sonovabitch out here. Behan ain't a lawman in Graham County." Whelan lifted his eyebrows. "Neither are his deputies."

"Well said, son," Doc chirped up. "Behan's not much of a lawman in Cochise County either."

Wyatt lowered his voice just for Whelan. "We don't intend to bring any trouble on Hooker. I want to hole up until my courier arrives with expense money . . . that's all."

Billy Whelan allowed an unrestrained smile. "Hell, we ain't afraid o' trouble at the Sierra Bonita. Mr. Hooker says you're welcome, and that's all we need to know." He neck-reined his horse and pivoted in place to lead out. "Come on with me. I'll take you boys to the ranch house." Then Whelan called over his shoulder to his men. "Two o' you boys get back up on that rise! The rest o' you can finish flushin' cattle out o' those arroyos to the west!"

The Hooker men rode off in their assigned directions, and Wyatt and his party followed the young foreman north up the valley. For the next hour they saw nothing but prime land, golden-hued grass swaying in the wind, and various breeds of English cattle spread out over the flats with the occasional Durham or Alderney bull strolling about as if he were royalty.

*****

The ranch compound was an island of buildings clustered tightly together amid the swale of the valley. Henry Hooker was waiting in the shade of the ramada that wrapped around the main house. Standing with him in the compound were four men wielding rifles. Seven more hovered at the outbuildings that collectively framed the open space of the yard. The layout of the structures suggested a palisade that could be used as a fortress if the need arose. The muscular limbs of an old cottonwood spread grandly into the air above the yard, its leafless branches casting a mosaic shadow across the entrance to the livery barn. Towering above all of it the blades of a metal-latticed windmill turned in the breeze, rendering a steady mechanical *clackety-clack* from its well-oiled parts. Chickens strutted and clucked as they scattered in the yard, dodging the incoming party with their wings flailing at the air.

Hatless, Hooker stepped forward into the light. He was a slight but handsome man with authority etched into his face. A neatly trimmed beard followed the line of his jaw and contrasted sharply against his white dress shirt and scarlet cravat. When he picked out Wyatt, he approached directly, stopped, and spread open the front of his gray woolen coat to splay his weathered hands on his hips.

"You must be Earp. I know your brother, Virgil."

Wyatt dismounted and gripped the man's outstretched hand. "Wyatt," he said.

"How is Virgil recovering from his wounds?"

Wyatt removed his hat and propped it over the bare metal of the horn-post jutting up from the front of his saddle. Raking the fingers of one hand back through his hair, he felt the weariness he had suppressed on the ride north now catch up to him. It trickled down through his body like a cascade of warm water, working its way from scalp to toes.

"He's comin' along . . . in California with the family. He'll find a doctor out there, I reckon, but I doubt he'll ever use that arm again."

The skin on Hooker's forehead tightened, and his gray eyes shone slate hard, giving Wyatt a glimpse of the kind of man who could build an independent cattle empire in the hinterlands of Apache territory. Stranded so far away from any town, the Sierra Bonita seemed a world complete unto itself.

"Hell of a thing," Hooker growled, "when your enemies are a rat's nest of God-less cowards . . . degenerates who would rather skulk around in the night and back-shoot you rather than face you like a man."

The rancher's countenance softened and flushed with color—the sudden change in demeanor seeming entirely unnatural for a man such as himself. After looking away briefly toward the mountains to the west, Hooker cleared his throat and then met Wyatt's eyes with the earnest glow of a gentleman's apology.

"I read about your other brother in the newspapers. I never met him, but I'm sorry for your loss."

"Morgan," Wyatt said, giving a name to his brother and putting the cattleman at ease. He took in a long breath and tried to push the fatigue from his voice. "We're ev'ning out that score as we go, Mr. Hooker."

Hooker nodded but spoke no more on the subject. Slipping his hands into the pockets of his trousers, he inspected each of the men in the posse.

"You men are welcome here. I'll have a meal served up for you within the hour. Meanwhile, you can picket your horses down by the creek. I'll have some good hay thrown out down there. Clean up all you want." Hooker pointed toward a long building extending from the far end of the barn. "We've got space for you in the north bunkhouse. Towels, too." He turned to Whelan. "Billy, why don't you go get these gentlemen some towels they can take down to the creek."

When the foreman strode off toward the bunkhouse, Hooker jerked a thumb over his shoulder at the hacienda behind him. "When you're ready, come into the main house and get something to eat. Then you can rest all you want. If you've got spare clothes to wear, you can give what you're wearing now to my washer women." He nodded toward the open door, where two stout Mexican women had appeared unnoticed. "You are among friends here," he said, turning back to his visitors. "My men will keep you apprised of anyone who sets foot on my land."

Billy Whelan reappeared in the yard with a stack of neatly folded towels hitched under one arm. He tossed a brick of lye soap to Charlie Smith and began doling out towels. When Whelan received a nod from his employer, he mounted his roan and kicked the horse into an easy lope out of the yard in the direction from which they had come. The posse men started their horses for the copse of willows on the low ground behind the compound—all but Wyatt, who remained behind with Hooker.

"I'm behind you all the way with what you're doing," Hooker said. "And the Stock Association, too." He leaned in closer and lowered his voice to a monotonic murmur. "If you can find your way to rid this country of Brocius and Ringo, the association will pay you a thousand dollars a head on those accounts." Hooker's mouth twisted with a wry grin. "When I say 'head,' I mean that literally."

"You don't need to worry about Brocius," Wyatt informed him. "He won't be stealin' any more cattle around here or anywhere else."

Hooker's eyes sharpened. "He's dead?"

Wyatt nodded. "Yesterday. Caught up to him in the Whetstones."

Hooker's expression remained contained and unreadable as he continued to study Wyatt. His gaze lowered to inspect the holes peppered into Wyatt's coat.

"And you're sure he's dead?"

Wyatt nodded. "Both barrels of a scattergun."

Henry Hooker flashed a row of straight teeth in what probably passed for a smile on the Sierra Bonita. Taking his hand from a trouser pocket he tossed a coin in a low arc and snatched it out of the air. Then he let go with a single laugh that sounded like the bark of a dog.

When he looked at Wyatt again, he began to nod, as though confirming something to himself about the man standing before him. "I'll give you that reward out of my own pocket right now and let the association reimburse me later."

Hooker started to back away toward the front door of his house, but he stopped when Wyatt raised one palm as a gesture to delay. The cattle baron waited with one hand resting on his door frame.

"Appreciate the offer," Wyatt said quietly. "But I've got expense money coming in from Tombstone in a day or two."

Hooker's expression was contemplative. He took a step toward Wyatt and then crossed his forearms over his chest.

"You won't take blood money for killin' the men who murdered your brother . . . Morgan. That about right?"

Wyatt said nothing. The two men stared at one another for the time it took one of the yard hens to scout for insects at the fringe of the plank porch. In that half minute of silence the two men learned more about one another than all their previous conversation had afforded.

Hooker turned to face the house, where the two women continued to hover in the doorway. "Consuela, bring us two shot glasses of bourbon, would you?"

When one woman disappeared into the dark interior of the house, Henry Hooker stepped down from the porch into the dusty yard. "I won't insult you again with any talk of money, but I *will* drink with the man who has rid this country of Curly Bill Brocius."

Within a minute, the Mexican housemaid brought the drinks on a hand-carved wooden tray and stood before the two men. Hooker scooped up both glasses and handed one to Wyatt. Even before the woman could return inside, Hooker began a formal toast.

"I speak for all the honest cattlemen in southern Arizona when I say 'thank you.' I want you and your men to take your meals and rest up here as long as you need. Then when you're ready to leave, pick out the best saddle horses from my remuda, and we'll consider it a fair trade for your mounts."

As Hooker threw back his drink, Wyatt balanced the amber liquid before him and thought back to the last time he had felt the burn of liquor in his throat. It was in Prescott with Virgil . . . on the turnaround of a freight haul from San Bernardino. Wyatt had been sixteen years old, and it was the sickest night he had ever experienced.

Hooker lowered his glass, exhaled heavily, and extended his forefinger to point at Wyatt's chest. "You just might have cut off the head of the snake, Wyatt."

Wyatt raised his shot glass to the gratitude in Hooker's face, and then, picturing Morgan smiling with that boyish twinkle in his eyes, he downed the bourbon in one quick swallow. The drink was smoother than he expected, the fire of it a delayed singe after he had handed the empty glass back to his host. Hooker looked around the yard as though he were not yet through celebrating. Wyatt returned his hat to his head and started to lead his mare to the creek.

"Wyatt," Hooker said, pointing toward the chestnut mare, "leave that saddle here. I've got a man who can build a new pommel for you." Hooker pulled two cigars from the breast pocket of his coat and pushed one on Wyatt. Then he struck a lucifer and cupped a hand around the flame as Wyatt nursed the tobacco into a steady burn.

When Wyatt began loosening the cinch on his saddle, Henry Hooker lighted his own cigar and tossed the dead lucifer into the yard. Turning back to the house he spoke in Spanish to the last female hovering in the doorway, and together they walked inside.

Wyatt perched the saddle and blanket on a fence rail at the side of the farrier's shop, removed his personals from his bedroll, and walked his horse toward the stream. The scorch of the whiskey had subsided in his belly, and he felt his body beginning to relax as the alcohol spread to his limbs like a dye bleeding into whole cloth.

The cigar offered a sweet, mellow flavor that Wyatt assumed was standard for a top of the line brand. It seemed that everything about Henry Hooker was high quality: his land, his cattle, the loyalty of his working crew. Even his whiskey and tobacco. There had been a time when Wyatt himself had considered entering the cattle business. In Kansas the prospect had always been an ill-fated one, because the very men he would be compelled to do business with were the same ones that he, as an officer of the law, sometimes slapped over the head with the barrel of his gun.

Now, in this private world of the Sierra Bonita, he was finally able to comprehend the monetary potential for such an undertaking. Henry Hooker had achieved something out here in the Sulphur Springs valley, and Wyatt took note of it. But he didn't envy it. Not now. A new occupation had taken over his life, and he was not ready to give it up. Not yet. There were still names on his list. Men he needed to find. Killers who had believed they could take away his brother and then go about their lives as if there were no price to pay for killing an Earp.

As he approached the creek, Wyatt heard the men talking in low tones, and then, unexpectedly, several of the voices broke into a raucous laughter that carried over the water like the honking of geese. It was the way men used to laugh at Morg when he shared one of the better jokes he liked to unleash on a special occasion.

"Hey, Wyatt," Creek Johnson called from the rocky edge of a bathing pool. "You ever see a plucked prairie chicken take his baptismal rites with a shot o' whiskey?"

Doc Holliday sat naked as a newborn in the center of the pool, the cold water lapping just below his washboard ribs. Upending his silver flask, Doc downed the contents in three quick gulps and then slapped at the surface to splash water toward the others.

"Johnson?" Doc drawled. "When you wade out here and lower yourself into the water, we just might have to change your name from 'Creek' to 'Tiny.' 'Tiny Johnson'! How's *that* sound?"

Everyone laughed but Wyatt. He led his mare upstream to drink with the other horses. While his companions joked downstream, he looked north to the mountains that capped off the valley. Thinking about Morgan, he wondered how many more men he would have to kill before he could fill the cavernous hole of loss that had opened up at the center of him.

CHAPTER 22

March 28, 1882

Sierra Bonita, Graham County, Arizona Territory

Billy Whelan took his mustang at a walk behind another rider slouching over the withers of a swaybacked bay. As they entered the compound just after dawn, Whelan kept his carbine trained on the back of the stranger. No one else stirred among the buildings.

"Turn there behind the barn and pull up at the bunkhouse," Billy ordered.

The lead rider lost his slump and sat his horse erectly. Following the foreman's command, he reined up before the bunkhouse and awaited further instructions.

"Marshal Earp!" Whelan called out. "Could you come out here and identify a man for me?"

When Wyatt stepped outside, he was shirtless with streaks of shaving soap running down one jaw and the side of his neck. His pistol butt jutted from the waistband of his trousers. He gripped a towel in his left hand. The morning chill seemed not to affect him.

"Tip," Wyatt said, greeting the man.

"Wyatt," Tipton replied, a little stoic, and at the same time a little irritated.

Wyatt began rubbing his neck with the towel and looked at the foreman. "This is Dan Tipton, one of my deputies."

Tipton turned his head to glower at Whelan. "Same thing I been tellin' you for the past hour."

Unapologetically, Billy Whelan smiled, slipped a Colt's revolver from the front of his cartridge belt, and made a quick swivel by the trigger guard to offer the gun handle forward. Tipton received the gun unceremoniously and returned it to his holster with an angry thrust. Then, in turn, Whelan returned his new guest's shotgun and lever-action rifle and watched the interloper stuff the Winchester in its scabbard and loop the shotgun over his pommel, all with the same brusque flair.

"No offense, mister," Whelan said agreeably. "Welcome to the Sierra Bonita." He turned to Wyatt. "Breakfast in an hour. I'll tell Consuela to set out another plate."

As Whelan rode off for the main house, Dan Tipton dismounted and began loosening a set of new tan saddlebags draped over his own worn-out pair. "Brought a thousand dollars from E. B. Gage and some of the businessmen in town." He hooked the bags over the hitching rail that ran a quarter the length of the building.

Wyatt lifted the leather bags and slung them over one shoulder. "You look wore out, Tip."

Tipton shrugged. "Rode all night. I was purty near to asleep in the saddle when that young blue-eyed buck jumped me."

Wyatt almost smiled. "He did the same to us. Just doin' his job. Hooker has made us welcome here."

The two men watched as a rider galloped into the courtyard and dismounted at the house. Billy Whelan came outside to greet him, and the two hands spoke briefly as the new arrival untied his saddlebags and handed them over to the foreman.

Whelan walked alone across the yard and held out the bags to Wyatt. "Got you some more money and some news," he said as Wyatt accepted the second delivery. "This here's from Wells, Fargo. Should be a thousand dollars."

Charlie Smith stood in the bunkhouse doorway dressed in gray long johns and boots. The pistol he gripped hung down by his leg. He smiled as Tipton sidled past him with his gear.

"Well, damn," Charlie laughed. "Maybe we just ought'a sit tight here and see how many times somebody sends us a thousand dollars."

"What's the news?" Wyatt asked Whelan.

The foreman pointed south down the long flume of the valley. "Sheriff's posse is about twelve miles out." He pursed his lips and let his eyebrows rise with the implications of his report. "Headed straight for us."

"How many?" Wyatt said.

"Seventeen riders," Billy reported. "Looks like Behan."

Wyatt flung the towel over his shoulder, and his mouth tightened to a grim line. "We'll have to pass on breakfast."

The door at the main house slammed, and Hooker marched across the yard in his shirt sleeves. His wet hair was neatly combed back over his hatless head. A fierce determination sharpened the angles of his face. Whelan took a deferential step back as his employer stopped and spread his boots in the sandy dirt.

"You can make your fight right here, Wyatt. We can hold off an army if we need to. With the men I've got working here at the compound right now, we'll come close to matching Behan's numbers."

Wyatt recognized the heat of battle rising in the cattleman's face. It was the same tacit contract of loyalty he had received unasked from each of his deputies.

"I appreciate the offer, Mr. Hooker, but there's no need for you to get tangled up in this. It could get complicated in the courts for you. Behan would see to that."

"Damn Behan, and damn the rabble who ride with him!" Hooker spat. "I'd be siding with a deputy US marshal."

Wyatt shook his head. "It'll come to a lot more complicated than that."

Hooker's lips pressed into a thin line. His eyes seemed to burn with a fever.

"There's eight of you, Wyatt. Behan's got more than double that."

Wyatt appeared to place no interest in the numbers. "Your man put any names to those faces?"

Hooker's mouth curled to a contemptuous smile. "Behan . . . his undersheriff, Woods . . . Ringo . . . and two of the Clantons. As to the others, hell, they could be Lucifer's in-laws."

Wyatt pushed the towel idly around his cheek and neck. He felt his blood start to run hot. He turned to Billy Whelan.

"Where would you go to make a fight?" Wyatt asked.

"Reilly Hill," Whelan replied without hesitation. He pointed west through the bunkhouse. "Three miles out. It's the first hill you'll see out there before you reach the Galiuro Mountains. There's a spring heads up just below the summit. From up top you can see anybody coming for miles around in every direction."

Wyatt turned to Tipton, who had returned to the doorway with Smith and Vermillion. McMaster rose up on his toes behind them and then shouldered his way through to hear the conversation.

"Tip, can you ride a little more this morning before restin' up?"

"Hell, I can rest anytime," Tip replied, "but I'm gonna need something to eat."

Henry Hooker swept one hand back toward the hacienda as an invitation. "Wyatt, you've got time. Get all of your men over to the house now. We'll feed you breakfast and pack up some food supplies to take with you."

Letting one of the saddlebags slide from his shoulder, Wyatt began to unlace the leather tie on one pouch. "Our horses are not rested. We'll be needin' to lease fresh mounts from you, Mr. Hooker."

Hooker raised a palm and pushed it toward Wyatt, much the way Wyatt had denied payment on the previous day. "Keep your money, Marshal," he said sharply. "I'm loaning you eight fast horses and holding yours as collateral." Looking past Wyatt, Hooker snapped an order. "Billy, get some of the men and cut out the fastest horses in our remuda for these gentlemen."

Whelan started for the main bunkhouse at a crisp walk. Hooker pointed through the compound gate.

"Wyatt, you get your men up there on that hill, and I'll handle Behan." Hooker gave a dry, rough laugh. "Maybe I'll send him off to look for you where the Chiricahuas are holed up at present." His smile turned sinister. "And don't think I don't know."

Wyatt flipped the saddlebag over his shoulder and shook his head. "Send him to us," he said quietly. "Ringo and Ike Clanton are two of the men I need to see."

Hooker's brow lowered over his eyes. "Why don't we take care of that right here?"

Wyatt stepped closer to his host and lowered his voice. "I'm not foolin' myself about going back to run for sheriff in Cochise. There's been too much bad press about us. When I finish my work here, I reckon I'll have to leave. For a time, at least. Wells, Fargo is petitioning the governor for a pardon for what I've done, but that may take some time." Wyatt nodded at Hooker. "You've got to stay here and fit into things." He broke eye contact with the cattleman long enough to scan the buildings that comprised the compound. "You've got a good thing here. We're not going to put that at risk."

Hooker offered his open hand, and the two men clasped with a show of strength. "I'll send Behan to you, if that's what you want," he said.

"It's what I want," Wyatt assured him.

*****

Atop Reilly Hill, Vermillion, Johnson, Warren, and Charlie Smith took over the job of laying out fortifications. They hauled rocks and stacked them into a crude wall that partially ringed the small butte. The result was like the crenellated turret of a hastily built castle. Though riddled with gaps, the makeshift breastwork provided a modicum of defense on whatever side attackers chose to approach.

Perched on a boulder by the spring twenty yards below the crest, Sherm McMaster remained on watch, scouring the valley to the south through a pair of field glasses. In the lee of a boulder, Holliday huddled out of the wind and coughed while Tipton slept inside a bundle of blankets. Wyatt sat on a flat, chunky stone by the picketed horses and drafted a written document that would transfer all his holdings to his sister, Adelia, should events turn against him.

"They're here!" McMaster called out.

Wyatt put away his papers and joined the others at the east edge of the crest. Far off in the south, a cloud of pale-pink dust rose from the bevel of the valley. No one spoke as they watched the progress of their pursuers. Charlie Smith poked a finger at the air as he counted the dark objects clustered at the bottom of the basin.

"I get seventeen," Charlie announced. "That'll be Behan, I reckon."

"Hell, yes, that's Behan." Doc laughed. "Look at the way the third man back sits his horse. I imagine ol' bureaucratic Johnny is nursin' more than a few saddle sores by now."

Johnson squinted one eye at Doc. "Your eyes are that good?"

Doc gave Creek a look. "Hell, there ought to be some part of me that works well enough to brag about."

As they stood together monitoring the movement of the Cochise posse toward Hooker's compound, a knot of horsemen rode out from the ranch, kicking up their own telltale cloud. When the two parties came together, a lull ensued until both groups coalesced into one and started for the compound at a leisurely pace.

"You reckon they told Behan where we are yet?" Vermillion said, directing his question to no one in particular.

Johnson grunted deep in his chest and shook his head. Then he sniffed and spat tobacco over the low wall of rocks stacked before him.

"Them Bonita boys're prob'ly tryin' to give us time to dig in up here."

The wind leaned on them from the west, molding their coats to their backs and coaxing an array of low hums and soft whistles through the gaps in the stones. Watching the procession below, Wyatt's men were quiet for the time it took the group on horseback to enter the compound of buildings and disappear from sight.

"Shouldn't be long now," Doc said.

But they waited for two hours before they saw movement again. Behan's posse galloped out of the main yard headed straight for Wyatt's position. Only a hundred yards from the buildings, they slowed and then stopped. As they grouped together, some of the riders milled about idly, allowing their horses to nose around the rocks for grass.

"What the hell're they doin'?" Vermillion said, his voice impatient and angry. Everyone looked down the hill at McMaster for a reply. After peering through the glasses for a time, he turned to let them see the frown on his face.

"They're turning east . . . away from us!" Mac yelled.

When no one commented on this unexpected maneuver, Doc sidled next to Wyatt. "What do you think?"

Keeping his eyes on the retreating party, Wyatt shook his head. "I got no idea."

McMaster scampered up the slope on his bowlegs. "Behan prob'ly saw how hot things could get for him on this hill."

"He must'a wet himself." Warren laughed. "Prob'ly needs to ride into Willcox for a change o' trousers."

Creek Johnson snorted. "That sounds about right." He tapped the butt of his rifle on the ground next to his boot and turned to where Doc and Wyatt stood together. "What do you wanna do, Wyatt? Should we go after 'em?"

Wyatt squinted off into the distance. Behan's men appeared to be angling north for the pass leading to Fort Grant.

"Could be a trick," Wyatt said quietly. "Let's give it some more time."

Just as twilight tinted the air, Wyatt and his men took their horses at a walk down the slope of the hill. When they reached the floor of the valley, they prodded the horses into an easy gallop and retraced their tracks to the ranch. McMaster spurred his mount up beside Wyatt's and pointed to the churned-up soil ahead of them.

"My grandmother could'a tracked us out to that hill! What the hell do you think they're doin'?"

Wyatt shook his head. "Keep your eyes open."

Inside the compound Hooker stood in the lamp-lit yard with his crew of men, as the Mexican women cleared the last of the plates and silverware from several tables that had been set up in front of the main house. Billy Whelan stood leaning against the blacksmith's shop, turning his hat in his hands, a crooked smile set on his smooth face.

When Wyatt reined up in the yard, his men stopped behind him. Hooker walked out to meet him, and Wyatt could see a vestige of anger smoldering in his eyes. The cattleman's face appeared carved out of oak.

"Behan is riding with a pack of murderers and thieves," Hooker reported. "Every last one of them ought to be in the Yuma prison."

"Did you tell them where we were?" Wyatt asked.

Hooker coughed a sharp laugh. "Hell, I walked Behan out past the gate and pointed out the hill."

Wyatt frowned. "Where did he go?"

Hooker spread his coat and forked his hands over the sides of his waistband. The walnut handle of a Colt's revolver jutted from a trouser pocket.

"Said he was heading to Fort Grant to hire some trackers," Hooker said, allowing a little amusement to play in his eyes.

Wyatt jerked a thumb back toward the gate. "We didn't hide our tracks. Anybody could have followed the trail we left . . . even Behan."

Hooker's knotted mouth managed a tight smile. "I guess Sheriff Behan didn't feel up to the task of arresting you."

Wyatt's frown only deepened. He watched the Mexican women take in the last of the tables.

"But you fed him," Wyatt said.

Hooker's expression remained businesslike. "Just like I fed you and your men. Doesn't mean I enjoyed it."

Wyatt studied the man's weathered face. "Ringo and Clanton?"

"They were with him. And a pig's sty of companions. I'll wager most of those saddle tramps have stolen cattle from me."

Wyatt looked over the tops of the buildings to the mountains rising in the northeast. Behan would be climbing up to the pass by now. With him were two or more of the men on Wyatt's list.

"Makes no sense," Wyatt mumbled.

A deep laugh scraped up from Hooker's throat. "No . . . not to a lawman. But it makes perfect sense if we're talking about a spineless politician like Behan." Hooker pointed at a small table standing alone in the courtyard, separated by ten yards from where the long line of tables had linked together in front of the hacienda. "Behan and his undersheriff claimed they really had no association with the boys riding with them . . . that they were simply a necessary evil if they hoped to bring in the Earp party." Hooker turned to the smithy's shed where Whelan still stood. "Billy!" Hooker called and waved his foreman over.

Billy Whelan swung his hat to his head, leisurely pushed off from the rock wall, and ambled toward the parley in the courtyard.

"Show them your new jewelry, Billy," Hooker suggested.

Whelan removed his hat and handed it up to Wyatt. Doc edged his horse forward and the other posse men coaxed their mounts closer. In the sparse lamp light Wyatt inspected a glittery pin stuck into the hat band and then looked up, waiting for an explanation.

"S'posed to be a diamond," the foreman said. "Worth at least a hun'erd dollars, so says Sheriff Be-hind. He's the one give it to me." He flashed a grin and nodded at the pin. "I reckon that's s'posed to shut me up 'bout what happened here."

Doc took the hat from Wyatt. After holding it close to his eye he broke into a dry laugh that segued into a series of coughs.

"It's a diamond, all right," Doc said, getting his breath. He raised the hat for the others to see. Then he leaned to return the hat to Whelan. "And what's the big secret about what happened here?"

Billy slapped the hat to his head and pursed his lips. Then he looked down at his boots as though sorting out the words. Finally he propped his hands on his hips, grinned, and looked back at Wyatt.

"I reckon it's that Behan ain't no more in charge of that crowd than a meal worm bedded down with rattlesnakes." His grin widened to a smile that showed a row of crooked teeth. "We might'a embarrassed the sheriff a little." Billy popped the brim of his hat with a flick of his forefinger. " 'Bout a hun'erd dollars worth, I'd say."

When Whelan offered no more, Hooker slipped his hands into his coat pockets, hooking his thumbs on the outside. "Ike Clanton tried to get pushy. Called me 'a son of a bitch' for harboring fugitives from the law." He hissed a laugh through his teeth and removed a hand from his coat to pat the pistol stuffed in his pocket. "I didn't have this at the time," he said and cocked his head toward his foreman. "Billy stuck his carbine in Clanton's ribs, levered a round into the chamber, and demanded a retraction." Hooker's eyes took on an amused slant when he looked at Whelan. "How did you put it, Billy?"

Billy Whelan lost his smile. "You don't come into a gentleman's yard for a meal and call 'im a sonovabitch. I told him to skin it back."

Doc laughed. "And I'll bet his tail went between his legs as he provided a prompt apology."

Whelan snorted. "Looked 'bout like he'd swallowed his spoon. Didn't have much to say after that."

"Ike could out-crow a rooster with his tail feathers on fire," Doc said, grinning broadly as he paused, ". . . until the shooting commences."

Hooker stepped closer to Wyatt and lowered his voice. "Behan doesn't want to catch you, Wyatt. He just wants to appear as if he's looking for you. He's more interested in the travel expenses he's piling up. But he'd love to take credit for your capture if he can. He's hoping the army can do that for him."

Warren removed his hat and slapped it across his thigh. "We got three posses on our tail. Now we got the army looking for us, too?"

Hooker shook his head. "I wouldn't worry about that. Colonel Biddle owes me a favor. Even before Behan's crowd finished eating, I dispatched a man to the fort to apprise the colonel of the situation." Hooker stepped into the center of the half-ring of horsemen. "Climb down and relax, gentlemen. You are welcome here for as long as you'd like to stay. We'll have a meal ready for you in ten minutes."

Wyatt and Doc sat their horses as the other posse members dismounted and walked their horses to the livery. Hooker moved closer to Wyatt.

"Wyatt, those men with Behan are claiming that Curly Bill is still alive."

Wyatt showed no reaction. He said nothing.

Doc laughed. "Unless someone has figured out how to put a man back together after he's been cut in half with a shotgun, I wouldn't bet on it."

Hooker nodded and smiled. "The newspapers in Tombstone are having a war of words over it. The *Nugget* has offered a hundred dollars to anyone who can prove Curly Bill is dead. The *Epitaph* put up two thousand if Brocius will make a personal appearance."

Wyatt twisted in the saddle to look over Hooker's outbuildings. "My men could use some sleep. Is your bunkhouse still available?"

Hooker offered his hand. "Long as you'd like, Wyatt."

Wyatt met the man's grip and shook. "Thank you, Henry."

Hooker and his foreman walked across the yard toward the hacienda, leaving Wyatt and Doc the only two in the yard under the spreading cottonwood.

"Doesn't sound like Ringo," Wyatt said, "riding away from us like that." He lifted his gaze to the mountains. "He might want me as much as I want him."

Doc followed his gaze. "You think we could catch them, Wyatt?"

Wyatt shook his head. "Only nine miles to the fort. Maybe after they leave there."

"They'll head for Willcox," Doc surmised. "I suspect Ringo would be low on whiskey about now."

"Good," Wyatt said. "I'd like to kill him when he's sober."

When Doc started into a coughing spell, Wyatt turned and watched his friend's eyes glaze over with the sheen of involuntary tears. He waited until Doc stuffed his handkerchief back into the inside pocket of his coat.

"We'll rest up here a while, Doc. Long as you need."

Doc produced an impish frown. "And miss all the fun?" He reined his horse around for the stables. "I'll tell the boys to be ready to pull out after we eat."

CHAPTER 23

Late March 1882

Graham County, Arizona Territory

The gibbous moon lighted the trail through the mountains. On their original mounts, the eight men in the Earp posse traveled without speaking over the Stockton Pass down into Sycamore Wash and its well-known watering hole on the west side of the San Simon Valley. They made camp in a grove of oaks a quarter mile from the spring, with McMaster and Johnson taking up look-out positions nearer the watering hole.

Just before dawn Wyatt heard horses at the low end of the grove. Thinking it to be one his watchmen, he rolled out of his blankets and pulled on his boots. Charlie Smith was already gathering sticks to lay over the few red coals glowing in the shallow fire pit. Everyone else was asleep.

Wyatt buckled on his gun belts, picked up his shotgun, and walked out into the dark to wait for any incoming message from his scouts, but the leisurely sound of horses' hooves seemed to be heading south, passing their camp to the east. He stopped and listened for a voice, but there was none.

Then Charlie called out from the clearing in a raspy whisper. "That you, Wyatt?"

Wyatt quickly looked back to quiet the man but said nothing. Behind Smith on the far side of the pit, Warren kicked out of his bedroll and sat screwing the heels of his hands into sleepy eyes.

"What the hell're you screechin' at, Charlie?" Warren said gruffly.

Gunfire exploded from the trees below. Wyatt leveled the shotgun barrels at the muzzle flashes out in the dark and fired off both rounds, the big ten-gauge booms filling the oak grove like a double clap of thunder. The wrenching scream of a horse filled the dark with an eerie sound—like the blare of a rusty horn. A man's voice cried out in pain, that followed by a string of muffled profanities.

All of Wyatt's men were returning fire now, each gunman crouched behind a chosen tree and making a stand in his stockinged feet. They emptied their rifles and then snapped off a flurry of shots with their revolvers. The fighting intensified for a quarter of a minute until the fusillade from the camp seemed to overpower the ambushers. Soon the staccato clack of hooves on rocks marked a hasty departure by the attackers. Wyatt could hear their escape all the way down into the open sandy grassland at the valley's bottom.

"I'm hit, goddamnit!" Warren yelled.

When Wyatt got to him, Warren was furious, doubled up on his blankets, holding the front of his thigh, and gritting his teeth. The whites of his eyes glowed moon-bright against his dark irises.

"The sonzabitches shot me before I could get out of my damned bed," Warren hissed.

Dan Tipton knelt over the youngest Earp and inspected the wound. "Sit still, dammit, so I can see how bad it is!"

"I already know how bad it is!" Warren shot back. "It's like a damned sledgehammer tried to take off my leg!"

Wyatt knelt to his brother and gripped his shoulder firmly. "Let him have a look, Warren."

Tipton struck a lucifer and leaned low. When he looked up at Wyatt, Tip shook his head.

"He's losin' a lot o' blood. We're gonna need a doctor."

Warren sat up and tried to stand, but Wyatt took a strong grip on both of his shoulders and lowered him back to the blankets. Then Doc Holliday was there, trying to allay the boy's fears so that he would stay down.

"Who the hell was it?" Warren demanded. "Was it Behan?"

"Don't know," Wyatt said. "Sounded like four or five riders." He looked at Tipton. "Tear up that cleaner blanket into strips, and let's get this wound tied off."

Warren cursed profusely as Doc and Tipton tried to stop the bleeding. Wyatt cautioned for quiet until he heard horses hurrying in from the north. Picking up his shotgun, he reloaded, cocked the hammers, and waited. There was enough light now to recognize McMaster's paint mare breaking into the grove. Then, behind McMaster, Creek Johnson's broad silhouette atop his stout roan stud emerged from the trees.

"What the hell happened?" Mac called out. "We heard shots." He swung down from the paint even before it had come to a stop. Johnson reined up and frowned down at the men wrapping Warren's leg.

"Somebody opened up on us from down the slope," Charlie volunteered. "Wyatt's little brother here is the only one got hit. I might'a shot one of 'em, but, hell, I know Wyatt hit somebody . . . and a horse, too. I ain't never heard a animal scream like that in my life."

"They came out of the north," Wyatt said and looked pointedly at McMaster and Johnson.

Mac scowled and puffed out his chest. "Didn' nobody get past us. We were at the springs the whole night. Whoever it was must'a skirted us to the east."

"Wyatt," Charlie said, "I think they prob'ly stumbled on us. Else they would'a come in on foot and picked us off proper while we slept."

McMaster spat and looked around the grove. "Might'a been some of Ringo's boys quittin' on Behan . . . now that they know he ain't really wantin' to face us."

"Could've been Ringo and Ike," Charlie said. "Maybe a few others."

"We could go after 'em, Wyatt," Johnson offered.

Wyatt looked down the hill where the ambuscade had erupted like an unexpected string of fireworks. The thought of John Ringo and Ike Clanton firing at them from the dark made his blood run hot.

"We're going to Fort Grant," he said simply. "There'll be a surgeon there." He turned and looked each man in the eye. No one questioned his decision. He knelt beside Warren again and gripped the boy's arm. "Can you ride?"

Warren cleared his throat roughly and spat to one side. "Hell, yeah, I can ride. Let's go after those bastards, Wyatt."

Wyatt shook his brother gently as though pulling him from a dream. "We're going to the fort, Warren, so get chasin' out of your head."

Wyatt stood and shivered once. He had not noticed the cold of the morning until now. Pulling on his shirt and vest, he began working the buttons with numbed fingers.

"Let's saddle up," he said, loud enough for all to hear. "Mac, Creek . . . can you get my brother mounted on his horse?"

Everyone went into motion with no thought of building a fire or preparing breakfast. Vermillion took his dapple gray at a walk down the slope and studied the tracks at the edge of the clearing. Wyatt walked to his bedroll and gathered his belongings. When he carried his saddle to his mare, Doc was there, tightening the cinch on his own mount.

"You made the right decision, Wyatt. There's plenty of time to get Ringo and Clanton. I just hope nobody else shoots Ike before we can settle with him." Doc huffed an airy laugh through his nose. "God knows there must be plenty of men who would jump at the opportunity."

One-handedly, Wyatt threw his saddle blanket over the mare's back and straightened it. Then he swung up the saddle and rocked it by the new pommel that had been fitted to the post. It was a wider horn than that to which he was accustomed—a cow-man's tool for turning loops on a lariat. Flipping the stirrup over the bow of the saddle, he began running the cinch strap through the double rings beneath the fender.

"I won't lose another brother," he said, his voice quiet but determined. He let the stirrup fall, toed into it, and mounted.

"I know," Doc said. "Getting Ringo isn't worth that . . . and certainly not Ike." Doc pulled himself up into the saddle and met Wyatt's eyes. "I'll ride beside Warren and keep an eye on him."

"Thanks, Doc," Wyatt said and coaxed his horse forward to where Vermillion sat his horse and waited.

"Dead horse down there, Wyatt," Vermillion reported and raised his arm to point downhill into the trees. "Shot through the lungs, looks like. And there was plenty of blood on the saddle and all over the withers. I figure the rider was gut shot. Found this down there, too . . . 'bout ten yards away from the horse . . . next to a rock streaked in blood." From under his coat Vermillion produced an old Remington revolver converted for self-contained cartridges. "We must'a hit a couple o' those bastards, sure as hell."

"Any identifying marks on the horse or saddle?"

Vermillion shook his head. "Prob'ly rented from a livery. That's standard for a posse, ain't it?" When Wyatt did not answer he added, "Blanket and slicker but no saddle bags. Somebody must'a took 'em."

Wyatt pursed his lips and nodded toward the Remington. "What about the pistol? You recognize it?"

"Don' know, Wyatt. I showed it to Mac and Creek." He shook his head again.

"Could it have been Ringo's gun . . . or Clanton's?"

"Mac said it wasn't Ringo's. Don't know about Clanton."

For a time Wyatt stared downhill into the trees. Finally he nodded.

"Let's move out," he said and led the way northwest back over the mountains.

*****

At Fort Grant the surgeon removed the bullet from Warren's leg and confined him to a hospital bed. Wyatt sat with his brother until the administered laudanum ushered Warren into a deep sleep of utter stillness. Even the boy's breathing was shallow—so much so that Wyatt had to lean in close several times to be assured that Warren had not slipped away from blood loss.

"That's the laudanum," the orderly explained. "It's why we get so many slackers come in for headache and dysentery and gout and whatever else they can dream up. These soldiers gamble so much in the barracks at night, they think they should be admitted to the hospital to catch up on their sleep." The soldier dressed in white chuckled. "Can't say I blame 'em. You can drift off on some pretty tall clouds on a spoonful of that stuff." He nodded at the bottle on the bedside table, the same kind of brown glass container that had been Mattie's bosom companion for most of her time in Tombstone.

Wyatt stood quietly and looked down at his brother. Such a peaceful countenance was a rarity for the Earp who was sometimes referred to as "the tiger" by the other posse men. Warren always put on a show, Wyatt knew, trying to live up to his older brothers. It made him rash and unpredictable. One day it was probably going to get him killed, unless he could be persuaded into a line of work that carried a minimum of liabilities.

Wyatt thought of Morgan lying on the sofa in Bob Hatch's card room. After a grueling hour of suffering, Morg's face had relaxed into this same visage of complete surrender. Sending his body to his parents in California had been a cruel errand of necessity. To have repeated this with Warren might have broken the elder Earps.

"Where can I find a notary public?" Wyatt asked the orderly.

The soldier laid a blanket over Warren and then stared out the window at the growing dark. He narrowed his eyes and ran his tongue along the inside of a cheek.

"Sutler over at the fort store. He can stamp something for you."

Wyatt picked up his hat off the bed behind him.

"Oh . . . Marshal Earp," the soldier said, turning quickly from the window. "The colonel is providing a meal for your men in the officers' mess. Said to tell you to join 'em when you're ready."

After attending to his documents and posting them through the fort's mail service, Wyatt walked the long line of buildings fronting the parade grounds until he found the mess hall. Upon entering he was met by the unexpected memory of his mother's cooking on the farm in Iowa. The air in the big room was thick with the richness of savory meat and cooked vegetables. His men were gathered in the back of the room under a carved wooden plaque that reserved the area for officers. With the hour so late, the rest of the tables were unoccupied, but Wyatt could hear the cooks banging pans in the kitchen, the sound like a thinly disguised complaint for an unexpected late meal duty. The room was warm from a combined source of heat: a stove burned wood in the main hall, and it was bolstered by the ovens in the back.

The bulk of the men eating at the table leaned into their trays, each man wholly dedicated to a meal that he himself did not have to prepare. Only Doc and McMaster looked up to read Wyatt's face. Every man wore his revolver on his person, and nearby a rifle leaned against a wall within easy reach.

Wyatt took off his coat and hat and laid them across a neighboring table stacked with the sundry garments of his deputies. Doc held up an empty metal plate and set it down at the vacant space beside him. Wyatt sat and began serving himself from the platters of beef, peas, potatoes, and flat bread.

"How is he?" Doc said, pouring Wyatt a glass of water.

"Asleep. Doctor said, long as we keep the wound clean, he'll be fine."

Doc nodded and set down the pitcher. "Dig in, Wyatt. You need it."

Charlie Smith leaned forward to talk past Tipton and Johnson. "Army food ain't half bad, Wyatt. Not like Hooker's spread, but a hellava lot better'n salt pork and beans."

The front door opened, and Colonel Biddle and another officer entered the room. Biddle, a portly man with sweeping gray moustaches, walked to the kitchen and spoke brusquely to the men on duty. The other officer stood by the door as Biddle crossed the room and took up a stiff position at the head of the table.

"I trust you men are getting what you need?"

Creek Johnson smiled and raised a fork weighted with a chunk of beef. "Almost makes me wanna enlist, Colonel." He stuffed the meat into his mouth and spoke around the chewing. "Almost," he added and shook once with a private laugh.

Biddle returned the smile, looked at each man, and then settled his gaze on Wyatt. "Could I have private word, Marshal?" Without waiting for a response, he turned on his heel and joined the other officer, who now waited at the center of the room. Wyatt wiped his mouth with a folded cloth ink-marked with a black "US," set the cloth aside, and rose to join the private parley.

Biddle seemed to be gathering his thoughts as he stared at the plank floor. Then his head came up with authority. His bloodshot eyes showed a contradictory mix of power and compassion.

"I know what you're up against. I got the story from Hooker's man. And I think I know what kind of man Sheriff Behan is. As little as I care for the man, he does have a warrant for you, and the warrant appears to be valid. I checked. I'm sure you'll understand when I tell you that I have to be careful of *my* moves that might interfere with civilian government. I've contacted my superiors in Washington, and it seems that you have friends that extend a long way from Arizona Territory."

Wyatt said nothing but wondered which of the Tombstone business-men might have tried to pull strings for him. Probably Wells, Fargo, which had the ear of the governor.

"Nevertheless," Biddle continued, "despite where my loyalties may lie, I can't be seen as an abettor to a fugitive from the law. Behan's warrant comes from Cochise County. There is a second warrant for you out of Pima. That only complicates the situation."

Wyatt nodded. "I would not want to put you at risk, Colonel."

Biddle's aide unfolded a telegram and held it for Wyatt to see. Wyatt glanced at it and then met Biddle's troubled eyes again.

"As you can see, my hands are tied by my superiors," Biddle said. He pursed his lips and stared past Wyatt at the men feasting off army food. When he turned back to Wyatt he seemed to lose some of the stiffness in his posture. "Look," the colonel sighed, "these are Arizona warrants. If you were to continue what you're doing in ridding this territory of its degenerates, I could be held complicit . . . putting you up here at the fort, feeding you, permitting my surgeon to work on your brother. If you rode east to New Mexico Territory, things would be out of my assigned jurisdiction. You'd be someone else's problem. It would take an extradi-tion order to get you back here to stand trial. And it sounds like that ball is already rolling. Do you hear what I'm saying?"

Wyatt took in a long breath of air and looked down at his boots for a time. When his head came back up, he stared into the threads of blue and red that webbed across the colonel's apologetic eyes.

"When Behan was here," Wyatt said in a flat tone, "was John Ringo with him? And a short man with a little goatee and whining voice—name of Ike Clanton?"

Biddle squinted at the change in direction. "Behan and his undersheriff came in with over a dozen hard cases. I don't know their names, but I'm pretty sure that most of them have had their hands on government cattle at some time."

The aide put away the telegram and cleared his throat. "If I may, sir . . . I think five or six of them rode off early this morning. Seems there was some kind of argument between them and the sheriff."

"Was it Ringo?" Wyatt pressed.

The man looked away for a moment and then looked firmly at Wyatt. "Tall with dark hair and moustaches. Kind of morose. Wouldn't look at you when he talked to you." The man arched his eyebrows at the memory. "Tell you the truth, he seemed the kind of man that you were better off if he *didn't* look at you."

Wyatt clenched his teeth at the missed opportunity in the grove of oaks. If he had known it was Ringo and Clanton, he might have sent Doc with Warren to the fort while he and the rest of the posse trailed them south.

But that was the past. Already he could feel his plans taking a new direction. There would be time for those men—Ringo and Clanton. And the men who had taken refuge in Behan's jail.

"Marshal Earp," Biddle said in a low, humming voice. "I urge you to consider carefully which way you'll be traveling from here."

"You don't need to worry, Colonel. I owe you a debt for my brother. We'll head east. And as far as the territory is concerned, we were never here at the fort."

Biddle offered a flaccid hand, and they shook. "Your horses have been fed, watered, and groomed at the livery," the colonel said and released his grip.

Then the aide took Wyatt's hand more firmly. "The doctor says your brother can travel when he wakes. May I suggest you depart before reveille? The fewer eyes on you, the better. Wouldn't you agree?"

Wyatt gestured toward his men at the table. "I'd like my men to have a few hours rest. Can you accommodate us?"

"I've already taken care of that," the aide said. "We've set up cots in the back of the hospital. You can keep watch on your brother there."

"Appreciate your hospitality," Wyatt said and nodded to both men. He turned to leave, but the colonel stepped forward and touched his sleeve.

"The way you've been scouring the country for this Cow-boy scum," Biddle whispered, "I imagine most of that crowd will be heading for Mexico soon. Some of the men in my livery heard them talking about that. Arizona will likely owe you a great debt, Marshal Earp."

Wyatt thought for a moment before answering. "I reckon that'll depend on who you ask, Colonel."

When the two officers left, Wyatt returned to his table and finished his meal. The others lighted cigars, all but Johnson, who preferred his tobacco chewed, and Doc who could no longer subject his lungs to the acrid smoke. Anxious to be off duty, the kitchen crew quickly cleared the table, leaving the civilian visitors to converse in the warmth of the hall.

"Here, Wyatt," Doc offered, holding out a cigar. Then Holliday slipped his flask from his coat and took a long pull of whiskey.

Wyatt lighted the stogie from the oil lamp on the table. As he worked the tobacco into a steady burn, the men around him quieted and settled in, waiting for him to speak.

"It's time we got out," Wyatt said. "The longer we cover the territory looking for these last few men, the better chance we have gettin' put behind bars. That or gettin' killed. I figure one's the same as the other. If we go into Behan's jail, we're not likely to get out alive."

Johnson leaned to spit into a tin cup. No one else moved.

"What about Ringo?" Creek said. "You think that was him opened up on you in the oak grove?"

"Half a dozen of Behan's posse split off," Wyatt explained. "Ringo was with 'em. I figure they missed the watering hole and ran into us by accident."

McMaster's ruddy face sharpened like an axe blade. "Maybe it was him you hit, Wyatt."

Wyatt shook his head. "We weren't there," he said, underscoring his words with a flat monotone.

Charlie Smith's face wrinkled like a balled up dish rag. "What do you mean 'we weren't there'? I shot one of the sonzabitches myself!"

"We weren't there," Wyatt repeated. "And my brother—Warren—was never shot." He looked at each man's bewildered expression in turn. "I don't want to leave a trail to Fort Grant. We never came here. Never needed the fort surgeon. Colonel Biddle never saw us." Wyatt paused and checked the burn on his cigar. "I owe the colonel that much."

One by one, each posse man began to nod. Wyatt took a draw on his cigar and blew a thin stream of smoke that rose with the heat wavering over the lamp.

"Besides that," Wyatt went on, "I see no need to give Ringo's crowd the satisfaction of knowing they hit one of us."

"That sounds like you think we didn't kill Ringo," Tipton said.

"If we did," Wyatt said, "those boys would never let the news get out. Same as they're doin' with Curly Bill." He set down his cigar. "If Ringo is still alive, he'll head for Mexico. Him and a lot of others. There'll be another time to settle those scores."

Doc Holliday smiled and raised his flask like a toast. "Amen to that," he said. "And all the while, they'll be runnin' from their own shadows and wonderin' when we're comin' for them."

"What do you wanna do, Wyatt?" Vermillion asked.

Wyatt flicked his cigar over the metal plate the men had appropriated for their ashes. "Sleep a few hours. There are beds set up for us at the hospital. After that we'll ride for New Mexico. I think all you boys should consider staying out of Arizona for a while."

The posse men looked at one another, but no one offered a comment. Wyatt stepped out from the bench and stood looking at his deputies.

"I owe you boys. I reckon I always will."

Doc pocketed his flask and waved away the gratitude Wyatt had laid bare on the table. "It was a hell of a party, Wyatt. I, for one, would not have missed it."

The other men said nothing, but in each of their eyes was the deep-seated glow of loyalty. The steady flame of the oil lamp was like an extension of their solidarity. Wyatt donned his vest and coat and then withdrew an envelope from his inside pocket. When he dropped it on the table, the sound seemed magnified by the stillness of the men gathered there. Everyone knew that the package contained a hefty stack of bills.

"Split this up among yourselves. It should get you where you want to go."

Charlie Smith rose and extended a hand across the table. "I ain't been with you as long as these ol' ki-yotes, but I can tell you it's been an honor."

Wyatt took his hand and shook. Then each man in turn stood and repeated the ritual—all but Doc, who watched the proceedings and smiled as if he were on a good run at the poker table. McMaster was last to pay his respects and walked with Wyatt to the door.

"I guess you know I got reason to go back to Tucson," McMaster said. "Me and Val, you know?"

Wyatt stopped walking and turned to face his ex-informant. "You're the one's got reason to go back, Mac. But I hope you'll use that money to get the two of you out o' there. Bob Paul is doin' his best *not* to catch us, but he may have to do something if you rub it in his face."

"Val and me used to talk about California. She lived there when she was a kid . . . outside San Bernardino."

Looking at the earnestness in his friend's face, Wyatt pushed from his mind the picture of the young Mexican girl who had dressed and spoken like someone twice her age in an outdoor cantina. Though she had taught him in a peach orchard the subtleties of the carnal equation between a man and a woman, she was no longer Wyatt's to remember. She belonged to McMaster.

"California sounds good, Mac. Lot o' opportunities there."

McMaster nodded. "Long as they got horses. I figure that's what I'm best cut out for . . . workin' with 'em from wild oats to snubbin' post."

Wyatt nodded. "You hang on to what you got, Mac . . . it's a hellava lot more than what most men have."

Wyatt reached for the door latch, but McMaster cleared his throat and sidestepped to stand squarely before Wyatt. The flushed skin on the ex-Cow-boy's face tightened, giving new angles and shadows to his ruddy countenance.

"Wyatt . . . you pulled me up out o' a bad place. I'm beholdin' to you." His eyes were bright and steady, like two candle flames in the stillness of an empty room.

Wyatt patted the upper arm of the smaller man. "I threw you one end of a rope, Mac. You're the one climbed out."

McMaster thrust out a hand, and the two men shook again. Then Mac offered a single brisk nod before returning to the table for his things.

Buttoning up against the night air, Wyatt stepped outside and strode onto the parade grounds until he could stand beyond the half halo of dim light spreading from the mess hall. He stood for a time letting the slight breeze of the desert night carve around the contours of his body like the anointing of a private ritual. From one of the distant barracks he could hear the laughter of soldiers rising above the steady whisper of the wind. Oddly, the muted sound of it made him feel more isolated from the line of buildings spread out behind him. The stars were scattered thickly across the night sky, like shattered jewels arranged across a black blanket. Some of the points of light flickered like distant campfires. It was a celestial show of infinite possibilities.

Morgan loved nights like these. He would smile up at the stars and talk about things he and Wyatt discussed with no other living person— not even Virgil. On those occasions Morg could hold up a conversation by himself for long stretches, and Wyatt loved nothing better than to learn about the private thoughts his favorite brother entertained.

Those were the memories Wyatt wanted most to hang onto. But as they always did, the recollections funneled inevitably to the end, where they were supplanted by Morg's last words as he lay bloodied and broken on the sofa at Hatch's Billiard Parlor.

Get out, Wyatt. Get away from—

Even then, with his labored breathing and grimace of unspeakable pain, Morg's voice had retained a trace of that personable warmth that had been a part of him since he was a young boy on the Iowa farm. It was as if Morg's good humor had been part of two brothers' plan to balance out the deficits of Wyatt's laconic character.

Wyatt raised his eyes to the stars again. *Time to get out, Morg*, he mouthed, almost saying the words aloud. *For a while, at least.*

So wrapped up in his thoughts was he, Wyatt heard the relaxed approach of a horse's hooves only after the animal was almost upon him. A soldier walked Wyatt's unsaddled mare through the short, stiff grass of the open field, leading the chestnut by a simple halter of supple leather.

"Marshal?" the soldier called out and stopped a few feet away. "I was walkin' your mount to see why she was favoring a foreleg, but it was only a little speck of rock wedged near the frog. She's lookin' fine. I'll lead her back to the stall."

"I'll take her," Wyatt said and moved to the mare's muzzle where she could smell him. "Thank you, Corporal."

When the soldier started back alone for the livery, Wyatt slowly reached up to the horse's neck and combed the mane with his fingers. She had been groomed well, leaving no tangles in the coarse hairs. When the mare shifted her stance and swung a slow quarter turn, Wyatt found himself looking into the liquid gold-brown of the animal's eye. Sadie's eye. The mare stared back at him with the same gentle devotion he had seen in Sadie's farewell gaze in the dining room at Brown's Hotel.

You'll know when it's time to leave, she had said.

Now that time had come, Wyatt knew. And with that knowledge came the revelation that he could choose whatever life he wanted. He had nothing now—just a horse and saddle, a few guns, and a coat riddled with bullet holes. There was just enough money in his pocket to make a quiet exit from Arizona Territory. As he thought about it, it seemed to Wyatt that a man with almost no assets might be freer than most to determine his direction.

He turned and rested his forearms over the shallow sway of the mare's spine and stared out into the dark of the desert. Everything had been lost in Tombstone. He had banked on becoming sheriff and amassing his wealth through that plum position of the law, but now such a position was an impossibility.

A sudden fatigue washed over him, and Wyatt leaned into the horse's ribs, taking a grip on the withers. He didn't know how he had survived the battle at Iron Springs. Just like he did not understand why Behan's superior force had not laid siege to him on the hill outside Hooker's ranch. Except for Warren's wound, none of his men had been hurt. It seemed improbable. They had lost only a horse. That was it. How could one man have been blessed with so much good fortune?

Finishing the job of finding Morgan's murderers did eat at him, but there would be time enough to finish it later. Spence, Bode, and Swilling. Ike Clanton and Ringo. Let those sons of bitches hide out in Mexico. Let them wonder which day he might be coming. They would keep. The threat would hover over them like a dark storm cloud shuddering with flashes of fire and brimstone.

Perhaps that was enough—to simply leave them to uncertainty. One-eyed jacks, always looking over one shoulder. Either that or, one day when the time was right, he would bring judgment down upon them like the fury of God.

The door opened behind him, and Wyatt pivoted to see Doc turn his back to the wind and cough into his handkerchief. For a long time he racked his lungs and alternately sucked in air to let the spell run its course. Doc had seemed to take strength from their task of scouring the country for the men who had killed Morg. Regardless of his cavalier attitude, the ex-dentist had not been able to hide his pride in wearing a badge. But now it seemed his disease had worsened. In the last few days, Doc's vitality had waned. All the men had noticed and had tried to take up some slack to let him rest more than the others.

When the coughing would not abate, Doc walked briskly for the far end of the fort, never seeing Wyatt and his horse. The tubercular hacking remained audible as Doc made his way along the parade field to the hospital.

"Time to get out," Wyatt said softly, much in the same way he had spoken to Morgan on those long nights of brotherly exchange.

The mare's ears stiffened at the words. She hooked her neck around to better see Wyatt. He took up the cheek strap on the halter and started the mare at a walk for the livery.

CHAPTER 24

Spring 1882

New Mexico Territory, Colorado, San Francisco

They skirted the Peloncillos and stole into New Mexico by way of the old Gila River Road to Silver City. There they sold their horses and took a specially arranged stage to Deming, courtesy of Wells, Fargo. In Deming, Charlie Smith said his goodbyes and outfitted himself for parts unknown.

From there the rail lines ran due north to Albuquerque, where Doc Holliday and Dan Tipton parted ways from the retired posse and declared themselves for Denver, where the gambling was said to be good.

"Well, Wyatt," Doc said, standing on the loading platform at the train station, "I'd say we made our mark back there in that Godforsaken place so aptly named 'Tombstone.' Maybe we even helped civilize it a bit. Do you suppose that's why fate brought us together in Fort Griffin all those years ago?"

Wyatt looked down at his friend from the small coupling platform on the back of the passenger car. "Don't know much about those things, Doc."

Holliday laughed at his own attempt to be philosophical. "Oh, that's just how some of us mortals pretend we can see some kind of order in the insanity we encounter all around us."

"What I do know," Wyatt said in his straightforward manner, "was how you saved my skin . . . and you stuck with me."

Doc's smile was so gentle and childlike, Wyatt felt an unexpected tightening in his chest. Looking at his pallid friend, Wyatt found it easy to imagine the peaceful look on Doc's face when he would one day lie stretched out in a casket.

"Wyatt, men look up to you. Either that or they want to kill you. You'll always have friends who'll want to help you, just like you'll probably always have enemies."

Doc climbed the two steps to offer his hand. When they gripped and shook, Wyatt was surprised at the strength his ailing friend was able to summon.

"I'm proud the cards fell the way they did," Doc said, "and put me on your side of things."

Wyatt averted his eyes and nodded. When Holliday would not slacken his grasp, Wyatt turned back to Doc's determined face.

"You gave me something I didn't have before, Wyatt." Doc cocked his head and mustered a theatrical voice. "*Raison d'être*," he said with a rising and then falling attempt at melody. "Do you know what that is?"

"Can't say as I do, Doc."

Holliday's face sobered into patent ingenuousness. "You gave me a reason to live, my friend."

The whistle howled from the head of the train, and the car made a small lurch that banged the coupling. The line of cars started to move, and Doc backed off to the depot's loading platform.

"Take care of yourself, Wyatt," Doc called out over the rumble of the wheels.

"So long, Doc," Wyatt returned and watched the frail man bend at the waist to cough into his ready handkerchief. Doc was still hacking into the cloth when the train took the gentle curve that put the depot out of sight from where Wyatt stood between the cars.

*****

Sometime in the night the train crossed into Colorado. In Trinidad, McMaster and Creek Johnson departed for the Texas panhandle, until the situation in Arizona could cool down. The Earp brothers and Vermillion pressed on for Gunnison, where the ex-carpenter exhumed his original trade by hiring on with a construction crew to erect a new gambling hall in the business district. Camping outside Gunnison, Wyatt stayed with Warren until he had convalesced enough to maneuver without a walking cane.

When Wyatt finally found himself alone on the train to California, he felt the extended tragedy of the Tombstone venture close up like a book. All his posse men had gone their separate ways, just as they should. They were hardened men all, and harder still for their executioner's ride across the outlands of Arizona. Brothers who had answered a call. None of Wyatt's coterie of gunmen had been lost, and for this he was most grateful. But now, until such time as a pardon could be engineered, each and every one of them was wanted by the law.

For the time, at least, he was done with killing. Maybe for all his days to come. If he never killed again, it would take a lifetime—or what was left of it—to wash the blood from his hands. If not that, he would simply have to learn to live with the stain.

As the train rumbled its way from the mountains across Utah and into the Great Basin, Wyatt stared out the window at the vastness of the desolate land. It was another sharp-edged and dry terrain, inhospitable to men, except where their lusty ambitions lured them to chip away at the earth's surface to steal whatever rich ores might lie below.

During the night, as the track angled northwest through the Sierras, he turned to mark the moon creeping above the great skillet of desert stretching back to Arizona. It rose like a sliver of red flame banished from hell, pausing to shed its specious glow over the legions of men and women who desperately scrambled for their fortunes. Somewhere back there was Tombstone, receiving a piece of that light, as if it were due some illumination on account of the silver that had been chiseled from the land.

Virgil's lost letter had found him in Gunnison, letting him know of Mattie's rebellion among the elder Earps and her subsequent return to Arizona. Why she would choose that place was a mystery to Wyatt. He would not see her again, but he would have to live with her ruin. No matter what angle he took to study the situation, he knew he was a part of her dissipation. But, of course, so was she. All he had wanted was to give her a hand up, but there were people who would never take control of their own destiny, and Mattie was one of those. She was a follower. Now, she would have to follow someone else.

The low hanging moon softened to the colors of the earth, and he thought of Valenzuela Cos. Not so much the woman, really, but her claim on that moon . . . and how she had brokered a share of its pale promise to him. To all men who dreamed.

Waiting for her man, McMaster, to return, she lived inside the very adobe walls with which she had expected to surround herself. She was likely there now, fulfilling that prophecy. He imagined McMaster talking to her in the quiet of a Sonora Desert night. Mud walls and dirt floor notwithstanding, Wyatt estimated they had something more valuable than all the silver that still lay under the land.

The moon was still up when the train pulled into San Francisco. Wearing his new clothes, he stepped onto the landing and was struck with the realization that he was now a man without a horse. Not even a saddlebag. Everything he owned fit into the one valise he carried. At the terminal desk, a clerk took the Marcus address from him, scratched directions on the back of his ticket envelope, and then walked him outside to point the way. It was as though the clerk recognized a man who, separated from his horse, was no longer entirely connected to the world.

Within the hour, Wyatt set his bag on the sidewalk and stood soaking up the details of Sadie's brick apartment building. Even in the dark, it was not charitable to the eye. Located in a transition section of town, the structure seemed to be sliding down from the lower class of white families, if not yet bottomed out in the slums of Chinatown. Bricks, too, were made of mud, he reminded himself. He pushed a quiet laugh through his nose. Still, it was Sadie's parents' home—her home—and, for that reason alone, he sought out its charm.

He imagined her moving through the small worn-out lawn, where someone had hung a chair-swing from a stout juniper limb. He pictured her moving through the alleyway leading to the piecemeal marketplace on the street below. He could almost hear her footsteps moving through the open hallway of the building itself, the soles of her shoes tapping each stair.

He checked his pocketwatch. It was 4:10 in the morning. Picking up his valise, he walked to the swing and stared at it. There was something silly about a man—who had so recently killed—sitting in a swing. Setting down the valise he turned to the building. Moonlight washed over the apartment in a ghostly white, and he thought it the purest glow he had ever witnessed. He eased down into the seat until his body went weightless in the small pendulum arc of the swing.

Each time the chair came to rest, his foot gently pushed the earth to reestablish the rhythm and the crackling stretch of the rope that kept him company. Eventually he favored the stillness of just waiting. And thinking. The moon had descended below the buildings in the west, and soon the dawn would come. And he would emerge from the dark, a man sitting in a swing, willing to start over again.

There was time.

AFTERWORD

Wyatt Earp never killed again. He lived out the rest of his eighty years with Sadie, moving with the tide of enterprise throughout the West, until his death in Los Angeles in 1929. Aside from a few more stints as a lawman, his varied occupations included managing saloons, mine investing, horse racing, gambling, prospecting, boxing referee, real estate investor, bodyguard, movie consultant, railroad special guard, and protector of his own reputation and that of his brothers by seeking out writers to print his version of the truth about the events of his life.

Remarkably, for a man of his calling and history, not a single bullet had scarred his body. His last words, as reported by his wife at his bedside, were "Suppose . . . suppose . . ."

Sadie spent the remainder of her life defending the honor of her husband and trying to secure his place in history through the efforts of biographers and the novelty of motion pictures. She died in 1944.

Doc Holliday aged prematurely as his consumption worsened. He met with Wyatt only once again, when the two old comrades crossed paths in a Denver hotel lobby. Doc died in bed, succumbing to his ravaging disease in Colorado in 1887.

Mattie died of an overdose of laudanum in Pinal, Arizona, in 1888.

Bat Masterson became a New York City sports writer and died at his desk in 1921.

In 1900, Warren Earp met a violent death in Arizona as a result of a personal feud with roots that may have reached back to his brothers' Tombstone difficulties with the Cow-boys.

Virgil died in a pneumonia outbreak in 1905, while he was serving as a deputy sheriff in Nevada.

Allie Earp lived to be ninety-eight. She was the source for the best-known book debunking the Earp legend; however, recent research has revealed that her collaborator had fulfilled a covert anti-Earp agenda by falsifying the facts and publishing an altered manuscript only after Allie's death in 1947.

Bessie Earp died in San Bernardino, California, in 1887.

James Earp, despite his dedicated intake of alcohol, reached the old age of eighty-four. He died in Los Angeles in 1926, while Wyatt was still alive.

Newton Earp became town marshal of Garden City, Kansas, and later lived in Nevada and California. In 1928 at age ninety-one, he died in Sacramento less than a month before Wyatt passed on.

Johnny Behan fell gracelessly from the sheriff's position but stayed afloat through political connections by securing government jobs. He died from syphilis and arteriosclerosis in 1912. His son, Albert—interestingly—remained a lasting friend to Sadie and Wyatt Earp.

Ike Clanton, wanted by the law for cattle rustling, was shot in the back and killed while fleeing a lawman in Arizona in 1887. He was buried at the site of his death in an unmarked grave.

John Ringo, after a drunken spree alone in the desert, was found dead by a gunshot to the head just months after Wyatt Earp had left Arizona in 1882. The mysterious circumstances surrounding his demise have puzzled historians to this day. Hank Swilling was killed during a robbery at Fronteras in the same year. Phin Clanton and Pete Spence found a new home at the hell-hole territorial prison in Yuma. The fate of assassin Bode has escaped history, but he is believed to have fled to Mexico.

The debate about Wyatt Earp's character and methods of seeking justice are debated to this day, but no one has convincingly cast doubt upon his courage and deliberation. Countless times, his name has been evoked in speeches around the world as a symbol of an unflinching approach to law and order. Many historians have rationalized his failings by calling him a complex man with diverse agendas, which often grated against one another to create, finally, an enigma.

On the contrary, my research has led me to the conclusion that he was, in fact, a simple man, who used the same direct approach for

whatever problems or challenges he confronted, no matter how complicated or fraught with political threat. For this reason he had a polarizing
effect upon others; most who knew him either admired or despised him.

Much of the negative press on Wyatt's career as a lawman has come
from Arizona old-timers, who soaked up anti-Earp cynicism from Cow-
boy descendants, who had either settled the southern Arizona Territory
and resented the temporary, opportunistic fortune seekers of a boom
town . . . or once run roughshod over that country, only to come up
against the law as dispensed by Wyatt Earp.

Virtually every named character in this book—with the one excep-
tion of Valenzuela Cos—is an historical part of the Earp record and is
represented in this work in an accurate manner, as far as I now understand his or her personality across this reach of time. Certain secondary
characters (bartenders and prostitutes, for instance, without surnames
introduced) have been assigned names for the sake of story flow, but,
of course, they lived, too (or people very much like them), though their
names may have been lost to history.

Further Reading

Ambivalence at the O.K. Corral by Jeff Morey: self, 1989.

And Die in the West by Paula Mitchell Marks: Simon & Schuster, 1989.

Bat Masterson, The Man and the Legend by Robert DeArment: University of Oklahoma, 1979.

Charleston and Millville: Hell on the San Pedro by John Rose: Self-published, 2017.

The Clantons of Tombstone by Ben Traywick: Red Marie's, 1996.

Cochise County Cowboy War by Roy Young: Young & Sons.

Doc Holliday, The Life and the Legend by Gary Roberts: John Wiley & Sons, 2006.

The Earp Brothers of Tombstone by Frank Waters: Bison, 1976.

The Earp Papers, In a Brother's Image by Don Chaput: Affiliated Writers of America, 1994.

The Earps Talk by Al Turner: Creative Publishing, 1980.

The 1882 Arizona Territorial Census of Cochise County, compiled by Carl Chafin: Cochise Classics.

Equivocation at the O.K. Corral by Jeff Morey: Arizona Historical Society files.

Helldorado, Bringing the Law to the Mesquite by William Breakenridge: Houghton Mifflin, 1928.

The Illustrated Life and Times of Wyatt Earp by Bob Boze Bell: Tri-Star Boze, 1993.

Inventing Wyatt Earp, His Life and Many Legends by Allen Barra: Carroll & Graf, 1998.

It All Happened in Tombstone by John Clum: Northland, 1965.

John Ringo, The Gunfighter Who Never Was by Jack Burrows: University of Arizona, 1987.

The Last Gunfight by Jeff Guinn: Simon & Schuster, 2011.

The McLaurys in Tombstone, Arizona, An O.K. Corral Obituary by Paul Johnson: University of North Texas, 2012.

The O.K. Corral Inquest by Al Turner: Creative Publishing Co., 1981.

Murder in Tombstone by Steven Lubet: Yale, 2004.

The Story of Texas Jack Vermillion by Peter Brand: Self, 2012.

Tombstone, A.T. by Wm. B. Schillinberg: Arthur H. Clark, 1999.

Tombstone: An Iliad of the Southwest by Walter Noble Burns: Garden City, 1927.

Tombstone's Early Years by John Myers Myers: Bison, 1950.

Tombstone's Epitaph by Douglas Martin: University of Oklahoma, 1951.

Travesty by S. J. Reidhead: Jinglebob Press, 2005.

The Truth About Wyatt Earp by Richard Erwin: The O.K. Press, 1993.

Undercover for Wells Fargo by Stuart/Carolyn Lake: Houghton Mifflin, 1969.

Virgil Earp, Western Peace Officer by Don Chaput: Affiliated Writers of America, 1994.

Wyatt Earp, A Biography of a Western Lawman by Steve Gatto: San Simon, 1997.

Wyatt Earp, A Biography of the Legend by Lee Silva: Graphic, 2002.

Wyatt Earp, Frontier Marshal, Stuart Lake: Houghton Mifflin, 1931.

Wyatt Earp, the Life Behind the Legend by Casey Tefertiller: John Wiley & Sons, 1997.

Wyatt Earp Speaks by John Stevens: Fern Canyon, 1998.

Wyatt Earp, The Untold Story, 1848–1880 by Ed Bartholomew: Frontier Book, 1964.

Wyatt Earp, A Vigilante Life by Andrew Isenberg: Hill and Wang, 2013.

ACKNOWLEDGMENTS

With gratitude

To my friends and fellow researchers who have dug so diligently for the truth:

Peter Brand, (the late) Jack Burrows, Anne Collier, (the late) Paul Cool, (the late) Mark Dworkin, Bill Evans, Tom Gaumer, Paul Andrew Hutton, (the late) Roger Jay, Billy "B.J." Johnson, Paul Johnson, Troy Kelley, Bob McCubbin, (the late) Carol Mitchell, Jeff Morey, Roger Myers, Bob Palmquist, Roger Peterson, Pam Potter, (the late) Cindy Reidhead, Gary Roberts, (the late) Lee Silva, Jean and Chuck Smith, Casey Tefertiller, Ben Traywick, Victoria Wilcox, and Roy Young. *Muchas gracias* to Marcelino Espelosin and to Julio for keeping my Spanish on track.

About the Author

Mark Warren is a teacher of Native American survival skills. He lives with his wife, Susan, and dog, Sadie, in the Appalachian Mountains of north Georgia. His research into the Earp story has spanned sixty-plus years. Through his travels and studies he has interviewed the storied writers of the Earp saga and trekked with them to sites where the actual events in Earp's life took place.

Warren is the author of *Two Winters in a Tipi* (Lyons Press, 2012), *Secrets of the Forest, Volumes I, II, III & IV* (Lyons Press, 2020), *Indigo Heaven* (Gale/Cengage Publishing, 2021), *Song of the Horseman* and *Last of the Pistoleers* (both from SV Original Publications, 2021), and the Earp trilogy: *The Long Road to Legend*, *Born to the Badge*, and *A Law Unto Himself* (TwoDot, 2021).